Kathleen Rowntree grew up in Grimsby, Lincolnshire. She has written eight previous novels, amongst them *Between Friends*, *Tell Mrs Poole I'm Sorry* and, most recently, *Mr Brightly's Evening Off*. She and her husband live in Northamptonshire.

Also by Kathleen Rowntree

THE QUIET WAR OF REBECCA SHELDON
BRIEF SHINING
A PRIZE FOR SISTER CATHERINE
BETWEEN FRIENDS
TELL MRS POOLE I'M SORRY
OUTSIDE, LOOKING IN
LAURIE AND CLAIRE
MR BRIGHTLY'S EVENING OFF

and published by Black Swan

AN INNOCENT DIVERSION

Kathleen Rowntree

BLACK SWAN

AN INNOCENT DIVERSION
A BLACK SWAN BOOK : 0 552 99814 1

Originally published in Great Britain by Doubleday,
a division of Transworld Publishers Ltd

PRINTING HISTORY
Doubleday edition published 1999
Black Swan edition published 1999

Typeset in 11pt Melior by Kestrel Data, Exeter, Devon.

Black Swan Books are published by Transworld Publishers Ltd,
61–63 Uxbridge Road, London W5 5SA,
in Australia by Transworld Publishers,
c/o Random House Australia Pty Ltd,
20 Alfred Street, Milsons Point, NSW 2061
and in New Zealand by Transworld Publishers,
c/o Random House New Zealand,
18 Poland Road, Glenfield, Auckland.

Reproduced, printed and bound in Great Britain by
Cox & Wyman Ltd, Reading, Berks.

To Leo and Dorothy

Black absence hides upon the past
I quite forget thy face
And memory like the angry blast
Will love's last smile erase
I try to think of what has been
But all is blank to me
And other faces pass between
My early love and thee

—John Clare

1

Long before the proper time, wakefulness claims
Sonia Garrs. She resists behind tightly closed eyelids.
Pretends to a belief that the images and notions
bombarding her brain are merely dreams. Some
women – mistaken women – might wake prematurely
and lie in bed a prey to anxiety. But not Sonia. For in
everything there is an ideal Sonia way of proceeding,
and in the case of waking up it is to open her eyes
between half seven and eight, slide upwards against
her pillows, stretch a little, jiggle a little, then spring
out of bed and get on with the day.

But now, the morning still less than seven hours
old, a milk float whines outside in the avenue. *Clunk*
goes the bottle deposited in Sonia's porch, and prompt
as an echo, *clunk* goes the lump which arrives in
Sonia's chest. Her eyes come open and she considers
this lump. Though in all probability born of last
night's gin and tonic and single glass of Soave
Classico, it is not the sort that is susceptible to a
BiSoDol tablet. She knows what sort it is. A silly sort.
She will not grace it with any other description.
Words such as *pang, melancholia, depression* hover at
the brink of her consciousness, but since Sonia dis-
approves of depression in any shape or form and
always deals brusquely with silliness, they fail to
form up. Flinging off the duvet – brisk action seeming
called for – she swings her feet to the carpet, swipes a

9

button on her transistor radio and potters about the bedroom selecting clothes and humming along to its outpourings. She continues to hum in the shower, tra-lahs breathlessly as she towels herself, and absently as she draws on lacy underwear and a raspberry-pink chenille tracksuit. Seated at her dressing table, patting in moisturizer and brushing her ash-blond hair, she joins in with relish the singing of a number whose words she knows.

'*You are the dancing queen, young and sweet, only seventeen,*' trills to her reflection, Sonia Garrs, aged fifty-five.

Satisfactorily groomed, transistor in hand, Sonia roams her house pulling back curtains. In this she is poorly rewarded, the daylight being grudgingly grey. Nevertheless, like an aunt setting an example to grizzling nephews and nieces, Sonia smiles at each bleak vista, and finally arrives in her kitchen not in the least downhearted by the necessity to bring artificial light on the scene. Because that, she reflects, is the sort of woman she is: optimistic, resilient. Take this morning. She awoke feeling not quite the ticket. (It could happen to anyone.) Did she sigh and brood and drag downstairs in her dressing-gown, sit in the half-light, hunched over a cup of tea feeling sorry for herself? Did she heck!

Sonia sweeps up her shiny kettle and holds it under the tap; returns it to its resting place, flicks down the switch. With forefinger and thumb she takes a pre-cut slice of wholemeal bread and drops it from a height into the toaster. Then from the fridge collects honey and easy-spread marge, a plate and a knife from the fitted units, and as an afterthought, from the window sill, a vase of roses – the season's last, removed from her garden to escape night frosts. She pauses with the roses for a moment, holds them to her nose, before placing them on the table near the plate. Her performance of all these actions is monitored via the usual medium: a film running more or less constantly in her mind's eye. And considering the day's tricky start, she awards herself a pat on the back, for what a vision of cheeriness she makes, nipping about in her raspberry togs and her light-as-air, white-kid, soft-soled lace-ups. Her satisfaction is such that some comments of David's come to mind (as they frequently do).

'The more I travel this world, Sonia, the more folk I come across, the more I learn about women, the more amazing you seem, my sweet. A one off. Always cheerful, always on the go. Easy on the eye and unfailingly gracious. Never been known to throw a tantrum or belly-ache. I often remark on it. I'm with a couple of chaps in some hotel – in Dallas, say, or KL or Sydney – and we're swapping stories, comparing notes. I tell 'em: next time you're in the UK, go and look up the Lady Sonia. Learn what a woman ought to be.'

The Lady Sonia is how David likes to refer to her. Joshingly of course, but if it wasn't apt would it occur to him? One of his friends, an American – one of the many to have taken him at his word and paid her a call – solemnly believed it to be her due title. 'It's an honour and a privilege, Lady Sonia,' he declared, 'to visit with you in your lovely home.' A few days later when David phoned from his hotel in Dubai, they giggled over this. 'But really, David, you are naughty. Foreigners can't always tell when you're joking, you know.' 'Hey listen, who's joking? If anyone's a lady, you are, Sonia. You're a lady by temperament.'

Such comments, to do justice to their significance for Sonia, ought to be written on parchment or etched in gold. They are her certificate of worth, her badge of merit. They make up for things. Chiefly they make up for David – though remaining constant in his high

11

opinion of her and in generous provision for her and in hundreds of little amusing thoughtfulnesses – having chosen long ago to become her ex-husband.

The lump in her chest is suddenly reactivated, feels larger, more uncomfortable. She bites into her honeyed toast and tells herself it's a bit thick if she can't enjoy a glass of wine with friends without repercussions. But to tell the truth this has happened before; a few drinks during the evening and she has awoken next morning hideously early. And soon a heaviness has come in her chest, and a feeling of – not panic exactly; and certainly not depression. Heavens, it isn't *in* her to feel depressed. Slightly under par. Yes, that's how she'd put it: slightly under par.

Inadvertently – and not yet aware of the lapse – Sonia has become introspective. From the radio '*I will always love you*' is pelting out, but she doesn't hear; honey has gathered at the edge of her toast and is about to drip, but she doesn't notice. Seizing its chance, like next-door's cat spying Sonia absent and her conservatory door open, Truth steals into her mind. Isn't it a fact, suggests Truth, that she often wakes feeling slightly under par, and has done so for months, with or without the aid of alcohol? Isn't it a fact that a gin and tonic before dinner and a glass of wine during, will merely aggravate a customary state of affairs? Isn't it a fact that, in order to climb back to par or hit a notch or two above, a great deal of energy has to be expended – a lot of scurrying round with vac and duster, some vigorous gardening or chinwagging to chums? And on the worst days a great deal of money – at Antoine's getting her hair done, at Wilson's Shoes and Huffington's Top Labels and Scobie's cosmetics and perfumery counter?

Discovering next-door's cat glaring defiance in a corner of her conservatory, Sonia without ceremony

12

will send it packing with a nifty kick and a hiss like a kettle coming to boil. And now, waking up to the presence of a metaphysical interloper, she acts with similar despatch: rises up, gathers the crockery, scoots toast into the waste bin, slops tea down the sink, spins on the hot water tap, creates a cleansing agitation of Fairy Liquid foam.

It's twenty to eight when Fran Topping's sleep is disrupted – by her husband Steve coming into the bedroom with a cup of tea. His tread over the floorboards shakes the bed (he is a big man and the joists are ancient with plenty of give). For a moment, the rampaging dreaming part of her brain, struggling to maintain dominance over the waking part, incorporates this disturbance, persuades that she is airborne and being buffeted by air currents. Then, as cup and saucer descend, there's a falling sensation, and she opens her eyes. On the bedside table close to her face, she sees the calloused hand on the smooth china. He says, 'Take your time, love. You had a bad night. Don't worry, I'll see to the hens.' She says nothing.

Leaving, he delays at the door, endeavouring to lower the iron latch soundlessly. She hears him cross the landing. Hears voices below, hears a door slamming. She waits to hear her daughter's car start up, but misses the moment as memories of the night take her over.

Last night she gave Steve hell. Kept him awake (never mind that a lie-in for Steve is well-nigh impossible), raging bitterly about the old man. Always under her feet, she ranted – in the kitchen, in the yard, up to the henhouse, down the garden. He'll even follow when she goes for a pee rather than let his yarn be interrupted, he'll carry on talking outside the door. But maybe it's unsociable of her to lock the door. Maybe it's inconsiderate to go for a pee in the first place—

'Shh, Fran, don't wake the girls.'

That did it – his pleading for peace, not for himself, but for their sleeping daughters. 'Oh aren't you good, aren't you nice; and aren't I the bitch? Well listen here, you plaster saint: *you* don't have him bending your ear day after day. Those endless stories, same things over and over. And will he accept he's told me it all a hundred times before? Will he buggery! *"Did I ever tell you, Fran, about the time me and Edna met the Lord Lieutenant at Towcester races?"* Yes, Hal, you did, you definitely did. *"Well, it were mizzlin that morning if I recollect rightly, so Edna had pulled her old mac on over her costume"* – Dear Christ! Today I had the one about the fat-stock sale in Banbury market. You know – the time after the war when he and Bill pulled a fast one on Stiggy Wright, the boobies? I know every next word. I know where he'll pause for breath, chuckle, sound pleased with himself. And I know it'll end: *"Poor old Stiggy; he never did get over it,"* and if I don't stop him quick, he'll go right ahead into Stiggy Wright's funeral.'

'Shh, I'm sorry. I do know, believe me. I'll have a word with him.'

Poor, contrite, humble Steve. But what can he do? Hardly ban his father from the farmhouse – the house that was Hal's own up to a decade ago. Hardly confine him to the bungalow, allowed up to the house for Sunday lunch on condition of not annoying Fran with stories. In any case, she wouldn't really want that. Her father-in-law doesn't always get on her nerves. Some days she finds his company soothing. Sometimes she revels in the storytelling, and at other times Hal's tales and her private thoughts run as smoothly together as railway lines.

If Hal had happened to make himself scarce yesterday – worked in his garden, say, or been transported by a crony to the club or the market – she'd have found some other weapon to batter her husband with. And whatever she'd latched on to, Steve would have apologized, promised to make amends, fix it, do better. Being perfectly safe to do so, she vents on him her pent up feelings. As bullies will.

She is just plain disgusting. What she is, is sick. Because it's no use pretending she'll make it up to him. The very next time her thoughts get pulled in a certain direction, the very next time these raw feelings wash over, she'll do it to him again. Simply because he's there and unresisting. If he weren't so handy she'd go for some other outlet. Maybe turn on herself, slash at her flesh— Though in fact, last night, she was not ranting at Steve in order to relieve her feelings so much as trying to prolong the night. To stave off the morning.

Well, here it is. The day. Upon her.

Closing her eyes, Fran submits to it.

And October the twenty-first duly gathers her in. Bends on her all its nuances. Speeds her back to the end of things and the beginning of things, to the heart of the matter.

Her breathing becomes minimal. And when she senses that he is just a hair's breadth out of reach, when, save for the shadow, he would not be invisible, when her bones and nerves ends and the hairs on her skin cry out that they are reconnected (as in a sense they can never be disconnected) she speaks, not quite out loud.

Happy birthday, she tells him. Happy birthday, wherever you are.

2

Sonia has polished most of the polishable surfaces in her house; she has made her bed and plumped up cushions; she has retrieved from the lawn all the leaves fallen since yesterday's collection. It is quite ridiculous how much there is to do in a house and garden this size. David has offered to buy her somewhere smaller, but Sonia declined, knowing that from David's point of view such a move would be inconvenient. When business brings him to the UK the house serves as his base; it is handy and discreet for business meetings, and a perfect place to entertain. And she, of course, is the ideal hostess, as David regularly reminds her.

The chores done, Sonia relaxes with a cup of coffee and ponders her next move. No sooner has she arranged herself against the cushions than the annoying lump gives an expansive sort of lurch, this time pressing right up into her throat. She is impelled to catch her breath, to give her chest some quick admonishing pats. It's too bad. Not a minute's peace. Obviously, it's no good messing about with chores and the like; she needs some sure-fire diversion, something guaranteed to take her mind off silly lumps. Without a shadow of a doubt, what she requires is a trip to the shops.

She springs up. Her spirits are rising already. She wonders if Deborah could possibly fit her in; it would be an even greater fillip to get her hair done. She makes for the telephone to find out.

'Oh dear, Mrs Garrs. I'm searching for a gap in Deborah's appointments, and I can't spot a single one. Does it have to be today?'

'Yes, it does,' says Sonia. 'Ordinarily, I'd book several days ahead: I know how busy Deborah gets. But something's come up.' She isn't lying, with her hand on the lump, 'Something unexpected,' she croaks.

'Oh, I realize you're one of Deborah's most faithful clients. Bear with me a moment, Mrs Garrs.'

A soft thud – which Sonia interprets as the receiver going down on the reception desk – followed faintly by the piping of Antoine's sound-system: sounds which conjure the scene her heart is set on, customers sipping their coffee and idly flicking through magazines, customers conveying their wishes to attentive stylists and observing their own cosseting via gilded mirrors, customers – those of long standing – being treated to the latest salon gossip. She burns to be part of it.

'Good news, Mrs Garrs. We've had a bit of a change round with the lunch breaks. Deborah says she'll take a late one, which means she can fit you in at twelve-thirty. Does that suit?'

'Perfectly. I really am ever so grateful.'

It's an omen, decides Sonia as she replaces the receiver, a signal that the normal pleasant orderliness of things has now resumed. Which should put paid to silly old lumps.

The house is peaceful. Long ago Fran's daughters left, one for school, the other for work. Steve is busy on the farm somewhere, and has evidently kept his promise to speak to his father, to ask him please not to be constantly under her feet. Though probably he didn't say this in so many words. Probably he said: 'Fran's not feeling too clever today, Dad.' Or: 'Fran's got a lot on her mind; give her some space for a day or two, will you?' Hal's absence won't last, but it doesn't have to. Only for a while.

She is comfortable in this house of her husband's forebears. She is reassured by its great age and the impressions left on it by people long dead – the salt hole cut into the dining-room wall, the hooks inside the vast chimney, knife marks on the beams, initials etched in the wavy glass of an upper-floor window. It is comfortable to feel merely part of a procession. Comfortable to know that only one or two taken-for-granted and insignificant aspects of a life will leave memorials.

It is a house she can live in easily because it makes no claims. It does not insist, This is your home. She will sometimes speak as though it were. 'What time will you be home?' she will say to her daughters, and to a friend she has lingered with too long, 'Time I went home.' But it is not and cannot be her home in the belonging and finally settled sense of the word. She has privately declined to have one of those.

Her mind leaps to the poet John Clare (as it frequently does). *Home* he wrote again and again, often as a culmination, all other words leading to that one. He was obstinate. He never gave up on home as an ambition. But he did know the hopelessness of it – he did, he did: *My home*, he wrote, *was love and Mary*. So there you have it, thinks Fran.

The day they came and fetched her – just her, her arms empty ('Home, dear,' they said, 'welcome back,') – was the day she decided no thanks. Not her home, ever. Not here, not anywhere. Impossible.

Now, in the kitchen of this other house twenty-six years later, she remembers that day and hundreds of days after, in a suburban house with her parents and grandmother. She remembers the insistence there was – 'Well, isn't this grand, a real homey Christmas?' 'Do bring your friends home, dear, it's so nice to meet them,' 'Oh, it suits her to work at home with her daddy; doesn't it suit you, our Francesca?' – and the muscles and sinews, the folded lining of her throat, swell and meet.

In danger of choking, she hurries to divert herself. Attacks the disorder left by family members – the crumbs, smears, spilled cereal, sticky frying pan, the jam pot and butter dish separated from their coverings. And in the lull this activity brings to her rushing mind, begins to impose some internal order. Composes and addresses her further thoughts as if to a listener.

It's different living here, she explains. This is a house sufficient to itself. It has had its fill of people, their births and deaths and rows and love-makings, their bellies stuffed and bellies empty, their paraded hopes and disappointments, their stored-away secrets, their contrariness in cramming it to the rafters over one generation and abandoning most of the rooms over the next to insects and dust and mould. Its timbers will hardly be set aquiver by ambivalence on the part of one temporary resident.

She's doing it again, of course. Talking to him (name unknown). Sometimes the habit worries her; it's probably unhealthy, certainly addictive. But today is not the day to quibble. She needs the release.

She starts to lead him through the house. Shows him the little parlour where she goes to read (novels and poetry, mostly) and to write (a journal of sorts, recording things she has done or seen or heard or thought of – anything that comes into her head really; sometimes in prose, sometimes in verse). Shows him the place in the dining room where her late mother-in-law would sit, going tetchily back and forth in her

Parker Knoll rocker, thinking how unrestrained and overblown the garden was looking with her daughter-in-law in charge. Shows him the wide front staircase, and points out a strange acoustic phenomenon: that the further up you rise (Listen!) the louder sounds the ticking of the hall long-case clock, as if, noting your ascent away from it, the clock rouses itself to remain in earshot. Shows him the bedrooms of her daughters, and the one she shares with Steve (aware of treachery in the fact of being able to speak of them in her head when, if they were to come upon her now, it would almost kill her to exchange a word). Shows him the big spare bedroom, and is surprised to find feeble sunlight slanting in and veiling the far corner which contains a washstand: china bowl and jug, border tiles depicting St George and Boadicea, glimmer faintly, whitely, in space.

Collecting herself, she suggests that since it's getting brighter they might as well go outside.

Sonia, changed into a smart ensemble of court shoes, skirt and jacket, all in red, is covering at a fair lick the road between her home and the town centre. She passes the dignified and strictly residential dwellings of Leacroft Avenue; passes the more imposing houses facing the park that are mostly given over to the practices of medical men and lawyers; passes indeed the very consulting rooms where she was once employed as greeter, usher in, telephone voice and tea maker. Whizzing by her former workplace, Sonia calls 'Toot-toot!', fondly recalling a nice little job. As nice a little job in its way as others she has held in a similar capacity: at the Laurels Preparatory School for Boys, at the solicitors Blincoe Worsnip and Partners, at Brian Hopwell distributor for Mercedes Benz. All of them nice little jobs.

This is no idle phrase. That a job be nice and be

little are Sonia's main requirements of paid employment. Thus she can reply in answer to queries: 'Oh,
I've got a nice little job at a preparatory school.
Heavens no, dear, I don't *teach*: I answer the phone,
make the tea, soothe anxious parents, disarm any
bolshy ones,' and it is immediately established that
she is employed to be her charming self and possesses
no boring earnest side to her personality. (God forbid
she should in the slightest way resemble those driven
women you sometimes come across at parties: hollow-
eyed and dead on their feet, worn out and stressed out
and no fun at all.) She needs also to convey the right
message when mentioning the matter of a job to
David. In her experience, 'Darling, I've landed such a
nice little job at Brian Hopwell's,' will elicit applause
for a gallant attempt to contribute to the cost of her
upkeep (and at one time that of their only child),
without implying an iota of dissatisfaction with the
standard he maintains.

Sonia is in fact very well satisfied with this
standard, and when chance arises likes to describe
details of her former husband's continuing generosity.
To people she has worked with, to people she meets
for one evening socially, to her hairdresser, to shop
assistants, to her next-door neighbours and to people
she finds herself sitting next to on planes, she likes to
mention how the boarding school David selected for
their daughter is one of the most expensive in the
land; how fees were paid without flinching and con-
sent given for every extra: the horse riding and
fencing lessons, the cultural and skiing trips; and, as
if that weren't enough, school was followed by an
exclusive secretarial course. All of which has paid
off, she will add. For, at twenty-nine, their daughter
Penny is a well paid PA to a high-ranking member of
the European Parliament, married to a rich and clever
husband, has one small son and a full-time nanny,

and lives in a swish apartment. It must be apparent to all who hear this account that it is not financially necessary for Sonia to work, that when she chooses to do so her purpose is to pass her time pleasantly in an approved fashion. Perhaps it was mischievous of her, but she used to enjoy making this plain to some of the people she worked with. For instance, to a couple of teachers at the Laurels who, mindful of their professional status, misunderstood Sonia's. And there was a trainee solicitor at Blincoe Worsnip and Partners who, on learning of Sonia's divorce, and of Sonia's ex-husband's two further failed marriages and his now being settled (very sensibly in Sonia's opinion) in a bachelor's existence relieved by brief liaisons, launched into a tirade against the behaviour of men in general. 'Don't dare include my ex in that,' cried Sonia. 'I don't feel in the least let down. I certainly wasn't deserted. In David's line there's no option but to travel. It's international, the arms and security market, you know. You can't sell to foreign governments and huge business concerns abroad, sitting at home on your backside. It's not anyone's fault, but marriage doesn't fit with that sort of life. We came to an agreement like sensible people. He's loyal to me, I'm loyal to him. David's been wonderful – considerate, generous, an excellent father. So what's to complain of? Sorry, but I don't see it. And if you don't mind my saying, shouldn't you be interviewing that accident-at-work case round about now?'

Stationary at traffic lights, Sonia recalls this exchange and the way it wiped a smug expression from the woman's face. The lights change to green. Chuckling, she slips into first.

The streets are meaner here. The main road is a broad thoroughfare on which directional lanes have been imposed; its two sides bristle with narrow terraced streets like a double-sided comb. Now come the boot and shoe factories, tall blackened-brick edifices; and now the hooded chimneys of a brewery. Shoes and ale: the two industries that have built this town to the size of a city, though without winning for it city status. Sonia, flicking her indicator, moving from lane to lane, circling traffic islands, obeying a series of lights, navigates a one-way system that is regularly the despair of strangers. A lack of memorable landmarks contributes to the disorientation of those unfamiliar with the town. For the heart of the place, which included many fine Georgian and Victorian buildings, was bombed to destruction during the war. Devastation lingered for a decade, cleared spaces spawned weeds and rubbish for a decade further, and then began the concrete spring: a growth of anonymous blocks whose function becomes clear only on close inspection – bus station, police station, newspaper office, leisure complex, multi-storey car-park, and somewhere in the middle a vast indoor shopping centre.

A spiralling ramp leads into the multi-storey car-park. Sonia isn't sure how many times the ramp circles the central column, she is always too queasy to count. It's worse to be a passenger on the ramp, particularly when her friend Natalie Bellamy is the driver; at such times Sonia has to close her eyes. Driving herself, she finds the best way to cope is to stare fixedly at a point on the windscreen just above the licence disc. On arriving at the floor where parking begins, she hunches forward and tries to look everywhere at once: across the floor for a far-flung space, near at hand for signs of a place about to be vacated, and ahead and in the driving mirror to keep check of her competitors. It's a fraught business. Sometimes, when a free place is slow to come her way, or, worse, when she loses a space that is rightfully hers to some usurping driver, Sonia gets upset.

Tears start in her eyes. She has a recurrence of a bad sensation she used to get in infants' school when no-one picked her to join the farmer in his den or no-one seized her hand when the teacher cried, 'Get into twos, children.' But today Sonia is spared such misery. Ahead of her, at the perfect moment when the car in front has passed by and Sonia can brake without incurring nastiness from the driver behind, a small white car creeps backwards from between two large dark ones. 'Yes, come, come,' cries Sonia, beaming and beckoning. When the space is clear, by happy coincidence, she finds she is perfectly poised for a single, swift and accomplished-looking manoeuvre that brings her to rest centrally between two white lines.

For a moment Sonia stares through the windscreen at the low brick car-park wall, so happy she could jump out and kiss it. Then she collects her purse, jumps out, activates the central locking system and runs across to the ticket machine. She feeds in the maximum amount of money allowed, takes her ticket and returns to her car. Her high spirits remain unalloyed during the trip to the lift, during the descent, and for her first fifty or so steps across the brightly lit and prettily paved floor of the shopping centre. She's here, she's arrived. The whole of the shopping centre and the part of town that lies outside are at her disposal.

Fran, walking up the rise behind the paddock, senses how he matches his stride to hers. She wants to show him how well her chickens are doing. Only nine weeks old, she tells him, and already strutting round the run like kings and queens. Soon after they were hatched some of this lot were invaded by the sort of worm that produces what is commonly called the gapes because of the effect it produces: tiny beaks stretched to their widest in a desperate attempt to draw in air. Fran managed to save every invaded chick. By the usual method: the tip of a wing feather that has been dipped in turpentine circled inside a straining gullet, winding up the worm as a fork winds spaghetti. Generally, at least one chick expires during the operation, but not this time. This time she was quick, sure, deft, and maybe lucky. She recounts for him the whole story, describes her relief and joy. But she can't resist ending on a wry note: Yep, I'm a great little rearer of chickens.

But never mind her tone of voice. When she rises from crouching by the chicken run, she's feeling brighter, buoyed by reliving a simple achievement. She knew what had to be done, and she damn well did it. No-one hindered her. No-one imposed any ifs and buts. She was purposeful. Effective.

She walks up the rising track to a five-bar gate. Her hands reach for the upper bar, her body leans. Her eyes are on the view, which is by no means stupendous: some undulating pasture, some hills and copses. At night you can see the glow on the horizon thrown by the lights of the town eighteen miles away to the south-west. On any sort of day except foggy you can see the spire of the village church a mile and a half off, and a neighbouring farmhouse and a couple of cottages.

From the point of view of background, this country-side isn't hers. The town over there is hers, the place where she grew up on its south-eastern fringe close to the river where her father's garden centre business was situated. But it *is* her countryside, she feels, vicariously. Hal's stories reach back to his grand-father's time. They tell of some of the characters who have shaped it: the labourers in the tied cottages, the itinerant hedgers and ditchers and harvest hands. They tell of the rivalries between neighbouring farmers and the passions ignited by a transaction involving a single beast; of alliances between families and some unfortunate liaisons; of children who thrived and some who failed to; and one child who was lost, possibly stolen by gypsies. For Fran, listening to Hal, a collie performs again his sideways lope along the farm track, his yellow eyes agleam with his own and not his master's ambitions. For Fran, one day is selected to stand for other days Hal has forgotten, and to spawn days that exist only in the imaginings of a listener.

In a sense, it is John Clare's countryside, too. Though committed to the asylum in town, and belonging to the fenny north of this county, the poet's words in Fran's inner ear as she walks the tracks and fields and woods, make the countryside indubitably his. For a time, of course, he was permitted to wander; and years earlier, absconding from an asylum in Epping, he'd walked the eighty-odd miles home. Did he ever take the paths that cross this farm?

The scene before her is infinitely accommodating. As easily as Hal's, it can assume John Clare's eye view. And become peopled, not with scheming dealer farmers and their satisfactory or otherwise wives and their robust or fragile children, and with hedgers and ditchers and cowmen and truculent dogs, but with the companions of a lonely existence: a tit, a robin, a cock lording it over a dungheap. In this perspective the farmhouses are forbidding fortresses; home is a dwelling whose stones are slowly collapsing back into the earth; and life is marked out in trailing, criss-crossing, battered paths.

Right now her companion is not one of her husband's forebears, nor on this autumn day a russet-coated robin. She has no name to give him, as he joins her at the gate. She tries to relate the view to her own history as far as possible. Over there is the town where she went to school. Has he ever been in that town? she wonders. No doubt he will have driven past it at some time on the motorway; most people have. But she doesn't ask. Questions beg answers. If no answer comes, your question has merely bought distance – distance when you were striving for closeness. She tells him about the place where she grew up, the large house at the side of the garden centre. About living there with her mother, father and grandmother, and going to school on the bus. She tells him painstakingly. He has a right to know.

Sonia, walking through the shopping precinct, sees her reflection coming towards her in a mirror-faced pillar. And with her reflection comes a renewal of the doubt she felt earlier when selecting this handbag today. Its shade of red is intended to match that of her shoes and suit. But does it? She hovers by the pillar, shifts the bag about, frowns. Not in this light, it doesn't. Which is annoying, because the bag was sold to her as a match for the shoes. But that was nearly two years ago, so she can't very well return and complain. Maybe it's her eyesight playing tricks. The entrance to Scobie's department store is near at hand. Sonia marches towards it in search of a second opinion.

'Could be,' hazards the saleslady in the handbag department, 'could be that different leathers age differently. I suppose the bag and the shoes were the exact same shade when you bought them? Did you purchase them here, madam?'

'No, no. In Oxford. And it'd be most inconvenient to take them back. Anyway, after all this time—'

'It's possible you could get a closer match,' – the saleslady looks doubtfully over her merchandise – 'but after a year or so, who's to say you wouldn't end up with the same problem? Reds are tricky. And different leathers age differently, you see.' (She has forgotten this idea began as a hunch; now she believes in it.)

'Well, thank you. I'll be sure and remember that another time. I suppose I'll just have to lump it,' sighs Sonia, taking leave of the saleslady with a brave smile.

She returns to the area near the store entrance where the cosmetic counters stand. She needs a jar of moisturizer, since the one at home is almost empty. This line is for openers, and both Sonia and the white-coated assistant know it. Sonia is given the latest news from the battlefront in the war against ageing, and invited to accept a trial size, free of charge, of a new anti-sag ointment to apply at bedtime. Perhaps thinking of the resulting clogging of her pores, Sonia decides to buy a bottle of toner called Wake Up! that she spies on the counter. Yes, Wake Up! is a brilliant way to start the day, the assistant confirms, she herself wouldn't think of starting one without it. Sonia is shown a new range of lipsticks and buys one she will turn against within a week and place at the back of a drawer with other rejects. Also she buys some mascara – though she has a plentiful supply at home – in response to the information that the wand has a new and revolutionary shape. 'Do let me know how you get on with it,' says the assistant, as if Sonia will be helping with vital research. The assistant tots up the damage, and Sonia produces her charge card. With the bill, a free and tiny phial of perfume is presented. 'Mm, thank you,' Sonia says vaguely while signing her name. She is wondering, not about the amount of money indicated, but whether she will ever want to smell of a thing called Perdition.

*   *   *

28

At a minute to twelve the studs in Steve's boots clang out in the yard. Rosie the retriever hauls to her feet and gears up for a tail-sweeping welcome, the cat raises its head looking offended, and Fran continues to race backwards and forwards between table, oven and pantry. Lunch on the farm is always eaten promptly at noon. It's the second most important meal of the day. Breakfast ranks first, the stoke-up for the morning, but lunch must also be hearty to prevent flagging in the face of heavy jobs, dispiriting weather and dwindling afternoon light. Steve pauses in the doorway to remove his boots, then pads across the kitchen to scrub up in the scullery. The air he disturbs is left faintly niffing of diesel oil and cow muck.

Fran has set out bread and cheese and butter and water. Now she brings a bowl containing the remains of last night's casserole, hastily reheated in the microwave, to the table. 'Sorry it's a bit scrappy,' she mumbles when he returns.

'Looks fine to me. Nice peaceful morning?'

'Mm.' She fills the kettle ready for his after-lunch cup of tea. 'Thanks,' she adds, remembering that her peaceful morning was largely due to his having a word with Hal.

'Aren't you going to have some?'

'Nuh,' says Fran. She'd like to leave him to it, but can't. Soon he'll be wanting his tea. And besides, he's been very considerate, letting her lie in, feeding her hens, warning off his father. 'I'll have a bit of Stilton,' she concedes, reaching for the cheese board, sitting down. She crumbles off a small chunk.

He studies her without looking at her directly. He's become expert at this. She takes a mouse-size bite of cheese then lays the rest down on her plate. While chewing, she holds the sides of her face in her hands. Her elbows are propped on the table, her bony shoulders jut upwards. This morning her hair has been gathered up and screwed back through one of those frilly elastic rings she sometimes lifts from their elder daughter's bedroom. This is always a bad sign. A dark curly mass standing out from her face and hanging wide of her shoulders is the style that denotes a buoyant Fran. Today she looks drawn, and every one of her forty-two years. Most of the time she looks many years younger: skinny and vivacious, funny and inquisitive, she seems to Steve to be nearer their daughters' ages than his (yet he is, after all, only ten years her senior). He remembers how she was a fortnight ago when a party of guests helped them celebrate their wedding anniversary (their twenty-second!). Light as air she seemed, skipping about in the damson-coloured velvety dress she'd bought for the occasion, and happy, on top of the world. He couldn't be kidding himself, could he? Mopping up gravy with a piece of bread, he frowns in concentration, trying to conjure up Fran of the party. If she wasn't happy, she was giving a damn good imitation. But Fran has never put on an act, she's honest and straightforward: brutally direct, according to the girls. 'At least you know where you are with your mother,' Steve has said to one or other of them from time to time. No, there are no tricks or undercurrents with Fran. It's just that every now and then she goes through a bad patch. These patches are always short-lived and afterwards she doesn't want to talk about them. 'Sorry, Steve,' she'll say. 'Sorry I was off. Sorry I gave you a bad time.' But that's it. All she wants then is to get on with her jobs in the house and the garden, see to the hens, discuss the farm, chat or tease or argue with the girls, call on the neighbours, or go in the parlour for a quiet read or a bit of a scribble. It's as if, once she's returned to her normal self, she wants not to be reminded that she can ever be otherwise.

Steve thinks he knows the cause of these bad patches. He is. Or rather, their early history together. It was the way he couldn't wait once the unbelievable happened: the delectable Fran Spencer agreed to go out with him. He had to make sure of her, put an engagement ring on her finger, walk her down the aisle. He didn't dare wait, since there she was, meekly falling in with his every suggestion; for how many chances like that do you get in a lifetime? Her agreement with his every suggestion was due, of course, to her recent trouble. He knew it, and so probably did plenty of others. But by God, if ever a woman threw herself into married life – Yes, that's what she did, *threw* herself— into Steve's life, into farm life, into the lives of her in-laws and neighbours, and eventually into the lives of their daughters (as far as they'll let her). Affectionate and supportive, always got time for you: that's Fran. So it stands to reason she's contented, doesn't it? Even now, after all these years of marriage, she'll look him in the eye and declare that she's lucky, he's a man in a million. Nevertheless, Fran wasn't meant to be a farmer's wife. She wasn't brought up to it. She was like one of her father's precious hothouse plants, carefully reared and protected. Attention was lavished on her. She was cultivated to perfection. She was meant for some delicate and beautiful pursuit. Steve recalls the medals she won for ballet, and how, at the request of her parents, she would recite verse after verse of poetry (this is going back a fair way, of course, to his first memories of Fran when she was ten or eleven years old); and her future husband was meant to be rich and well-educated, someone who would continue where her father left off. The only reason Steve got her was because, at the time, she was vulnerable.

This is how it goes, imagines Steve: Fran is sitting opposite him at the table, or lying beside him in bed –

or something happens to remind her of the past, such as their wedding anniversary – and she starts feeling angry, trapped. Soon she's feeling mad as hell, and it has to come out. So she picks on an incident – like Hal getting on her nerves, or one of the girls playing up, or a succession of nights in the lambing shed – and she rants and raves till she's exhausted, and then, being whacked, she is naturally uncommunicative for a while. She can never voice the real cause of her fury – that Steve took advantage of her at a low point in her life – because she remembers how she encouraged him, how glad and grateful she was to be rescued from a tense situation at home, from a life (in her own words) that had run off the rails. It wouldn't be Fran to twist history, to blame him and excuse herself. Maybe when she's going through one of her rages she truly believes that Hal dogging her footsteps, or one of the girls being surly or everyone too demanding, is her sole cause of complaint. But Steve knows better. He *knows*.

'Any plans for this afternoon?' he asks as she pours him a cup of tea. 'Thanks, love. Just what I need.'

Fran hesitates. A longing springs up in her, sharp and urgent. A longing that cannot be directly satisfied (she cannot go and seek him out) but, it occurs to her, that she can indulge retrospectively. She can walk, she can sit and stand, she can hang about, in places where she and he were briefly a unit. She carefully refrains from looking beyond such an expedition, from asking herself what possible benefit might accrue (her mind takes a step in this direction but she hauls it back in case the answer is none); her desire to go ahead is too immense. 'I'm, er, thinking of going into town,' she says, not looking at him.

Steve is surprised. Fran hates shopping, hates traffic, hates crowds. 'Something you want? I'll probably have to go in myself in a day or so. The Land Rover needs a couple of tyres.'

'No. Just fancy it,' says Fran, begrudging every word. 'OK if I take the car?'

'Of course. Yeah, you go, love. Do you good.' It is a surprising fancy for Fran to have, but maybe it's one to encourage. 'There's some cash in the desk drawer, if you need some.'

Fran shakes her head to indicate that as far as money is concerned she is all right. Being spoken to is bad enough, having to reply is hateful. 'May as well get going, then.'

'Yes. I shouldn't hang about. Make the best of the light while it lasts.'

So off she goes: upstairs to exchange her old trousers for an equally old but clean long skirt, and to collect her long dark mac, a scarf and bag; then outside, across the yard and down to the barn where the car is garaged.

It feels purposeful to be driving. Almost hopeful. She tries not to set too great a store on this.

It's time to go and get her hair done. Savouring the weight of her purchases in the black and gold plastic carrier hanging from her hand – a small weight but satisfying, the feel of a result – Sonia walks down the main shopping street towards the square. The square is lined with shops, banks and estate agencies, and it encloses the parish church. On the far side, an alley-way the width of a cart or carriage runs between two tall buildings, and at the bottom of this beyond a courtyard lies Antoine's in what was once probably a stable block. But it is not Sonia's habit to wonder about former uses, or to think for long about anything outside her own time or experience. She turns into the alley. She spies the smokey plate-glass wall at the far end. And her step quickens, and the smile that is almost always lurking at the corners of her lips, blossoms.

'So – a special occasion,' remarks Deborah, a few minutes later. For a moment Sonia can't think what she means. Then she tumbles, recalls the white lie she told – 'Something's come up,' – in order to secure a last minute appointment. Her hand goes to her chest – though the lump took itself off long ago when her mind was elsewhere – and she hurries to agree without being specific. 'Yes, quite out of the blue. A total surprise.'

Deborah leans over. She fingers Sonia's hair. 'You could lose half an inch. Want to keep it the same?'

'I think so, yes,' says Sonia.

'See you in a few minutes, then. Paul'll be along to shampoo.'

Paul duly arrives. He wets her hair, squeezes shampoo onto it, and begins to massage her scalp. He does this well, she has to concede. As a rule Sonia does not appreciate being intimately handled by male persons. It has always puzzled her that some women, of their own free will, elect to have a man stylist. There are a couple of these at Antoine's, which in spite of its name is owned and managed by a woman and largely employs female staff. Sonia has often observed how men stylists behave differently: stand with their feet wide apart, thrust stiff stubby fingers through wet hair so that a client's head is dragged backwards, how they adopt offhand or imperious mannerisms, and how their clients are invariably subdued and obedient-looking. This lad who is now wrapping her hair in a towel will no doubt in time become one of those pony-tailed gods. But for the moment he's meek. Would she like coffee? he asks. Would madam like to go down to the styling area?

Down to that area now goes Sonia. Into the chair

34

vacated two minutes ago by Deborah's last client. Her coffee arrives, which she sips. Deborah arrives, all smiles – and straight away enquires as to the nature of Sonia's last minute big occasion.

'Oh,' says Sonia, cursing herself for not having anticipated the query. 'David's making a flying visit.' She isn't happy to lie, but can't spot any way out of it. If she weren't so straightforward an escape route might occur to her. But there you go. A twinge of guilt is the penalty you pay for being a basically truthful person.

'Your ex? Oh fantastic! We won't cut it too short, then. Just a little tidy up. What've you got planned? Dinner for two in a gorgeous restaurant, or a cosy night in?'

It occurs to Sonia that she isn't so much lying as repaying a debt. The fantasy is owed to Deborah for kindly fitting her in at short notice. So she relaxes, allows herself to elaborate, and draws, for authenticity's sake, on anecdotes drawn from David's past and actual visits.

Deborah, combing and snipping, listens intently, and at last comments that she thinks it's very romantic the way Mrs Garrs and her ex continue to see each other. Mr Garrs must be ever such an interesting person, travelling about the world the way he does. Sonia agrees that he is. She laughs, feeling delicious and light-hearted and fortunate. Her eyes in the mirror sparkle back at her. Very romantic, she makes Deborah say again in her head.

Deborah stops snipping and starts on the drying and shaping process. She tells Sonia about plans for a girls' night out, a hen party for Suzie, another stylist, who is getting married on Saturday. A table has been booked at Dimitri's where they specialize in hen parties and the highlight of the evening is a male stripper. In Deborah's opinion the venue is a mistake and will not prove the sort of surprise Suzie is hoping for. Deborah has suggested going for a meal and then on to a club, but has been overruled.

Sonia is enormously gratified to be let into Deborah's confidence, and enormously grateful that the story didn't take the tacky turn she foresaw the moment a male stripper was mentioned – she has a horror, a terror almost, of having sprung on her anything of a smutty nature. It's a relief to know Deborah is as nice as she's always supposed. Sonia commiserates, tells Deborah she knows how she feels. And makes the helpful suggestion that should the evening go wrong they could always phone for a taxi to take them somewhere more tasteful.

'That's a thought,' Deborah nods. 'I'll take my mobile.'

Sonia feels wonderful. It's good to have made a positive contribution. Good to have shared something, however small.

Fran drives onto an uncovered car-park, a piece of waste ground which, because of its distance from the shops, is seldom completely full. She drives into a space and turns off the engine. But instead of the silence her ears expect there is a disconcerting roar. A motorbike zooms up, swirls round the parked cars, and finally comes to rest at the rear of Fran's. She watches in her driving mirror the rider dismount. She watches him remove his helmet and make the vehicle secure. She watches until he is gone.

Then there is only the motorbike. The spread arms, the shapely undulating and intestinal middle, the back cylinder where its energy is exhausted. Black and silver and gleaming. An image grabs her – she might have known it would – of herself straddling it.

She might have known, because this is an image

she deliberately conjures at certain times, on certain occasions. Sometimes, conjugal sex can seem a dismal affair. Not wanting to be overly demanding when Steve is tired, and not wanting him to sense any lack of engagement on her part (certainly not wanting him to be hurt by it), she occasionally resorts to a mental trick. It's a convenience, like pushing the override button to bring on the central heating. Afterwards, tiredness and sleep usually close the wraps on such an episode, and morning brings many more pressing matters to think about. So it is only once in a while that she is brought face to face with the nature of this image, and the fact of its being lodged in a recess of her mind. And then she is filled with an amazed shame. As happens now. But perhaps she should be grateful it's only the bike her fantasy features, that no rider – other than herself – is involved. Even so, it's an image she would dearly like cleaned from her mind. Is she alone in her furtive harbouring? Or are there others out there who inadvertently became hooked on their first experience of sexual arousal? Depends, she supposes. Depends on the amount of surprise there was, on the depth of intensity when the pleasure gates opened.

She cranes forward, until her view of the bike is lost from the mirror, until all to be seen is her own face – which looks naked and exposed with her hair pulled back: the face of a green girl. Abruptly, she raises her hands and pulls off the elastic ring. Her hair flies, then settles, and a brief re-examination satisfies her that the girl is no longer on show. Nothing is on show beyond features, freckles, shadows.

Look, she tells herself, she is not going to beat her breast about a fantasy. She doesn't hurt anyone by it, except possibly now and then herself. The important thing is, it serves. She loves Steve deeply. If at times this love is insufficient to motivate her body then it's

37

a good job her mind can come up with something that will inject the necessary pep.

She falls back in her seat and takes another, harder, look at the motorbike. It's her perversity in harbouring *that*, of all images, that is bothering, of course. But she didn't go out of her way, she didn't leaf through magazines and cry to herself, Eureka, oh yes, I could really go for a motorbike. She was landed with the thing. And if life didn't persist in being downright cussed she might never have discovered she had been so landed. It serves life – fate – right if she has found a use. Turned it into an accommodation.

She picks up her bag, opens the car door, steps out and goes to the ticket machine. And while she does so, thinks to herself that she is about to embark on another sort of accommodation, in this case to the anxiety that has temporarily got the better of her. Or perhaps a propitiation – *if I put myself through it, let me emerge from this agony calmer and lighter and focussed on the future*. A pact with fate, thinks Fran, as she applies the ticket to the windscreen. She has made plenty of those in her time.

She locks the car door, then walks from the car-park into the street.

And here on the pavement, deliberately and without difficulty, becomes two versions of herself: a forty-two-year-old woman who has arrived at this point by car, and a sixteen-year-old girl who has illicitly walked into town instead of catching the bus to school. They start up the hill. They pass terraced houses of blackened red brick that are mostly used as offices of some sort, and some odd little shops. They pass the theatre, then a café. At the top of the road, where the girl might choose to turn right and head for the library (hours and hours she spends in the library, reading books, flipping through magazines, staring at public notices, trying to sneak a visit

38

to the John Clare collection without drawing attention to herself and her truancy, trying to keep warm, or dry, or cool), the woman holds back (the library stands in the very same street where her elder daughter works, who might now be taking her lunch break; the last thing she wants is to be accosted and hauled into the present: 'Mum, what are you doing here?'). The woman prevails. To the church now, to the library later.

At the end of the square, Fran the woman and Fran the girl climb the steps to the church forecourt. A portico extends across the west wall of the church and under this, set in the outside wall, are two niches with seats, one on either side of the main door. When John Clare was an inmate of the asylum – and when he was allowed out, which was during those periods when his demeanour was considered inoffensive – he would regularly walk the mile into town to sit in one of these niches and watch the bustle below and smoke a pipe of tobacco. Whether he preferred one niche over the other isn't known. Most probably he settled for whichever was vacant; no doubt there were plenty of others glad of a chance to rest here awhile.

Today there is a choice. They take the right-hand niche.

Perched on the stone slab, the sixteen-year-old Fran shivers in her uniform. She has come here with a purpose. She wants to be at one with the stricken poet; someone who knew, as she herself has learnt, what it is to be cornered, to be up against it. The noise of the traffic makes concentration difficult. But it would have been noisy here in John Clare's day too, with horses and carts, and drays with barrels, and people in iron-tipped shoes all clattering past. In any case, he wouldn't have come expecting peace; he'd have come to taste life, is the thought of the lonely sixteen-year-old.

It is a strange turn-up to find herself willingly re-entering a terrified girl, is the thought of Fran the forty-two-year-old. And to be almost envying her.

Sonia has paid her bill, and in the cloakroom has spent several minutes smoothing her clothes and mending her make-up. Now she leaves Antoine's, sallies forth into the alley, and thence into the street.

She passes the church. She does not raise her eyes to its forecourt and portico. Ahead of her she notices two girls walking, both in black leggings and short black jackets, both with eye-catching pale-blond hair. They nudge shoulders as they scurry along, they laugh together. The girl on the left is Deborah, the one on the right another stylist whose name Sonia doesn't know. It's their lunch hour, Sonia remembers, quickening her pace. But then she slows down, falls back. There is something about them, something about the way they nudge and laugh, something about the portion of Deborah's face that is visible, that tells her this is a Deborah she doesn't know and has no access to. An image flashes through her mind: she has caught up with the laughing pair, she has spoken to them; but Deborah is staring at her vaguely, not recalling who the person detaining her is.

Suddenly Sonia feels ghastly. The blessed lump has come back. When the hairdressers have crossed to the other side of the square taking a leftwards direction, Sonia crosses also but turns rightwards.

Fran has seen the young women in black, nudging each other and laughing, their blond hair mingling. She has seen the middle-aged woman, smartly dressed in red, who hesitated then hurried onwards. She has watched a young man clad only in T-shirt and jeans go by, and shivered at the sight; and another in a coat to his ankles with a violin case under his arm; and two elderly women loaded down with carrier bags; and a man with a briefcase climbing out of a taxi. She has watched these and many other passers-by.

None of them meant a thing to her.

3

Thank heaven, thinks Sonia, for another friendly and familiar place. Thank heaven for Wilson's Shoes.

This is a shop where over the years Sonia has spent a good deal of money. It has all the best makes, and some shoes that are made exclusively for the firm in Florence. Now why, she wonders, did she not think of Wilson's sooner as the very place to take her matching handbag problem? What Wilson's doesn't know about leather is nobody's business. And Heather, one of Wilson's assistants, is a girl who will move heaven and earth to ensure a customer's satisfaction. Yes, a very determined young lass is Heather. Some might say pushy, but Sonia knows how to turn Heather's keenness to her own advantage. Crucially, Heather understands the difficulties that can be experienced if one is blessed with high arches. And she'll give Sonia time, she'll stick to her unswervingly, run backwards and forwards finding more and more shoes for Sonia to try on, however many other people come into the shop. *Someone else can deal with them: I'm attending to a valued customer*, is Heather's attitude. An attitude Sonia finds endearing.

As she approaches the shop, Sonia once more holds the handbag against her shoes. In the clear light of day it is worse than ever, bag and shoes scream at each other, it's a wonder she ever accepted them as a match. That day in Oxford was a mistake. She went with Natalie Bellamy, and should have stuck to window-shopping. It is always a mistake to buy things when you're not concentrating, when someone you're with is causing distractions and offering opinions and ganging up against you with a saleslady.

Her mind is made up – the lump is forgotten – and she walks resolutely into Wilson's recessed entrance. Though before proceeding to the door, she glances quickly at the window display on both sides of the entrance, to see whether there are any items that weren't on show when she last took a look. And indeed, some shapely boots, which might go nicely with her winter camel coat, draw her eye.

From inside the shop, Heather has seen her. Her eyes were alerted the moment Sonia paused a few yards away on the pavement. They monitored the placing of the bag against the shoes, and Sonia's hesitation in front of the window display. Now they register the exact pair of boots that has attracted attention.

Heather has the leisure for all this monitoring because the shop for the moment is empty of customers. It often is. This is a high class shop, a purveyor of luxurious items. As she explained to her mother who came in one day and was bemused by the lack of bustle: 'Wilson's doesn't need a lot of customers, Mum. Just a few with big wads.' And this particular customer, this perky little grandma, flash and neat as a paradise bird, nipping about town on her twiggy legs, eager eyes on the lookout for treasure, this one is *hers*.

Heather quickly checks on the position of her co-workers in case she is not the only one keeping watch on the outside world. If she weren't she would issue a warning, which would go unchallenged because authority is on her side – she and John are the seniors in the women's and men's departments respectively. The shop manager, Mr Nuttall, is seldom around, being frequently called to confer at the parent store in Bond Street, visit suppliers abroad and keep in touch with the local shoe factories, the ones that produce top quality goods. Heather is just nineteen years old. This is only her second job since leaving school (her first, in a department store with a preference for cheap part-timers, did not offer the opportunities she craved). On the strength of her stunning sales record at Wilson's, when Miss Petheridge retired, Mr Nuttall chose Heather to replace her as senior in preference to either of two others who had worked here longer. One of these promptly left. The other remains, fearful and jealous of Heather and sulkily doing as little as possible (Heather punishes her by sending her to check stock in the freezing back rooms). The girl who left in a huff was replaced by a school leaver, who also finds Heather formidable, and regards flirting with John as her best hope of survival. There is one other assistant, male, working mostly under John – though in theory every assistant stands ready to work anywhere in the shop when occasion demands – and he, too, is in awe of Heather.

Why does Heather inspire such trepidation? She is not physically outstanding – slightly taller than average, and on the stocky side, with a fleshy weather-hardened face, and brows and lashes so fair as to be invisible, and hair that also is fair and is generally caught up at the back of her head by a fancy elasticized ring of ribbon. Maybe it's her eyes, their blankness, their neutrality; the way, in their watery fastness, they seldom require to blink. Maybe it's her manner of planting herself when she's talking to you, seeming weighty and immovable.

No, no-one else is on the lookout for customers. So there's no need for Heather to hiss *this one's mine* as the door comes open. She can take matters slowly, amble over.

'Hello,' she greets Sonia. 'Nice to see you again. I noticed you eyeing the boots. They've just come in. Fabulous, aren't they?'

'They're certainly smart. I wonder if they're comfortable?'

'You should try them on. Why not come and sit down? Have the lace-ups been satisfactory, the little white Skippies?'

'Oh, blissfully. I simply live in them at home.'

'Maybe you should have another pair, then. They come in baby blue and sugar pink.'

'Possibly,' says Sonia, taking a seat on one of the gilt-and-red plush chairs. 'But to tell the truth, Heather, I've come in to tap your expertise. See this bag, these shoes? They were sold to me as a match.'

'Not by us,' Heather observes. Her voice doesn't change, nor does her expression; nevertheless she manages to convey that the articles fall short of Wilson's standard.

'I know, dear. Silly me. A friend took me to Oxford for the day – oh, this was getting on for a couple of years ago I should think. They were an impulse buy. Well, I was more or less talked into it. But I thought they matched this suit. Now the shoes *do* match it, wouldn't you say? It's just this darn bag that's gone a bit purpley. Tell me if I'm mistaken.'

'No, there's definitely a bluish tinge in the dye,' says Heather holding the bag up to the light.

'I knew it!' cries Sonia. 'Oh, I could kick myself. It was my friend's fault. Hers and the saleslady's. Well, it's taught me a lesson: stick to the shops you know you can trust. So what do you advise? A different bag? I don't suppose it could be redyed.'

'Why don't you make yourself comfy a moment?' says Heather. 'I think I know where you went wrong.'

Sonia settles back. She exchanges smiles with an assistant who is dusting a nearby display shelf. She feels better already with Heather applying herself to the problem. A problem shared is a problem halved.

'Here's what I wanted to show you.'

'Oh,' says Sonia, surprised to have a magazine thrust into her hands. On the open page is a photograph of a model stunningly attired in a red two-piece with shiny black accessories.

'See what I mean? Black patent is perfect with red.'

'Hm, do you think so?'

'What I think this shows,' says Heather, tapping the photograph, 'is, you can overdo it with red.'

'Mm? Mind you, I do sometimes opt for black with this outfit—'

'Black patent? Matt would be no good. Red sort of swallows a matt finish.'

'My goodness, what a fount of information you are, Heather.'

'But your red ones needn't be wasted. They'd be great with navy. In fact, I bet you could get away with the bag as well, if you teamed them with navy. John?' she yells, lifting her head. 'Come over here. Lend us your jacket a minute.' John, frowning, approaches, and Heather lays firm hands on him and briskly removes his navy jacket. She is then equally firm with Sonia: 'Shoes?' she demands, holding out her hand. 'Bag?'

Heather takes the articles to the window and arranges them on the floor of the display area so that a large plane of navy blue separates shoes and bag.

'That . . . is . . . a . . . mazing!' says Sonia. 'I defy anyone to say they don't match now.' She shakes her head at the cleverness of this plain plump girl. 'Thank you, Heather. You've saved me a great deal of trouble and a great deal of expense. As it happens, I have a very good Jaeger two-piece in navy.'

'That's good,' Heather says. 'Sit down, and I'll fetch

out some black patent shoes. Then you can see if I'm right about that, as well.'

Sonia cannot believe how right Heather proves. Shod in black patent leather, she studies her full-length reflection. Her skirt and jacket seem lifted into a classier league; especially when Heather sidles up and suspends a black patent bag from her shoulder – small bag, long strap. 'Oh, yes,' she breathes. All in red she must have looked like a walking pillar box.

'Seems a shame not to keep them on,' hints Heather.

'Go on then, wrap the red ones up. Bag as well; I'll swap over the contents.'

'In that case, if you'd like to wait a couple of minutes I'll give them a spray. You'd like a can of water repellent? Best to put some on before you wear them outside. It's no trouble. It soon dries.'

'That's what I call service.'

'While you're waiting, why not try on the boots? And you might as well see the Skippies – they're really sweet in pink and blue.'

Thirty minutes later, Sonia is laden and Heather is satisfied. The purchases today comprise one pair of black patent shoes, one matching shoulder bag, one pair of Skippies in sugar pink, one can of water repellent, two jars of shoe cream and a pair of the best quality solid wood shoe-trees. (One of the reasons Heather rates Sonia highly as a customer is that she always buys the extras, never claims to have an ample supply at home.) Also Sonia has promised to come in soon wearing her winter camel coat to assess the boots.

But on the way to the door, a gasp from Sonia gives Heather a momentary misgiving.

However, it is not her depleted bank balance that is paining Sonia, but her empty stomach. A determined gripe reminds her that she hasn't eaten since break-fast, and then rather minimally. 'No lunch,' she explains, stifling a groan. 'My stomach's complaining. Dear me, I'll have to eat something pretty darn quick. Don't think I can make it to Quigley's.'

'The Tasty Bite's nice, in Brewer's Yard. They do homemade soup, and dish of the day and jacket spuds with fillings, and you can help yourself to as much as you like from the salad trolley. I often go there. Lots of office people use it. You can leave your purchases here, if you like.'

Expressing her fervent thanks, Sonia dumps her parcels and heads for the Tasty Bite.

Mike's Coach – with its gold-lettered undertaking to convey parties in luxury throughout Europe and the UK made wistful by caked-on dust and a school-bus symbol in the rear window – pulls up at the top of the farm road. Janie Topping alights. The bus grinds onwards. Janie crosses the cattle grid and remembers to keep her toes turned upwards. Sometimes she forgets, even though the grid has to be crossed twice every school day; sometimes her mind is just too involved with matters of importance. This afternoon her mind is active, but as it happens, when she arrives at the grid she is between thought sequences.

On the bus, Janie had been mentally decrying the behaviour and dress of some fellow passengers, a couple of sixth-formers. (Janie, at fifteen, has recently entered the fifth form.) Though obediently clothed in the statutory navy blue, these girls had knotted the belts of their macs in a ridiculously tight fashion, they had stood up their collars under their hanging hair; in fact everything about them, including their dinky laughs, denoted membership of the affected *fem* brigade. Janie herself is dressed in an interpretation of the school uniform; in her case, heavy-duty boots and a padded bomber jacket many sizes too large denote adherence to the *tough girl* school of thought; a short spikey haircut and owl-eye spectacles are further signs. But as she jumped from the bus her natural irritation with the sixth-formers vanished, and once over the cattle grid, her mind embraced a more pleasing topic.

This afternoon a discussion was inaugurated by Janie's favourite teacher on the subject of being comfortable with one's body. It was a girls' only session, held in response, Janie suspects, to a directive to schools from the Department of Education that steps be taken to discourage anorexic tendencies. (Nothing much gets past Janie.) Janie has not been feeling too comfortable with her own body recently. In fact, she's pretty fed up with it, specially after the way it chose to ooze away strength on the very morning of a grudge match with St Mary's girls, at a time when her regular inclusion in the hockey team was in question, for though she is fleet on the wing and a great feinter and dodger, there are doubts over her ability to withstand heavyweight tackles. However, a healthy personality will accommodate these bodily inconveniences, Janie appreciates, having studied *An Introduction To Psychology* lent to her by Miss Simons. She argued for this line very effectively in the debate, and afterwards received Miss Simons's congratulations. Janie is frequently praised by her teachers, she is a highly intelligent and diligent student; but praise from Miss Simons is specially sweet. Janie reveres her. If she, Janie, were the sort to require a role model – she is aware that given her tough independence of mind she is not – but if she were, Miss Simons would be it.

The private farm road takes her past the modern bungalow where her grandfather lives. But she does not study its windows and prepare to wave because she is suddenly taken by a contrary thought. That it is all very well for people like Miss Simons whose bodily inheritance is already known (and in the case

49

of Miss Simons is, frankly, brilliant). Some people are in the position of not being sure how they will finally turn out. Just suppose, worries Janie, fate were to drop on her her sister's body. She'd have to drown herself. She would, really. (A decision arrived at as the road swings to the right and the willow-edged pond comes into view.) Fortunately, this is not a likely outcome. Heather is clearly a full-blown Topping. Janie appears to favour her mother.

At least, so far as looks are concerned she does: they are both small, both skinny, both dark. In other matters Janie perceives a very great difference. On imaginary scales she weighs such qualities as intellectual rigour and evenness of temperament; and sees her own side drop with a satisfying thump, while her mother's soars. Poor Mum, up in the air as usual, thinks Janie. It about sums her up.

Janie is more than half convinced that her mother's bouts of preoccupation and moodiness are the fault of her father. Most trouble in the world comes down to men, is the opinion that unites the members of Janie's gang – an opinion honed by a wide range of reading, by the output of television, and by ironic remarks dropped by Miss Simons – an opinion confirmed by their experience of co-education (boys are noisy, boys are greedy, boys will carelessly do disgusting things; they think they own the space, they are selfish and arrogant and disruptive; most damning of all, they don't give a toss, they think everything they do or say is either correct or hilarious). It stands to reason therefore that living with her father must be deleterious to her mother in some way. Living with any man would be. The only thing this theory lacks is evidence. Unfortunately, her father's manner to her mother is unfailingly loving and courteous. But Janie isn't fooled, she knows there must be some subtle way he has of unsettling her.

The road has brought her to the farmyard. There is a branch off to the house, which Janie takes. Beyond the farmyard, the road continues to service the farther fields, and from this direction a Land Rover arrives.

Steve has brought down a couple of hay bales from the Dutch barn. He backs up to the milking parlour and turns off the engine. 'Janie?' he calls as he springs out.

Rosie the retriever jumps out also. With her head down and her tail waving, she lollops across the yard, eager to be let into the house: she is an elderly dog and keen on her comforts. From her knowledge of this, Janie deduces that her mother is out. She stoops down and holds out her arms. 'Hi, Rosie.'

'*Janie*,' yells Steve, annoyed at being ignored, annoyed that his daughter doesn't come over, annoyed that she will waste his time messing with the dog. Work doesn't stop on a farm at four-thirty.

Janie hears her name bouncing among the farm buildings – in her father's unpleasant tone of voice. She hates the way he says *Janie*, as if she's an aberration or something. He never says *Heather* in that nasty tone. Oh no, his voice is soft when he addresses to his pet.

'Janie, get here!'

'Why?' asks Janie, straightening up.

'*Here.*'

'Anyone would think I was the dog,' she complains, taking unwilling steps.

'Your mother's out.'

'I know.'

'Oh you know, do you? Then I suppose you know where she went, Miss Clever Sides.'

'No?'

'Never mind. Just give the place a bit of a tidy. She left during lunch, I didn't have time to clear up after. Oh, and see if you can do something about tonight's meal – I expect she'll be tired when she gets home – maybe peel a panful of spuds.'

'Christ Almighty!' cries Janie. 'Mock GCSEs start tomorrow, I've only got an English exam first thing. But I suppose you've forgotten a tiny detail like that; my life's not important.'

'I've told you before to watch your language,' shouts Steve. Then he sighs and goes towards the back of the jeep, saying, 'I haven't got time to argue the toss, but I don't see what exams have to do with it.'

'No, I don't suppose you do. Well, for one thing I've got to swot, and for another Miss Simons said we should avoid getting overtired. Exams are stressful, in case you didn't know.'

'If you can't help your mum when she's feeling low,' puffs Steve, hauling out a bale, 'I reckon it's a pity.'

'Don't tell *me* about Mum. It's not my fault she goes funny.'

'What's that?' he cries indistinctly, while making a hobbling run for the milk parlour doorway with the bale propped on his thighs.

But Janie decides to leave matters to his conscience, and turns and stomps back to the house.

While Janie is letting herself into the farmhouse, her mother is speeding towards it – speeding, impatient to be home, impatient to resume normal life.

Fran was released from depression in a single instant at around half-past three. The battering ram through the door, the knife cutting her free, was a slight and unassuming instrument. Merely an idea. A connection. It rose in her mind as cleanly and swiftly as a lark from grass.

She had been reading for over an hour – reading John Clare, naturally enough – the set of poems he began writing while incarcerated in the Epping asylum and completed after his long hike home. The set he called *Prison Amusements.*

Life is to me a dream that never wakes
Night finds me on this lengthening road alone—

She was struck by his frequent use of the name Mary. Again and again in these poems it appears. John Clare himself remarks on this:

Mary how oft with fondness I repeat
That name alone to give my troubles rest—

But his motive was surely more than this, much more than heart's ease, thought Fran. She raised her head and peered at the shadowy shelving beyond the flat exposure granted by the strip-lighting. And her mind gave birth to a novel idea. That, by incorporating Mary's name into his writing, Clare was bringing into being, securing for himself, her actual presence.

A very modest idea, and doubtless novel only to herself, but the getting of it – the twitch and grind of her brain's muscle, the convulsive leap, the snatch of recognition – was a heady experience. It shot her clean from her despair. For a while she even forgot she had been in despair, so arousing was her idea's corollary: that writing can achieve such a thing. And that if she too were in possession of a name she could attempt to do likewise. The fact that a name was not in her possession didn't at all have the appearance of a stumbling block, for it was immediately apparent she should exploit what she did have: a sense of him, his amorphous presence. Lacking a name, lacking a face, she would invoke him obliquely.

A little while later she replaced the book she'd been reading and gathered her bag. She felt sated and grateful, as if, after much tortuous searching, she had finally been pointed in the right direction. Which was to take her writing more seriously, to make time for it, and to hold fast to the knowledge that had come to her this afternoon that its possibilities are limitless.

Outside in the street she discovered she was teeming with energy. And hungry, hungry. She made for a baker's, the very same shop where she had pacified her hunger as a truanting schoolgirl. It was still there, still displaying the same type of cakes. The taste of the doughy Danish she bought filled her mouth before she had got it out of its paper bag. She straight away began to eat, resting her back against a shop's window ledge. At first her eyes were greedily fixed on the pastry, marking out successive mouthfuls, but as her hunger abated they slid to the pavement, to the feet of passers-by. And her ears picked out above the din of traffic and commerce the sound of a violin. She began to walk towards the sound, out of the lane containing the baker's shop, into the wide pedestrianized street; and eventually she noticed a busker – tall, gaunt, youngish, in a long black coat – outside one of the stores. She had a feeling she'd glimpsed him somewhere earlier this afternoon, but couldn't be sure.

At a distance from the violin player she stopped to finish her pastry. There was a ceaseless passage of people, some on their own, some in twos or in larger groups, some with children. A few dawdled and looked about them, a few paused to examine the contents of shop windows; most walked by quickly, intent on where they were going.

Were they all, every one, here for the strict purpose of shopping? Fran wondered. Or had some, like herself, come to town for a more complicated reason? To take the edge off a loneliness by rubbing shoulders with strangers, perhaps; or as a distraction from worry or depression or a painful memory; or simply to be somewhere, no other place being available. If so, Fran wished them luck, wished them to find as happy a resolution as she had. She screwed up the empty paper bag and dropped it into a litter bin. Moved on.

In the car-park the empty space at the rear of her car seemed to leap at her. The motorbike was potent in its absence, able to assume a disproportionate size, to lean indecently towards her, almost brushing her back as she unlocked her car. Guilt, she explained it to herself. Guilt and shame.

But then, having manoeuvred into the one-way traffic system, the car-park and its spaces falling further and further behind, she denied she had any reason to feel guilt or shame. After all, she had not invented the fantasy for any vicious motive. She hadn't invented it deliberately at all. Her mind had made her a gift of it, to get her out of a hole. The same way it came up with the idea about John Clare's use of the name Mary this afternoon, to get her out of a much worse hole. Maybe her mind likes to oblige in this way because it tries to make up for landing her in so much trouble in the first place, all those years ago. It often seems to Fran that there is more going on inside her head – convolutions, improbabilities, histories, fantasticalities – than outside. But maybe the stuff inside is just more successful at grabbing her attention.

She leaves the ring road, choosing the dual carriage-way in preference to the country route, and the town dwindles to a straggle of houses. She keeps in the fast lane, bearing down on the accelerator.

Fran enters the house via the kitchen door and makes straight for the tap where she pours and drinks a glass of water.

'Anyone home?' she calls, filling the kettle. She turns, noticing packets, tins, jars and various vegetables spread over the table. 'What's going on?'

Janie comes in from the scullery carrying a large saucepan. 'I'm making supper. Dad said do some potatoes. But I thought what's the use? You've got to have something to go with potatoes. So I looked through the books and found this recipe. It's going to be great, a healthy risotto. I hope you're not going to get in my way, making tea and stuff.'

'I'll try not to, but I'm thirsty,' Fran says, while thinking to herself Risotto, eh? Steve and Heather aren't going to like it. Steve and Heather will ask if it's just the starter. Where's the meat? they'll say, Where's the potato? Well she herself can do something about that; she can say Risotto, how scrumptious, just what I fancied. With luck, Steve will follow her lead and Heather will follow her father's. 'Terrific,' she tells Janie. 'What a clever and thoughtful daughter I've got. Fancy a cup?'

'No thanks. I'm glad somebody round here appreciates me. Dad even forgot it's my English exam tomorrow.'

'Poor baby. I'll test you on your quotes later, if you like.'

'Thanks, but no sweat. We had free periods this morning and me and Char tested each other. I say, Mum.' Janie blinks and pushes up her spectacles. 'You sound quite normal.'

'Do I? Then perhaps I am.'

'That's a relief.'

'Mm. Well, I'll just go and change, then see to the hens. If I don't get a move on I'll be feeding them in the dark.' But in the doorway she pauses, sips from the mug of tea she is holding and observes her daughter; observes that she doesn't look the cleanest of mortals.

'I suppose you did wash your hands before handling that food?'

'Yes, *Mother*,' growls Janie.

'Just checking, my scary cherub,' says Fran.

Ten minutes later Fran has swopped her skirt and shoes for trousers and wellingtons, and is hastening through the yard. She treads the cobbles that line the way in front of the former wash-house and stables. It's a path she treads every morning and evening (unless someone has opted to feed the hens for her), but tonight it feels different; tonight the knobbliness of the cobbles and the way they throw her feet out of line seem like new sensations. Arriving at the barn where the chicken feed is stored, she swings each leg in turn over the low barrier across the threshold. They feel weightless, her whole body refreshed.

From the milking-parlour window Steve has caught sight of her. 'Hello,' he calls, coming over. 'What are you doing?'

'Seeing to the hens, of course.'

'Darn,' says Steve, climbing over the barrier into the barn. 'That was the other thing I meant to tell Janie: Hal's seen to the poultry. Pity I forgot, and you had to drag out here. But that girl was so blimmin argumentative—'

'That was nice of him. After all I said.'

'So how are things, love? You sound more like your self.'

'I'm fine. Sorry I—' But she's said it too often, the phrase has a worn-out sound. Instead, she reaches up with a kiss.

'Fran,' he says, gathering her. 'Oh, Fran.'

She hugs him hard, then pulls free. 'Yep. Well, I'll go and give Janie a hand. She's making risotto – a special treat for me, she knows I love it.'

'Ah,' says Steve. 'Right.'

'Or maybe I'll have a bath. She was coping fine, why interfere? See you later, love.'

*   *   *

Sonia is sipping tea while perched on the arm of a gold and aqua brocade settee. She's much too animated to sink her behind in its squashy seat.

After her lunch in the Tasty Bite (surprisingly nice) she went window-shopping. There was a busker on the pavement outside British Home Stores. Not the usual kind – tatty old geezer or grim-looking youth with a mouth organ or guitar – no, this busker was a tall, lean, nice-looking boy in a long dark coat, playing some classical tune on a violin. Sonia was so struck that she stopped right there on the pavement, causing a passing couple to separate and other shoppers to swerve. She got out her purse (not as easy as it sounds: the new bag is smaller than her others and stiff and retentive), selected a pound coin, walked up to the young man and carefully let the money drop into the open violin case. Yes, a full pound: not a 20p or even a 50, but the full whack as coins go. 'It's a treat to hear good music,' she told him – loudly, so that he should register the size of her donation and others might be prompted into similar largesse.

'Thanks,' acknowledged the lad.

'Oh, the pleasure's mine,' beamed Sonia. Moving away, she tried to hum the tune.

It eluded her. Classical tunes usually do. In truth she dislikes classical music – except for one or two familiar numbers, such as Vivaldi's *Four Seasons* which is always playing when she eats at the Ca D'Oro, and those pieces that have been used as theme music for films. Mostly, a classical sort of sound makes her feel glum. What she loves are the pops; the good old numbers with a strong melody and a beat to set her feet tapping. Her favourites are the ones that conjure happy times: parties, dances, charity balls, Conservative Party shindigs. (Sonia is famous in her circle as a dancer; light on her feet, and adaptable and kind to the worst clodhopper of a partner.) No, what she really and truly meant was, it was a treat to see a nicely brought up boy (after all, someone must have paid for his music lessons) standing up for respectable standards, giving them an airing. Such a pleasant change from the *I demand a handout* attitude that is so often thrust in one's face. That's what she meant, and that is what she is confident she conveyed.

She continued on to Marks & Spencer, where she purchased a dinner for one – chicken cordon bleu, temptingly illustrated on its cardboard jacket – and a pair of tights, and spent ages trying to make up her mind about a nightdress. Until something made her look at her watch. Whereupon she ran like the dickens, hurled herself into Wilson's Shoes to pick up her parcels, then skittered as fast as her brand-new Cuban heels would allow over the shopping centre's slippery floor tiles. She just made it into a lift as the doors were closing. 'Sorry, everyone,' she told the crowd inside, apologizing for causing the doors to fling open again, and sending round her best supplicatory smile. 'I need level five, somewhat urgently. My time's run out. I'm in danger of getting a ticket.'

Not a flicker. Not a murmur. Straight up to level six without anyone lifting a finger. Talk to yourself, Sonia, she thought. At level six an overweight couple got out, and she quickly shoved her own finger against the button marked five. Naturally, to no avail. Up they went to level seven. Really, the lack of common courtesy these days could make you weep.

Level five at last. Out she flew, and over the tarmac to her parked car. No ticket. Thank you, thank you, she silently serenaded an absent warden who was obviously taking an extended tea-break. It's silly, and she knows it, but she just can't bear getting a parking ticket. It isn't the fine – which is not all that severe when you think about it, only a tiny proportion of a good day's spend; it's the unpleasantness of receiving

59

a telling off. However much she tells herself it's only money, see a ticket tucked under her wipers and she has to cry. She does this discreetly, gasping and sobbing behind the steering-wheel at the unfairness of being picked on, while carefully stopping up with a tissue any tears that might be harming her make-up.

So there she was: not crying this time, but with her parking ticket expired and a disinclination to go home. Huffington's Top Labels, came the obvious answer. She drove straight over, out of the centre proper to this characterful area of town, where disused warehouses have been turned into ultra-smart or ultra-arty shops and cafés. She came not to make purchases, but to show off her new patent accessories to Maureen (Maureen Huffington, the store's owner) and Jill and Jenny (her assistants), while casting an eye over the newest stock. Well, it's a boost to be admired. It's nice, once in a while, to bask in a little praise. There's no-one at home to give her any.

Maureen and Jill and Jenny came up trumps. Maureen recognized the red two-piece at once: 'Doesn't it look fabulous? And it must be, what? – at least two seasons ago you bought it. Looks great with the shoes and bag.' And when Sonia had worked her way diligently through the racks and promised to think seriously about one or two items, Jill brought her a cup of tea, and Jenny brought over some glossy leaflets and pointed to pictures of some of the garments the store has on order. They are such dears in this shop. She is always made welcome, even when she has only come to browse.

It strikes her all at once that Maureen, Jill and Jenny are making clearing up moves. She looks at her watch. Blow if she isn't going to be caught in the rush hour! It'll be dark outside by now.

'Thanks, that was lovely,' she says, depositing her cup on the counter. 'I have to fly. Bye, everyone.' And she dashes down the stairs and out into Huffington's section of the car-park.

Sonia is driving in heavy traffic at about twenty miles an hour when it occurs to her: those are her brand new eighty-quid patent leather shoes working the pedals. A vision hits her of cracked uppers, scuffed heels. Thoughtless woman! She reaches round into the pocket on the back of her seat and draws out the pair of old shoes she keeps handy for when the shoes she has on aren't suitable for driving. She lays them ready in her lap.

The traffic is crawling now, the traffic lights ahead are showing red. What's the betting they'll be green by the time she arrives? Deciding to proceed at once, she reaches down, pulls off her left shoe and tosses it onto the passenger seat, then fits on the substitute shoe. It's a panicky sort of snatch and grab operation, but she manages, just, to keep her eyes on the windscreen throughout.

As she predicted, soon as she approaches, the lights go green. A bit of a spurt happens now, as the line of traffic she's in swoops round to the right. A minute later and the speed's back down to twenty, then fifteen. She wishes she'd changed the right shoe first; it's the right shoe, constantly prodding accelerator and brake, that's most at risk. Damn. But at this pathetic speed she could manage it, surely? Yes, she tells herself, give it a go. Raising her right foot slightly, she reaches down and yanks off the shoe— And is shocked by the consequent loss of momentum, by headlights zooming close in her rear-view mirror. In her scramble to get her foot back on the pedal and both hands on the wheel, the shoe is let slip. And there it lies, on the loose in the footwell.

For the moment she is simply relieved that her car is moving smoothly at the correct pace. Then she thinks of the abandoned shoe, and worries that it might get caught and therefore damaged under the pedals or the seat. She reaches down and gropes about, first with her right hand, then with her left. Both fail to locate it. She tuts in annoyance. Brake lights come on in the row of cars ahead. Sonia shifts her shoeless foot to make her own car follow suit, but instead of engaging the brake, stabs into something slippery and yielding.

Now both her feet are fighting and fumbling, and in her head, with her will and every nerve in her body, she is shrieking *Brake*!

But the blessed car – blind, deaf – carries dumbly onwards. Until brought to rest by the inability of its nose to penetrate any further the rear of the car in front.

4

In one crowded instant:

Jason pulls down on his steering-wheel – hard and leftwards – and thus avoids shunting into the car ahead; consternation breaks out in the near-side lane – swerving, braking, honking – and, though no further impact occurs, traffic there is brought to a halt. Jason's engine dies; someone raps on his window – 'You all right, mate?' – and Jason nods and mouths a thank-you to indicate that he is.

Then a curtain falls. As ever, Jason's father takes full advantage:

'Can't say I'm surprised. Can't think why you had to go buying a car in the first place. They're a liability, cars. What's wrong with the bus? Young lad like you with your health and strength, what's wrong with shanks's pony, eh? You know how old I was when I got my first car? Thirty bloody nine. I take it you're properly insured? Eh, might have known; third party only. Which means, if I'm not mistaken, this little lot is going to cost. Well, don't look at me. Haven't finished paying for it yet, I suppose? Like you haven't finished paying off that overdraft; like you haven't made a start paying off that student loan. Gordon Bennet! What'd I tell you, more times than I care to remember? Never, never get into debt. I knew it'd happen; but there weren't any stopping you, you were bent on going. Yewni-poxy-versity! Fastest way to

incur debt man ever invented. Stands to reason: raw youth, told it's God's gift cos it's passed some exams, given tax-payers' money, let loose unrestricted, no rules, no time sheet. A fools' paradise, that's what your university peddles. And now look at you: up to your ears in debt and a job that hardly covers your rent and food. And to cap it all you buy a car – cos a car's indispensable. Do me a favour, you must want your head examining. I bet your employers'd take a pretty dim view – or is it happy, your bank, having a member of staff up to his ears in debt? Cos if it is, I tell you here and now, it can whistle for my custom—'

But this is all wrong, says Jason to himself as the curtain lifts. This is rubbish. His father doesn't know about his job in the bank. His father doesn't know he lives in this town. His father is a hundred odd miles away and doesn't know, and probably never wonders, whether his son Jason is alive or dead. (Why should he? He never wondered about his wife. *Good riddance, I say. We're well off without her. Not to mince words, your mother, lad, was a slut and a whore.*) More to the point, since his father is ignorant of the purchase of this car, he cannot know its up-to-the-minute history – that someone has run into it, inflicting God knows how many pounds' worth of damage.

Damage is galvanizing. It jolts Jason completely out of his daze. It restores his ability to move.

Sonia has been engulfed by the world of men. The driver of a bus coming the other way leant out of his cab and shouted a comment. Sonia is sure it was a derisive comment even though she didn't catch the words. A man from the car behind got out and rapped on her window – 'All right, darling?' – but the look he gave her was not sympathetic. More men have arrived and are standing and gazing by the area of impact. Any minute now they will be joined by the irate driver of the car she has pranged. It'll be just her luck if a *police*man turns up. Men en masse, it seems, are converging to pass judgement on yet another example of inept female behaviour; to be persuaded more surely than ever of their belief that women and cars don't mix. *Good grief. Just look at the dizzy cow. I ask you.*

And then Sonia recalls the cause of her accident, the rogue shoe that somehow got trapped between the pedals; recalls also the shoeless condition of her right foot. Swiftly she rectifies both these matters, then, taking a deep breath, unlatches the door of her car. If only David were here, she is wishing, as her feet land in the road. Or if only these men could be David's sort. Then she'd be all right, she'd know how to be: rueful and smiley, sorrowful and sweet, she'd be mistress of the situation. Sadly, these men do not look promising.

It strikes her that the driver of the car she pranged is taking the dickens of a time to emerge. Surely he can't be injured? No, no. If anyone was going to be injured it would be herself, taking the impact head on. And after all, it wasn't such a big impact, quite a gentle one really. Maybe he's slow because he's big and cumbersome. A cheesy sort of man, to go with this cheesy old car. She conjures him: florid, fleshy, hulking. And her insides tighten like ravelled up knitting. Wishing herself a million miles away, she goes dutifully forward.

Jason gets out of his car and dream-walks round to its rear. It looks bad. And it's not even his car, properly speaking. It's the finance company's car. But since this accident wasn't his fault, surely the other driver's insurance will pay. Hasn't he read somewhere though, or heard on a radio programme, that insurance companies often split the damage between them, regardless of fault? So what if you've only got third party insurance? In a despairing gesture Jason runs his fingers through his hair. He knows in his bones that he's going to come out of this badly. Because that's how life is for young people on their own who are trying to make a go of things, who haven't a bean in the world, who have nothing and no-one to fall back on, not even a well-disposed parent who'll slip the odd handout.

Just a boy, thinks Sonia. A slim, floppy-haired, mild-looking boy. Attractive, too, in spite of his woe-begone expression. *Thank you, God*, she prays – for such has been her dread of confronting a bludgeon-faced stocky individual, that she feels let off; as if the Divine Hand has made a quick substitution.

'I'm terribly sorry,' she chirrups, raising her voice against the traffic noise. 'The most horrid thing happened, I got cramp in my foot. Have you ever suffered from foot cramp?'

Only the nosey parkers look at her. The injured party continues to examine his car. 'Agony,' shouts Sonia, pulling a face. 'Could I get my foot to the brake? Not to save my life, I couldn't. Seems hard to credit, I expect, but that's how an attack of cramp can take you. It was a mercy we were only crawling along, or it might literally have been my life at stake.' (All right, she's lying. But she's up against it – the law, possibly, and certainly these cold-eyed men.) 'Luckily, it was just a minor prang.'

'Don't know about minor. Bet his boot won't open. And he'll need new panels. Your bumper don't look too healthy, neither.'

'That's what I mean – surface damage only. I mean, their vital organs couldn't be affected, not by a bump at that speed; the things will still *go*. They will, won't they?'

The men confer. They agree the cars are probably drivable, once Sonia's has been lifted free of Jason's.

'I reckon we could shift it off between us,' says one. 'Go and take your brake off, missus.'

'They better exchange details first,' says another.

They are less stern now, cheered by the prospect of the obstacles being cleared from their path: pulling out from their zig-zagged nose-to-bumper line-up would be difficult, given the traffic density, but if these two move off and sort their problem out elsewhere things will become easier. The last speaker nudges Jason. 'Got something to write with?'

Jason jumps. 'I've only had it a week,' he says, voicing the aspect of the situation that is impressing him most.

Sonia picks up that he is not so much complaining as overwhelmed. She also registers that his voice is pleasantly modulated. 'Only a week? Oh dear. I really am most dreadfully sorry.'

'That's all right,' says Jason automatically. 'I mean, you had cramp, you couldn't help it.'

What a sweet, forgiving boy! 'Dear, don't look so tragic. It's not the end of the world. My garage will fix it in no time. Good as new, I promise. I'm Sonia Garrs, by the way.'

'Oh, um, how do you do. I'm Jason Caulfield.'

'Well, Jason. First, as this gentleman has pointed out, you and I have to confide to each other our vital statistics.' Sonia's feeling is, a little roguishness might persuade him to smile. Pleasant, well spoken, courteous young men normally do smile, in Sonia's experience. If she could only restore Jason's, then she mightn't feel so guilty.

'Just follow me. Got that? Follow *me*,' Sonia has yelled to Jason, because Jason has explained that he has

67

never heard of Bellamy's Motors; he has lived in the town for only a few weeks, and still finds the one-way system confusing. In fact, the only route he can follow with confidence is the one between the staff car-park behind Barclays where he works (his first job, he told her, since graduating last July) and his bedsit in Florence Street.

Sonia found his address faintly shocking – not that she let it show. Florence Street is one of those dreadful dingy backstreets near the shoe factories. The young have to start somewhere, she supposes; even so – nice boy, nice family, one presumes – you'd think his parents would help him out till he lands on his feet, you'd think they'd want to see him installed in a pleasant area with other young professionals. Take Sally Bellamy, whose father owns the very garage they are now driving towards. Sally, also a recent graduate, working for Martin Pask a well-known solicitor in the town, has a three-room apartment at the top of one of the Victorian houses near the park – though mum and dad do help with the rent, of course.

Sonia checks her rear-view mirror. And is reassured that Jason is managing to keep close to her tail despite the density of the traffic and all the stops and starts they need to make. Poor boy, he did look upset. But she soon changed that, soon had him smiling. Probably because her own smile was infectious. She's often noticed this to be the case.

'Follow *me*,' she told him. And as if his life depends on it, Jason is following. Whatever the situation on the road, he permits no other vehicle to come between hers and his. They arrive at a roundabout, a huge one with five exits, three of them major routes. Cars edge forward in turn and wait for the chance to nip into the circular flow. When Sonia goes, Jason follows; and a white van whizzing round from the right is forced to brake. There's an angry honking. But Jason doesn't care. He's far too elated.

It isn't because he doesn't trust her that he keeps so close. He has no sense at all of her trying to evade him; if he gets held up he knows she'll pull into the side and wait while he catches up. It's the mood she has cast that is making him feel light-hearted and reckless. 'Follow *me*,' she commanded, and an answering voice in Jason cried, Yes, *ma'am*!

He recalls another thing she said: 'It's not the end of the world.' It was brilliant, that. The complete opposite of the attitude he was brought up with, the *You've gone and done it now, lad*, and *I told you so*, and *Don't come crying to me* line, dished out by his father.

All that gloom and doom, the blight of his teenage years. Literally a blight. Because it blighted his memory, withered it away, leaving the years that went before, the years when his mother was around, a total blank. Seven years of his life, his first seven years of life (which were definitely idyllic, must have been, *she* was part of them), completely blotted out by mind-numbing bombardment. *Stop that whining you snivelling little sod, she ent coming back and a good job too. I warn you, you'll come to nothing. You're bone idle, just like your mother. Go on like that and you'll be out on your ear. Lying little bastard. Blithering idiot.* It was like living with a vengeful binman – the least show of spirit, and he had a wheeliebin's smothering muck flung over him. No wonder his mother left home. The reasons his father gave were just rubbish. *She was a hussy, your mother. One and only thing she cared about was having a good time. Got herself a fancy man. Well, I wish the poor bastard joy of her. Cos it won't last; there's not a man born could satisfy her appetites.* It was rubbish, all of it. What really drove her off was the thought of being tied to old misery-guts. She got to the stage where she couldn't stand it any more. Jason can picture how it must have happened, how she'd have planned to take her seven-year-old son with her, but was prevented by her husband – not out of fatherly affection but dog-in-the-manger vindictiveness. In a mood of defiance, Jason put this theory to his father once. *Oh yeah? And what do you think she'd have wanted with you, may I ask? A seven-year-old kid would've cramped madam's style.* But Jason hardly bothered to listen to the reply. In any case, he didn't need to test the theory, because by this time he'd already started having his intuitions – the waves of conviction about his mother's personality that rush to his head and drain warmly through his body, leaving him with a well set-up feeling, as if he and she have enjoyed a satisfying conversation, as if she has confided in him. As a result, memories have become unnecessary; he has learned all he needs to know of her intuitively. This is why he is sometimes able to recognize aspects of his mother in other women. Like in Miss Nyree Purcell who was his English teacher at school and on whose speech patterns he modelled his own (how desolate he felt when she left to get married); and in Mrs Pam James, mother of his close friend Kevin (terrible the way he and Kevin fell out); and in Dr Janet Drinkwater, lecturer in economics, who was his personal tutor at university (till she took a sabbatical). And now this evening, in perhaps the most dramatic example of all (Christ, she actually crashed into him!) he has met another: someone so like *her*, it's uncanny. It's not that this Sonia resembles his mother physically. Jason knows that she doesn't, because he has in his possession a photo of a pretty young woman with her longish fair hair being blown about and a face not at all like Sonia's. (Jason pocketed the photo when he came across it one afternoon during the school holidays – his father being at work, he'd taken the opportunity to search

70

the sideboard drawers.) But the image doesn't really tell him anything. It doesn't stir memories. The portrait he has built of his mother is the one that counts, which is really a portrait of attributes. It's because of this, the portrait of attributes, that when Sonia said, 'It's not the end of the world,' a lurch came inside him. Of recognition.

And in a way, *she* seemed almost to recognize *him* – which was also uncanny: the way she took hold of his name the moment he spoke it. 'Well, Jason,' she said – by way of introducing a jokey remark about vital statistics – which was a nice touch, too: it showed she's not the sort to stand on her dignity, that she's willing to take a bit of a gamble, friendship-wise; that she's open and generous and fun. Being with his mother must have felt like that: fun and a bit of an adventure. Just as flying round in tandem through these ill-lit streets is fun and a bit of an adventure.

No way is any car or van going to come between them!

As soon as they arrive – Sonia springing out of her car and beckoning her follower to get out of his – the idea comes to her that this is not the right place. Bellamy's Motors supplies and maintains BMWs – nippy coupés like Sonia's, sleek medium-sized saloons, and big powerful jobs. What on earth will they make of this used-looking C-reg Ford? But – never say die – the Bellamys are personal friends of Sonia's. (Which is the reason she drives a BMW. 'Isn't it rather an extravagance, the few miles I clock up in a year?' she has suggested to David. But David says it's an investment in friendship and goodwill. David was at school with Ronnie Bellamy.)

Now, a mechanic working late in the service department having been summoned to explain to her the facts of life regarding horses for courses, or old bangers for back-street garages, she plays her trump card. Not to the mechanic, but to the glossy haired, over-painted young woman in a swivel chair on the far side of the vast and low reception desk. 'Is Ronnie around?' she asks.

'Mr Bellamy?' The expression in the receptionist's eyes changes, from glazed-over sorrow at being unable to assist this dotty lady customer (except in the matter of her BMW's damaged bumper, and that only when the job is booked in) to wide-awake caution.

'That's right. Give him a buzz will you? Tell him it's Sonia Garrs come to beg a favour.'

'I think Mr Bellamy's taking a call in the sales office.'

'That's all right. We'll wait.' Sonia takes a chair and indicates to Jason to do likewise. 'I don't suppose Natalie's anywhere about – Mrs Bellamy?' she asks casually.

'Er, shouldn't think so. I tell you what,' – the receptionist gets to her feet, her expression has changed again, this time to keen and helpful – 'I'll just pop over to the sales suite myself and tell Mr Bellamy you're here.'

'Oh will you? That is kind.'

You see? asks the smile Sonia flashes at Jason. Oh, she is in her element.

'Mr Bellamy says he won't be long and would you like to wait in his office?' announces the receptionist, all smiles on her return.

'Certainly.'

Sonia and Jason are led up a flight of stairs, along a corridor and into a room dominated by a desk and a leather sofa. 'Oh yes, I remember this room,' says Sonia.

'Can I get you some coffee?'

'That would be lovely. Right, Jason; we might as well make ourselves comfy.' Sonia plonks down on the sofa and pats the space beside her. 'Now,' she says. 'Tell me about yourself. You're not from round here, I can tell that from your voice.'

Jason smiles. 'No, I'm from Aldershot. My father's an army man. Or *was*, I should say: he retired some years ago, after the sudden death of my mother. He took that very hard, it was a terrific shock, he being a good bit older than my mother.' Jason speaks smoothly without hesitation, and without his eyes darting the way people's eyes often do dart when they are embroidering – he can be confident of this because he's practised various accounts of himself in a mirror. Accuracy, in any case, is not on his mind. As always, he's concerned with one thing only: how to respond in a way that will make him attractive – he is particularly avid to be successful in this when the enquirer is one of those women he has linked to his mother. How to capture her attention and approval: this is his only concern. Once, he based his method principally on being as different as possible in every way to his father (since his father is obnoxious it seemed a fair bet). But these days his father doesn't come into it: the pleasant and accentless voice he has acquired, together with considerate and engaging manners, would make him a foreigner in the Caulfield household. Having had so much practice, he feels pretty confident during these early stages of a relationship. It's later on he has to watch out. It's later on when there's a danger of the thing that he dreads most of all occurring: another door closing, another desertion.

Sonia, whose face has changed from pleased interest to sad surprise, waits until the receptionist who has brought in the coffee goes out before commenting on the loss of his mother. 'Oh Jason, I am sorry. How old were you when she died? If you don't mind talking about it.'

'Not at all. I was seven. We were abroad, my father

73

was serving in Germany. My mother caught a viral infection. It nearly destroyed my father. He and I came home, and Dad retired soon afterwards. He's become a bit of a recluse, chiefly interested in the garden.'

Sonia demurs. 'Surely, his chief interest is *you*. He must be enormously proud—'

'Oh Dad does his best. He's supportive and all that. He just can't help being out of touch.' Jason laughs. 'I bet most kids think that about their parents. Do you have any children?'

'One daughter. She's married, with a two-year-old son. She works for the European Parliament. A confident and happy young woman. The world's her oyster, you might say. But then her father simply lavished money on her schooling and so forth. She was a lucky girl. Her childhood was very different to mine. Both my parents worked for Church's, the shoe company. A lot of people round here are connected with shoes, mostly in a humble way. My grandparents were factory hands. My parents were wages clerks – they considered they'd gone up in the world. My husband's people, now, were in brewing, the town's other big industry. I thought them posh; they actually owned the brewery, you see. Though it was taken over years ago.'

Her frankness, for one moment, makes Jason thoughtful. He wonders whether she'd have warmed to an unvarnished account of his background – life as a child in married quarters, his father's former devotion to the parade ground and present devotion, as gardener and handyman, to keeping spruce the homes of the top brass of Aldershot. But that would leave out so much – the truth about his mother, her gaiety and love of life, all her appealing ways, which cannot be backed up by facts and memories. The facts and memories he still possesses are centred round a parent he loathes. They sicken him to recall, never mind speak out loud. How will he ever become the person he aspires to be dragging that stuff after him? He won't. The facts have to be shed. They have to be obliterated.

In his thoughtfulness, Jason has turned his head to one side. Sonia studies his profile and sees a gauntness that isn't noticeable when he's giving his attractive full-faced smile. 'Are you comfortable in your digs?' she asks. 'It's not the nicest part of town.'

'They'll do me for a start,' he smiles.

'Do you cook for yourself, or is there a landlady?'

'Oh, no landlady. The house is divided into bedsits. Most of those houses are. Not that I do cook. Too lazy, I'm afraid. Anyway, communal kitchens are just so much hassle – your stuff's always being nicked, people start accusing one another. No, what I do, I have an enormous lunch, and take home a sandwich and maybe a cake to eat in the evening. There's this terrific place near the bank that does home cooking and serves huge portions. Someone at work put me on to it. The Tasty Bite.'

'Well now, if that isn't a coincidence! I went there myself today, for the first time. Yes, it's terrific value, and very nice wholesome food. But don't you get peckish during the evening on just a snack? I should've thought—'

She pauses as the door opens smartly, and a large handsome middle-aged man comes in, stomach first.

'Now then, Sonia. What have you been up to?'

'Ronnie, darling.' She darts up to be kissed. 'I've been terribly naughty. I've got this young man into all sorts of bother. This is Jason Caulfield, by the way. Jason – Ronald Bellamy. Jason's from Aldershot. He's come to work in our lovely town, at Barclays in the square. Imagine: it's his first job, he hasn't got his bearings (and who can wonder, with our traffic

75

system?), he's just bought a car, and what do you think? He's driving home, minding his own business, when a scatty lady comes up behind, gets cramp in her foot, can't use the brake, and ploughs – wham – into his back end.'

'Sounds painful,' says Ronnie. 'Glad to meet you, young man.'

'Glad to meet you, sir.'

'I made up my mind then and there, Ronnie. I thought: this poor boy shan't be put to a load of inconvenience on account of stupid old me. I insisted that he follow me here to Bellamy's.'

'I see. What sort of car do you drive?'

'A C-reg Escort,' says Jason promptly, looking BMW man square in the eye.

'Right. Well, Dodd's garage on the Wellingborough Road will look after you.'

'Oh but, Ronnie,' says Sonia, 'you'll do me a great favour, I hope, and have one of your men drive it to this garage place? I refuse to let Jason take time off work – it's his first job, mind, he needs to make a good impression. He can't go taking time off work to chase after car repairs.'

Ronnie sighs softly.

Jason makes as if to speak, but Sonia waves him to silence. 'And you know, I don't actually feel all that confident about going there myself. Having to deal with men I don't know.'

'Righty-oh. Leave it with me. I'll see to it in the morning.'

'Oh thank you, darling. That's wonderful of you. Tell the garage to send me the bill – it's lucky you can vouch for me. Oh, and ask them to ring up Mr Caulfield at the bank and inform him when it's ready.'

'Where have you left it?' Ronnie asks Jason.

'Outside reception.'

'We'd better move it. No, don't bother, just leave me

your keys. Better jot down your details before you go.'
He goes to his desk and produces biro and paper.

Jason writes down his name and address and the bank's telephone number. He wonders whether Mr Bellamy is thinking him a bit of a weed for letting Sonia take over. But no, he and Sonia are obviously old friends, he'll be familiar with Sonia's ways. He gave in to her pretty sharply himself. Right now they're chatting like good old chums about someone called David.

'No I haven't. Not a word for – oo, I don't know, it must be getting on for three months. Why, have you?'

'Not a dicky. Natalie and I were only saying the other evening: must be six months since David was in touch. He's probably mixed up in some cloak and dagger business. I bet we don't know the half of it.'

'We'll hear soon enough, when he's ready to tell us,' says Sonia in the unflappable tone she knows she is admired for. (*Sonia's such a brick. No wonder David thinks so much of her. Now if it were me— Oh David can't stand anyone flapping. Remember Josie going bananas and calling in the Foreign Office? Was he livid!* went a conversation overheard by Sonia in the ladies powder room at a Rotary do. Josie was wife number two, someone David met and married in Canada and brought to live – or maybe dumped – in his home town. Soon after the Foreign Office fiasco, Josie very sensibly returned to Canada.)

'Sure we'll hear,' says Ronnie. 'We always do, the old dog.'

'Thanks,' says Jason passing over his keys and note of information. 'It's amazingly good of you to go to this trouble. I would gladly see to it myself, but—'

'I know, the lady insists. Barclays, eh? How does my old mucker Colin Whitehouse treat you? Decent enough boss?'

'Oh, certainly. A most excellent boss. And I don't mind in the least if you tell him I said so.'

Ronnie Bellamy laughs and claps Jason on the back.

Which delights Sonia, who sees that not only has she saved Jason from the consequences of her silliness, but might also have done him a bit of good. 'I think you made an impression,' she confides when they are alone together on the forecourt. 'Which can't be bad. Ronnie's a very big wheel in this town. Now, let me drive you home.'

'No, really, Mrs Garrs.'

'Please, *Sonia*.'

'Sonia, I can perfectly well get a bus.'

'A bus? Are there buses? Well yes, I suppose there must be, but heaven only knows the routes they take, and on this I can't advise you. No, you are coming with me and no argument.'

'OK, then. Thanks.'

They run to their respective doors – both in a festive mood for some reason – and jump into Sonia's car.

'Have you ever been in there?' asks Sonia thoughtfully. They have driven to the end of Bellamy's forecourt. Straight ahead looms a tall old building, formerly a malt house, now a pub and restaurant of the roadhouse type. The lights at the square upper-storey windows look warm and inviting, as does the floodlit old red brickwork and the hanging blue tiles and new dark-green paintwork. In big brass letters the name of the place is simply announced: Connor's. 'Sounds Irish to me,' says Sonia. 'But it looks like they've done it up beautifully. Must have cost them a mint. Shall we go in and check it over? I've always wanted to.'

'Well,' begins Jason.

'Oh, come on. Live dangerously.' Sonia drives briskly onto Connor's forecourt. Then she thinks of something. 'I say, I do have a cheek. How do I know you haven't made other arrangements? Honestly, Jason, do say if you've a reason to go straight home.'

'Well, no I haven't.'

In the semi-darkness Sonia beams. 'Splendid. Then let's go and investigate, shall we? If it's ghastly we can always walk out.'

'Yeah,' he says. 'Why not?'

5

On the following afternoon at half-past two, Fran enters the farmhouse by the kitchen door and discovers Janie, calmly reading from a file of notes spread open on the table and nursing her cat. Fran is both dismayed and perplexed. Two hours of peace at least, she'd anticipated. A chance to collect her thoughts and get on with some writing. Now such an idea fades. How does Janie come to be here, is what she wants to know. Specifically, by what means of transport. For only one bus passes by the farm in the afternoon, and that not until twenty-past four. However, it is Janie who is first in with a question.

'Where've you been? That's two days running you've been out.'

The tone of this prompts Fran to proceed warily. 'I've been delivering envelopes since one o'clock. I promised Liz I'd cover the farms between here and the village, so I decided to get it over with,' she says while dumping a bag on the table and unbuttoning her coat. 'And I stayed for a while at Sue Goddard's. Would you believe she still hasn't got a date for that hip replacement?'

Over the granny spectacles that invariably slide to rest near the tip of her small bumpless nose, and from under her fall of gelled curls (intended to be gelled spikes, but nature will out), Janie glowers, and Fran wonders which aspect of her afternoon – delivering charity envelopes or spending time with a neighbour – will be selected for mockery and condemnation. But then something behind her daughter's cross expression, something less certain, causes Fran a pang. It's only plastered on, she thinks; one wrong word and that stern act will crumble. So what can be the matter? Overtired from too much swotting? Today's exam surely can't have upset her; this after all is little Miss Brainbox.

From her bag Fran removes a greaseproof-paper parcel; she opens this to reveal some cakes. 'Sue had been baking. She insisted on giving me these for "the girls' tea". Fancy one now with a cuppa?'

'No, I do not.' Evidently put into a huff by the very suggestion, Janie dumps the cat on the floor and flounces up from the table. Army boots thump over the quarry floor tiles, tiny fingers, the nails bitten to the quick, emerge just sufficiently from straggly woollen sleeves to yank open the fridge door.

'Suit yourself,' says Fran. 'I'll have one anyway.' She fills the kettle.

Janie slams the fridge door shut. 'There's never anything decent to eat in this house.'

'What do you call decent?'

'Healthy stuff. Stuff that doesn't clog up your arteries. Like that special light yoghurt.'

'Right. Well now you've told me I'll put it on the list. Anything else?'

'Honestly, how can I say off the top of my head?'

'*You* write it down, then, when you've had time to think.'

'Lite and Lovely it's called. It's been on the telly. But I only like the vanilla flavour.' She sounds cross and accusing, as if a sensitive mother would be aware of her latest food fad without needing to have it spelt out for her.

But her grumbles are losing their bluster. In another

moment, Fran senses, the picture could be changed, and Janie sharing a joke or a confidence. She is a volatile creature. What she says and does can seem full of contradictions. This is because she very often gives precedence to what is going on inside her, is Fran's hunch, based on her own similar tendency. For Janie reminds her, in a worrying sort of way, of herself at fifteen. Not that Fran was specially clever – good at some things, hopeless at others. Janie gets A grades in every subject. Except Home Economics. Crass stupidity in Home Economics is Janie's pet affectation. Particularly it wins Janie's black spot, Fran suspects, because it happens to be the one school subject at which her sister excelled. Janie and Heather are deadly enemies. At least, their enmity is deadly to Fran and Steve, particularly when it erupts at mealtimes.

'May as well have one, I suppose. Seeing as you're making it,' says Janie. And Fran puts out two mugs.

'What sort of cakes are they?'

'Butterfly cakes. Pieces of sponge held together with lemon curd. Homemade lemon curd.'

'Oh, natch,' Janie says, casually helping herself.

Fran whips out two plates and puts them on the table. 'How did the exam go this morning?'

'No probs,' Janie says with her upper lip lifted away from her teeth and her head rocking, like Patsy on TV in *Absolutely Fabulous*.

Not the exam, then. So she might as well ask the question that's really bothering her – the omens look kind, the cake's vanishing without mishap. She fills the mugs, and says casually, 'How did you get home so early? I'd have come and picked you up, only you said you wanted to work in the library this afternoon.'

Janie's humorous look vanishes.

'You didn't hitch a lift, Janie? You promised me faithfully you'd never—'

'Mrs Whitehead dropped me off at the gate, if you want chapter and verse. Their Range Rover came up the school drive, so I dashed out and asked for a lift to the village. She'd come for Pip. She said she'd bring me to the farm gate.'

'Nice of her. But you only had to ring me.'

'No answer, was there.'

'But I was here until one. What time did the exam finish?'

Janie raises her mug to her mouth and leaves it there. Fran waits.

'Mu-um?' Putting the mug down at last.

'U-huh?'

'I had a blazing row with Char.'

'Oh, you didn't!' Charlotte Timms is Janie's best friend. 'Never mind, you'll make it up.'

'She was a cow. Totally unreasonable. She got the others on to me. They were all foul.'

'Why? What was it about, love?'

'Well, it was the English exam, right? A brilliant paper. Everyone said it was a doddle afterwards. Then Char goes, "Fancy setting us the exact same question she gave us for homework." "What same question?" I said. "The one on Hamlet," said Char. "But it wasn't the same question, you twit," I told her. Cos, Mum, it wasn't. Char couldn't've read it properly. She probably saw *Hamlet*, then *guilt*, and thought, *Cool. Done it*. I said, "You had to discuss motives *other* than guilt – like jealousy, say; jealousy of his uncle having it off with his mother." Char went scarlet. And you know what? She said I'm a bighead, I act like I know everything, and I – I crawl to teachers. THAT IS A LIE. Honestly, Mum, I've never crawled to anyone in my life. "You're only saying it," I told Char, "cos you're pissed off you messed up." Then Char started crying. And the others were like, *Never mind, Char, Janie's a show-off. Just ignore her*. And Katie said she'd thought the same as Char, only she didn't do it cos when it was homework she got C minus. I said, "But it wasn't the same as homework, you thickhead." And God, Mum, they went ballistic. All of 'em. Really really vicious. It was so horrible I went and hid in the bogs. After a bit I went to the phone – but you didn't answer. Then I saw Mrs Whitehead drive up, so I ran out and asked her for a lift. Pip said, "Huh, it's *you*," when she saw it was me in the back, but nothing worse, not in front of her mum.'

Her arms and head collapse over the table. 'What'm I going to do?' she wails. 'Everyone hates me, and it's so unfair, it's totally unreasonable. *Cos I was right.*'

Fran waits for a long moment. Then she says diffidently, 'I suppose you could try saying you're sorry.'

Janie snaps upright, her eyes ablaze. 'You don't get it, do you? I am actually in the right about that question, *Mother*.'

'I know, dear, I don't doubt it for a moment. I don't mean sorry because you were wrong. Sorry for her feelings. Sorry to have given her bad news.'

'Oh,' says Janie, and her jaw slews. She chews her lip for a while. Then, 'I see now what happened,' she says.

'Yes?' says Fran.

'Yeah. I forgot to use my People Skills.'

'Your what?'

'People Skills – you know? When I told Miss Simons I was thinking of doing psychology at university, only I wasn't sure what psychology is, exactly, she lent me this book. There was a chapter in it called People Skills. Incredibly interesting. You want to read it, Mum.'

'You'd better lend it to me some time. Anyway, love, why not give it a try? Saying sorry, I mean. Will Char be home yet?'

'I'll ring her later, when she's had time to calm

down. Thanks for the suggestion, though. I'll go and swot some History now.'

'Hey, Janie,' Fran calls after her. 'Do you think you could operate some People Skills tonight? I mean with regard to your sister. Can you try not to stir things, and not to take umbrage. What do you think?'

Janie retraces her last few steps. 'You mean you actually want me to humour the Heifer? Good God, Mum, you don't want much.'

'Janie—'

'OK, OK, I'll give it a go.'

'A nice quiet mealtime, that's all I ask.'

'That's all she asks, folks. It's a modest request. Tune in tomorrow and discover whether Mrs Fran Topping has been granted her dearest wish.'

'She better have been, you little tyke.'

An hour and a half later, Fran is trudging through the gloom with a pail of chicken meal. The dog follows but loses heart, and before the top of the rise is reached stops to yawn in an embarrassed sort of way, then turns and lopes back.

Fran is thinking about Janie's upset with Char Timms, in particular she is thinking of the way Janie continued to insist on her rightness despite her friend's distress. And she thinks what a fool she is to imagine Janie as a rerun of herself. Just because they have a similar sense of humour and share a desire to play the fool and be what Hal would term 'contrary', just because she and Janie will catch the other's eye at certain moments knowing they are on the same wavelength and wanting to exchange a grin, and just because Janie is uncertain about some things and disturbed by others (where Heather is all too certain and scornfully dismissive), it doesn't mean they are altogether alike. And thank heaven for it, thinks Fran.

She tosses handfuls of grain into a low trough, and

calls, 'Chucky chucky chuck,' to a couple of reluctant feeders. 'Don't hang about, there's good girls. It's blimmin parky out here this evening.'

Thank heavens also that in one important respect Janie is the complete opposite of herself at fifteen. Janie knows who she is. Her sense of self is larger and more pressing than her sense of anyone else. Furthermore she knows her own mind, and has no inhibitions about making this clear. Just contrast this with the silly baby that was once Fran Spencer. *Francesca* Spencer she corrects herself, because the affected Italianate name her parents chose for her and always insisted upon seems to sum up the burden of expectation they laid on her. And not only her parents: mustn't forget the Grandmother Spencer, my goodness me, no. What a household – the son with his doting mother and his ambitious wife (ambitious for other people, that is) and his anxious appeasing daughter. Pretty, dainty, obliging little daughter; diligently accomplished, too. Ballet lessons, tap, elocution, piano. Not too hot at her schoolwork, mind, but who's bothered about that? With her looks and talent our Francesca's set to be a star, the father, the mother, the grandmother aver. *Have you seen our Francesca's ballet certificate? Grade five, Royal Academy, passed with distinction. She was really too young to go in for it, being only eleven, but her teacher had every faith. Come here, our Francesca. Show Mrs Burnet your matelot outfit. Put it on for Mrs Burnet, there's a sweet girl; show her the Sailor's Hornpipe. Did you know our Francesca got first place at the East Mids Dancing Festival for her Sailor's Hornpipe, Mrs Burnet? We were ever so thrilled, weren't we, Mother? What's that, Mother? Oh yes, quite right, it was no more than her teacher expected. I'll just put the record on. Ready now, our Francesca?*

Standing there in the wire pen, in her wellington

boots and torn waxed jacket, her nose dripping from the cold, her hair sprinkled by the dust kicked up by two old hens flying at each other's throats, Fran is visualizing a large and comfortable suburban sitting room. The room has a small girl in it. She has dark curls and an eager-to-please smile. Behind a settee she is removing her shoes and her kilt and jumper; she is putting on a sailor's outfit and a pair of red ballet pumps. She is coming out now to stand before the ladies who are seated on the settee, to look to her mother who has the arm of the needle poised over a revolving record. Her feet are placed in third position, her arms raised crosswise at chest level. Yes, our Francesca is ready; ready at the first note of music to leap into a sprightly jig.

Quickly, before it can start, Fran turns her back on the image. She goes to open the flaps on the roosting boxes, and finds five eggs; gently, she lays them in the base of the empty pail. 'Not a brilliant work rate, girls. More effort, please.' She shoos the hens up the wooden ramp, then shuts the henhouse door and wedges it securely with a stout stick. She walks round the perimeter of the wire enclosure, making sure there are no gaps, no sign that a fox has paid a preliminary visit. There is nothing amiss. As if there could be. A day can hardly go by without Hal giving the pens a check over. In near darkness, she returns down the track, carrying the pail and its fragile load.

Where's Daddy's little Francesca, eh? Oh, been to elocution lesson. Learned a new poem? Say us *Little Trotty Wagtail*. Come on in, Steve – never mind your boots – come in, lad, and hear our Francesca tell us her poem. You'll like this one,' her father winks, thinking the poem a bit of hoot. *Little trotty wagtail he went in the rain and tittering tottering sideways he ne'er got straight again* – but even then, at twelve years old and not over-bright (recently just scraped her way into grammar school), even then she knew the poem was not a hoot. It was a miracle; movements made by words, words that were delicious to utter, even under your breath, even silently. It was one of the asylum poems: she knows that now, but didn't then. It is doubtful whether in those days she connected the poetry she enjoyed with the facts that were dinned into her about the poet's life – facts which were regularly expounded during school assembly and went as follows: John Clare was a native of Northamptonshire (Hooray!), and was a living miracle because, though an uneducated peasant, his verses passed muster with the highest literary pundits of the day (Hooray again!); sad to say he went mad, and spent his last twenty-three years just round the corner from this very school, girls, in the hospital that was then a lunatic asylum (Just fancy!). But in spite of her ignorance, somewhere inside, under the elocuted voice and winsome smile and practised prettiness, lay private knowledge that in *Little Trotty Wagtail* more was to be found than any of the adults around her conceived of.

Perhaps this was her undoing – the bits of private knowledge she carried inside; knowledge that couldn't be talked about or shown to anyone, so was never examined in the light of day. Maybe it was keeping so much of herself inside her head that made her develop into a nebulous creature, unsure whether she was a person in her own right, unable to express her wants, unclear as to what her wants were. And made her end up as the sort of fifteen-year-old who, on discovering a certain motorbike rider was not the princely creature she had originally supposed, would feel obliged to pretend a continuing interest in case he should guess her disappointment and have his feelings hurt. The sort of fifteen-year-old who would let him go right ahead and fuck her rather than state plainly, no beating about the bush, that she'd prefer him not to.

Janie like her? Not in this world. *Piss off* would be Janie's instruction to any chancer on a motorbike. *Piss off* is what Janie conveys to most male persons having the misfortune to cross her path. She and her chums think men are a waste of space; they look to make them redundant; though what they then intend doing with the poor unwanted souls Fran is too soft-hearted to ask. Janie and her chums pride themselves on being the embodiment of girl power; they strut, they snarl, they dress for combat. No lad in his right mind would bother to slow-drive past Janie, and then make a point of slow-driving past her again on following days, same time, same stretch of road.

Francesca steps down from the bus. Two other girls also get off here; a girl who is a year older and in the lower sixth, and a much younger girl, a second-former. They are all three dressed in the winter school uniform, but because it is unseasonably warm, Francesca and the sixth-former have removed their gaberdine macs and bundled them into their satchels. The younger girl, mindful of the rule, has kept hers on but left it unbuttoned (not wanting to seem overly conformist perhaps). Mini skirts are the fashion. In obedience to this the sixth-former (now stalking away ahead) has jacked her school skirt higher by folding the waist band over several times, thus exposing a large expanse of mottled bare flesh between the hem of her skirt and the top of her knee-length socks. Observing her from the back, Francesca thinks she is misguided. The younger girl keeps pace at Francesca's side, not venturing to strike up a conversation; but when she turns off, calls, 'See you on Monday, Francesca,' in a breathless shy voice, and Francesca responds vaguely, 'Oh yes, bye-bye.'

Now she is alone, Francesca walks more slowly. She transfers her satchel to her left shoulder, the shoulder away from the road. In a moment he'll arrive. As she climbs the hill she ponders on her certainty – it's very light-hearted, there's no trace of anxiety in it: obviously, it wouldn't be the end of the world if he didn't come. And since she herself wasn't here at this time yesterday (her father collected her from school and drove her to the dentist), perhaps, deciding she's unreliable, he won't bother coming to seek her out this afternoon.

And yet he will come. She knows it.

Silent glee bubbles up through her chest and throat. It's hilarious, when you come to think of it, the way he behaves: zooming round the corner at a normal motorbike speed, then rapidly decelerating as he catches sight of her, driving past her so slowly that the bike wobbles and he has to skim the ground with his feet; then, at a distance a little way ahead of her, coming to rest and removing his helmet, letting his long brown hair fly out over his black leather jacket; looking back at her then, watching as she draws level; and when she has walked by, driving past for the final time, his hand raised briefly as he gathers speed.

And never, ever speaking. Francesca finds this the most mysterious and entrancing aspect of their encounter. The first time it all happened, a Friday, exactly two weeks ago today, she found it bizarre and even a little alarming. She thought then that she might have seen him previously, she had a vague recollection of a motorcyclist looking back at her over his shoulder. Perhaps he'd decided he wanted a closer look. When the whole thing – the slow drive past, the pause and the scrutiny – happened all over again on the following Monday, she was very surprised. And yet not surprised. Perhaps it was this mixture of being surprised and not surprised that caused her, before she knew what she was doing, to break into a smile. Astride his machine, he smiled back. Drawing level with him she looked away, feeling nervous and awkward. But it was all right; he didn't say anything. He didn't try to detain her. Nor did he whistle after her like the yobs do on building sites. Simply, he came on by with his hand raised in salute. And so, when on Tuesday, and again on Wednesday – and every following weekday since, apart from yesterday when she went to the dentist – her alert ears picked up the noise of the approaching engine, she felt thoroughly confident in her pleasure, knowing she could rely on an unaltered procedure.

It's perfectly delicious the way they limit themselves to an exchange of smiles. And romantic that he understands as well as she does that any words spoken would ruin the magic. She's thought about him a lot when lying in bed before going to sleep. Her imagination always retains him on the motorbike. Nothing happens in her fantasies that doesn't happen on the street; she has no curiosity about him. In bed, she merely prolongs and lengthens their customary encounter. Which is rather like a dance: she steadily walking towards him and smiling ever more broadly, he astride the bike, passing, then waiting, removing his helmet, airing his face and hair, and at last sending her his smile (a smile that is warm and appreciative, yet has a hint in it of rueful amusement at there only being this smile between them); and then the dance's conclusion, the hand lifted in farewell and the flourish of noise that carries him away over the brow of the hill. Yes, a dance, she thinks. Or an atmospheric film.

What was his reaction yesterday, she wonders, when he came by and there was no sign of her? Did he travel back and forth for a while hoping she'd turn up? Or did he shrug and give up, putting her out of his mind, perhaps concluding that she's changed the route or time of her home-going? Maybe he's decided to take a different route himself from now on, in view of yesterday's disappointment.

And yet she knows that exactly as before their pas de deux will take place. By the time she's drawn level with the pillar box ahead she will hear the noise of the bike. She calculates: about twenty more steps.

Father and daughter step in from the cold. Their faces are rosy, their eyes animated, an air of excitement and satisfaction bonds them into one unit. It is plain to Fran that the ventures Steve and Heather have shared today are more vivid to them than the scene in this kitchen, with herself running to turn up the heat under the potatoes and then to the back stairs to yell to her younger daughter that, the wanderers being returned, she will be dishing up in five minutes.

'We sold the bullocks, Mum,' cries Heather, throwing her arms round the welcoming retriever. 'Yes, Rosie we did! And made a good profit.'

'You're kidding!'

'Not. It was the records proving no history of BSE that did it. And being registered grass-fed only. Earned us a premium, didn't it, Dad?' Heather's proud and admiring face turned up to her father is as smooth and gleaming as polished pink marble. 'There were a few jealous comments going around. Terry Carver got a dig in at Dad. But some farmers are just sloppy. I've no time for 'em.'

There speaks your actual authentic Heifer, says Fran to herself. Clearly spent a rewarding day with her favourite person. And in a favourite setting, too. For a day to be top-hole it has to feature a trip to the market, is the opinion of this particular father and daughter. Fran herself hasn't been near it for years. She abominates the place, hates the whole pitiless procedure: the human participants looking on with indifference as terrified beasts are cursed, beaten, punched, into the ring; the animals' dazed and desperate gait, and the stench coming off them in their dire stress. She's none too keen on the niff coming off some of the farmers there, either, the ones who are more or less permanently zipped into nylon coveralls and have their feet stuck for ever in heavy-duty wellies. And the chat and banter leave her cold; it's always the same, always predictable, both in content and assumptions. But she is very glad indeed that the market appeals to Heather and that she often tries to arrange her day off work for when her father plans a visit. And it's great for Steve to have the company of a knowledgeable daughter, a daughter he can show off to his cronies, a daughter he will be envied for and congratulated on. Steve has reported the sort of thing that is said: 'You've reared a clever 'un there, Steve Topping. She's got her head screwed on, has Heather. She'll make some fella a cracking good wife one of these days. Nice lookin' an' all; not one of your modern-day beanpoles.' Well, thanks be to Heather, thinks Fran. Lets me off nicely.

Fran was surprised when Heather left school and got herself a job. Because she was mad keen on farming, everyone assumed that Heather would work with her father, perhaps going to agricultural college first. But Heather, of course, was much too sensible. She'd been over the figures, she'd worked things out. Maybe one day she will join forces with Steve, but in the meantime she wants to earn money, get something behind her. And so she will, Fran doesn't doubt it. Not clever in the way that Janie is, Heather is determined, single-minded, resourceful. She is *a good girl*, Fran tells herself firmly as she hands her elder daughter a plate of casseroled lamb. And – her younger daughter now comes galloping, late as usual to table – it is *very bad of her indeed* to mentally use some of Janie's terms: the Heifer, the Heffalump, the Bishop. (This last, arrived at via the colour of heather, is the one Fran finds most amusing.) But it's appalling to be seduced by these childish terms, and to joke to herself about her own daughter. Though maybe it's a sort of release – they do say you poke fun at things you find troubling. And it is very troubling to Fran, troubling and odd, the way a child you've nurtured and felt passionately for can grow into someone so very *other*. How can Heather be a child of mine? Fran has sometimes wondered. Though wasn't Heather always, even as a little one, startlingly self-contained? Fran pictures a podgy three-year-old, dispassionate eyes fixed on the mother who is trying in vain to interest her in Christopher Robin.

'Exam go all right?' Steve asks Janie.

'Yeah, thanks. How was the market?' There is a note of disapproval in Janie's voice.

'They had a marvellous day. Heather came back full of it, didn't you, dear?' Addressing her elder daughter, Fran manages also to flash a reminder at her younger one.

'Yes,' shortly answers Heather, who has no wish to elaborate for Janie's benefit and get sneered at for her pains.

'A terrific day,' confirms Steve. 'Any spare gravy?'

Fran says there's heaps and holds out her hand for his plate.

Janie, who has been frowning to herself, suddenly recollects her mother's desire to see People Skills in action. So she cocks her head in an alert and interested manner, and says, 'Really? So what happened?'

'We sold the fat stock,' says Steve, before hunger forces him to pile in another mouthful.

Janie looks down at her braised lamb. She thinks

the term *fat stock* is disgusting. Now and then she announces an intention of becoming a vegetarian.

'Yep, every last steer,' says Steve, cutting another chunk of meat from his chop. 'And we didn't give 'em away, neither. Bidding was brisk. They made a good price.'

With an effort Janie banishes her scrupulous line of thought and applies herself to the matter in hand. 'Gosh,' she comments with enthusiasm while looking straight at her sister. 'I bet it was good watching the bidding, eh? Were you excited?'

'Why?'

'Um – I just imagine you would be.'

'You do, eh?'

'Yeah. I mean, I thought when I came down just now: Heather looks like she's had a really interesting day.'

'So what you're saying is, I don't usually, right? You're saying that anyone who'd find selling the fat stock exciting can't have a life. I know your game, you sly little twister—'

'Well, bugger me, honestly! Anyway, *you* said it,' Janie fires off to Heather, as Steve points his knife and says, 'None of that, young lady!'

'And don't bother asking me to humour her again,' Janie cries to her mother.

'I'd read that chapter more carefully, if I were you. *After you've eaten*,' Fran adds, as Janie's chair scrapes backwards.

But Janie takes off regardless, and Fran is left facing her older daughter's wrath.

'You been discussing me with that kid.'

'Of course I haven't – it wasn't like that. Oh please. All right, I asked Janie not to be provocative. Because I know she can be very provocative—'

'You didn't tell her to humour me, then?'

'The word never crossed my lips. Swear to God.'

'Huh,' says Heather.

'That it?' asks Steve. 'Temporary all clear? Safe to carry on eating?'

'I'll put Janie's to keep warm,' says Fran.

As usual, the telly comes on soon after dinner.

Janie is upstairs in her room going over her History notes and essays, assisted by a mug of coffee brought in by Fran and by the singing of a female – if the noise issuing from the amplifier can be described as singing; to Fran's ears it's more like a diatribe on a monotone; ordinary speech with its natural inflections would be easier on the ear; silence, thinks Fran, would be even better. But what does she know, wife, mother, hen-keeper, basic cook, cleaner up of household dirt, failed peacekeeper? Failed student, too, in her time. Failed daughter. Janie might function best with her ears full of garbage, but at least she continues, in the manner expected of her, to function with purpose. Fortunately, in view of the row that comes out of it, Janie's room, which is over the kitchen and accessed by the back stairs, is well away from the rest of the house.

For the look of the thing, before sneaking off up-stairs, Fran lingers in front of the television in the living room with Steve and Heather. Father and elder daughter share a similar taste. This is inevitable; anything Steve would consider worth viewing Heather would watch as a matter of course. Fran has a reputation for disliking the telly. Family members joke about it, as if it's an aversion she has to the machine itself. Lacking any desire to give explanations, Fran lets it go at this.

In fact there are programmes she loves and tries not to miss. And when she's tired she'll watch almost anything. The family would be surprised by some of the stuff she looks at while propped up in bed – as rough and as spine-chilling as anything that might be appearing on the box downstairs, and sometimes the very same. But – and this is the point – by viewing alone Fran keeps control of the set. She can press the off button without argument.

Sometimes, though, she forgets to use it. And sometimes not till it's far too late does she understand that she should have used it. Like the time she switched on and found a film just beginning with a favourite actress playing one of the leading roles. She was immediately hooked. It was about a search for runaway teenage children: the mother of a runaway girl joins a support group and strikes up a friendship with the father of a runaway son; they join forces, go to London, and hang about the mainline train and bus terminals, questioning children of the streets. Fran watched it through to the end, sympathetically engaged, but normally so. It was hours afterwards, three o'clock in the morning to be precise, that the thought jerked her awake that *he* could have been such a runaway. Thousands of teenagers disappear every year, she learned while watching the film. Some are never traced, never make contact with their families; they enter the unseen world of dossers and drug-users, prostitutes and rent boys; they get locked away for persistent offending; and some get murdered, their bodies never found. *It could have happened*. Most probably it hadn't. Most probably he passed the teen-age years in perfect safety, content and secure in the home provided by his adoptive parents – as content and secure as Heather and Janie are in this, their birth home. *But how can she know?* She can't. If he had died, she would not have been informed.

A thought like this cannot be dealt with. Once it takes hold, no amount of conjuring a happy boyhood and a confident young manhood can calm the trapped bird of panic banging away in her rib cage. Only in the aftermath of a full-blown panic attack will she be able to leave such a thought alone, too weary, too numb, to care any longer.

So it's better to be on her guard while telly watching. Better to keep charge of the remote. Because you never know. The most innocent seeming story can turn subversive. A story utterly foreign to a normal person's sense of reality can all of a sudden hit home.

Tonight, after the news, there will be an episode of *Blackadder*. She'll definitely watch it, it's one of her favourites. If, that is, after the weather forecast and the regional news round-up, she's still awake.

'What happened to you, then, yesterday?'

Funny how she knew, as soon as he pulled into the kerb and removed his helmet, that this afternoon he was going to break their pact, going to speak to her. And funny how she knew that as soon as he did whatever it was she imagined she saw in him would abruptly vanish and there'd be no more dwelling on him when she lay in bed with a sense of deliciousness. Funny how a sinking feeling came inside her as she went towards him. Funny, all that.

Today as she moved forward she didn't smile. And neither did he. He was frowning, wanting to know something. And she, anticipating the question, was briefly shocked that he could chuck away something so precious and undefinable for the sake of curiosity. For one second, the second before he spoke, her feelings were focussed and uncomplicated. Pure anger.

'What happened to you, then, yesterday?'

There. It's done. Smashed. Over. And in such a banal way.

She stands there, dazed by her perspicacity. Then has a keen desire to hurry off, finding she is not only jarred by the fact of him speaking but also by the sound. But her knowledge that he hasn't a clue of having put a foot wrong, keeps her from doing so, tells her that she has to be nice to him for a moment, and that at all costs she must cover up her unfavourable reaction. Because it isn't really very fair, in fact it's rather shameful, to take against someone because of how they speak.

'I had a dental appointment.'

'Uh?'

'My father took me in the car. To the dentist. He met me from school.'

'Oh.'

'Yes. Well, um—'

'Have any out?'

'What?'

'Teeth. Have any out?'

'Oh no. It was only a check-up.'

He shuts his mouth at this. So maybe he's satisfied. Maybe that's all he wants to know. Maybe *he* is put off by the way *she* speaks: all those elocution lessons, perhaps he's thinking she sounds a bit snotty. It should be all right to leave him now, so long as she does it pleasantly. 'Funny the way we keep seeing each other when I'm on my way home. Anyway—'

'Like the bike?'

'What? Oh— Mm, very nice. Um, big. I expect it goes pretty fast.'

Becoming voluble, he confirms that it does, and goes on to enumerate several special features and indicates these by pointing with a foot or a hand. He revs the engine to give her an idea of its awesome power. 'Want a ride?' he says.

'Oh, no thanks,' she laughs.

'Why not? You'd be OK.'

She backs away, still nervously laughing. 'I wouldn't know what to do. I expect I'd fall off.'

'Ner, you wouldn't. 'S easy. You just hang onto me, keep yer body in line, lean when I lean.'

She laughs again, shaking her head.

'You can have the helmet, see?'

Sure enough there is a helmet, strapped to the ledge behind the pillion seat, which he now proceeds to unstrap.

'I really,' she says. 'I honestly—'

'Here.'

The helmet comes to her emphatically, allowing her hands no option but to clasp it. Then begins the difficulty of handing it back. 'No, I really don't think—' She shivers, and is suddenly aware of the brilliant red orb, only inches above the skyline at the top of the road. 'Gosh, it's getting late. I have to go—'

He reaches out and slips the strap of her satchel from her left shoulder. In order not to drop the helmet as the strap comes down over her left arm, her right hand clamps the helmet to her chest. And she continues to clutch it against her as her eyes take in the stunning fact that he is hooking the strap of her satchel round the bike's handlebars.

He looks at her. He looks at the helmet. 'If you're worried it's me girlfriend's, well, it was, but she isn't me girlfriend any more. We've split. Finished.'

'But I wasn't— I mean—'

'So put it on.'

She puts it on.

'Fits fine,' he says, and turns to put on his own helmet.

The engine revs.

'Look I can't,' she shouts, worried to death about her satchel, and the gaberdine mac inside, and the text books, property of the school, and envisaging having to account for the loss to teachers and parents, and the total impossibility of confessing that a motorbike rider made off with her property while she was idly chatting to him in the street. 'Please, they're expecting me at home. Can I, could I—?'

'What?'

'I'm expected back.'

'We shan't be long. Just up the road and back. Ten minutes.'

It sounds quick and simple. It is probably the quickest and simplest way of getting her property back and putting an end to the situation. Gingerly, she climbs up behind him.

'Hang on tight.'

She hangs on tight indeed – as her body falls back with the bike's surge, and they rush forwards, up-wards, towards the blood-red sun.

The place is familiar, she's passed by it many times in her father's car. It's an area of grassed-over wasteland, full of humps and hollows; probably something was quarried from the ground here once, but she doesn't know, she's never wondered or thought about it. However, it is excellent ground for dirt-driving over when you want to show off your machine.

'All right?' he yells at one point over his shoulder. She can hardly answer for the laughter bumping out of her. 'Aghh!' she screams as the bike skids on the sunless side of a mound where a night frost has persisted. 'Whee-ee. Woo-hey!' as they hit a bank and soar into the air, bang down to earth and go racing onwards. In the cooling air her breath spurts out in clouds; and every thought in her head evaporates also – thoughts of her kidnapped belongings, of people waiting for her at home, of the uncongenial person-ality of her companion; even that she *has* a human companion: the body that is pressed against hers seems merely an extension of the roaring beast be-tween her legs. An audacious beast, treating her to the time of her life. They leap through the air, zoom over the ground, and an ecstasy of sensation leaps and zooms inside her.

She is still weakly exclaiming when he brings the bike to a halt.

'You enjoyed that.'

'Phew, yes, gosh.'

As the bike tips, her left foot lands on the ground and forces her to swing her other leg over. She stands among the stones and weeds, laughing and panting. Her legs are trembling so much they have a hard job bearing her. The engine's reverberations continue through her bones.

In fact he has switched the engine off. He removes his helmet, clears his legs from the bike, then props the bike up and leans back against it. 'Come here.' He reaches out and takes off her helmet, and at some length studies her.

'You're a doll,' he says.

This strikes her as hysterically funny. She laughs so hard that she starts to topple over, but he catches her and pulls her hard against him between his legs. 'You're a doll, all right,' he repeats, then covers her mouth with his and inserts his tongue.

After a while he removes his tongue and puts it into her ear. One of his hands explores her breasts. 'Ever had it?'

The question arrives in her ear on hot steam. Just in time she prevents herself from asking, 'Had what?' Grasping his meaning, she indicates that she hasn't, while exclaiming Heavens! to herself.

'Thought you hadn't. Want it though, don't yer?'

She would need to have been very quick off the mark to have got in a reply, because now he's kissing her again, and squeezing and pressing the breath out of her, and rolling her body against his. Suddenly his hand is touching her bare flesh, and in another few seconds he's crying out hoarsely, 'God, you do want it!'

She is still wondering how to put it to him – that really she doesn't, or possibly she might but doesn't think she'd better, at least not today, not at this moment, if he doesn't mind – when, with a swiftness that she can't comprehend, having formed the opinion during discussions with schoolfriends and their shared perusal of certain reading matter that love-making is a lengthy procedure involving a number of clearly defined stages – before her mind can sift through all this, the thing is suddenly happening. It actually is. He is actually doing it to her. Standing up, too, which until this minute she was not aware was a possibility. Eventually, though, they more or less tumble to the ground, and continue, first with her on top of him, then him on top of her.

'Cor, bloody heck,' he puffs at last. 'That was summat, wa'n't it?'

It's unreal.

'Hey, don't you go worrying. You can't get caught on your first go – it's a well-known fact. Next time I'll bring us a rubber.'

So unreal she scarcely hears.

6

Lunchtime on Friday. And in the Tasty Bite Heather is on edge with suspense. Teeth, tongue and digestive system are doing the business on a tuna-stuffed jacket potato, Heather is even aware of a growing satisfying fullness, but her eyes scarcely flicker from a view of the alleyway outside, along which Jason must come if he is to eat his lunch here today, which, he gave her to understand when she mentioned the subject to him earlier this morning, was his intention. She watches for him as jealously as she watches for a likely customer in Wilson's Shoes. And just as in the shop she will shoo off a rival colleague, now, for the benefit of the girls from the bank who are eating and gossiping at the next table, her arm is braced to gesture possessively to the chair opposite. *This one's mine*, she will hiss at work – meaning: any dealings involving the transfer of money from this person's bank account are mine. Similarly, *this one's mine* will be signalled by her quick arm when Jason appears – meaning: for better or worse, from this day forward, till death us do part, this one's mine.

It was actually in here, in the Tasty Bite, that Heather decided on her ownership of Jason. Decided in an instant, quickly as snapping her fingers. She already knew him in a way. He'd often received the shop's takings from her when it was her turn to take them to the bank. After the first time she always tried to manoeuvre her progress in the queue to coincide with his window coming free at the counter, though of course this wasn't always possible. Then one lunch hour she walked into the Tasty Bite and there he was, eating his lunch. Looking up and meeting her eyes, he smiled in recognition. And later, in response to her arrival with a tray of food and her question 'Mind if I sit here?', he said 'Not at all,' and half rose, and courteously dashed a piece of lettuce to the floor that had fallen from the plate of a previous diner. Heather, who had already noted his attractive looks and pleasantness in the bank, now became aware of other attributes: beautiful manners, nice way of speaking, deep blue eyes, and hair so floppy and silky your fingers itched to run through it. And with his job in the bank and polished voice screaming to her good education, surely he had prospects, too. This is *it*, she cried to herself, while chewing her food and hungrily eyeing him. *Mine*.

Heather has finished her potato. Resting hands and mouth, she leaves for the moment her slice of passion cake. Now she is feeling not only suspenseful but agitated too. Even a bit annoyed. Though to be fair to Jason, he has no inkling at this stage of being Heather's property, or indeed the property of anyone; if the matter were put to him, he would no doubt claim to be a free agent. Heather admits the truth of this and that therefore annoyance on her part is unreasonable. But she goes on to think that if he carries on like this, failing to be good as his word, letting her down after she's taken the trouble to run across to the bank during her coffee break to establish exactly when his lunch hour will be and exactly where he'll be spending it – then annoyance will definitely be justified. If he didn't intend eating in the Tasty Bite, he should have come right out and said so. After all, they've been spending their lunch together now on and off for almost a month. It seems to Heather that it's about time things moved on to the next stage, to a trip to the cinema and supper at the Pizza Hut. Then, after a few dates of that nature, she could ask him home for Sunday tea; introduce him to Dad (also to her mother – but Heather's focus tends to be stuck on her male parent; it's her father's opinion of her selected mate that she cares about). She feels strongly that her expectation of matters proceeding in this direction is only reasonable, only what any girl would expect. She pulls forward her portion of cake and brings a fork down through it, hard. And promises herself that when things do so proceed he'd better not try turning up late and messing her about. Because she'd be good and annoyed then with every right. And just let him try it once they're engaged. By Christ, then he'd know about it.

In the British Home Stores cafeteria, behind a newspaper and over a plate of cod and chips, Jason is keeping his head down – so far down that the food is scooped into rather than raised to his mouth – so far down that only the lower lines of newsprint are readable with ease. But Jason has no thought of reading, the state of the world is not on his mind; his only purpose when he propped *The Times* against the salt and pepper shakers was to effect a screen. (In fact, Jason seldom finds *The Times* a compelling read, but likes to carry a copy into work with him each morning. It says something about him, he feels, a positive thing of the sort that the right school tie might say, if he possessed such an article.)

It is not that he expects Heather to track him down to this cafeteria. He imagines her stolidly eating in the Tasty Bite, and stolidly keeping watch at the Tasty Bite's window, wondering where the hell he has got to. He doesn't think Heather has ever mentioned

British Home Stores as a possible venue for lunch during their conversations, and she did state her intention when she came into the bank mid-morning of eating today in the Tasty Bite. So the position of *The Times* is merely a precaution against an unlikely event. A token of his wish for privacy.

Fortunately, there was no chance this morning of a detailed discussion with Heather. 'You on twelve to one? Tasty Bite, all right?' she mouthed interrogatively from the far side of the counter towards his desk. He simply nodded and smiled and indicated urgent on-going paperwork. When they eventually meet up and she takes him to task, he will claim to have been too distracted by his workload to catch her meaning. With luck he will get away with it.

He certainly hopes he will get away with it. He would be very sorry if they stopped being friends. Heather, after all, is just about the only friend he has made in this town – up to now, he reminds himself joyously. And Heather is not at all a bad sort. Her company can come as a relief after the sort of stuff he has to put up with from the girls at work. They, after initially friendly overtures, now shoot silly questions at him, raise eyebrows at his answers, and generally milk every aspect of his presence for their shared amusement. Michael on the foreign currency desk is a pretty good bloke, but too burdened by his new status as a father to have the time and energy for proper mateyness. All the other men at the bank are older. Unfortunately, there are no women at the bank who are older – Jason usually gets on splendidly with women of middle years. Quite honestly, he would have had a very lonely time of it these past few weeks were it not for shared lunchtimes with Heather. These became a habit without either of them noticing (as they have both remarked). Though recently Heather has wanted to make firm arrangements and not leave matters to chance. Now she wants to know if his lunch hour is twelve to one, or one to two (as the holder of a senior position in the shoe shop where she works, she can arrange her lunchtimes to suit herself). Now she wants to know whether they will be eating in the Tasty Bite or the coffee shop in the precinct, or, if it's a nice day, taking sandwiches from Marks & Spencer to a bench in the churchyard. In fact, so proprietorial has Heather become that she assumes she has only to mention a place to have him turn up. 'You on one to two?' she will mouth towards his desk from the counter. 'Coffee shop OK? Cos I need to pop into Boots.'

Recently, Jason has caught Heather looking at him under a furrowed brow. Sometimes he hears impatience in her tone. He has guessed the reason: Heather expects their friendship to go further, she thinks it's about time he asked for a date. Well, maybe he will ask, all in good time, because there are several things to be said in Heather's favour. For a start, she takes him seriously (no archness, no girly giggles, no hint of a send-up). And she clearly finds him attractive – doesn't care if her frank appraisal lets this show, either. And he feels secure with her, that she's sensible and reliable. That he could depend on her if ever he got into a scrape.

However, now is not the moment to have a girlfriend in tow. Something has turned up. Something he wants to dwell on, be free for. So although he doesn't want to end his friendship with Heather, he can't for the time being let it go further. Whether Heather will co-operate is another question; she strikes Jason as a pretty determined character. But he hasn't come here to worry about Heather.

Having eaten every edible scrap on his plate, Jason lays down knife and fork and draws up his mug of coffee. Cups his hands round it, and urges his attention towards the task that has brought him here to eat alone undisturbed.

Which is, to psyche himself up. To recall every detail of last Tuesday evening, to relive their amazing rapport, and finally convince himself that it will be quite OK, the most natural thing in the world, when he collects his repaired car from the garage this evening, to drive straight round to Sonia's and give her his thanks in person.

He looks into his mug at the fawn-coloured liquid, then across the room to where a group of young mothers are talking and smoking while their tiny children ravenously stuff chips into their mouths. He looks at them and through them, and fails to hear any of the noise swirling round – music through the sound system interrupted by customer announcements, the rumble from dedicated gossipers, a child wailing, its mother issuing threats. What he hears is the sound of traffic and the thump of his heart in his ears. What he sees is a dark road lit by street lamps and headlights, and two cars improperly connected. Traffic is passing, slowly and unnervingly closely. Men are standing round; they speak to him, expect things of him. Then a woman appears. She is smiling. It is incongruous and even deplorable of her to smile in the circumstances – this is clearly the opinion of the men who are present. But to Jason, stranded in outlandish territory, the effect of her smile is like that of a message coming through from civilization.

'This is not the end of the world,' the woman says. 'Fix it up, good as new, in no time, I promise.'

In the cafeteria, Jason returns Sonia's smile. He watches her sort the men out, persuading them to lift the cars apart and then to test them. He sees her get into hers and wind down the window. 'Follow *me*,' she shouts.

A shiver goes through him, and he relives the buzz

of racing after her, keeping right on her tail, jumping
lights and cutting in front of other vehicles on round-
abouts; careless, reckless, as greedy for his chosen
route as a joyrider. Then they arrive at Bellamy's
Motors, and a new mood takes hold, one of calm
persistence, of determination to get what they want
from this place. Get what *they* want; have *their* way:
for her impulses have become his. It's almost as if, by
banging into him and claiming him and leading him
away, she has completely taken him over. Now they're
alone in Mr Bellamy's office, and she wants to know
everything about him. Jason gives his story, and her
encouragement and sympathy lead him to come up
with the most perfect version yet. Perfect for *him*, for
the him he feels himself really and truly to be – and
would have been, if he hadn't been saddled with a sod
of a father who drove away his mother because she
couldn't stand the life he made them lead, which was
too far removed from the life they ought to have led,
the sort of life Jason is painting now for Sonia. Sonia's
grasp and appreciation of this version that his mother
would have preferred link them in a way. This, and
his rapport with Sonia, and hers with him, go round
and round in a reinforcing circle. Everything fitting.
Everything telling him that of course he must drive
straight over and thank her when he gets his car back
after work, no question. Not to would be impolite,
ungrateful. Not to would go against his dawning
hunch that she is half expecting him.

'You remember – they brought her to the Atkinson's
party, the girl who went to Paul for six weeks' experience. Mm, she got that all right – not the sort her
father had in mind for her, though. It was her father
fixed it up with Paul, asked him to take her on as a
favour – he and Paul were at school together or
something – because the girl had to observe how an

outfit like that operates, it was part of her university course. You know, Sonia, I think it's the fact of her having a brain, and coming from a decent sort of family – not the usual tart or bimbo – I think it's that aspect Annie finds so truly upsetting. Not to mention the girl being only a couple of years older than their own daughter. Not to mention the breach of trust. Poor Annie. You know, she's even had the girl's mother on to her? Yes, the woman rang her up, got really abusive, from what Annie said. Mind you, Annie gave as good as she got. Pity your husband can't keep his trousers zipped style of thing from the mother, and quick as a flash Annie comes back with a similar line re the girl's knickers.'

'Dear dear,' murmurs Sonia, dropping freshly cooked *fusilli* into a bowl of *pesto*.

'Not too much of that for fat old *moi*, darling. Remember my diet.'

'But pasta is good for you. So's olive oil. It's the unhealthy foods you ought to cut back on, Natalie.'

'It's all right for you. Anyway, where was I?'

Sonia stirs the pasta then arranges it on two pre-warmed plates. She puts these on the kitchen table – not on the dining-room table because this is an impromptu lunch. Her friend Natalie Bellamy dropped round an hour ago 'just for ten minutes', but found much longer was needed to relate her news. With a kindly smile to acknowledge that, yes, it is all right for her, since unlike Natalie's, her own figure is trim, she motions her friend to be seated.

They eat: Natalie quickly, as if a shorter length of time in her mouth will afford the food less opportunity to affect her bulk; Sonia slowly, appreciatively, daintily. Natalie, while gobbling, continues to explore every nuance of their friend's discomfiture, some nuances more than once.

From time to time Sonia makes a comment. Annie

111

must not be provoked into ugly displays of wrath or anguish. At all costs Annie must keep her dignity. That way, when she looks back on the affair she will at least have nothing to reproach herself with. This is the burden of Sonia's contribution. But both women know it cannot apply to Annie, whose nature is spontaneous and passionate. Both know Sonia is really talking about herself, about the ideal Sonia way to behave in such circumstances.

'We can't all be saints,' says Natalie at one point.

'Hardly a saint,' demurs Sonia.

'You know what I mean. Not everyone's blessed with your sunny temperament.'

Sonia lets this go. The ins and outs of the affair, though of great interest, do not command her rapt attention as normally such a story would. Another matter is rattling round at the back of her mind, and every so often rattles right to the fore – as it does at this moment: He'll have been told by now, she thinks. They'll have phoned the bank. 'Message for Mr Caulfield. Will you tell him his car will be ready by the end of the afternoon?' The garage rang her earlier with this news. They asked, as though she hadn't already informed them, where they should send the bill. 'To me, of course,' she cried. She checked they had kept her address, asked them to be sure and phone Mr Caulfield at work, and reminded them of the bank's number. No doubt he'll pick it up after work, Sonia says to herself. Yes, that's most likely what he'll do.

'Poor Annie,' she says with some heat to Natalie – as a private reproof to her wandering mind. 'I do sympathize, believe me. It's a lamentable lapse on Paul's part. I'm surprised at him. And I'm sure David will be, too, when he hears of it. It was probably one of those mid-life crisis thingies. It'll soon blow over. If Annie can just sit tight—'

Natalie belches behind her hand and looks sourly at her friend. The story has gone limp on her, all its goodness extracted. And Sonia, who is lively and entertaining enough in her way – good company on a shopping trip, an asset at parties because the men always take to her – can sometimes come over as a trifle smug. Though if Sonia has anything to be smug about after the way David ditched her and then used her as a convenience all these years, Natalie would like to hear of it. 'The other night, Ronnie came home with a funny little story about *you*,' she says abruptly. 'As a matter of fact.'

'About me?'

'About you and a good-looking young man.'

'Oh *that*,' laughs Sonia. 'Ronnie was such a sweetie, coming to the rescue.'

'Sounded more like it was you coming to the rescue – in a very large way. Poor old Ronnie didn't know quite what to make of it.'

A few seconds elapse before Sonia reactivates her trilling laugh. 'But I had to make amends. Surely Ronnie told you? I bashed into the poor boy's car. You see, I was wearing these new patent shoes—' Sonia pauses, and recalls that the true version, which she would normally confide to a woman friend, cannot be told on this occasion, since this friend's husband has already been given the version more suitable for a man's ears. 'They set off the most shocking, the most vile cramp,' she continues, and goes on to relate more of the story – though she does not go on to describe how she treated the young man to a road-house supper.

'Well, I hope that'll be the end of it. I hope you haven't let yourself in for something.'

'What on earth do you mean?'

'You being so generous. It might have given him ideas. But I suppose he couldn't get in touch all that easily. I mean, he doesn't know your address?'

'What, dear?'

When Natalie has repeated the question, Sonia makes a negative sort of sound, and leaves the table and goes to switch on the kettle.

'So that card can't be from him?' says Natalie, speaking of a card on the window sill just above the kettle, a card depicting a vase of roses and with *Thank you* printed across the top in large italic. She has only just noticed this card. But now that she has, she knows – it's one of those blinding intuitions she gets – that the card most definitely came from the young man. And how else if not by post? By hand, possibly, but that would be even more dodgy.

'Good heavens, no,' says Sonia. 'That card's from a friend – well, more of an acquaintance really. Someone I used to work with. No-one you'd know. Her husband's fallen ill, so I wired her some flowers. Which she obviously appreciated.'

Liar, thinks Natalie. When I know a thing, I *know*.

Sonia, with her eyes on the kettle, is thinking she must get Natalie out of the kitchen pronto. And until she has, she must keep her body between Natalie and the card. Sonia wouldn't put it past Natalie to seize it on some pretext and take a squint inside, she's blatant enough. It was stupid to have left it on show. But how was she to know Natalie would come round and more or less invite herself to lunch?

'We'll have our coffee in the conservatory. You go through.'

'I need the little girls' room first.'

'Help yourself,' says Sonia. She starts stacking the dishwasher. She will not leave the kitchen until Natalie's large behind is parked in the cushions of the cane recliner. She closes the dishwasher, then raises her eyes to the source of her difficulty. In spite of the awkwardness that it's causing her at this moment, she is glad to see it there, glad to see its pastel prettiness and slanting script, glad to recall what is written inside. *You must be magic, Sonia, to turn an unfortunate accident into such a fun event. I can't tell you how much I appreciate your kindness. Regards, Jason.*

'So tell me,' Sonia says firmly when at last they are sitting in the conservatory, 'tell me what Annie is going to do. Surely she won't kick Paul out?'

'She already has, I thought I told you,' says Natalie, who is bored with the Annie and Paul topic.

'Oh, in the heat of the moment, I know. But once the affair's over and done with, once she's calmed down—'

Natalie shrugs. She leans forward and reaches for the sugar bowl. She declined sugar when Sonia offered it, but now thinks half a teaspoon might perk her up. She stirs, then sips, then puts her head on one side and cocks an eyebrow. 'I still think it's a bit peculiar of you, Sonia, to go to such trouble for a perfect stranger.'

'Stranger?'

'The lad whose car you pranged the other night. I said to Ronnie, anyone else but Sonia and I'd have my suspicions. Hey up, I'd think, she fancies herself with a toy boy.'

'Natalie!' cries Sonia with frank annoyance.

'Don't worry, I said anyone *but*. We all know you'd never stoop. Not the Lady Sonia.'

'Natalie,' reproves Sonia again, but this time faintly, with a pleased little smile.

Natalie has been seen safely off the premises. When she said she had to go, Sonia insisted on the garden route, said she wanted Natalie to look at the conifer by the side of the house and advise her what to do about its brown patch. Now, thankful to be alone, Sonia looks at her watch. It is ten minutes to three.

115

She wonders what Jason is doing. She imagines him asking permission to leave work early in order to have plenty of time to inspect the car before the garage closes. What time, anyway, do bank employees finish these days? Sonia has no idea. But, there's surely enough time to go upstairs and do her hair and check her face, and maybe change into something else – she's gone off this trouser and tunic outfit after sitting about in it for so long with Natalie. She'd like to feel different for when Jason comes round—

Hang on a minute. What the heck is she saying? Doesn't she mean *if* he comes round? It's only the teeniest hunch, this feeling that he might. She has absolutely nothing to go on – except that she can imagine him wanting to make some sort of gesture once he is reunited with his car. Some sort of charming gesture.

She goes upstairs. Looking into her built-in wardrobe, she strives to conjure in her mind the sort of look that would enhance a possible encounter. *Nothing too young* slots into her mind like a perfectly grooved sliding door. This surprises her, but after a second's thought she affirms its correctness – and that it has nothing to do with wanting to disprove Natalie's coarse remark (Natalie is inclined to be coarse, it's the one thing about her Sonia doesn't care for). Not too young, but reasonably jaunty nevertheless. Something that is simple, bright-looking and confident. She settles on a neat little shift dress – long sleeves, high neck, knee-length hem – in soft coral-coloured wool.

Spot on, she tells her reflection. She tidies up after herself, puts clothes away, wipes a drop of lotion from the glass top of her dressing table, humming as she goes. The song that has popped into her head – *'I'd like to teach the world to sing'* – strikes her as wonderfully apt. For she could teach it, she could. What did Natalie say? Not everyone is blessed with your sunny temperament. What people don't realize, says Sonia to herself, is that her sunnyness has to be worked for. Not too many days ago she was having to contend with a draggy lump in her chest. Did she allow it to get the better of her? She did not. When one solution failed, why, she embarked on another. And now look at her; merry as a songbird. She's been chirpy as a sparrow ever since – well, ever since bashing into Jason's car; it's almost as if the jolt sent the blessed lump packing. But what she prefers to think is, if you engage with other people, take an interest in them and stop brooding about your own affairs – which, unfortunately, too many people are inclined to do these days; didn't she read somewhere about a me generation? – then of course you feel better. Cheerful, even. Stands to reason, because your horizon has broadened. You get a lift, like the sort you get on a clear day when you can see for miles.

Jason has collected his car. On the seat beside him lies a bunch of flowers. He bought them on impulse when he stopped to fill up with petrol. Spotting cellophane bunches packed into a bucket outside the pay kiosk it seemed the least he could do was take her some flowers. God knows she's been decent – arranging instantly for the repair, paying up, no messing with estimates, no hassle to him.

After leaving the bank he called in at the estate agent's next door to consult their wall-mounted street map. He needed to work out a route from the garage to Leacroft Avenue where Sonia lives. (There was no need to consult the bit of paper she handed him after the accident; he knows her address by heart.) But despite this foresight, he is now completely lost. The one-way system keeps insisting on a turn to the right or the left when what he needs to do is drive straight on, and his fellow road-users are too impatient to get home to allow him the leeway for a last minute change of mind. It's beginning to feel like one of those nightmares that have you trapped in an irrational situation with no way out, when, while he's waiting for the lights to change, he sees beyond the intersection a row of tall trees and an expanse of grass: obviously the fringes of a park. So the road ahead must surely be the Park Road he's been looking for, with Leacroft Avenue the fourth turning off.

Fortunately, at this particular intersection it is permissible to continue straight ahead. In his relief he almost shoots across when the lights change. And finds that this is indeed Park Road. He slows down sharply in order to count off the turnings.

It strikes him that the houses on the right overlooking the park are extremely grand. Some have turrets, some are castellated, all have deep wide drives. Doubt creeps over. Is he right to have come? Will her heart sink when she opens the door? Will she think, Oh God what a bore?

Leacroft Avenue arrives too suddenly. He turns into it, but in two minds. Perhaps it would be better to drive home and phone her from work in the morning, to report, out of courtesy, on the excellence of the car repair. Oh, but here already is number twenty-seven. Automatically, it seems, his feet hit the brake and the clutch.

With the engine still running, he peers at her house, trying to make up his mind. These houses in Leacroft Avenue are less imposing than the ones on the park, but they're still pretty smart. Sonia's, though, strikes him as somehow friendly – maybe it's the pinkish light showing low down and faintly behind the bay window curtains. His fingers hovering over the ignition suddenly decide the matter: they switch it off, and then there's nothing for it but to gather up the flowers and get out of the car. He doesn't lock it, though; a locked car might seem presumptuous. And if by any chance she asks him in (as she did when he was fantasizing the scene over lunch in British Home Stores) it will look good to need to return to lock it. It will look as if the invitation comes as a surprise. As if it wasn't anticipated.

Only when he has virtually committed himself – with his feet on her path and the gate shut behind him – does the thought occur that she might have company. After all, there's an ex-husband in the picture, isn't there? With whom she's still on friendly terms. And a married daughter who works abroad and is married to a foreigner. Did she mention any other relatives? Or any close friends? Hell's teeth, she might live with someone, might have a lodger, just have chosen not to mention the fact. Actually, she could very well have mentioned it without him registering the information, because while they were in the restaurant, when it became Sonia's turn to recount life history, his mind was seized by a stunning idea: that the waitress and nearby diners were taking Sonia and himself for mother and son. Mother treating son to a meal. Mother and son on the razzle together. Covertly looking around, Jason watched for the odd glance coming in their direction. Then tried to assess it, and to assess the manner of the waitress when she brought the dessert menu. It was difficult to be certain, but on the whole he was inclined to think it more probable than not. So he ventured a little mild teasing, the way an indulged son would tease his mother. Sonia adored it. He can still hear her pleased laugh.

There's a yellow label stuck in her window. It says *Neighbourhood Watch*. What a twit, to be standing here dithering. A neighbour could be watching right now. Might be picking up the phone: *There's a young chap on your path, Sonia. I saw him draw up and go through your gate. But he hasn't rung the bell. Looks suspicious. Like me to investigate?* Jason steels himself. Tells himself he had better get on with it.

Three steps, and he's standing under her porch. And then – maybe it's the proximity of the doorbell – something triggers another contrary thought. How can he be sure that she really took to him the other night? Just because she made a fuss of him, it doesn't really prove anything. It wouldn't be the first time he's got the wrong end of the stick—

A feeling he recognizes lands in his stomach: not in its upsetting full-blown form, but a hollow sort of echo of it. His muscles clench. He tells himself to stop being stupid, to simply ring the bell, show her the repair, and tell her he's pleased with it.

His hand obeys him. Inside the house there's a ding-dong of chimes. And Jason summons a more businesslike manner than the one, a few hours ago, he had seen himself using.

'Jason, how nice! Have you—'

'I've just picked up the car from the garage. They've made a very good job of it. I thought it right, in view of your kindness, to bring it over straight away. I thought you'd want to see.'

'Well, I'm delighted to see *you*, but really there was no need—'

'It's just here. Right by the gate.'

A bemused Sonia follows him down the path. In the brightness cast by a street lamp, she notices he is carrying a bunch of flowers. Sweet of him, she thinks.

'There,' he says, waving with the flowers at the rear of his vehicle. 'What do you think?'

'More to the point, what do you think? Are you satisfied?'

'Good heavens, yes. They've fitted a brand new panel – see?'

'So they have. Blatantly new, blatantly shiny. They might have tried to distress it a bit. Though I suppose it's not like furniture; the distressed look isn't in vogue for cars.'

This is obviously a joke, though Jason doesn't understand it. He smiles politely and tells her once more he is enormously grateful, that not many people would have jumped to remedy the situation as she did.

Sonia listens with her head on one side. This doesn't sound like Jason, she thinks. Not the Jason she remembers from the other night. Where's the light touch, the boyish charm? Then she tumbles: of course, he's embarrassed. At the garage they probably let slip the cost of the repair. This has made him feel awkward. It's crossed his mind that he shouldn't have accepted so much munificence, with supper on top of everything else. The poor boy. He's only young.

'Forget the car. Come in and have a drink,' she tells him. 'Are those flowers for me, by the way?'

'Oh. Yes. But I've got a nasty feeling they're rather tatty. They were on the forecourt when I stopped for petrol. Seemed a nice idea at the time.'

'It is a nice idea. Hand them over, please. Now come in and relax. Tell me the news. Any hold-ups at the bank since I saw you last? Any masked robbers? Any of your colleagues eloped with the contents of the night safe?'

Jason laughs. 'No-oh,' he says as he follows her into the house. 'But a woman attacked one of the cash-point machines. Gave it a hiding with her brass-studded handbag. Said it had swallowed her card, and it wasn't the first time. Said she was sick of being picked on and had to teach it a lesson. Oh, and one of the girls at work got a warning. She was rude to a customer, who happened to be a fellow Rotarian of Mr Whitehouse's.'

'Lord, Jason, you do see life.'

'Those flowers definitely are tatty. They're a hotch-potch. What's the blue one doing with those pink and yellow jobs? They must be florists' leftovers. Sorry about that.'

'Fear not, dear boy,' says Sonia, coming up with two vases. Into one she puts all the pink carnations, into the other the single blue daisy and the piece of golden rod. 'Not bad, eh? These on the window sill, I think. And the carnations in their silver flute will be very happy on the dining-room table. Come and see. Then we'll have that drink.' And afterwards, she thinks, you can join me for supper. Silly boy, spending money on rubbishy flowers. Should've bought himself fish and chips with it. Look at his bones sticking out. What he needs is feeding up.

'Drive safely. Try not to get bumped by some scatter-brain old lady,' she calls to him, just before he gets into his car.

Jason laughs and promises to be on his guard. 'See you on Sunday,' he adds, having promised to come round and help her cut the brown patch out of her conifer and tie green branches over the resulting gap, as per the instructions of her friend Mrs Bellamy.

How right he was to come, he reflects as he drives at a lick down Park Road. No worries now as to whether she really likes him. That's been thoroughly tested out. When she answered the door, he was cautious, merely polite, giving her every opportunity to offer politeness back, to say thanks for calling, bye-bye. But she didn't. She invited him in, pressed him to stay. She's even booked him to come back.

This time, plainly he has got it right.

7

Hal marks the passing of three whole days. He countermands several impulses – to take this or that up to the house, to ask if Fran would like this or that doing, and while he's at it describe an incident that has come back to him vividly and explosively. Taking a walk he gives a wide berth to the house, and also to the yard and barns. After once feeding the poultry as a favour to Steve – Fran, apparently, having gone into town – he keeps well away from the hen coops which normally he would check over daily, for no-one appreciates better than Hal the cunning and determination of a hungry vixen.

But on the fourth day, Saturday, he digs up some late potatoes. And before he knows it, he's heading up the farm road, crossing the yard, going in at the kitchen door, placing a soily newspaper bundle on Fran's shiny clean draining board. 'I'm not stopping, mind,' he calls out virtuously. 'I just brought you a boiling. They're fresh dug.'

Follow through, for pity's sake. There's such a thing as follow through! The cry quickens on Fran's tongue as she lifts her head from the store cupboard and spots what he's left her. She utters these or similar words whenever a man dumps vegetables on her draining board together with half the garden. She is especially roused when the gift is accompanied by a look of soft pride. 'Thanks, but you might have scraped off the mud. You might have swilled them first. There's a tap in the yard, there are knives in the outhouse,' she will remind husband, father-in-law, and David the cowman who is another keen vegetable grower. (She herself would never dream of taking fly-ridden lettuce or mud-encrusted carrots to a friend or neighbour; she would get the worst off first.) Such things need to be said because men need to learn. And as the mother of daughters it is her duty within her small sphere of influence (and whenever she remembers it) to see that they do. Not that her daughters are particularly appreciative. Janie claims she is inconsistent. And it is true that many of the problematic habits and attitudes of men, which so consume Janie, tend to escape Fran; it just so happens that finding earth on the draining board is a sharp reminder. Heather, of course, would fail to be moved by any ideas or actions of Fran's. In any case, Heather regards her father as the single most admirable person on earth. And who is to say, Fran has sometimes asked herself, that Heather's not right?

But this morning the admonition to follow through is stillborn. She gulps it back. She remembers why her father-in-law has kept clear of the house for the past four days, and what this may have cost him. 'Wait, Hal. Hang on.'

'I shan't dwell.' He is already out of the door.

She leaps after him, calls from the doorway, 'Hal, come back here. Come in and talk to me a while.'

'I dursn't. I was warned off.'

'Oh, get back in here, you stubborn old cuss. Come on, now. I'm going to put the kettle on.'

He comes back slowly, watching her from under his brows. And she watches him till he is almost level, when she turns on her heel and goes inside ahead of him.

'Stubborn old cuss, is it? You wouldn't have used that sort of language when my Edna were alive. Leastways not in this house.'

'No, I wouldn't,' says Fran. 'Your Edna scared me rigid.'

'She couldn't abide language, couldn't Edna.'

'No, she wasn't a great fan of the spoken word. But then she hadn't the same need as ordinary mortals. Her flinty stare saw off any opposition. The snort expressed her opinion adequately on most matters, as I recall. I'll never forget the first time Steve brought me over. For Sunday tea. For the great inspection. Those eyes! You could see what she was thinking: That girl'll never cut the mustard as a farmer's wife. Like to see *her* get up at six to cook a man-sized breakfast, like to see *her* trundle a bale of hay. Our Steve's gone and saddled himself with a useless article there, all right.'

Fran speaks without rancour, simply stating the facts. For Edna herself liked to confess that her initial judgement had been unfavourable. Right up to the end it was one of those things that tickled her memory and she enjoyed repeating. The last such occasion, Fran remembers, was one morning in the bathroom – herself perched on the edge of the bath, Edna on the lavatory. Fran was waiting for her to finish so that she could then wash and dress her and help her into the chair she occupied most of the day. Edna at the time was dying slowly of stomach cancer, and for some reason the nurse was unable to attend that morning. There was no hint of embarrassment in Edna's re-telling. Nor did Edna claim to have dramatically revised her verdict over the years.

'She were *wrong*,' blurts out Hal, drawing up his chest.

'What?'

'Edna. She were wrong about you. And she knew it.

You been a brilliant wife, by God you have, Fran. Our Steve picked himself a champion.'

'Bloody hell, Hal, you'll have me blubbing in a minute.' Fran reaches across the table, clasps his horny old hand.

Primly, Hal withdraws it. 'Just one thing I've got against you: the language you come out with. It's not ladylike.'

'Nobody's poi-fect,' pleads Fran, with a grin.

But Hal shakes his head. He is not a Tony Curtis fan.

'Stay to lunch,' Fran tells Hal some time later.

When he is reassured that Steve won't be annoyed to find him at the table – 'Of course he won't. He'll be relieved, he'll see it as proof positive I'm over my bad turn,' – Hal accepts the invitation.

Steve registers his father's presence without comment. They eat their lamb and barley soup and wholemeal bread, and discuss the beef crisis. It's gloom all round for farmers, Steve and his father are agreed.

'So what's new?' says Fran cheerfully. She collects their plates and stacks them in the dishwasher. 'Anyone for cheese? Piece of cake?'

They see off the last of Fran's Danish apple cake and a chunk apiece of extra strong Cheddar. Then Hal offers to feed and shut up Fran's hens later on.

'That'd be great. There's a thing I've been wanting to do, and I'm just in the mood for it this afternoon. Thanks, Hal, you're a brick.'

'Sounds mysterious,' says Steve. His face is pink with pleasure at his wife's and father's resumed affection.

'Oh, just a bit of writing. Some time to myself is what I'm hankering for.'

'You have it, then, love.'

'Well, it's a good opportunity, with Janie gone over to Char's. You remember Janie's friend, Char, Hal? They had a bit of a tiff the other day but they've patched it up. They're swotting together for the physics exam.'

'Heather went with you to market then, I hear,' says Hal to Steve.

'Aye, Dad, she did. Enjoyed herself, too. Got quite excited – unusually so, for Heather. She doesn't give away much as a rule. Chip off the old block, that one, eh?'

'Chip off which old block?' asks Fran.

'Mother, of course.'

'Of course! Same implacable attitude.'

'You two've lost me,' Hal complains. 'Who're you talking about now?'

'Mum and Heather,' says Steve.

'Heather and Edna,' says Fran.

'Oh, I'm with you,' says Hal.

When the house is quiet, Fran goes down the hall and enters the musty-smelling parlour – a room where fires are seldom lit and only sun in the late afternoon can suspend its air of purposeful mouldering. She flicks on the light and closes the door. From a cupboard let into the wall and from under her sewing box she pulls out the uppermost of a pile of exercise books, and from a box at the bottom of the cupboard a ballpoint pen. Then she sits in a low chair by the window and spreads the notebook open at a clean page, resting it on her knees.

The first thing she writes is the day's date. Underneath she refers to a story Hal has told many times before and which already appears in an earlier notebook. Hal told the tale again today when she was preparing lunch, but she didn't actively listen until her ears were caught by some new material. It's been buzzing away in her head more or less ever since.

On hot summer afternoons Hal and his school pals would often play truant to go bathing in the nearby blow-wells. Fran knows by heart about their horse-play, about a near drowning and the ensuing punishment. She can vividly picture the scene having often visited the blow-wells herself. They are grown-over with sedge and reeds and iris now, but in Hal's day were kept clear for the sake of the watercress that was cultivated in trough-like run-offs. Today she learned that sometimes bubbles were seen rising to the surface of the largest well, a series of plopping, breathy eruptions. The story grew amongst the truants that these were caused by the farts of a monster living in the well's depths, a jelly-like monster, jumpy and tentacled. It was Old Gelid Rump loosing off, the lads would cry, seeing the bubbles come. For this reason, mindful of the tentacles, they conducted their horse-play in the smaller wells, reserving the largest piece of water for a daredevil swim or for tossing some un-popular lad into.

Fran sets it all down, this new information concern-ing Old Gelid Rump's farts. Then, aided by a volume of John Clare's poems, with a sense of triumph she writes: *gelid*: from *To the Snipe*, fifth verse. After this she leaves several lines blank and begins a report of their earlier conversation, the one about Edna and her disparaging judgement of Fran, and Hal blurting out suddenly that Edna was wrong.

This done, Fran looks up. She lays down her pen. She stares out of the window between the cotoneaster stems that drape it, to the bit of garden she can see from her low chair – the buddleia with its blossoms gone rusty, a few pickled-looking rose heads, a dark wall of laurel. She thinks about her bad turn, the form it took, and where it led her. Why, she asks herself, was the pain more intense than usual? The birthday precipitated her anxiety, of course. But the birthday happens every year, and it doesn't always affect her so fiercely. What then?

It starts to come to her, the reason. It comes, she resists, it comes again; and this time she allows it. The reason she despaired was her sudden realization that almost a year has passed since she placed a letter with the Adoption Contact Register. It was soon after the last birthday that she placed it, a letter setting out her name and address and a few personal details and expressing the hope that one day he will contact her. What's a year? she asks herself now. It's nothing.

An image comes into her mind, then a phrase. She turns the words about, takes the image further, distorts and lengthens it. At last she picks up her pen. She writes, pauses, writes again; writes in short building phrases, and afterwards, reading it through, asks Does it work? Does it invoke him? Is it poetry?

Possibly. There are layers of meaning, like a recession of hills in hazy light, that excite and please her. Anyway, it's a start. She will work and work. She will get better at this.

8

It is six thirty-five on Sunday morning when Sonia wakes. She squints at the illuminated dial of her bedside clock and is informed of this. Damn, she says, returning her head vigorously to the pillow. Damn and darn everything. But especially, and with bells on, damn and darn Alistair Rogers.

In the dream she was having prior to waking, Alistair Rogers, stark naked, was chasing her all over her house. His thing was sticking out from him at right angles and was so rigid and huge you'd be justified in terming it an offensive weapon. A hideous dream. Terrifying. Probably it was doing her actual harm. With her heart going like the clappers, maybe it was a mercy she woke when she did. It could kill you having a dream like that.

As it happens, blame for the dream can be laid fairly and squarely at Alistair's door – indirectly on one count, very directly on another. Indirectly, because it was Elaine and Alistair who took her along to that terrible party last year, thrown by those terrible people. New to the town, these people were, just bought a house on the park which was sold to them through the Rogers's estate agency. She'd had an instinct from the start about these newcomers – the famished-looking wife, the leery husband. One thing she did miss though, and has never since been able to recall, was how the photographs came to be going around. One moment she was discussing with some-body the feasibility of a park and ride scheme for the town like the one they have in Oxford, the next she noticed that most people had clustered together amid a nervy sort of silence – though the odd snigger and shout of laughter broke out. She and her companion joined the group and found photographs passing from hand to hand. Only one photo ever reached Sonia. For a moment, when her eyes met it, she failed to cotton on. (Well, you don't always when you're suddenly faced with something totally outside your ken, some-thing you'd never expect to be shown in your entire life, never mind at a respectable party in a respectable house with people who in the main are your friends.) Then it clicked what the photo showed (the male of the species in the exact same state as Alistair Rogers in her dream). The breath shot out of her. She dropped the photo, of course, dropped it to the floor; but that didn't somehow feel enough, her hands needed to be rid of its slimy feel. Many times since that evening she has imagined how she must have looked to the bystanders, whimpering and wringing her hands, then opening her mouth and starting to screech – quite unable to stop, screeching on and on. It must have turned her face purple. Probably, spit came out.

It's not that she was shown the photograph that she can't forgive, it's that she was trapped into making herself ugly, into losing control. It took a piece of smut to do that to her.

Obviously, the photograph is where Alistair's aggressive nakedness came from. If she hadn't seen it she could never have dreamed anything so, well, *literal*. It could not be said that the beastly sighting was his fault exactly, only in so far as it was he and Elaine who persuaded her to attend the party. But where Alistair Rogers is wholly to blame, is for last night's shenanigan, putting his hand on her knee and saying he'd always carried a torch for her. It was surely that that triggered the dream in the first place. Admittedly, she wasn't aware of feeling upset when the incident was occurring; she was too delighted with the way she was handling it, remaining the Lady Sonia to the last ditch; but it is possible that underneath it was unsettling.

It had been arranged that Elaine and Alastair, who live fairly close by, should take her in their car to and fro from the Assembly Rooms, venue of the Rotarian Quiz Night. Actually, she hadn't been all that keen to go, but several friends pressed her. 'No need to get the car out, Alistair will be chauffeur,' Elaine promised. Seconds after she climbed into the back of their Lexus, Sonia guessed the Rogers's were having one of their famous rows: Elaine was very short, Alistair very hearty. Sonia made good and sure she was not put into the same team as the Rogers's. Halfway through the evening Elaine complained of a splitting headache and wanted to go home. That didn't matter too much because the team the Rogers were in had already been eliminated, but it was awkward for Sonia whose team was by then in a winning position. Ronnie Bellamy, her team captain, quickly said there'd be no difficulty about a lift, and Sonia herself said she could always get a taxi. In spite of this, having disposed of his wife at home, twenty minutes later Alistair was back. It was rather embarrassing; not only because he'd returned, but because he then hung about at Sonia's elbow. She noticed people exchanging looks, evidently wondering. (Not that they'd have been wondering about her, of course – her reputation is safe as a strong box; no, they'd have been wondering about him.) Actually, she rather enjoyed the secret attention. It gave her a chance to demonstrate the characteristics David always praises to the skies – her feminine poise, her tact, her steadfast cheeriness, all coming to the fore in these testing circumstances. (Alistair was already behaving like a chump, keeping his arm on the back of her chair, looking at her too much, teasing and trying to get a rise out of her.) When the time came, she calmly agreed he should drive her home. Not to have agreed would have meant causing a fuss – he was being pretty pushy about it – and the Lady Sonia does not cause a fuss. In any case she knew she could handle him; and she knew everyone present knew that she could.

Once in the car, Alistair embarked on a whole list of grievances against Elaine. Sonia let him talk, merely chipping in with the odd neutral comment or joky objection. But Alistair wouldn't have it. Wouldn't have it that he and his wife were just having a tiff and would soon be the best of friends again. Certainly there was no chance of them ever being *more* than friends, he said darkly; that side of things came to a halt years ago, what with Elaine's headaches and stomach pains and arthritic joints. Not that he was particularly bothered, he couldn't fancy her anymore. And would anyone blame him, the way Elaine had piled on the weight? One of their clients had actually assumed she was his mother. She ought to have more pride. Not every woman of her age lets herself go. 'Look at yourself, Sonia,' he invited, taking his eyes from the road to do some looking, with the aid of the street lighting, on his own account. 'Slim and attractive as ever you were. A fine-looking woman, if you don't mind my saying. David must want his head examining; I've always thought so.'

He was still singing her praises and venturing to describe his long-held admiration when he drew up outside her house and turned off the engine. Politely she waited for a chance to conclude matters, and remained perfectly calm when his protestations grew warm and he turned in his seat to face her. 'Now, Alistair,' she only murmured. Even when his hand came on her knee she stayed unflustered, simply returned it to his own knee and gave it a merry little smack. He understood then that he hadn't a chance. 'I suppose I'm not about to be asked in for a nightcap,' he said. 'Indeed, you are not, Alistair,' she agreed. Whereupon, with pretty good grace, he stepped out of the car and went round it to help her out. Fortunately, she'd had the presence of mind earlier to put her key in her coat pocket. Grasping but not revealing it, she reached up and pecked his cheek and said 'Goodnight,' then stood stock-still on the pavement, demonstrating an intention not to budge an inch until he himself budged in the direction of his car. Which he soon did, and, like a gent, waited behind the steering-wheel until she'd unlocked her front door. Sadly, not like a gent, more like one of those nasty flashy young men, he drove away tooting his horn.

She stood in her hall, the *toot-toot* offending her ears, asking herself What will the neighbours be thinking? But in the end she forgave him, recognizing the noise as a salute to herself. Disappointed though he was, he'd felt compelled to hail a woman who knew how to stick to her guns without being unpleasant about it.

As she prepared for bed she became elated. She kept herself awake going over the whole thing, picturing the way she'd handled it, often laughing out loud with delight.

So it's a blow to wake up now and find it still early, when she would have hoped to sleep in and make up for her late night. The hideous dream is to blame for that. And it's upsetting to think that her unconscious mind would thoroughly distort reality, would turn a skilfully resolved episode into something crude and alarming—

Botheration if the lump hasn't come back in her chest. That makes two shocks to her system already this morning. It's a shock having the lump return because she really thought she'd seen the back of it, she hasn't been bothered that way for ages. To be precise – and as it happens she can pinpoint it exactly – the last visitation was over a month ago, in the morning of the day when she bumped into Jason's car.

Aspects of that collision float through her mind, and the lump eases slightly. She sees the unknown boy's look of hopelessness, and herself anxious to put matters right. She sees them getting to know each other at Bellamy's Motors, and later in the roadhouse over blackened swordfish with Cajun spices. She recalls his subsequent visits to her house – there have been half a dozen of these at least – and the lump eases further. What an engaging chap he is. It's no wonder she seems to blossom in his company. They have a similar sense of humour. With Jason along for company, the carrying out of most ordinary chore can be turned into a festive occasion. The reason she finds his company fun is that she has stayed young for her years and energetic. The trouble with many of her friends is, they haven't. They've aged and grown inactive, and some, sad to say, have grown sour. Jason calls to her lively optimistic nature, and she to his. In the nicest possible way, of course.

It strikes her suddenly that the lump has dispersed, and in a light-hearted vein she jumps out of bed, turns on her radio, hums to the music, prepares her bath and lays out clean clothes.

Some two hours later she is cleaning up in the kitchen, her mind on nothing in particular, when Alistair comes by. He is naked all over. His thing jutting out is livid crimson. She blinks, cries out 'No!' and Alistair goes. But the panicky feeling that came with his brief apparition remains. Also, the lump is hovering.

Not again, she thinks wearily, noting that since it is Sunday there are very few courses open to her that might provide an antidote: the right sort of shop is closed, the right sort of friend is engaged in coupledom. As a single you can be asked out to lunch on the occasional Sunday, but it's not done to butt in. You can't even very well phone. Except to phone another single—

The phone's ringing breaks into Jason's doze. For a moment he thinks it must be ringing for some other occupant of the house, not having possessed a phone of his own very long. Then: Sonia, he tells himself, and grins. It has to be Sonia, because only Sonia knows he has a mobile. It was Sonia who gave it to him, plus a year's subscription, as a present for helping her deal with a bogey: the clearing out of her so-called box room.

Sonia has a phobia about clutter. Receipts and communications from way back; magazine articles and special offers clipped out aeons ago in the belief they might come in handy; letters from people she's lost touch with; bits of material intended for heaven knows what; things her daughter abandoned, ditto her husband; articles removed in a fit of sentimentality from her parents' home after the second one died – never looked at since, of course; old theatre programmes, mementoes from Ladies' Nights, invitations to weddings (the senders now grandparents or divorced); information and equipment to do with the various jobs she's held and, you never know, might need again: they are all just too awful for words.

'So much rubbishy *stuff*, Jason. You feel it could burst out of the boxes, fly out of the drawers; you could drown in it. I know I ought to get rid. I lie

136

awake sometimes thinking I ought to get rid. But what it comes down to: I can't darn well face it. Those nagging reminders, horrid guilt twinges; the sad old past looming right up in your face. Hark at me: "sad"! No, when I say *sad* what I mean is *stale*. And that is one thing I cannot abide. Staleness, sourness – urghh, makes me shudder. You see, Jason, I've always been forward in my outlook, and I've always been attracted to nice new things. That's why sorting through junk is such a beastly chore. Now some people love it. Some people are drawn to sorting through clutter, picking up bygones, wallowing in nostalgia. Not me. I don't know whether you've noticed, Jason, but there are very few antiques in this house. The furniture's traditional, I grant you, and top-notch quality, but it's all first-hand. I admit I'm a bit of a collector; adore my Capodimonte pieces (isn't my lady with a dove exquisite? – just look at her tranquil expression). And my first edition plates. And my porcelain bells from all over the world – from David, most of them, collected on his travels. I think whenever he sees a bell, *Sonia* rings in his head. And now Penny's started following suit, brings me a bell from wherever she's been on holiday. Just between you and me, Jason, I sometimes wish I'd never begun my bell collection. Now, my funny teapots I couldn't have enough of. And fortunately teapots don't appear to be as popular abroad as they are here. You're rather taken with the crocus teapot, aren't you, Jason? – I've noticed you picking it up. Actually that one is rather valuable because it's a Clarice Cliff; and it's an exception because it was second-hand when I got it – in mint condition though, or I wouldn't have given it house room. But apart from that, each and every object in my collection came to me spanking new. You see what I'm getting at? No dead person's dust and gunge in the cracks, everything clean and sparkling. Now you'll appreciate why that clutter up there preys on my mind, why I keep putting off having a sort out?

All this was confided to Jason one evening three or four weeks ago. Jason said he did see, and suggested that a way to overcome the depressing aspect of the job might be to turn it into a bit of a party – he and Sonia doing it together with a bottle of wine on the go and music to sing along to. He could do the hands-on rooting through, Sonia could sit in judgement on whether to chuck a thing out or file it away. They'd fill big plastic bags and take them to the tip. But they ought to get on with it: the longer Sonia put it off, the more it would haunt her.

Afterwards, Sonia was tremendously relieved. Grateful, too. It was naughty of her to give him the phone, but she enjoys spoiling him.

In a leisurely fashion he raises himself up in the bed and reaches to the chair and retrieves the mobile from a jacket pocket. 'Hello, Sonia,' he says.

'Gracious you knew it was me!'

'I'm telepathic.'

'I bet I woke you up.'

'You'd be lucky, I've been up since six. Been for a jog, read the papers, done a load of work—'

'Stop pulling my leg. Young men always lie in on a Sunday.'

'Well, yes, I admit it. But it's lovely to hear you nevertheless.'

'You're sweet to say so. Look, the reason I phoned: a friend rang me just now to cry off lunch – which is particularly vexing because now I've got masses of food going begging. Don't suppose you're free today?'

'Well, I was only going to catch up with some banking quarterlies, dull stuff like that.'

'Really? Then why not come over for a late lunch? Do your boring old reading first, and then relax.'

'Lovely idea, Sonia. I'll bring a bottle.'

'Don't bring a thing, only yourself. How does lunch about three suit?'

'Terrific.'

'Grand. See you then.'

'See you, Sonia.'

9

Saturday afternoon, two weeks later. A woman is standing in the middle of a farm track, waving her arms and making her slight body as wide as possible, wide enough to block off the section of track behind her to a pack of headstrong bullocks that are on the move towards their winter quarters. Planting herself down and waving at cattle is a thing Fran is often called upon to do. Steve made the request on only her second visit to the farm, she at the time merely his intended. Sometimes it feels like her prime function in life. Sometimes, as she takes up position and stamps her feet and thrusts her hands deep into her jacket's front pockets (like this afternoon, it's nearly always cold), waiting to deflect the first bovine foray, Here I go again, she tells herself; and all the dinners got and washing done, all the attendance upon family members and poultry, seem mere faffings about performed between taking up cattle-barring stations. This is probably due to the weighty boredom of the task. But the task is better kept boring. If she doesn't resist for the duration her habit of drifting off on a daydream, some determined beast will likely outflank her. Experience has taught her this.

Today, just when her stint appears to be over, there's a disturbance down the line. Steve's shouting takes on a new quality. Soon, Janie zooms into view on her purple and pink mountain-bike. Seeing Fran she brakes hard. 'I thought I was doing the right thing,' she says, frowning over her granny specs, her gelled hair standing on end, 'but Dad doing his nut, I wish I hadn't bothered.'

It is plain to Fran that her daughter has cycled head-on through the cattle procession, causing beasts to panic and father to fume. 'What is it?'

'Grandpa's come.'

Fran is puzzled: so much fuss for Hal?

'Grandpa Spencer,' says Janie. 'And *Brenda*,' she adds, pulling down her mouth.

'Oh Lord. Why ever didn't they phone?'

'Called on the off-chance on their way to see her mother, they said; before flying off to Tenerife for the winter, lucky pigs.'

'Couldn't you have entertained them for a while?' (Couldn't she have entertained them period, told them her mother had gone to the moon?) 'You knew what I was doing. You knew I wouldn't be long. I suppose you couldn't be bothered. You decided it was Mum's place to be bothered, as usual.'

'Well, it is your father! God, I'm pissed off. It's impossible to please anyone round here.' She hoicks her bike round to face the way she has come.

'*Don't* go upsetting the animals again, please. Get off and walk. It looks like my job's over, anyway – we can walk back together. You can help me entertain. It won't hurt you. We see little enough of Grandpa Spencer.'

'Why's it always got to be me?'

'Because Heather's at work and your father's busy with the cattle,' cries Fran, her voice rising. 'Just do me a favour, right?'

An entirely different expression now comes over Janie's face. 'Sure, Mum, 'course I will, you can rely on me,' she says sweetly. 'I'll show them my seeds project. They're bound to be interested. Specially Grandpa.'

'Thanks, love. That'd be nice.'

No, this is not an instance of Janie recalling her People Skills. Nothing so calculated. Ever since she entered her teens Janie has been capable of rapid mood changes, surly one minute, sunny the next. These are more marked in her encounters with her mother (with Heather and Steve she's more likely to be unrelentingly surly). Although it is weak and foolish of her, Fran can't help feeling specially privileged when the black clouds melt and there is a period of mother-and-daughterly warmth. For a teenager who can be such a pain to live with – provocative to her sister, curt to her father, crass with her friends – Janie's ability to pick up and respond to some of Fran's emotions seems touching and amazing. Just now, thinks Fran, Janie sensed her sinking heart and was moved to take pity.

When they catch up with Steve and the rump of the cattle procession, Fran and Janie cut across the paddock to avoid causing a distraction. 'Why don't I bike on ahead and make them feel at home? I'll tell them you're on your way,' Janie suggests, and Fran agrees this is a good idea.

Janie jumps on her bike. 'You don't need to worry Mum, honestly.' And off she goes, standing on the pedals, bouncing over the tussocks, flying down the slope. A witch on a bicycle. A witch because she knows things without being told.

Just how much does Janie know? Fran wonders. But this is not an appropriate question. It's not facts Janie knows, but that her mother has a dread of the coming meeting. She knows there is danger in a visit from Grandpa Spencer. She knows it can cost.

*   *   *

Some miles away in town, Sonia, who has been feeling restless and a little aimless, comes to a decision. She picks up the phone.

'Jason, dear, it's Sonia. Hope I'm not interrupting anything, I know it's your afternoon off – Really? Well, I was just leafing through the telly magazine, wondering if there's anything to look forward to tonight (brute of a day, isn't it?), and I noticed that film actress you mentioned is on: Ellen Burstyn. Nine o'clock, Channel Four. It's a film about a spy: *Web of Lies? Pack of Lies?* Something like that. The funny thing is, someone I like is in it too: Alan Bates – Oh do you? Good; I've always admired him. What I wondered, Jason: would it be fun if you came over here to watch it? – Lovely, oh, grand! Round about seven? We'll have a bite to eat first – No, I shouldn't dream of it: just something simple and warming. Now, you're quite sure you haven't got something better planned? – I don't believe you for a minute, Jason, you're a shocking tease – All right, dear. See you later. Bye-bye now.'

Fran and Brenda touch cheeks. They say hi to each other and lovely to see you. Then Fran turns to her father, who, having put down the cat and risen to his feet, now opens his arms. 'Hello, Daddy,' she says.

Almost beyond anything she hates having to call him that. *Daddy* marries her to several of her former selves: her pretty-baby self, her sweet seven-year-old self, her anxious twelve-year-old self, her sullied but obedient (God help her) sixteen-year-old self. What else could she call him, though? *Father* would signal coldness; he would search for a reason and erroneously conclude that she disapproved of his remarrying too promptly after her mother died; or disapproved of his selecting a wife young enough to be his daughter. *Dad* is too easy going; it's what Heather and Janie call

Steve, and what Steve calls Hal; *Dad* is from a different world. Certainly she could never bring herself to use his first name. So there she is, stuck with *Daddy*, whenever necessity and politeness force it out of her.

'Francesca, love,' he says huskily, and pulls her into a hug. Possibly he says other things besides, but any further words are drowned by the sound of her own voice saying *Daddy*, a sound which continues to beat in her aural passages, causing them to feel hotly and abnormally wide.

Now he studies her at arm's length. Or pretends to: his verdict on what he sees comes immediately and predictably. 'You're looking marvellous. Isn't she looking great, Brenda? How's Steve? Busy housing the cattle, I understand. Heather all right? Janie here has been showing us her work. I'm impressed. I reckon this little lady could be set to follow in her grandpa's footsteps.'

'Not likely, Grandpa. I'm going to be a psychologist,' Janie corrects him, seriously and pedantically. 'And even if I was thinking of horticulture, which I am quite interested in, I'd never consider garden-centre work. I don't approve of it. A nursery, yes – so long as it's linked to conservation. You see, the trouble with garden centres—'

'OK, Janie,' warns Fran. 'Why don't you go and put the kettle on? I'm sure Brenda and Grandpa would welcome some tea.'

'Oh yeah. Right.'

'Quite a little character, our Janie. She certainly knows her own mind,' Fran's father comments when his granddaughter has left the room.

'No bad thing,' Fran says, before turning to Brenda. 'So it's back to Tenerife?'

Brenda confirms that soon it will be, and mentions that they are on their way to visit her mother.

While Brenda is talking, Fran in her tense and super-charged state picks up the noise of Steve's boots crossing the yard. Her heart lifts. Her husband has spotted the Spencers' car and has left the bullocks to come to her rescue. He is a very dear man. She scarcely deserves such thoughtfulness. But she'll make it up to him. Whatever his misdeeds – even putting shirts in the laundry box without first un-doing the buttons – she won't shout and swear for at least a week. She'll allow him to get away with one or two things. This is a promise.

'Sorry I'm not dressed for company,' Steve says, coming into the room on a whiff of soap and cowshed. He hasn't even stopped to find his shoes, but simply pulled off his boots and walked in in his socks. Nor has he stopped to change his clothing, just stepped out of overalls and rolled up his shirt sleeves. His forearms, neck and face are red from their brisk lathering and towelling.

'Steve, lad! Good to see you. How's the farming business? No, don't tell me; when was farming ever good news? You're looking well on it, though. And so, I must say, is my lovely daughter. Amazes me how the life suits her. Who'd have thought it, eh? Our little Francesca a farmer's wife. When I think back – well, you remember, same as me: spit of a girl, eleven years old, dainty as a fairy in her ballet frock—'

'Yes, glad to say we're both thriving, thanks. And so are the girls. How's yourself, Brenda?'

'I'll just go and give Janie a hand,' puts in Fran, stepping towards the door.

'Can I be of any assist?' her father jovially enquires.

'Oh no, stay and talk to Steve. Shan't be long.'

He needs to believe it, thinks Fran on her way to the kitchen. Her father needs to believe that she is happy and blooming, and would not swop life as it is for any other on earth. He needs to believe that despite a brief coming to grief, everything has turned out for the very best. Well, perhaps it has and perhaps it hasn't. Fran finds it easy to contemplate other courses she might have taken and to speculate on their possible outcomes, but she can understand it would be intolerable for her father to dwell on her might-have-beens. Perhaps, without his willing it, some do jump into his mind. But if they do, Fran is willing to bet they are the same old dreams that were indulged in when his daughter was small – she becomes a ballet dancer, or famous in some other glamorous way, and marries well and leads a cosseted life.

What ever possessed her? What ever got into her? How in God's name did it happen: my tenderly nurtured plant turned overnight into a common weed? At only sixteen, Lord help us! Which means she was only fifteen when it happened, when she turned wild and threw a sport. Who'd have foreseen it? To what lengths in the way of precautions was I supposed to go? Didn't I fetch and carry her everywhere in the car, often leaving the business at inconvenient moments? She had only the few yards to walk between the bus stop and home – like several other nicely brought up, intelligent grammar-school girls. Did any of these climb onto the backs of motorbikes and lie down on waste ground with their legs spread open? Then why in heaven's name should a daughter of mine? Why? Why mine?

In her head, Fran makes him torture himself, guessing at the way his lines would go. She knows when to stop. She knows the question he will never pass beyond. She knows it will never occur to him to go further and ask whether they were right to bring so much pressure to bear, forcing her to give up the child, putting forward all the reasons why it was better for her father as well as for herself to do so.

Though it was always expressed the other way round, of course. *'It's you we're thinking of, our Francesca,'* they said, the mother, the father, the grandmother. Over and over they said it. But the most forceful impression left with Fran was the disappointment that must come her father's way if she refused to relinquish the evidence of her offence – the effect on his standing in the business community and as a town councillor and as chairman of public amenities. Daddy's standing with the Masons would also take a knock; there'd be no question of high office if her misdeed got out. With the Masons, one breath of scandal and you're good as dead.

Fran would lay any sum anyone cared to mention that it never entered her father's head to wonder if it had made a difference to her life, the way his standing had been thrown into the equation and given such weight.

'Oh, well done, love. You can take in the china, and the cake and the jam, but leave the tea for a moment while I heat up some scones. Oh and Janie, try and keep off the hobby horses while your grandfather's here, there's my sweet girl.'

'God, you're so bloody twitchy! Why shouldn't I give my opinions? Just cos I'm young—'

'Hey! And we'll both of us try not to swear, OK? Just for the duration.' *Both of us* is right, thinks Fran. Where did Janie get her propensity to swear? From her mother, is the shaming truth. Obviously the habit is catching.

Though not, as it happens, in her own case. Fran adopted the practice as a deliberate policy. A swear word would fly to her tongue whenever she needed a handy missile. And with a swear word she could hit them so hard. It was the surest way she could devise of smashing any notion they might retain of a dream-daughter. Perhaps it's unfortunate that the words have

147

stuck – Steve probably thinks so, Hal definitely does. But she can't give them up, they seem like old friends. She's fond of them.

And *There's my sweet girl*. Now how the hell did that pop out? Courtesy of present company, of course. *There's my sweet girl*, they would coax in the old days – though not with the irony she put into it just now, speaking to Janie. And by way of variation it was sometimes *Daddy's sweet girl*, and sometimes it was *Mummy's*.

'Do go to your ballet lesson, there's Mummy's sweet girl. You've missed ever so many, and you don't want to get behind. It'll buck you up. You're looking quite pasty. Don't you think she's looking pasty, Mother? I say, isn't our Francesca looking pasty?'

'Looking stout, if you ask me.'

Stout?

But Francesca's had tummy trouble. Trouble keeping down her food. It's made her listless. She's had to be excused from ballet, and she's had to be excused PE and games at school. It's no wonder she's looking pasty. But stout? Wouldn't thinner be what you'd expect, the way she's been picky at mealtimes, the way she's complained of feeling sick? Mind you, she hasn't actually been sick for weeks. And there were those screwed up chocolate wrappers in her waste-paper basket. Odd that, the wrappers. Because she's never been one for sweets, our Francesca. But Mother's right, she does look a bit odd. And yes, you could say plumper than normal – though isn't that just the effect of those big frumpy cardies she's taken to wearing lately, claiming to be feeling the cold? 'Mumps?' wonders Francesca's mother aloud. 'Could she have mumps? Is your neck sore, love? Have you got glands?'

'Ay, could be glandular,' puts in Francesca's father,

thereby revealing that he too, on reflection, finds his mother's observation to be correct. 'Glandular trouble can alter a person.'

'I've thought for some time she could be putting on weight,' Mrs Spencer senior claims again. 'Only I didn't like to remark.'

Before they can postulate further, the subject of their discussion abandons her breakfast and bolts from the room.

'Sorry and all, folks, but I'm afraid you'll have to excuse me. Time to feed the hens.'

Steve starts to make an offer, but is quickly silenced by his wife's grin. 'Life on the farm,' explains Fran mock-ruefully.

'Actually,' says Brenda, 'we ought to be getting along. Didn't we, pet? We don't want to be late for Mother.'

Mr Spencer heaves himself out of his chair. 'I'll just get the, er, you-know-whats out of the car.'

Fran and Janie exchange glances. Christmas presents are being referred to, of course; because at Christmas the Spencers will be in Tenerife.

A performance is then gone through, of bringing into the house some conspicuously wrapped parcels in as inconspicuous a manner as possible. Fran, Steve and Janie observe it, and Fran offers her regrets that a similar foresight has not occurred in the other direction. 'If we'd known you were coming—'

Not to worry in the slightest, indicate the visitors. It's their own fault for deciding to do things in a rush this year. 'Your father's had a bit of a scare,' says Brenda in an aside to Fran, placing a hand on her left bosom. 'The doctor said it was nothing much, but it might not be a bad idea to bring the holiday forward. Cold weather thickens the blood, you know.'

Fran lowers her eyes and murmurs, 'I see.' The

news embarrasses rather than alarms her. She knows this is unnatural of her. Later on of course she may well be struck by more appropriate emotions and regret that she didn't manage to fake some at the proper time. But that's life.

'Goodbye, Daddy,' she says. 'Have a nice trip. Enjoy the sun.'

She's packing some things.

No, she's changed her mind, she's unpacking, stuffing the clothes back in the drawers. What's the point of them, when already they hardly go round her?

Oh God, help.

She's packing again. Loose clothes, clothes that will fit her for a while longer.

Hang on, though. Think. Where can she go?

Why hasn't she worked this out already? Why hasn't she got a plan? Why is she such an idiot?

Because she didn't believe it. Didn't, couldn't believe it. Couldn't believe it even when her stomach wouldn't go in however hard she pulled. It had to be wind. Or maybe that sickness she suffered from a while back was the herald of something. Like cancer. Even cancer would be better than—

No, she won't even think of it. Because it couldn't be, *couldn't* – not from one single dream-walking mistake. And didn't he tell her not to worry, that nothing could have happened on her first go? She can't really recall him properly (she half believes he doesn't exist), it was too long ago, way back in the summer term when she was still only a kid. How long ago actually was it? Five months? For God's sake wake up!

But she didn't wake up, not properly, even when, with the aid of reference books in the town library, she convinced herself of her condition. She spends a lot of time in the library, also in the town parks and hanging around the shops. She hasn't been to school for a fortnight; she's pretended to set off for the bus, then walked instead straight on into town. One morning she phoned the school secretary pretending to be her mother, putting tissues over the mouthpiece and apologizing for the poor line. Francesca's under the doctor, she said, feeling poorly and undergoing tests. Please pass the news on to the head and all teachers concerned.

He was wrong about it not being possible on your first go; though the misapprehension is quite a common one, so it said in one of the books she consulted. In her first throes of desperation she wondered how to find him and tell him of her plight. But it soon came to her that if she saw him across the street or in the park she'd run away and hide.

No, there is no-one she can turn to. There's not even a friend she can confide in. It is sometimes known that a girl at school has been caught in such a predicament, but it is always a girl of a particular type: the type who is poorly regarded, the type she and her friends never mix with. It is enjoyable to speculate about such girls, but it goes without saying they are not to be emulated. If her friends knew of her condition they would be horrified. Ultimately, they would shun her.

On a notice board in the library there was a phone number girls in trouble could ring. She has visualized ringing it, but only hazily. This is her trouble: everything is hazy, nothing real. The start of it wasn't real and no more is this, the outcome. But neither does her former untroubled life seem real. Looked at now, from the far side of the rift carved by the trouble she has fallen into, this is what she sees: herself performing, dancing, reciting, smilingly complying with the pattern laid down for her, in a kind of daze.

*   *   *

151

'Can I come in, love?'

'Just a minute, Mummy.' She pushes the holdall under the bed behind the frills of the bedcover. She shuts the drawers.

'All right,' she calls, 'decent now.'

Mrs Spencer comes in.

'Hello, dear. Daddy's going to run us to the doctor's. We think it's best. I spoke to Doctor on the phone. "I know it's Saturday, Dr Smalley," I said, "but could you possibly take a look at our Francesca? We're most concerned, we're sure she's not right." He's agreed to meet us at the surgery at ten-thirty, so get yourself ready, there's Mummy's sweet girl. Have a nice bath and tidy your hair. Put something warm on, mind: it's parky out.' Leaving nothing to chance, Mrs Spencer opens the door of her daughter's wardrobe in order to point out some suitable articles.

Yes, thinks Francesca, let the doctor tell them. And she sees at once that she has been waiting all along for something of this sort to happen, for her parents to be told so that they in their turn can tell her what has to be done. Ideas about packing a bag and phoning a number for girls in trouble were only self-delusion. They helped to ease the stress while the time passed. There is no other course that she can picture with any clarity. She always has done as they have told her.

'This nice grey wool would suit, I should think.'

'Yes, all right, Mummy.'

When the doctor says in a careful tone, 'Your daughter is pregnant, Mrs Spencer,' Francesca, recumbent on an examination table in a screened off part of the room, hears her mother's sharp intake of breath. Nothing else for a moment but chair legs scraping. 'The pregnancy is well advanced. Twenty-four weeks I should estimate.'

'Francesca!' comes her mother's howl, and the

curtain secluding her is ripped back. 'You heard the doctor? Say it isn't possible.'

Mutely, she indicates that she cannot.

'I'm going to fetch her daddy. He's waiting in the car.'

'Good idea,' agrees the doctor. He steps up to redraw the curtain and repeats to Francesca that she should now get dressed.

She climbs off the table, acknowledging to herself that facing her parents cannot be postponed and reflecting that it's a mercy her grandmother isn't also waiting outside. Her father is in the room by the time she emerges. She notices that his hands are trembling. It frightens her to know she is the cause of this.

The doctor is saying, 'Take a seat, Mr Spencer,' and is being ignored. 'You'd better tell us about it,' her father commands.

So, with many a hesitation, she does her best. She tells how a motorbike-rider often came along the road as she made her way home from the school bus, how he would pull up just ahead of her and watch as she drew level, how one day he detained her and relieved her of her satchel and hooked its strap round his handlebars. At this point her listeners crane forward in their chairs, her father having seated himself as she began talking. 'Go on,' he instructs. So she explains how it struck her that the simplest means of getting her satchel back was to comply with his demand that she accept a ride. 'Only for ten minutes,' he said. She climbed on board and he drove to some wasteground. After a while he stopped— And that's when it happened. She explains that she tried to find the words to prevent him, but they wouldn't come; probably because she couldn't really believe what was happening to her.

'Shock and inexperience,' interprets the doctor. 'Sounds to me a clear case of abduction and rape. A matter for the police. It's particularly serious in view of her being underage at the time.' He looks down at his notes. 'I'm right in thinking Francesca has only recently passed her sixteenth birthday?'

'What do you know of this fellow?' barks Mr Spencer. The whole of him is trembling now, even his voice is trembling. 'Did he tell you his name? Did he say where he lives? Describe him,' he orders, as Francesca continues to shake her head.

She is saved by the doctor's intervention. 'I think questions of this nature could be left for the police. My concern is for Francesca's health, and to offer you all the advice and help I can.'

'My daughter has been abducted and raped. I think it's plain the help we need from you. I was never in favour of that Act they brought in, but I'm beginning to see the sense of it.'

'Mm. If you're referring to a termination, Mr Spencer, I have to tell you that it's out of the question. The pregnancy is too far advanced.'

'What the devil was it for, then? You said yourself, we're talking about rape.'

'And I must repeat it isn't an option. Not at this late stage. We have to think first of your daughter's health and safety. It's a pity, of course, that I wasn't consulted earlier—'

'Oh, why ever didn't you, Francesca? Why ever didn't you *say*?' wails Mrs Spencer.

Francesca, keeping her head lowered, mumbles, 'I thought – not much harm was done, not really. And I didn't want to worry you—'

'Surely,' protests the doctor, 'when you missed your periods—?'

'But I don't have them all that often.'

He takes another swift glance at the notes. 'Ah no. I remember now.'

A new tension springs up in the room, tension

154

between the doctor and Mrs Spencer. Both recall an occasion over a year ago when he was consulted on the subject of Francesca's irregularity. In the doctor's opinion too much ballet dancing was the cause, an opinion, he now concludes, that was foolishly disregarded. Mrs Spencer, who did so disregard it, is hotly aware of the doctor's conclusion.

Mr Spencer clears his throat to remind them that he is present and ought not to be embarrassed by mention of a girl's monthlies. 'What's this help you can give us then, if it's too late for the other?'

'Obviously the medical care and attention Francesca is going to need. But also, if, for example, adoption is decided on, or that a confinement outside this locality would be appropriate, I can put you in touch with certain agencies. In fact, I have some leaflets somewhere that might be useful—'

'I see,' says Mr Spencer, sounding a little brighter and a lot less hostile.

The doctor produces the leaflets, and suggests they go home and talk things over. He reminds them about the police's probable interest, and asks to see Francesca again on Monday.

Going across the forecourt Mrs Spencer holds herself at an odd angle and proceeds, half running, in a weaving motion – as if she isn't sure any more of her right way up, or of backwards and forwards. 'I'm sorry, Mummy,' says Francesca, stumbling after her.

'Get in,' says her father, holding open a rear door of the car. 'I'm sorry, Daddy,' she says as she steps past him.

Mr Spencer drives out of the forecourt onto a busy road. The pavements are thronged with Saturday shoppers. Now and then he glances at his daughter's reflection in the driving mirror. 'Think we ought to call at the police station?' he asks his wife.

'Oh, I don't know, dear.'

'Better if they come to us, maybe.'

Francesca bites her lip and stares out of the window. This idea that she was raped doesn't seem quite right. She wonders how her parents and the doctor can be so certain, just from her brief account. It was the brevity that did it, she suspects. Lots of details make for a more complete picture but make it harder to judge things in black and white. How, though, can she possibly go into details? How can she explain the way the joyride caught her up – the thrill of swerving and swooping at a terrific speed, at times flying through the air, and helplessly bumping over the hard ground? How can she explain that when he started to touch her, part of her went on thrilling, while the more sensible part of her, the part that wanted him to stop, remained tongue-tied and inhibited? She can't, and that's the trouble.

In fits and starts the car continues through the traffic. And a way out of her difficulty occurs to Francesca. If the police are called to the house and she is asked for a description, she will give a false one. She will say her abductor had red hair (not brown) and a large mole on his (mole-free) chin. If by any remote chance such a man is ever produced she will be able to declare truthfully that they have the wrong person.

By the time they arrive home Mr Spencer finds he is in two minds about calling in the police. 'Might be better to keep things quiet,' he says to his wife. Nevertheless, for his own satisfaction, he instructs his daughter to describe the fellow.

Francesca complies by mentioning the two features she claims have lodged in her memory: red hair and a mole on the chin. In doing so, she startles herself. For the first time in her life she is acting according to a personal view of a situation that is contrary to her parents' view.

After further reflection Mr Spencer concludes that the police needn't be troubled.

Fran returns to the farmhouse from the chicken coops to find Janie in the kitchen looking virtuous. She has cleared up after the visitors, everywhere is shipshape, and she has made her mother some tea.

'Did you notice?' she asks with a beaming smile. 'I didn't say a word when he slagged off the Manchester runway protesters. And I told them, when I didn't have to, about the Heifer getting the Best Sales Record Of The Year Award.'

'You played a blinder, my little chuck.'

'I did it for you, Mum. So you wouldn't get het up and go into one of your funnies afterwards.'

'What do you mean?'

'Funny moods, you know. Cos I remembered: you were in a mood for days after Grandpa came last time.'

Fran sips her tea and doesn't comment. One of these days she might explain a few things to Janie. She can imagine doing so. But she can't imagine sharing confidences with Heather. This strikes her as sad, and she resolves to try harder with her elder daughter. Yes, she really must make a positive effort in that direction.

When Heather comes home from work, she takes the cup of tea her mother pours out for her, and grunts – a noise which may or may not indicate thanks. When her mother starts up a conversation she cuts her off. She has to go and lie down, she says. She thinks she's starting a cold.

10

Jason drops his newspaper and the plastic bag containing his sandwiches (bought this lunchtime in the Tasty Bite) onto the only suitable surface in the room – a small rickety table. He removes his jacket and drapes it over the room's only chair. While he is smoothing out the jacket's creases a ringing goes off in one of the pockets.

'Hi,' says Jason, after pulling up the mobile's aerial.

'Only me,' says Sonia. 'Guess what I did today?'

'Booked yourself on a cruise. Bought a hat you'll never wear in your life.'

'Went mad in Sainsbury's! I was pushing my trolley past the butcher's counter – just looking, you know? – and there was this gorgeous juicy *huge* hunk of sirloin. Aberdeen Angus, guaranteed grass fed. I haven't tasted a cut off a joint of beef for ages, what with this BSE crisis. I stood there looking and drooling, then I flipped, bought it; now it's cooking in the oven. And, Jason, it smells heavenly. Do come over and help me eat it. There's roast potatoes and parsnips and Yorkshire pudding and sprouts— If you're not too busy of course.'

'Oh my goodness, am I too busy? I can never think with my mouth watering. But look, I can't keep eating your food, Sonia—'

'Rubbish. Which do you prefer, mustard or horse-radish?'

'Definitely horseradish.'

'Me too. So you'll come?'

'How can I resist?'

'Your coffee, Mrs Garrs.'

'Oh, thank you, my man.'

'That beef was scrumptious. Cooked to a turn.'

'Mm, good, glad you enjoyed it. Gosh, this article's interesting. Know what I've a yen to do, Jason?'

'Tell me, Sonia.'

'Decorate the kitchen. I mean, radically. I'm tired of this heavy colonial look. What I fancy is *provençal*, something fresh and pretty. *How to achieve the French Country Look* it says in this mag. Here, take a gander. What do you reckon?'

'I see, yes. Oh, very you. But you don't mean do-it-yourself? This would mean a professional job.'

'By heck, Jason, how long have you known me? No job too tough for this little lady.'

'Well, if you need a hand.'

'Funny you should say that, Jason. How're you fixed at the weekend?'

'The weekend? You mean the whole of it? After a meal like that what can I say? I'm entirely at your disposal, ma'am.'

'You're booked.'

'Hello,' says Heather. 'All right if I sit here?'

The query is sarcastic, she's not really asking permission, she has already dumped her tray on the table and her bag on a chair. But Jason takes it at face value.

'Heather. Of course. Here let me—' He helps to unload her tray, then makes off with it to the stack. He returns to his chair, takes up his knife and fork, and beams at her across the table. 'How've you been?'

It's only a few days since they last met at

lunchtime, so she doesn't bother to answer. She forks food into her mouth, chews it, observes him.

'It's great to see you.'

There's nothing in that worth responding to either, so again she doesn't.

'You're looking well. You're over that cold.'

'I was over it last time.'

'Yes, I thought you were. Good.'

He eats, she eats. She eats while keeping her eyes on him, he while looking about or inspecting his plate. She notes that he constantly smiles, so much so that his face is lit up. It's as if he is seeing something huge and wonderful that she can't. Or as if he knows something huge and wonderful.

Heather grabs her glass and swallows some water, as it suddenly becomes clear that there's more to her problem with Jason than his evident wish for nothing beyond friendship between them, as it suddenly becomes clear that there's Someone Else.

For the first time in her life with a plate of food in front of her Heather loses her appetite. She can no longer fancy the eggy quiche with bits of pink ham in it, or the green leaves glistening with dressing and sprinkled with croutons. Her only craving is to discover her rival's identity. Who is she, the cow? The girls in the bank appear in her mind, lifting their heads from counting out notes and tapping into computers to stare at her brazenly. She zooms in on the one who has always given her misgivings – Gina, he's mentioned her once or twice: dark hair, red slash of a mouth, pointy breasts. Jason has mentioned her, but always in a disparaging way, giving the impression he thinks she's the worst of the bunch: his female colleagues are all airheads, according to Jason. What's the betting he was really trying to pull the wool over her eyes?

But then she realizes she's barking up the wrong

tree, thinking her rival could be someone he works with. Her rival can't be anyone who works in the town centre, otherwise he wouldn't be eating here on his own. He'd be sitting with *her*, perhaps with his arm on the back of her chair, perhaps holding her hand. 'Heather,' he'd have said, beckoning her over. 'Come and meet—'

So how did *they* manage to meet? wonders Heather. Whenever she mentioned clubs and pubs he claimed to be too busy or too tired – too busy studying in the evenings for some banking exam, too tired from working unpaid overtime in the hope of winning his boss's approval. 'A degree doesn't take you anywhere these days,' he said. 'You need qualifications on top. You have to put yourself out.' Heather couldn't help being heartened by this, in spite of her frustration at not securing a date, because it confirmed to her that he was excellent husband material.

She sees now she's been an idiot. Fancy swallowing all that. Fancy letting him alone. He was bound to get bored one evening and go out on the town, bound to be snapped up first time he did. She shouldn't have pussyfooted around. She should've just come out with it. Like, 'I fancy going for a Chinese tonight. Want to come with us, Jason?'

God, if she hasn't actually gone and said it! She clenches her fists in her lap and waits for him to answer, certain of a refusal, dreading one all the same.

' 'Fraid I can't, Heather, sorry. I've promised to work late tonight. We're downloading the computer.'

'Tomorrow, then. Weekend. We could see a film.'

'Ah.' His smile is directed at his plate for a moment, then comes shyly across to her. 'At the weekend I'm all tied up. Um, a friend of mine, she wants to do out her kitchen; strip down the units and use this special-effect paint. She's after the French country look. I've promised to help.'

161

'Oh,' squeaks Heather, and forces herself to ask: 'Got her own place, then?'

'Er, yeah.'

Lucky cow! Got her own place where she can have him all to herself.

'The apple pie looks good,' says Jason with his eyes on Heather's untouched portion. 'Think I'll get a piece. I wasn't sure I'd have room before. Shan't be a sec.'

'Have mine. Go on, have it.'

'You sure?'

'Yes.'

'Let me get you something else.'

'I've gone off a sweet.'

'OK, let me pay you for it then.'

'Forget it,' says Heather. She watches Jason draw up the apple pie portion, watches him spoon a piece into his mouth, watches him chew with enjoyment while his free hand flicks back his hair – beautiful pale, incredibly silken, boyishly floppy hair. Heat shoots through her, starting in the pit of her stomach, seeping downwards to her toes and upwards to her scalp. Then she goes clammy and prickly, as her whole notion of Jason and what she wants from him undergoes change. Never mind all that stuff about getting engaged. Never mind showing him off in front of girls she went to school with, prettier, thinner girls. Never mind the pats on the back she expected from her dad, and striking her mother and sister dumb. Never mind the dreams about her and Jason getting a place together, and later, when Grandpa passes on (as has to happen some day), moving into the farm bungalow. Scrub all of that. All she wants is Jason himself. No strings.

She wants, in fact, what some crafty slag is all set to get this coming weekend. 'I have to go,' she tells him, grabbing her things.

'But you haven't finished your lunch. You all right, Heather?'

'No, I'm not, actually. I need some air.'

'Hey, I didn't realize. Sorry. Shall I walk you back to the shop?'

'No thanks. See you.'

'Yes, see you. Hope you feel better soon.'

Fat chance of that, thinks Heather.

'You've got paint on your nose, Mrs Garrs.'

'I haven't. Flip, I *have*.'

'Suits you, madam.'

'I don't think it's going to come off. Help, what am I going to do?'

'Start a fashion for green noses? Shall I have a go at it?'

'All right. Ow! Do bear in mind, this is *skin* you're stripping—'

'Hold still.'

'Delicate human skin, Jason.'

'There you go, clean as a whistle.'

'Let's see. Oh dear. How about a fashion for scarlet noses? I say, shall we call it a day? No need to kill ourselves, we've got all tomorrow. My tummy tells me it's time we ate.'

'Why don't I go for some fish and chips?'

'Now there's an idea.'

'We'll sit on the floor and eat them straight from the bag.'

'Mm, don't know about that. Let's see, where did I put my purse? Everything's topsy-turvy. I know I had it—'

'I'm paying.'

'You're certainly not. All the help you're giving me—'

'All the meals you've given me. Anyway, I'm enjoying it. So where do you think is the nearest chippy?'

'Gosh, I haven't the faintest. I should go to the end of the avenue and turn left, if I were you. You'll come to a parade of shops eventually, might be one there. Or you could ask at the Texaco. Look, are you sure? I think maybe my purse is upstairs.'

'I told you, Sonia, this is my treat. Cod, chips, mushy peas?'

'Lovely. All right then, just this once. I think I'll take a shower while you're gone. Try not to get lost.'

It is not plain sailing on the drive back from the chippy. Almost immediately a NO RIGHT TURN forces him into new territory. It is beginning to seem like there's no course open other than heading on into the town centre, when the Texaco where he made his enquiries on the outward trip surprises him, and he regains his bearings. Relieved, he breathes easily again, and an appetizing fragrance comes to him from the warm parcel on the seat at his side.

On the seat behind lies another parcel, consisting of pyjamas, shaver, flannel, toothbrush. He put it in the car this morning, thinking that, as it was to be a two-day job on her kitchen, it made sense for him to stay over. Surely she'd ask him. It's not as if she's hard up for space. Surely at some point in the day the sense of him staying over would occur to her.

He remembers this reasoning as he drives back to Sonia's with the fish and chips. So far it has not occurred to her.

But he tells himself that it's bound to, perhaps when they are eating their supper and talking over the day's work and what needs to be achieved tomorrow. Once an early start is mentioned the penny will drop. 'Why don't you bunk down in the spare room, Jason? It's pointless you driving back to your bedsit only to drive back again first thing in the morning.' It would be natural for her to say that. He can hear her doing so. A mother would not expect a son to drive back at nightfall halfway through a weekend spent in a joint task. 'There's plenty of hot water,' she'd say. 'Here's a clean towel. Got everything else you need? Eggs and bacon all right in the morning?'

Although he is confident that she will press him to stay (because it makes good sense, because it would be peculiar of her not to), he can't help feeling rather tense. As if something hinges on it.

What fun this has been. She loves messing about with paint. Decorating always gives her a warm virtuous feeling. She likes to imagine David's pleased surprise, and his saying that she ought to have got in a firm to do it. She likes having an opportunity to point out that she can't bear to waste money, she'd much rather do a job herself and know it's been done properly. And she likes to imagine David's private response: *Sonia's such a tonic, she'll roll up her sleeves and tackle anything, that girl. Nothing bothers her. Terrific taste, too. She can achieve an effect good as anything you'll see in the glossy magazines, and all on a shoe-string*— But Sonia has to admit that it is extra fun having Jason along for company.

'I really enjoyed that,' she tells him, referring to the fish and chip supper she has eaten. 'But I feel guilty about you paying for it after the help you've given, the time you're putting in. It doesn't seem right.'

'I wanted to,' says Jason. He gets up and starts gathering their plates and utensils.

'Leave that. You've a drive ahead of you. Go home and rest. You'll need plenty of vim and vigour in the morning – all the paint to rub down before we get cracking on the next coat.'

When he says nothing to this, but continues to hold the used plates, staring as if transfixed by them, she has a sudden misgiving. Is she taking him for granted?

'Gosh, Jason, do I sound like a slave-driver? Look, dear, if there's something else you could be doing tomorrow please don't let me and my kitchen stand in your way. I was only teasing. I can get on with it perfectly well in my own sweet time, which is what I usually do. Not that it isn't fun having you along. But please don't for one minute feel obliged. If something's cropped up—'

'Nothing's cropped up. I've every intention— At least I had. I thought that's what we'd planned. I thought we were going to spend the weekend *together*, doing up the kitchen, like you said. But if you've changed your mind, if you'd rather finish it on your own, you've only got to say, I can take a hint—'

'Jason!' Sonia has never known him like this: peevish, somehow childish. She's completely at a loss. And a little alarmed. 'Of course I – I want you to help me, of course. I didn't mean— Um, I don't know how—'

Already Jason is regretting showing his disappointment. He knows he just couldn't help it, he knows there were too many questions bombarding his brain. *Why is she kicking me out? Doesn't she understand what our relationship is, that it's quite OK for me to stay over? Is she trying to deny it? Or does she think I'm the type who'd steal the silver?* Even so, it was a mistake; he can see that from the look on her face. Mend it, he instructs himself, quickly, before everything's lost.

'That's OK. I thought for a minute you were trying to tell me something – maybe I was getting on your nerves.' He laughs, activating his most engaging smile. 'I'll be off, then. See you in the morning. And do make sure, Mrs Garrs, that *you're* full of vim. No slacking allowed!'

She must have imagined it, thinks Sonia, going with him to the front door. It must have been a shadow on his face, a trick of the light, that caused her to imagine an unpleasant scowl.

But after they've said their goodbyes and she's waved and closed the door behind her, Sonia stands stock-still in the hall remembering that her ears, as well as her eyes, picked up something unpleasant. Her ears picked up that he sounded put out. Most put out. As if he might turn on her.

Then she wonders whether she isn't being silly. What did he actually *say*? She has to confess that she can't recall.

There you are then, goose.

She returns to the dining room to collect their plates. While she is clearing up, his explanation comes back to her, his remark about wondering if he got on her nerves. It must have been something *she* said to make him wonder that. Which isn't surprising. You do go on and on, Sonia, chatter, chatter, chatter.

She decides to forget it.

'Day four was the visit to Orlando,' says Mr Gretton, pushing home the relevant slide.

A whimpering sets up in Fran's head: Why am I here? Why have I come? This is so-oh boring. She lifts her buttocks in turn, allowing each a moment's respite from the chair's moulded plastic.

Then pulls herself together. She is here because this is a village do, and you have to support the village. She is here to chat to some of the elderly afterwards over a cup of coffee and a slice of cake. Any failure to be here hastens the death, that is surely approaching anyway, of a sense of community in this place: and where, then, will these poor old souls go for an apology of an evening out, stuck as they are in their council bungalows and draughty cottages with no means of transport, no car, no proper bus service?

Funny, though, how the responsibility for keeping it

going seems to rest on women. As usual it's mostly females here tonight, though the person in charge of village hall events is a male, and it is a male – also as usual – who is giving the talk. Men's place to expound on the world, women's to fill the seats, Fran supposes. A few elderly men turn up regularly, it's true; widowers mostly, they come for a warm-up free of charge and refreshments at rock-bottom prices. Wild horses wouldn't get Steve here on a bitterly cold December night, though he thinks it's great that Fran will turn out to show the flag for the Toppings. Hal comes occasionally. Once a year during the Flower Festival he comes to present the Edna Topping Trophy for the best arrangement, and sometimes he cadges a lift in Fran's car, having a wish to contribute to the proceedings. As he did when there was a talk on bygone farming practices.

The evening they had the farming reminiscences wasn't too bad, Fran remembers. And she enjoyed the talk a local historian gave on place names. Subjects such as these are fit topics for a country gathering. But Florida? she marvels. I ask you.

Mr Gretton, though, appears to have a rapt audience. 'On day six it was the trip to the Everglades,' he continues. 'There we are in the boat. That's me – the wife took this one, sorry it's not as clear as it should be – looking through me binoculars. Sad to say we didn't actually witness any alligators, but we were assured they were about. You see those tall reeds sticking out of the water?'

Fran closes her eyes, not wishing to see – at least, not via the lens of Mr Gretton's camera. Mr Gretton made heavy use of the promotional material while preparing his report. Most of what he says is too monotonous to latch on to, but some words lodge in her ears and chime in her head and throw familiar images. Marshy, for instance, conjures fenland, not

Everglades: the fenny north of the county that she has never physically set eyes on. We must drive up there sometime, she has often said to Steve, but, for some reason, only half-heartedly. Now she knows why her heart was never in it: it was some sixth sense telling her the experience would be pointless, even depressing. Viewing the Fens from a road or footpath, she guesses, even with the help of binoculars, would be about as rewarding as surveying the Everglades from a tourist launch with half a ton of photographic equipment slung from your neck. Probably what she would want to see isn't there any more. Perhaps it wasn't ever for ordinary mortals. The observation that mattered was made nearly two hundred years ago, intimately and tenderly, by the one who could make pictures no camera could match. Pictures better than anything it's possible to physically see – or mentally, come to that. Because isn't there something a degree more magical than the pictures sprung in your mind's eye by *washy flag sown marshes*, and *pudges fringed with moss*, and *tiney islands just hilling from the mud and rancid streams*? Something a degree more magical even than the sounds of the words and their conjunction? Something beyond seeing and hearing? Something you experience, but only just and very briefly, with a sense you can't pin down?

The lights come back on – it seems very suddenly, and people blink and shuffle and start to clap.

'Wasn't that interesting?' 'Most enjoyable,' Fran's neighbours say to one another, speaking across her. She smiles and adds her agreement.

And yes, it was all right, she says to herself. Quite a useful evening, really. It could have saved her a lot of bother. No need to go to the Everglades. No need to take that day trip either.

*   *   *

When the seat at the side of her wheelchair becomes vacant – Doris Sadler having excused herself to go and chat elsewhere – Mrs Clews seeks another's attention: 'Mrs Topping, Mrs Topping.'

Fran nods to her and smiles, and waits out the remainder of the tale Sam Hetherage is telling. Then, free at last, she steps across the room.

'I'm going into a home,' Mrs Clews announces – the news bursting from her even before Fran is properly seated. 'It's all arranged. I go in on Monday.'

It's like a door opening in Fran's heart, the word home, uttered that way. It's like a door opening on empty cavernous space.

'It's for the best,' says Mrs Clews. 'I haven't been managing too well lately. And our Maggie's got her work cut out with their Paul. It's quite nice really, the home. Very clean and bright. Everything laid on you could wish for. And not everyone there's— I mean, some of the residents seem very alert, very with it.'

'So you've had a good look?'

'Oh yes, dear. Our Maggie took us. You'll know it, I dare say, The Limes in Market Spretton?'

'Of course. Well, you won't be very far away.'

'I never dreamed I'd end up in a home. Well, you don't, do you? It's not how you picture yourself at all. Only other folk. But there you are. You make the best of it. Very pleasant the people running it were. Very pleasant.'

'I'll come and see you. I'm sure you'll have lots of visits from people in the village. And I expect Maggie will bring you over to see us.'

'Oh yes, you get taken out. And you can have your own things, up to a point. I wonder if that includes a budgie? They never said.'

'I'll come and see you,' Fran repeats, thinking to herself: home's a common enough word, amazing it can be so charged. As she spoke it, Mrs Clews's eyes were locked on to hers like twin limpets: *Never dreamed I'd end up in a home*. It's a charged word also for John Clare, charged with longing, almost with a sense of the sacred; *a still and quiet home*, he wrote, denoting a place to aspire to, to come beautifully to rest in. For Mrs Clews it's charged with something else. Fran knows what else, but doesn't attempt to put it in words.

The home changed everything. Principally it changed her idea of herself. Even now, looking back, she knows how it feels to be Francesca-before-the-home and Francesca-the-inmate.

To Francesca-before-the-home, her condition set her so far apart from the normal run of girls as to make her virtually unique. Set beside girls she knew well, girls whose lives she could imagine in detail, she *was* unique. And even if she included girls from less comfortable backgrounds in her sample she was surely pretty unusual: pregnant with only a hazy idea of how she got that way; pregnant without a clue as to the man's name or whereabouts, or any clear picture or knowledge of him at all except as connected to a motorbike. (No idea of the make of the motorbike, either.) This sense of being odd, of being different, was reinforced by her parents' attitude. They would look at her when they thought she wasn't noticing as if they didn't know her any more, as if in the dead of night a creature from another planet had invaded their home and devoured the soul of their only child, and now inhabited her body rendering it every day more grotesque. And of course, for the few weeks it took to make the necessary arrangements, she was kept out of sight of ordinary normal people.

Arrangements, that is, for her entry into the home.

The moment she stepped over the home's threshold she seemed to grasp that she wasn't unique, nor even particularly unusual: that her condition and its circumstances were predictable; that she was one of a whole drab army of girls, stretching back into history and forward into the future. She didn't learn this from anything she was told (though as time went on she was told lots). The home itself came rushing to tell her – with its particular odour and its tired appearance and its endless background noise of female voices (confiding, agreeing, sobbing, railing, rallying, conceding) pierced now and then by an infant's cry. Maybe by the cries of more than one infant: Fran at this stage couldn't tell.

As an inmate of the home you spent the days preparing for Afterwards. What sort of Afterwards depended on whether you were going for Keeping or going for Adoption. Girls who were going for Keeping remained every day in the home, receiving instructions in baby care and cooking and mending and so on. Girls whose babies were going for Adoption attended either the local college of further education or a private secretarial college. Fran, directed by her parents, went to the latter. (Already they'd worked out her future: daughter at home helping out in her father's garden centre and recovering from the illness that had unfortunately removed her from the local scene for a while and brought an end to her education.) With three or four others from the home, Fran pursued a course in office skills. She wore a wedding ring to go to the college (supplied by the home), and, as instructed, called herself Mrs Spencer. It was plain the college had entered into an arrangement, but wished even so to be preserved from any slur on its name or other embarrassment.

Fran was glad every weekday morning to be getting out of the home for some hours. She pitied the girls who were going for Keeping.

*   *   *

Fran turns in at the gateway and rattles over the cattle grid, and thinks to herself that Willow Bank Farm is not too bad a hole to have ended up in. She greets the pile of slate and stone looming up in her headlights – not with the fervour of John Clare: *at home at last* – but with reasonable contentment.

11

It was meant to have been the most fantastic Christmas. He'd worked it all out, imagined how they'd give
each other presents and toast one another before the
Queen came on, how they'd eat together and clear up
together and laugh and grumble at the programmes on
telly. For Boxing Day he'd planned a surprise visit to
the pantomime. *Puss in Boots*. He's already booked the
seats.

But last night she mentioned in passing that she'd
be flying out to Switzerland on the twenty-second, to
spend Christmas with her daughter and young grandson at the place belonging to her son-in-law's family.

It knocked him sideways. She was standing by the
hob stirring something in a saucepan at the time, so
was deprived of a view of him – fortunately, as it
turned out. *How could she?* he was screaming to
himself, as she talked on and on about the grandson,
and her excitement at her ex-husband's promise to do
his darndest to join the party on Christmas Eve. How
could she be like this? Ringing him up whenever
she felt like it, because she was bored or needed a
job doing, and then, something better and more exciting turning up, casually setting him aside, not even
featuring him in her calculations? He'd experienced
this sort of thing before (Miss Nyree Purcell, Mrs Pam
James, Dr Janet Drinkwater) but he'd never expected it
from Sonia.

Just as his feelings reached bursting point, she stopped raving on about how much she was looking forward to seeing the ex-husband again, and interrupted herself, as if she'd just remembered he had a life too. 'Of course, Jason, you'll be spending Christmas with your father,' she said. 'I expect he's looking forward to it. You haven't seen him, have you, since you came up here to work? You'll have lots to tell him. He'll be so proud hearing about the progress you're making at the bank – those nice compliments you've had from Mr Whitehouse (which don't surprise me in the least, the amount of overtime you put in). Don't forget to tell him all that, Jason. Don't go hiding your light under a bushel. Parents do need to know their children are thriving in the big wide world. It'll be a pleasure to him for days just thinking about it, really!'

And then he tumbled. This was his own fault entirely. No wonder she thought nothing of going away for Christmas. Naturally she'd assumed he would be spending his with the widower father he'd told her about, the retired army man in Aldershot. He calmed down. It was still a bitter disappointment, but no longer a crisis.

After a while he told her he wasn't looking forward to staying with his father, who was a man of few words and had difficulty expressing his feelings. His father had always been inclined that way, he said, but had grown worse since his mother died. But you had to make an effort at Christmas, didn't you?

Privately, Jason resolved to kill the father off sometime in the summer, and thereby ensure that he wasn't in a position to ruin the following Christmas. On second thoughts he saw that the deed would yield better results if left till the autumn, that way Jason's bereavement would be fresh in Sonia's mind when Christmas plans came up. Feeling sorry for him and full of motherly concern, she'd want to personally make sure he didn't feel mournful over the holiday period; she'd tell her daughter it wasn't possible for her to fly out to Switzerland on this occasion.

It still rankles, though, that Sonia's daughter can crook her little finger and have Sonia winging over. He can't stop thinking about it as he potters round his bedsit, sorting out things he will need in the morning. He decides to call at the theatre box office in his lunch break and ask to change the pantomime tickets for a performance in mid-January; there shouldn't be a difficulty with more than two weeks' notice. Then it strikes him that two weeks' notice was precisely what he was given of Sonia's desertion. Wouldn't you think she'd have mentioned it earlier, say when Christmassy things started appearing in the shops? Wouldn't her mind have been jogged then into thinking of Christmas plans? Still, as became clear to him earlier this evening, she'd made a natural assumption which she shouldn't be blamed for.

Finding Sonia absolved and needing to focus his bitterness somewhere, he thinks again of the daughter. Penny, her name is. There's a photo of her in a wedding dress on a side table in Sonia's sitting room. A hard little piece, very pleased with herself, was Jason's verdict when he studied it. His jealousy of her intensifies, gathers into it every other feeling he has. Preparing for bed and climbing in, he is wishing Penny ill, very terrible ill. He turns off the light, and in the darkness soothes himself with an invented example.

An intruder climbs into a swish apartment and creeps around, helping himself to valuables. It is Penny's apartment. They are Penny's valuables. In the bedroom of the apartment, Penny wakes. Thirsty, she goes into the kitchen and pours herself a glass of water. The intruder watches from behind a door. There's something about Penny that enrages him – the way her avaricious little eyes sweep possessively about the flat perhaps? Part of Jason wants to hold back at this point, experiencing distaste and even fear at this urging onwards towards violence. But another part has to proceed. So the man steps out – it's inevitable, isn't it? – and he seizes Penny from behind, one hand clamping her mouth to prevent her from making a sound, the other clutching her neck. His fingers round her neck tighten—

But here the unwilling part of his mind interferes with the sequence of events in Penny's apartment, pours blankness over like thick paint. Soon, however, the blankness acquires significance. Jason perceives that it is a *piece* of blankness, in fact a piece of blank pavement. The pavement now gains length, and a pair of small feet come scurrying along it. Viewing them from above, Jason knows whose feet they are. His feet. His feet at about four years old. His left arm is being held very tightly by someone much taller. Fingers dig in. 'Hurry up, you little sod,' his mother's voice snarls, while his arm is given a cruel yank. It's a voice without a vestige of love in it.

It's not true, of course. It must be an invention of his dreaming mind, working ahead of his falling asleep – no doubt stimulated by the upset earlier. Because his mother was never like that. For confirmation he brings the photograph to mind, the photograph he stole from a sideboard drawer at home. There she is, fair and smiling. A breeze lifts a section of her hair, she puts up a hand and smooths it down, giving a light, easy laugh. Jason feels certain now that he was present when the photo was taken, so vividly does he see her adjusting her pose. It's him she must be smiling at, he sees that now, with her chin tilted upwards slightly and her eyes looking downwards. Downwards, not to the camera, but to someone small. That other thing he imagined just now, having his arm yanked and being spoken to harshly, was rubbish. He can't think where it came from. This is the picture that states the case: lips smiling, hair gently lifting, eyes sending affection.

Jason phones Sonia and asks whether she'd like a lift to the airport on the twenty-second; he can easily get the day off, he claims. Certainly not, cries Sonia, tut-tutting to indicate that she wouldn't hear of Barclays being incommoded on her behalf. In any case, Ronnie Bellamy has already offered her a lift and she has accepted.

'Oh,' says Jason. 'Well I just wanted, I just thought, I, er—'

And Sonia is guilt smitten – as well she might be: Jason has scarcely figured in her considerations during the past two weeks. Ever since the arrival of David's marvellous letter describing his intention of joining the family celebration on Christmas Eve, she has been on the go: dashing to the shops to buy clothes, wrapping presents, visiting friends to regale them with her delicious news, planning a little drinks party, securing a hairdressing appointment (she was lucky Deborah managed to fit her in so near to Christmas), ensuring the cleanliness of her house for her return (there is nothing worse than coming home from a Christmas break – a tinsy bit glum, as one is in the aftermath – to be confronted by remnants of pre-Christmas panic: the paper, the tinsel, the Sellotape, the lists). What a whirlwind! The funny thing is, she wasn't looking forward all that much to Christmas with Penny's in-laws, suspecting she was the subject of pity. ('Poor Mum, all alone in England, I can't help feeling guilty. Do you think we could invite her over here? It wouldn't be too much of a drag, would it?') But the picture changed completely once she heard of David's intention to join the party. In her head she hears him singing her praises, referring to her in front of the in-laws as the Lady Sonia. And any notions of pity are squashed flat.

So, busy bee that she is right now, Jason has been rather forgotten. The poor boy is wanting an opportunity to give her a prezzy, no doubt, and to be given his. He is hankering after some homely cheer before going to stay with that father of his, who does not sound a whole heap of fun. Quickly, she searches her schedule for a free moment: she's off on Friday, at the hairdresser's Thursday, Wednesday she's giving her drinks party, today is Monday— 'Come round tomorrow, Jason. We'll have a nice cosy supper, a little celebration all of our own. Can you manage that?'

Jason says he'll be with her around seven.

At five minutes to seven the doorbell rings. Sonia rushes downstairs, assuming Jason has arrived early.

'Hello, Sonia, I've just popped round with these glasses.' Natalie Bellamy sweeps past her into the hall, not waiting to be asked, confident of her welcome. 'I know I said I'd bring them in the morning, but morning was the only time I could get my hair done, and as you know Wednesday afternoons I visit Mother.'

She has brought the champagne flutes she agreed to lend for Sonia's drinks party, Sonia having felt that only champagne could reflect her mood.

'Oh, thanks, but you could have left it till the evening, you could have brought them with you.'

'Didn't I warn you we might be late? Don't worry, we're definitely coming, but Ronnie's pre-Christmas schedule is simply crippling. I'll put them in here, shall I? Oh, I see you've been busy. What's this – dinner for two? I do believe I've caught you out. Caught you at it, Sonia. Anyone I know, you sly little cat? Go on, you can trust me—'

Sonia is frantically considering her options, when the doorbell rings a second time.

'My, you are making an early start. Going to make a long evening of it?' asks Natalie, adding, 'Well, do go and answer it, dear.'

In a daze Sonia complies.

'Sonia,' beams Jason, mischievously dangling from his raised hand a sprig of mistletoe. He keeps it high over their heads as he bends to kiss her cheek. 'I wish you weren't going, but at least we have tonight.' He is determined to make the best of it, to remain the charming tease she always delightedly responds to and will surely wish to hurry back to.

But now he sees there is someone else in the hall, and Sonia is gulping and turning a funny colour.

'Well, there's a surprise,' dryly declares this other person. 'Aren't you going to introduce us, Sonia? Natalie Bellamy,' the woman tells him. 'I rather believe you've met my husband.'

'Sonia, love, don't think I'm poking my nose in,' Natalie says, when the drinks party is in full swing. She staggers slightly and puts out a hand to steady herself against the whatnot – for whose safety Sonia's heart leaps, for the whatnot is not of robust construction and it supports some of Sonia's favourite ornaments.

'Come away,' she urges her friend, pretending to a wish for greater privacy.

Natalie wobbles after her and is finally stabilized against a kitchen cabinet. The cabinet provides Sonia with sudden inspiration. Also she recollects that attack is the best form of defence.

'I know what you're on about, Natalie, and I want to say here and now that I'm cross. You were downright embarrassing yesterday evening. You mortified that poor boy with your insinuations. Just because he was larking about with a bit of mistletoe he'd snitched from an office party— See this kitchen, newly decorated? Nice job, eh? Well, Jason did that, with help and direction from me, of course. And he fixed that conifer I was worried about. It's his way of paying me back for helping out over the car. And I've let him. The young must be allowed to keep their pride, you know, even if it is hard going for them nowadays. I've given him the odd meal by way of remuneration, because strictly speaking he didn't have to repay me – I did bump into him, after all. Though I have been glad of his help. You know as well as I do, Natalie, what a bind it can be having the workmen in – specially in the kitchen. Aren't I right? So now that you're in the picture, if you want us to stay friends, please cut it out. Because if there's one thing I can't abide it's smutty insinuations. I've never been one to see smut where there isn't any myself, and I take it very ill if people don't show me the same courtesy. Very ill indeed, Natalie, if you take my meaning.'

'Well!' In her indignation, Natalie almost topples over. 'I'm sorry, I'm sure. But I'll tell you this, you want to be careful. What do you know about this young bloke? Having him in the house, doing jobs all over, woman on her own—' Tears start in Natalie's eyes as her words encourage an unpleasant vision: her friend being stealthily robbed of a prized piece of porcelain due to inviting an unknown quantity into her house. 'I'd never forgive myself – David wouldn't forgive me – if I saw a danger to one of my closest friends and didn't do anything.'

The mention of her ex-husband's name in this context sends a shiver through Sonia. 'You're half-cut, Natalie,' she declares. 'I'm going to find Ronnie.'

Ronnie is found and is brought to his wife. His face creases in distaste. 'Too many drinks parties, this time of year,' he comments in an undertone. 'We were at the town hall bash earlier. Trouble with Natalie, she misses the point. I tell her: we're here to press the flesh, I say, we're here to glad hand with the fleet users, not to sup their blimmin booze.'

'Don't worry about it, Ronnie,' says Sonia calmly. 'She was a bit OTT in what she was saying just now, but I refused to take offence.'

Ronnie gratefully grips her arm. 'Like the man always says, you're a lady, Sonia. Have a beautiful trip, darling. Pass on my regards. Tell David it's about time we saw him over here again, eh?'

'I will indeed.'

Sonia sees them off. If Natalie persists in casting aspersions, it will be remembered that she was in her cups, she reflects. And feels somewhat cheered.

All the same, when she returns from her holiday it might be prudent to ease up a little on the friendship with Jason. Not have him round here so often. Let things cool down. Anyway, the probability is, by then other interests will have seized his attention. He's young, he's good-looking; any minute now some girl will take him in hand.

Sonia sincerely hopes it will be a nice type of girl.

On Friday Jason is still feeling low – the way he's been feeling ever since Tuesday night and his supper date with Sonia, the date she promised would be a cosy little Christmas celebration all of their own.

It was that woman who spoiled it. The woman who was there when he arrived, Natalie Bellamy, wife of the owner of Bellamy's Motors, making comments and questioning him about the repairs to his car and about Sonia crashing into him. What she was really doing was pumping him about something else. Probably, about how close he and Sonia are. The most upsetting thing, though, was the effect of this on Sonia. She kept butting in, laughing and contradicting things he said. Twitchy, was how he'd describe her. He'd felt belittled.

Even when the woman went, Sonia didn't revert to her happy self. She remained preoccupied, and Jason wondered aloud whether she'd prefer him to go. Sonia flushed and said no. But she couldn't keep off the subject: Natalie Bellamy was a fearful gossip, she said, and it was more than likely she'd try and make something sinister out of Jason coming round for supper.

A vision came to him: Natalie Bellamy and her loose tongue laying waste to the most precious thing he had in his life. And a soaring anger took hold. He started ranting, saying he'd a good mind to go after Natalie bloody Bellamy and damn well put her straight.

Sonia told him not to be ridiculous.

It was a shock, her speaking coldly like that. 'I think I *had* better go,' he said.

At this she made an effort. 'Look, dear, I'm sorry. I'm tired, I admit it. I've had a thousand and one things to do trying to be ready in time for Friday. But you and I are going to have a lovely evening. We're going to forget about silly old Natalie.'

So he simmered down and produced the Christmas present he'd bought her. She loved it – a piece of her beloved Capodimonte, a country boy, posed with one foot propped on a log – but scolded him about the expense. She gave him a present in return and asked him not to open it till Christmas Day, thinking, he supposed, that it would brighten up a drear occasion.

'I hope you have a lovely time,' he said as he was leaving, and couldn't help adding, 'You'll tell me all about it when you come back?' After the edgy little episode between them he needed the reassurance.

'Of course, dear,' said Sonia. 'But do try and enjoy

yourself. I'm sure it won't be as bad as you expect. Merry Christmas.'

Merry! Sonia will be the merry one, thinks Jason. She's probably getting into the swing of things right this minute, up there above the clouds. He looks at his watch and estimates that she'll be well into her flight by now, somewhere above France. He pictures her wineglass in hand, chatting to and captivating the stranger beside her. He on the other hand couldn't be less merry, couldn't be more depressed if he really were destined to spend Christmas in Aldershot – with his father, his real one, the ex-squaddie himself, presently employed by pukka army types as oddjob man and gardener.

Oh it's you, is it? Turned up like a bad penny. Hope you're not expecting anything laid on, I never bother with Christmas meself. Don't tell me that's your car outside. You blithering idiot! I knew you'd do it. Knew you'd go chucking your money away soon as you got your hands on a bit. Easy come, easy go – just like your mother. Daft young devil.

Yeah, things could be worse. Christmas in the bedsit has to be better than Christmas with that. With the old bastard grinding on.

There's always the telly.

'Jayce? Someone trying to catch your attention,' says Michael as he passes Jason's desk.

It's Heather, pink in the face, biting her lip, frowning. Determined but nervous is how she looks. Jason gets up and goes over.

'I've brought your present, 'case I don't see you later. Don't suppose I'll have time for lunch. Hell, isn't it?'

She means the crush on the pavements and in the shopping centre, and the queues at the cash point – people desperate for further supplies of the readies in order to carry on shopping till the very last minute.

Taken by surprise, Jason stutters out thanks.

'It's nothing. Looking forward to the break? Got much planned?'

'Not really.'

'Oh,' says Heather, carefully filing this information. She hesitates. 'Love you and leave you, then.'

'Yeah. I was going to drop yours in later,' he lies, telling himself that there goes his lunch hour. Today is Christmas Eve. Only seven shopping hours left.

Heather shrugs. 'You don't have to. Anyway, cheers.'

'See you,' he promises.

In the staff lavatory, Jason peels off the wrapping paper. Not because he can't wait to see what Heather has got him, but because he needs to calculate how much she spent and how much he needs to lay out in return.

Inside is a flap-over purse made from pigskin. His initials have been embossed on it in gold.

He's amazed. He's touched. He's amazed she remembered that time in the Tasty Bite when coins fell through a hole in his trouser pocket and they both went scrambling over the floor looking for them. She said then he needed a purse. He said only women had purses, but she put him right, said Wilson's sold lots to men of the flap-over sort. She'll have got it at cost, of course. Even so, the purse has a really nice feel, and it smells expensive. And though it couldn't have been very much trouble picking one out of stock, she did go to the bother of getting it embossed. It really is a classy little number. He'll enjoy flipping it open in front of people.

He stands with his back to the lavatory, practising flipping it open and shut. It comes to him as he does so, that of his two Christmas presents, this from Heather, the sweater from Sonia, it's the purse he likes best. (He couldn't wait until Christmas Day to

185

open Sonia's present. He was overcome by misery on Saturday night, thinking of her in Switzerland and knowing he was the last thing on her mind. So he opened her present in search of solace. The sweater's quite nice, warm, sensible, from Marks & Sparks. She got it there on purpose, it said in her note, because they'll always exchange things, no question; and if he wants to exchange it for something else, he should go right ahead, she won't be in the least offended. There could well be more exciting sweaters, but he hasn't been to look. He wants the sweater that Sonia has handled.) He puts the purse in his pocket. He only has the lunch hour to find a present for Heather and take it round to Wilson's. There's a jewellers next door to the bank. Maybe they'll have something.

At five minutes to two in Wilson's Shoes, Christmas becomes all too much for one female customer. 'What sort of shop *is* this?' she screams. 'Shoe shop or crap shop? Call yourself a shoe shop and not have *slippers*? I don't want to know you've got them in size seven. If sixes were selling out you should've got more. No, Ray, I won't be quiet, they need telling. What's the point traipsing all over town when this is the main stockist? *Let go my arm.*'

Heather rises swiftly from her knees and, leaving her customer to try out the various shoes she has brought her, hurries to the trouble spot. She interposes her body between the heated complainant and the trembling junior.

'What seems to be the trouble, madam?'

'Seems to be? *Seems?*'

'I'm afraid we've had an unexpected rush on ladies' slippers. Size six were you after?'

'Six! Yes!'

'Get me Squashies, size six, every colour,' Heather orders the junior out of the side of her mouth. She

186

looks the stroppy customer hard in the eye. 'Have you ever considered an alternative, madam?' (The firmness of her voice implies that not to have done so is a foolish oversight.) 'Personally – were the slippers for an older person or someone more youthful like yourself? – personally, I think our Squashies are preferable every time. They're soft and warm, light as a feather, and they look so much nicer than bedroom slippers; not quite so, well, *bedroomy*, if you take my meaning. You feel right in them all over the house. And if you happen to slip outside, no worries at all. Wearing 'em outside is ruination to a regular slipper. People do it, I know, but the makers specifically advise against; they issue a disclaimer. But really nothing looks worse than bedroom slippers worn outside, don't you agree?' asks Heather, who has never worn a pair of slippers in any location, but pads round the house, like her mother and sister, in heavy-duty socks.

The Squashies arrive.

'Thank you, Paula, Now, madam, I'd be interested to hear your opinion of these. I swear by 'em myself. Ever so comfy. See how they fold up in your hand. Aren't they attractive?'

'I like the gold ones,' concedes the customer.

'Why not try them on? There's a seat over here.'

'Well, seeing as you've gone to the trouble. Actually the slippers weren't for me, they were for my mother-in-law. She's so blimmin difficult to please— Oo, yes, see what you mean. Lovely and soft, they sort of mould to the foot. Pretty, too. Aren't they pretty, Ray? Ray, I say, aren't these pretty? I reckon I'll have 'em. Why not? Think of something else for Ma-in-law. Why don't *you* think of something, Ray? It's your flipping mother. God, aren't they awful? You have to do their thinking for 'em. And their shopping. Hopeless men are, specially at Christmas. Yes, I'll take 'em. My poor old feet deserve a treat.'

187

'Certainly, madam. Glad to have been of assistance. See to it please, Paula.'

With which Heather sets off across the floor, back to her own customer. The manager is in today. She saw him taking note. Her colleague and rival, the senior assistant in men's, is clocking her too. She juts her chin at him, just a bit, just enough to signal *How's that?*

'Gosh, I'm really sorry, leaving you. How're you getting on? How do they feel?'

The customer hums and haws and thinks that maybe she needs a half-size larger. Heather rushes off to the stockroom.

When she returns, Jason is standing in the shop.

'Oh, hi,' she calls. ''Fraid I can't stop.'

'Can I just give you this?'

He hands her a small package, saying, 'Happy Christmas,' which she stuffs into her skirt pocket. 'You shouldn't have. But thanks. I hope—' She's recalling his reply – not really – when she asked him earlier if he'd got much planned. Maybe it's all off between him and the woman he's seeing. If only she weren't in a rush.

'I hope you do too,' says Jason, making an assumption, in his haste (he can see he's in the way) about how she intended to complete her sentence. 'See you when it's over,' he calls as he departs.

Yeah, see you, Heather thinks to herself glumly. 'Here we are, madam, size five and a half.' She drops to her knees in front of her neglected customer, and something hard is caught between her thigh and stomach.

It's Jason's present in her skirt pocket. A Christmassy feeling rushes right over her.

Fran opens the door. It isn't an easy thing to do with fingers like raw stumps, fingers howling for a soak in hot water, howling for it *now*. Those weather fore-casters who've been insisting Christmas won't be white this year ought to have spent the past half-hour as she has, up the field with the poultry; it might have changed their minds. She shuts the door and leans back against it and stoops to remove her boots. Her mind is on one thing only: the next step, the reviving of her fingers at the scullery sink.

Then a sound pours through the house. A treble voice, stealthy as a predator, cutting straight to her heart. It cuts, not with a thrust, but with remorseless gentleness. A killer just the same.

'*Once in Royal David's City*' – the sound empties her, she forgets her frozen fingers; she is pinned to the door, anger and loathing rushing to fill the space in roughly equal parts.

First and foremost she is angry with Hal who has obviously opened the living-room door while she's been out, and has left it open – after she expressly told him she wanted it kept closed. 'There you are,' she said to him earlier. 'It starts in half an hour. I'm off to deal with the hens, but the telly's all set on the right channel. If you want it louder press this button.' (Hal, who is getting deaf, always wants the volume up.) 'But do me a favour and keep the door shut, eh? That particular noise gives me the willies.' Why couldn't he accept this? Because he thinks her odd, no doubt. But we all have our foibles; he's funny about swearing, she's funny about church music (specially when it's nine lessons and carols from Kings). Doesn't she do her darndest to guard her tongue while Hal is around? Just good solid wood in the hole is all she asked for.

Anger at Hal is quickly consumed by her loathing of the sound and its message. That unctuous tone. In a lowly cattle shed, eh? And, strap me, only a manger for a bed! Anyone would think there were no home-less mothers with babies, no homeless kids, in this very locality at this very minute. As usual it's the one probably mythical example that people take to heart, and crooners croon over, and elevated voices decry in elevated buildings. *There was no room at the inn*. The congregation will presently be invited by some plummy-voiced cleric to dwell on this fact. Never mind no room at the inn, there are commodious suburban homes that can't spare a corner for an infant conceived in irregular circumstances. Like once upon a time, and not so very far away, in a house most people would consider spacious (four bedrooms, one en suite plus family bathroom, luxury kitchen, utility, downstairs cloak, two well-proportioned living rooms with garden aspect, garaging for three vehicles with granny flat over), once upon a time in just such a house there was no room at all. Not that she protested on that score, then or since. But, by God, she's thought about it. Once she was over the shock of parturition, once the finality of her loss hit her, once she stopped thinking of herself as a pariah who didn't deserve to have her feelings considered, she thought about it hard. And soon worked out the reason. It was the vast pride of certain people (the sort who are suckers for the babe in the manger story) reaching into the house's every corner, stuffing its every last nook and cranny. No wonder no room could be found.

Goaded up this particular blind alley by the voice of a choirboy, Fran goes skimming over the floor in her socks, through the kitchen, through the hall to the living room. She reaches in for the door handle – it's the second verse beginning now, the full choir coming in – and carefully draws the door to. She doesn't want to distract Hal. Nine lessons and carols from Kings is the highlight of his Christmas. It is for a lot of people. She herself is warped, that's all.

This conclusion sends her limp and empty. Her cussedness is revealed to her as a lonely condition. In the dim hall she stops and waits. But he doesn't come to her. She guessed he wouldn't.

Depression, a swelling dark wave of it, is rising inside her. She recognizes the feeling and starts to panic. It's Christmas, for heaven's sake. People depend on her. Whatever the cost, she will have to pretend to be feeling fine and dandy.

Her formerly frozen fingers are full of jumping blood. Their nerve ends screech. She tries to quieten them by stuffing them under her armpits. As she does so she remembers that a better course than pretence is open to her. She can work off her depression. She can lose her self-dissatisfaction by earning satisfaction. Four good lines would be enough to do it. In any case, she'd already earmarked this afternoon for a writing session in the parlour. This is why she dealt with the hens an hour before the usual time; why she stuffed the turkey this morning and baked the mince pies; why she asked Janie to deliver Christmas cards in the village and Steve to collect Janie after milking; why she was eager to see Hal installed in front of the television and the dog at his feet. With a solid family day lined up for tomorrow, friends coming in on Boxing Day and a lunch invitation to a neighbouring farm the day after, she saw this afternoon as a last chance for several days. What she had not foreseen was that it would prove a lifesaver.

In the scullery she puts away her boots and coat. She ties on her shoes, collects a glass of water, goes back through the hall. And enters the parlour where – crowning piece of planning this – she has a fire laid.

'Ent any of us going to Midnight, then?' says Hal, not for the first time.

'Grandpa!' growls Janie.

Janie, Heather and Steve are watching television, a comedian's Christmas special. Hal, it seems, is not watching. Fran definitely isn't. She's not sure why her daughters and husband are, it can't be for the jokes; the studio audience may be splitting their sides, but not this lot.

Steve now rebukes Janie for rudeness.

Janie protests that the way Grandpa keeps on asking the same thing over and over is getting on her nerves.

Steve rebukes Janie for compounded rudeness.

Heather sighs and jabs the volume button.

When the programme ends, Fran lays aside her book, gets up and turns the television off. 'Right, Hal. You'd like to go to Midnight Mass, I take it. Any volunteers to go with him, folks?'

Silence. So, curses, *she*'ll have to.

It isn't fair, of course. Steve and Heather are the nominal churchgoers in this household (Janie has been devoutly religious in her time – for about six months at the age of twelve – but now brands religion as crappy superstition). But for Fran the midnight service will be real punishment, loathing as she does all forms of churchiness. She's never made a secret of her position on this, or of her position on God: namely, that the odds are He doesn't exist; but if it turns out He does, then He's a sadistic pig, and she'll be pleased to tell Him so when the time comes and take what's coming to her.

For Hal, though, she'll grin and bear it. Anything to make him feel wanted, to feel part of the family. As usual Hal has moved into the farmhouse for Christmas. It gets harder every year for him to leave it and return to the bungalow. This is the house where he grew up, and spent the larger part of his married life and raised his son and daughter (daughter Eileen, now in Australia). He was pleased enough to swap residences with Fran and Steve and their young daughters fourteen years ago – at least, Edna was pleased, pleased to have all the modern conveniences and to order brand new curtains and carpets and bedcovers. Since Edna died Hal seems less enamoured. When he speaks of home he means the farmhouse, as in, 'You'll be wanting me home for Christmas, then? I'll come a few days early if you like, give you a hand.'

'Seems it's just you and me, Hal, unless—' Fran hesitates. Steve has to be up at six, so it wouldn't be fair to put pressure on him, but one of the girls for company would be nice. It's on the tip of her tongue to prevail on Janie, the daughter who secretly enjoys putting herself out for mum, when it occurs to Fran that this could be the opportunity she's been seeking, a chance to share something with her elder daughter. 'It'd be really nice if you came with us, Heather.'

Heather blows out her lips in indignation. 'Why pick on me – after the most hellish shopping day of the year? I've been rushed off my feet, people were going frantic. Why not ask *her*? Been on her backside all day.'

'No, I haven't. I delivered cards all round the village, didn't I, Mum? And I cleaned the upstairs, including your foul bedroom.'

'You're not supposed to go in there. Mum, she's not supposed to—'

'For Christ's sake! Oh sorry, Hal.'

'I'll go. No need for you to come, Fran.'

'No, Steve, you have to be up early. I don't mind going, I just thought it'd be nice if one of the girls—'

'No, love, you stay home. I quite fancy it, matter of fact.'

'Well, in that case—'

Heather feels a change of heart coming on. She was looking forward to bedtime and a private opening of Jason's present. But now it seems Dad is going to Midnight, and she thinks it won't hurt to postpone her treat; it might make it even more special. And so what if she's tired? Tomorrow she can lie in as long as she likes.

'I been thinking, Dad. I don't mind coming. In fact it'd be good. Quite, you know, Christmassy.'

'Great,' says Steve. 'D'you hear that, Dad? It's you and me and Heather going to Midnight. Come on. Better make tracks.'

Shit, says Fran. But only to herself.

It's a thin gold chain. In the centre of the links there's an H – H for Heather. She holds the initial between finger and thumb and imagines Jason lingering over her name. Watching herself in the mirror, she fastens it round her neck.

She'll wear it always.

12

Sonia is happy. Happy in the very best way. Happy and *right*.

Yes, it's the rightness of things that is giving the way she is happy at present the edge – the edge over some previously happy states which, frankly, were only attained by her determination and strength of character. Sometimes, because of her circumstances (which not everybody interprets in the correct light), she has heard herself described as happy and brave. She has even thought of herself as happy and brave; certainly she did last autumn when she was having to contend with bouts of silliness. Well, thank goodness those dull days and long evenings at the tag end of the year are behind her now. The year ahead already looks promising. Treats are in store and delightful rewards.

Though it could be said that the treatment she got in Lucerne – all thanks to David – was sufficient reward to be going on with. My goodness, he did her proud. 'This here is one heck of a little lady,' he declared to Penny's in-laws and assembled company one evening as Sonia concluded an amusing anecdote. And he topped that with an anecdote of his own, the one about the time he clinched a deal worth heaven knows how many millions of dollars with an Arabian arms-buying syndicate, crucially assisted by Sonia's charming but discreet hospitality. No chance after that of anyone noting her down as the mark-one wife, the wife who gets dumped for more exciting material. Probably did her a bit of good in her daughter's eyes, too. (It might be her imagination, but ever since she landed her glamorous job Penny has seemed just a teensy bit patronizing.) So all right, marriage to David didn't last. But she'd like to meet any woman, now or in history, who could claim greater loyalty and support, greater *respect*, from the man in her life. Mind you, we're not talking any man here. Remember the way those German women couldn't keep their eyes off him? David is *some* man. The goods, as the Americans say.

On the plane home it occurred to her that really and truly she has the best of both worlds: David's constancy without the risk of daily wear and tear. As for sex – well, speak the truth and shame the devil: hasn't she always considered it overrated? Face it. What a man requires in that department can be bought, custom-tailored. Not an area the Lady Sonia needs to get into. It's a pity so few wives nowadays can see it this way; they'd be a darn sight happier if they could. (Back to that word again!) But maybe it's true we make our own happiness, by and large. Her own experience is a case in point: for by no means has life been all plain sailing, there have been times when she could easily have succumbed to negativity. But thankfully she's a fighter, determined to make the best of whatever life dishes out. If you look for the bright side, chances are you'll find it, is her philosophy.

There was a lot of turbulence on the flight home from Lucerne, which kept them strapped in their seats and meant the stewards were unable to wheel out the duty frees. But the bumps and plunges couldn't jolt her happy frame of mind; not with a visit from David brightening the horizon. A nice long visit around the end of March is what he's promised. He'll be bringing a client, hoping to strike a deal. 'But once the business is out of the way we'll have ourselves a ball, have the crowd round, hit the town, maybe take a trip to Ireland. Would a few nights in Dublin suit my lady's fancy?'

Her reverie is interrupted by a summons from the phone. She jumps and looks at the instrument, but doesn't go near. She knows who is calling. Once the ringing stops she'll dial 1471 to make certain. It's a flipping nuisance the way he won't take a hint.

The ringing stops. After a moment she picks up the receiver, and soon a stilted voice confirms her suspicions: *We do not have the caller's number to return the call.* So it came from a mobile, she thinks, walking away from the phone, walking upstairs. As she reaches the landing, the ringing starts again. Botheration. She hates the obsessive way he persists, and she hates the way this reminds her of her own weird state at the end of last year. It's as if her difficulties then are trying to pull her back, staking a claim. It occurs to her that he might have rung back immediately after the first time, while she was ringing the 1471 number; in which case he'd have got the engaged signal, in which case he'd know she's at home. This is not an appealing thought, and coming face to face with the dressing-table mirror she catches herself with a deep frown. Dear me Sonia, she cries to herself crossly, for goodness' sake buck up. Do something positive!

She decides to go out. It might be an idea to call at Huffington's Top Labels. True, the rails will be full of marked-down winter leftovers, but she'll let Maureen know she's anxious for news of the spring collection. She has to look her absolute best for David's visit. It'll be fun talking about that to Maureen, too.

She flicks on her bedside radio and jigs over to the wardrobe, checking her reflection as she passes a mirror. That's the ticket, she encourages, seeing the smile back in place, noting that it's a chirpy Lady Sonia glancing back as she prances. Chirpy, *happy*.

He activates her doorbell. There's no answer. He thought there wouldn't be. Soon as he saw the garage doors open and the empty space inside he knew it would be the same story as yesterday (the garage then in the same state as now): let down, no Sonia. You wouldn't expect, though, that she'd be out two days running; out yesterday, more than likely she'll be in today, he'd reasoned before setting off. But of course, she's got a lot on her plate at the moment. He recalls her telling him this, saying certain of her friends were in difficulties and required her attention; also that she had things to see to on behalf of her ex-husband, preparatory to his visit in the spring. They must be very demanding these friends, and the ex-husband's requirements very complicated, to judge by the number of times she doesn't answer her phone. From being a lady with time on her hands who would ring him up on the least pretext, she's become virtually impossible to access. Well, life can be like that; it happens. But he does think she could show some regret. She could give him the odd call just to say hello, just to show he's not forgotten. Still, at least today's lunch hour won't be wasted. He has come prepared. He has a letter written.

He takes it now from his pocket and inserts it, under the flap of her letter box, into the space of her hall. Letting it go, he visualizes her reaction when she returns and discovers it. *Oh, a letter from Jason. Would you believe, the poor boy has to write to me these days to get in touch? Now what does he say? Oh, he's got pantomime tickets – how very thoughtful, what a nice surprise! I must ring him up this very minute.*

He returns to his car with his mind adhering to this

version of the coming event. No other version is allowed to intrude as he drives speedily back to work.

That evening, as he waits in the bedsit for her anticipated phone call, his mind returns to the territory of their last meeting – the one and only meeting achieved since her return from Switzerland. This came to pass after he had rung her three times. On the third occasion, sounding flustered, she invited him round for 'a bite of supper'. She went to a fair amount of trouble over this, producing a cheese fondue, something he'd never tried before. It proved fun to eat as well as heady and tasty. Throughout the meal she talked of her holiday, the grand time she had had, and how David, her ex, had been the life and soul. Only when the last chunk of bread had mopped up the last morsel of cheesy goo did she ask about his Christmas. He told her his father had been glum company. He'd been glad to escape, even glad to return to work. No, he answered in reply to the rather surprising turn her questions took: he had not been out 'clubbing it'. (Where on earth did she pick up that expression?) He hadn't the time, the cash, or the inclination. Yes, maybe one day the sort of girl who wasn't too bothered about flashy nights out would materialize for him, but so far she hadn't. Nor was he particularly bothered on this score. He had Sonia for a friend. Need he say more?

But this failed to amuse. She didn't laugh, as she would have done once, didn't accept it and embroider it as a joke. His quip was left in the air as silence grew between them and her eyes went flinty. Eventually she got up to clear away, and he to help her. But however hard he tried, relating amusing incidents that had happened in the bank, he failed to restore them to their old footing. His throat went tight with the effort. His ears detected that his voice sounded forced. A frantic feeling came in his guts as the marvellous world he had built seemed to be slipping away.

He could only conclude that there had been something in his answers that Sonia hadn't liked. What and why, when he had only spoken the truth (or the truth as it would be if the details he'd related about his background were correct in every particular), were beyond him. And he wondered about her peculiar insistence on the subject of girlfriends. Could it have been due to a comment the Bellamy woman had made (the woman who'd been present when he called waving mistletoe that evening)? Had the woman hinted at something going on between him and Sonia? Which might have worried Sonia and made her want to be reassured that he didn't harbour funny ideas about her. It made him feel uncomfortable and indignant thinking this might be so, and somehow sad. He needed her to be as clear as he was about the nature of their mother-son closeness. It shouldn't be necessary to spell it out. Come to that, he didn't think he *could* spell it out. Then an alternative explanation came to him: had it crossed Sonia's mind that he might be gay? Perhaps with her hints about girlfriends she was testing out the theory. This was not such an uncomfortable idea as the first, it didn't demonstrate a hurtful misunderstanding of their friendship; it was just rather awkward, gayness being definitely not part of his make-up. Mind you, if he could be sure of shoring up their friendship by affecting otherwise, he'd give it a go. But on second thoughts he probably wouldn't; you could never be sure where such a pose might lead; she might suddenly produce gay friends: which could prove dodgy. In the end he decided, next time he got the chance, to introduce a past girlfriend into the conversation, since Sonia seemed so keen on the subject. Lissa, for instance, the girl he went out with for a couple of terms at university, who in fact consoled him when Dr Janet Drinkwater took herself off. Rather conveniently Lissa now works abroad. They've lost touch since graduation, but Sonia doesn't need to be told this. He could invent letters passing between them and talk of a possible future.

(It was odd what happened when he got this idea of resurrecting Lissa as someone he thinks of in girl-friend terms. Try as he might he couldn't hang on to her features; they faintly came and swiftly went. Then another face arrived, and, however much he blinked and shook his head at it, stubbornly persisted. It was Heather's face. Yes, very odd, that.)

Sonia wouldn't be pinned down when he left that evening about a further meeting. He has rung her many times, but only caught her on two occasions – unfortunately both times she was on the point of going out. Mentally, he's had several chats with her, which usually proceed along similar lines: he issuing gentle rebukes, she apologizing and offering one of a series of explanations. Always the air is cleared be-tween them. In the real world, however, with the date of the pantomime performance they are booked to see fast approaching (and Sonia still unaware of their being booked to see any performance), he saw no alternative but to drive to her house. He'd planned to surprise her with the tickets at the last moment – in the days when he could bank on there being lots of moments. He'd much rather not be so desperate as to call on her uninvited, but what other course was there?

This was where his reasoning had led on the evening before his first lunchtime dash to her house. It's the point he reaches still; there's no getting beyond it. Not until she phones.

Which she must do soon. Surely.

*   *   *

Hampered by large rectangular lilac-coloured plastic bags, Huffington's Top Labels in simple beige capitals stated across them, and by a rather large G and T drunk with poor Annie Noble (who is still misguidedly bitter about Paul's misdemeanour with a girl who worked in his office), Sonia turns her key in the lock. She manoeuvres through the opening into the hall, turns to close the door, and spots a letter on the carpet. Frowning, she observes it, noting its lack of stamp and address. She leaves it where it is, goes upstairs with her purchases.

She hadn't intended to make any purchases today. She had intended to discuss her spring wardrobe with Maureen and get a feel for the coming look. One or two things proved irresistible, however, particularly with their sale price tags. She unfolds each item from layers of tissue and hangs or lays them away. Then she slips out of her town outfit and pulls on loose fitting trousers and top.

When she runs downstairs the letter comes into view. She goes to collect it, her frown returning. It'll be from him, of course. Which means he's been round. With the phone bothering her this morning an instinct told her to go out. Obviously a sound instinct.

She rips open the envelope and reads *Dear Sonia*. Her eyes skip to the bottom of the page where *With love from Jason* appears. She sucks in her breath. This is beginning to feel like persecution.

Her spirits sink even further when she sits down in the kitchen and reads the letter thoroughly. He proposes to take her to the theatre, she discovers, the Westgate in town, a pantomime performance. He's bought the tickets already. He seems to think this news will excite her. And so it jolly well does. This is the limit, she cries to herself. He only proposes to escort her to the best-known theatre in town, on the most popular night of the week. Anyone could be there. People who know her. Friends of herself and David.

The tickets, he says, are for this coming Saturday. Today is Tuesday. He apologizes for the short notice but says he has tried on numerous occasions to contact her, all without success. Well, that explains the constant phoning. She feels relieved to an extent; a sensible motive shows she isn't dealing with a crazed person. Even so, she's glad this wasn't sprung on her over the phone; this way she has time to consider how to react. How to put him off.

An hour later while eating her supper, Sonia experiences a prick of guilt. The boy has spent money on her in an attempt to please. She wonders how much, calculating that he would go for the most expensive seats; but she has absolutely no idea, never having purchased theatre tickets personally, always having had them bought for her. A telephone call to the box office soon enlightens. Fifteen pounds is the top price for the pantomime, with a reduction for OAPs at matinée performances. 'Is it possible to return tickets already purchased?' Sonia asks. And learns that it is only possible to exchange them, given seven days notice, for a performance on a different date. Sonia says, 'Thank you so much,' and replaces the receiver.

Thirty pounds is a heck of a lot of money for a boy in Jason's position to forfeit. But even that consideration is not going to persuade her to risk being seen with him in public – at the panto, for heaven's sake, *Puss in Boots*. Lord, how juvenile, she scoffs, forgetting that not very long ago she and he watched several *Carry On* videos together, laughing so hard they were nearly sick: her mind is more pressingly engaged with her knotty problem. At last it comes up with a fair solution. She'll ring him up and ask him to come over. She'll have some invented problem ready, the sort of problem that prevents people from entering places such as theatres – claustrophobia, something like that. She'll insist on buying the tickets from him, saying she'd like to make a present of them to a hard-up friend who would just love to treat her grandchild.

Invigorated by her creativity, Sonia heads for the phone.

'Hello, Jason,' she trills – 'Yes, of course it's me, dear. Thank you for the note. Look, I'm in a spot of difficulty about Saturday evening. Can you come over for supper tomorrow so I can put you in the picture? – No, nothing to worry about; just be sure and bring the panto tickets. – Well, I don't mean to be mysterious, all will be explained. – Yes, it'll be nice to see you, too. I'm terribly busy these days, as you know, but it's good to keep in touch – But that's what I *said*, Jason: it's good to keep in touch. About seven shall we say? – Yes, dear, that's fine. Must fly. Bye now.'

The meal is over. Sonia has begun to explain matters to Jason which will help him understand why a visit to the pantomime would be impossible for her. Her tale is thoroughly rehearsed, she has no feeling of launching on a fabrication.

'It was pulled down years ago, the Roxy,' she reflects happily. 'It stopped being a cinema well before that – they had bingo there. Now it's shops on the site.' Her eyes go misty at the memory of schoolgirl viewings of X-certificate films – preceded by sessions in the public toilets when age-enhancing mascara and lipstick were applied in order to fool the cashier that they were over sixteen. Because Sonia was small and stayed young-looking however much make-up was plastered on, another girl, usually her best friend Mavis, would present herself at the ticket window, saying, 'Two three-and-sixes, please.' Safely inside the auditorium they would break into the giggles of fourteen-year-olds. Sonia sketches in the scene for Jason, recalling much more than she relates. Then she comes to the crucial invented part, the incident that never did happen to Sonia, though it happened to scores of other girls visiting cinemas in those days, according to reports in *The Evening Chronicle*. Apparently, girls were molested on a regular basis in the Roxy and the Regal, the Gaumont and the Savoy, under cover of cinematic darkness and noise.

'We were a threesome that evening: me and Mavis and a girl called Daphne Payne. We had a tiff; heaven knows what about. Though – you know what girls are – I think I took the hump because Daphne Payne seemed to be muscling in on my friendship with Mavis. Anyway, I stomped off and sat on my own, a few rows behind the others. Once the film got going, a man left his seat across the gangway and came and sat next to mine. I won't go into details of what happened next, if you don't mind, Jason. I'd rather draw a veil. Suffice it to say that from that day to this I have never lasted more than a few minutes in a theatre or cinema. Once the lights go down, that's it, I'm finished. 'Course there's a word nowadays for an upset like the one I suffered. *Trauma*. And what you go through afterwards is *post traumatic stress*. Think of it like that, Jason, and you'll understand. Much as I appreciate your thoughtfulness, there's no way I'd put myself through another dose of *post traumatic stress*. And I know you wouldn't want me to.'

Jason says nothing. His eyes leave her face and drop to the tickets, which at her request he earlier placed on the table between them. When Sonia's little hand smartly shoots out and whips them away, his eyes are unable to leave the spot. He registers that she's off again, on to a new tack. Her words land in his ears. His brain labours to extract their meaning – something about a friend of hers who is hard up and a grandson

205

from a one-parent family. Sonia wants to treat them both. She wants to treat them with the pantomime tickets. She proposes to reimburse him for their cost.

His eyes seem heavy lidded as they rise again to her face. All his senses are lumbering. She's too quick for him. She's like a champion sprinter who knows she can't be beaten: at any rate, not by present company, he's not in her class. Now she's reaching for her handbag, bringing out her purse. She's claiming the tickets as her trophy; she's accepting his silence as conceding he's lost. When she brings out the money he's reminded of a winner who insists on buying the loser a drink.

He didn't disbelieve her from the outset. When she began explaining her situation, he started looking for a solution: a cinema is a cinema but a theatre a theatre, he was waiting to point out; maybe they could explain her difficulty to the theatre management and be given different seats, seats by an exit or near some lighting or maybe in a box. He'd assumed that finding a solution was the point of this tête-à-tête. Only slowly did it dawn on him that the point of it for Sonia was to set up an insuperable obstacle to their outing. Or set him up? When her hand snatched the tickets, he knew he'd been set up. Stitched up. Bound and gagged. And now it's plain to him what all this is about, this little farce: she doesn't want or intend to go to the pantomime with him. Or anywhere else, come to that.

'I've checked it's the right money, Jason,' she says, passing the notes over and smiling.

Of course she's checked. She's worked it all out in advance, every sodding detail. Every sodding lie. If she can lie to him so blithely this is because he means nothing whatever to her. Except a damn nuisance.

'Can I see the tickets for a moment?' he asks, keeping his voice steady.

She hesitates, looking surprised.

'They are my property.'

For the first time she looks less than sublimely sure of herself. 'Well of course you can, Jason.' She takes the tickets out of her handbag, and after a moment's indecision, lays them on the table beside the money. She affects a little laugh. 'See? I'm not diddling you, dear. Really I'm not.'

'Aren't you, Sonia?' he asks, noting with interest that his voice sounds calm, as if it's detached from the rest of him. His hands, though, are a dead give-away. When they take the tickets and hold them up in front of both their faces, they jig like they're having a private fit. But at least they do as they're told.

What they do is rip the tickets in two – this way, that way, this, that. Finally they toss all the bits in the air.

Pieces of pink paper drift down like tired rose petals.

He is filled with sadness. Looking at the scraps which were once his tickets, he remembers all they have meant to him over the past weeks. Oblivious of the Sonia who is present, the Sonia he suspects of lying, the Sonia who has fallen silent, a sequence of events flows through his mind such as a sight of the tickets would always conjure: Sonia and Jason arm in arm running up theatre steps, laughing together at abysmal jokes, their fingers colliding in a shared box of chocolates. But the sequence does not, as formerly, have a consoling effect. There is no little leap of anticipation. It seems fitting that the tickets should lie there in bits.

'I'm sorry,' he says to her at last. 'I'm sorry for your friend, but I couldn't let them go to anyone else. They meant something, you see. I bought them ages ago, well before Christmas; it was going to be my surprise.

You know how you were always springing nice surprises on me, giving me little treats?' He mentions a few of these. 'The thought of doing this for you kept me going over a bloody awful Christmas. Then you came home and were too busy for me all of a sudden, but I wasn't too bothered, not with the panto coming up. The money's not important, not the point. You'll easily think of something else for your friend. You're good at treating people, Sonia.'

Sonia is in so many minds at once, she hardly knows which to articulate. She is relieved that apparently he didn't see through her ruse. For a nasty moment she thought he had. For a nasty moment she thought he'd taken umbrage and when he'd finished ripping up the tickets he'd start ripping something else. She's also relieved that the tickets are now dead meat, so to speak. But mixed with all this relief is a fair smattering of guilt. He has reminded her of many things she's pretended to herself never happened. Yes, she was always phoning him. 'Come and share this joint of beef. Jason, come and watch this film on TV.' It was very stupid of her. It's been a lesson. But obviously it's a different story from Jason's point of view. She sees this now.

'I've been insensitive, Jason. I'm sorry. I should have thought.'

'Don't worry. It's nobody's fault you can't go. Just bad luck.'

'But I should've— The trouble is, what with the holiday, and now David coming—' Hell's teeth, David coming! Just because of a few guilt twinges she mustn't start encouraging the boy all over again. What would David make of a young fellow turning up at the house and constantly ringing her up? By the light, Sonia, get this sorted! Before there's a chance of anything of that nature happening.

'The reason I've been a bit tactless, Jason: I've got so

much to do. I hardly know whether I'm coming or going—'

'I know, Sonia, you've said. Don't worry, I understand. I might be a bit pushed myself round about Easter – when Lissa comes home. And I know you'll be equally understanding, because good friends are, aren't they? They fit in with one another, make allowances—'

'Lissa? Did you say Lissa, dear? I don't think I—'

'My girlfriend, yeah. I didn't mention her before because I wasn't sure how things stood. I mean, we were together at university, then I got a job here, and she went to Japan – she teaches English as a foreign language. Anyway, she's coming home for three weeks, so *hopefully*—'

'Oh, I am glad, Jason. No wonder you weren't too keen when I quizzed you about meeting girls. All the time you were— Well I think that's sweet, staying so loyal. You've missed her, haven't you?'

Her fears have melted like magic. As she expresses her enthusiasm she is expressing other things to herself: here is an ordinary, nice young man. What an idiot she's been, building him up into a sort of monster.

She jumps to her feet. 'Good lord, we haven't had our coffee yet. What on earth must you think of me?' And she swoops up the kettle, eager to make amends.

Amazing, the transformation his mention of a girlfriend brought. Jason doesn't know why this should be, and he's not sure he wants to. Least said, soonest mended. He's lucky it *is* mended, because a few moments back he nearly lost it. He could have ripped up just about anything, never mind the tickets; rip his heart out was what he wanted to do, the way it was hurting. He was saved by those torn pieces of paper floating down, slowly, lingeringly, imposing a change

209

of pace. By the time they'd fluttered to rest, the desperation had gone out of him. There's a power in things that are light as air that heavy things don't have. Heavy things just reflect back your energy. You chuck 'em up, and *wham* they come down. Weightless things take their own sweet time. You're forced to watch and wait. And while you're waiting the steam goes out of you. It would probably be like that scattering a loved one's ashes. They'd fall, slowly and gently as snowflakes, and by the time they'd landed you'd be empty, numb.

Funny though, how once he got talking, trying to explain to her why he'd torn up the tickets, he started reviving. And then he knew he'd give anything not to be stuck with that bereft feeling. He had to salvage something to ward it off, something of what they'd had. It was sheer inspiration the way he hit on Lissa. And the way Sonia immediately came round, *snap*, like that— It was amazing.

Sonia says the floor tiles in the guest bathroom are looking tatty. She wants to cover them with some of that natural fibre – sisal or coir – aiming for a masculine look. She's going to lay it herself. There's a warehouse she's heard of in Oxfordshire where you can get cheap offcuts.

All this is because of her ex coming. David is so good about letting her keep the house and not stinting her over its upkeep that she likes to demonstrate the great care she takes of it while never wasting a penny. She explained all this when Jason called round this afternoon. For once she was at home, taking it easy with the Sunday papers. He said straight off that he couldn't stop, he was expecting a call from Lissa's mother in a couple of hours giving him news of the coming visit. 'Just time for a cuppa, then,' said Sonia.

They sat in the conservatory, which was warm as

toast with the heater on and the sun coming in; you'd never have thought there was an icy wind outside. She started talking about her ex coming and bringing a guest, and it was then she mentioned her worries about the state of the bathroom floor.

He offered to go with her to the warehouse in case there should be difficulty getting the carpet into her car. She said there wouldn't be, there were bound to be assistants. He said, 'What about this end? You'll need a hand here.'

She thought about it for a moment, then said it was very kind of him. So she's going to postpone her trip to the warehouse until his day off. He's promised to arrive at her place around half-past eleven. Probably he'll stay on and lend a hand with the laying. Probably they'll have a spot of lunch.

It looks like things are getting back to normal.

Blast it, blast it, thinks Sonia, silently cursing the brand new covering on the guest bathroom floor. Things are as bad as ever they were, and it's all the fault of that flipping sisal.

No, it's her fault. She should never have agreed he could help her unload it. She should never have gone on to him about the state of the bathroom floor in the first place. Chatter chatter chatter: you let your tongue run away with you, Sonia. You'd think you'd have learned. Give that lad an inch and he takes a whopping mile. He had to stay and help lay it, of course. Had to go get them a pizza. Had to come back two days later because he'd read some article saying there's a spray you can get for sisal that guards against stains. And then there's the phone calls. What is her opinion of his trying for a bigger place before his girlfriend comes home? Can he bring over some details of studio flats he got from the estate agent? And when that subject's exhausted, back he comes with a complete change of tack: a book from the library on Clarice Cliff – as if she couldn't have taken out a book on Clarice Cliff for herself, if she'd been interested. Good grief, it was the teapot she fancied, *the teapot*: far as she's concerned it was just an accident it was made by some pottery person that people go mad over. He left the book here, of course. Which means he'll soon be back to collect it. Any excuse. She really believes he makes them up. He's probably at it this very minute, hunched in his bedsit, dreaming up more irritating nonsense to plague her with. All right, he's a nice enough lad. She doesn't mean to be nasty. But will he please, *please*, get off her back?

Sonia sighs and goes on with her dusting. She's going to have to say something. She's going to have to drop a pretty hefty hint. It's March the first tomorrow, by crikey. Time's getting short.

13

Steve's snores reach Fran before she's out of the bathroom. He's fallen asleep on his back. These days he invariably falls dead asleep after they've made love – flops on to his back, manages, 'Lovely, darling,' or some other message of appreciation, then he's gone, zonked out, because he's so dead beat. Usually she remembers to tip him gently onto his side. Tonight she forgot.

This is a shame because now she will have to disturb him. Snoring is a danger sign, she has read, indicating blocked airways and a heart coming under stress.

The moment she slides her arms beneath him, he jerks awake. 'What's matter. What—?'

'Shh.' She knows what he's thinking: What has she heard? Rosie barking? Rustlers about? A cow gone into labour? A fox got into the hencoop? 'Nothing's the matter. You were snoring, that's all. Lie on your side and go back to sleep.'

But he remains awake. After all these years, she can tell the subtle difference in bed weight between a dead-to-the-world Steve and a Steve lying awake. 'Something bothering you, love?'

His arm comes over her. 'I'm thinking it's time Hal went back to the bungalow. I'll have a word with him tomorrow.'

'He's still a bit chesty.'

'He's spinning it out. He finished the antibiotics a week ago. Must be the longest Christmas break on record, this. I don't want you getting tense.'

'Tense? Me?'

'Hal has been known to get you down.'

'Yeah. But let's be honest: whatever's in my face gets me down when the mood comes over. It's not Hal per se. Oh, I'm a trial to you, Steve.'

'Never.'

'Liar.'

'Let's just say, I like it when you're happy and relaxed. I like the fringe benefits.'

'OK. But you've had all the fringe benefits you're getting for one night. It'll be time to get up before you know what's hit you. Get some sleep.'

'Night, sweetheart.'

'Night, love.' She brushes her hand down the length of him – an affectionate swipe, but also a means of making sure he has adopted the correct sleeping posture. Steve's heart is precious. The idea of it coming under strain makes her own thump with anxiety. Must be because she loves him.

Well, of course she does. She's loved him for years and years. Why is it then, that whenever she's reminded of the fact a splinter of surprise tweaks her?

Because of the *way* she loved him when she first knew she did. Which was different to the way, during the last years of her teens, she loved Kevin and Josh and Dave and Rob and Adam and Timothy – thrillingly, breathlessly, briefly. Loved them particularly, is what she suspects now, for the ego-bolstering image of Fran Spencer they projected back to her – a lively party-going, tennis-playing creature, always in demand, always on the go. In those days an hour of solitude was an ordeal and a punishment. Leeway for memories.

Steve was older. All the time she was growing up he

214

was a business associate of her father's, a supplier of best quality turf to the garden-centre business. It's amazing really that the connection didn't put her off. But no, she thought that Steve was nice. She liked the twinkly way he looked at her, as if while saying very little he was thinking lots. She also regarded him as terrifically handsome. But she was a little shy of him; it never occurred to her to think of him as someone she might go out with, much less that he'd be interested. It was an enormous surprise when he asked her for a date.

The biggest surprise of all, though, was her own behaviour. That very first time she spilled out her story to him, the details of how she got pregnant and was then put in the home, and how after the birth she changed her mind about adoption, passionately wanting to keep the baby, but how in the end she submitted to the pressure that was put on her to give him up. Even, she described the feverish resentment she has borne her father ever since, the aversion pulsing under her skin like a blind boil.

Steve accepted every word. He didn't show shock or embarrassment, didn't try to minimize or soothe, didn't say she'd grow out of the bad feelings or in time get over the episode. He simply accepted everything she said as statements of fact.

He took it all to heart, though. Straight away she saw evidence of this. Solidarity is what you'd call it, she supposes, extended in very small ways, ways that only she would notice. For instance, in placing himself bodily when he came into the room between herself and her father, or in answering for her when one of her father's heavy jocularities came her way; and sometimes, sensing a tense family moment, Steve would make a point of addressing her privately, thus affording her another less painful level of existence. Small things, but as obvious to Fran as specks of mica

215

in dull rock. He does it still, thinks Fran, recalling her father's last visit, the day he and Brenda called with Christmas presents. As soon as he saw the Spencers' car in the yard, Steve came tearing over to the house – in the middle of moving the bullocks, too. 'You remember, Steve,' her father said, 'the little girl in her ballet frock, dainty as a fairy—' 'Yes, glad to say we're both thriving,' said Steve, cutting short a dangerous reminiscence. No wonder she loves him.

But maybe she always did. Maybe that's why she singled him out to tell her story to. Maybe loving him just gradually crept over, like a tenacious plant. Like periwinkle – not very showy on top but underneath busily rooting.

'You know how it is, Jason? Sometimes we all need to take a breather from people—'

Before she can get out another word, he comes bounding across the room. Not quite *at* her – which for one frightening moment it looked like – but to the whatnot close by her chair.

He picks up one of her china bells, puts it down; adjusts the position of the piece of Capodimonte he bought her for Christmas; pokes a finger into the pot that is home to a sansevieria plant—

'This poor plant is gasping, Sonia. Don't you ever water it?' He gathers it up and makes off with it to the kitchen.

'Jason!' Rather late, she hurries after. 'Jason, what are you doing with that plant? It shouldn't be over-watered in winter.'

'Have a heart, Sonia. It must have a few drops now and again.'

'Tepid then, *tepid*,' she almost screams, as he puts it to the cold tap. He switches to the other tap, testing with his finger the temperature of the running water.

She watches, feeling helpless, knowing it would be

useless to try and dissuade him. If he wasn't interfering with her sansevieria, he'd be interfering with
one of her other possessions. Anything to create a
diversion. He is determined not to hear what she is
trying to say.

She catches her breath as he swings past, the plant
whisked inches from her nose, a draught from it
brushing her skin.

He's not just the ticket, she says to herself. He's
touched, he must be. Normal people don't go on like
this.

She did it again this evening. She's always doing it.
It's like, everything's going fine, they've had a lovely
chat, a bit of a laugh, taken a bit of interest in the
other one's doings, when out of the blue this look
comes over her face – sort of nose-twitchy, as if she's
spotted something not quite right, and calculating, as
if she's wondering how to phrase a complaint. Then
her mouth turns down and words come out; words
that jar with the nice time they've been having.

Not many words, mind. Because after the first few,
soon as he hears their negative tone, he can't stand to
let her continue. Agitation takes hold, panic almost,
and he has to dash about, he has to *do* something.

Usually he manages to steer them back onto a fairly
safe footing. But Sonia stays quiet, not recovering her
true warm nature. So naturally, after a dodgy episode
like that, he has to return the following evening, or at
the very least ring her up, to make sure things are OK
between them. He has to check – same way as you
would if you'd fixed an appliance, a faulty switch or a
loose connection; you'd test to see if it was properly
mended. She probably thinks he's overdoing it, going
round there or phoning too often. But she brings it on
herself.

If only she wouldn't. It's so unnecessary.

217

*   *   *

Three o'clock in the morning. Again.

Sonia heaves out of bed and goes to the bathroom.
Then she does a few stretching exercises, then a
few breathing exercises. She encourages a yawn, and
climbs back under the duvet.

But some time later she's still awake. She's been
trying to pretend otherwise, but nameless worry keeps
breaking through. Eventually the worry crystallizes in
one hard question: if she goes on like this, what is she
going to look like by the time David arrives? Certainly
not like her usual self. The Lady Sonia does not have
bags under her eyes.

Why the what's-name is she doing this anyway?
Springing wide awake in the small hours. First time it
happened she put it down to her after-supper cup
of coffee. The following evening she went without
coffee. Maybe it was due to watching a stimulating TV
programme too late at night, was her next excuse. So,
no telly either; at least not beyond half-past ten. Face
it, Sonia, she says to herself, it's that pest of a boy
ringing you up three nights on the trot.

Last evening she didn't answer. When the ringing
stopped she pressed 1471, and received a shock.
It had been the Bellamys' number calling. 'Sorry,
Ronnie,' she said. 'I was just coming in as the phone
stopped. It was you was it, not Natalie?' It had indeed
been Ronnie ringing to ask if she could throw any
light on David's plans. Ronnie and the chums are
trying to arrange a boys' night out. Five minutes after
she'd stopped speaking to Ronnie, the phone went
again. Naturally, she answered it, thinking it might be
one of David's other old pals phoning with a similar
request. But of course it was Jason.

Jason said he wants to call round tomorrow
after work. (*Today*, yells Sonia silently, as she recalls
what time it is.) He said he's bringing something

218

to show her that he thinks will be of interest.

'Well, Jason, if it's all the same I'd rather—'

It was as far as she got. Only a bald 'Don't!' might have stood a chance of beating the load of blather that followed.

Sonia turns her head into her pillow. 'What the heck are you going to do?' she groans into it. 'You have to do something, Sonia. You have to do it sharp.'

'Da-*dum*!' cries Jason, bringing an object into view from behind his back. 'What do you think?'

'Oh. Nice. But—'

'Perfect for your kitchen, eh? *Provençal*. Let's see.'

He passes her, setting off through the hall.

'Jason—'

'Do I have an eye or do I have an eye?' he demands, holding up an ornamental plaque against a space on the kitchen wall.

'Jason,' says Sonia, recalling her strictures of the night and enunciating very clearly, 'I – don't – *want it*.'

His showmanship crumbles. A petulant boy's face comes through. 'But I *bought* it for you, Sonia. My treat for your kitchen. *Our* kitchen,' he amends coyly, 'the kitchen Sonia and Jason built, right? A little finishing touch. Admit you love it.'

'I have to go out,' Sonia says, looking closely at her watch. 'I have to leave in five minutes flat.'

'Oh? You never said.'

'Something cropped up,' she begins, before it occurs to her that he is not someone she ought to be accountable to. That she'd begun to speak as though he were makes her angry.

'Look here, Jason. I don't need to *say* – not to you, not to anyone. If I decide to go out, I just do, that's all. And I have, and I'm going, so would you please—'

But the word *leave* is never said. Sonia falls silent,

though open-mouthed, as a fit of sorts takes Jason, and the wall plaque drops and lands ringingly in pieces over the tiled floor.

Sonia's hand rises. It clutches the material of her shirt tightly to her throat. The thought jumps into her mind that she ought to have left the front door open. She'd had the perfect excuse ('I won't shut the door as I'm on the point of leaving, Jason'). Her trouble is, she doesn't think quickly enough. But why should she need to? Why should she be in this frightful position?

She catches her breath and steps backwards as he swings towards her.

'Silly me, butterfingers. Where's the pan and brush? Got some old newspapers?'

He sounds like a hysterical person trying to act normally.

'In here is it? Surely you have such an article as a dustpan, Sonia.'

The reason why she can't move and can't speak, it dawns on her, is that she is locked rigid by sheer terror.

'Here we are. I'll sweep, you be a dear and fetch something to wrap it in. We don't want the bin men injuring themselves. Don't want to be sued. Parcel it up all neat and tidy—'

Sonia steps jerkily towards a drawer. Shakily she opens it and produces a roll of plastic bags.

'Yes, one of them'll do.'

She watches as he fussily completes the job.

'Dustbin,' he then says, moving confidently in the direction of her garden door.

It galvanizes her, the sight of his hand shooting back the bolt. 'Leave it,' she cries. 'I'll deal with it tomorrow. I'm late as it is. I was expected at a friend's several minutes ago.'

He hesitates, nodding as if recalling this, then

dumps the bag on the floor. 'Right-oh. Don't worry about the breakage, Sonia. It wasn't your fault.'

She goes towards the hall and then along it, willing herself to act as a magnet, to draw him after.

'Your tone was a bit startling, but I was plain clumsy. Please don't give it a thought.'

She jerks the front door open. 'Goodbye,' she says as he draws near.

'*Au revoir*,' he corrects her. 'Never fear, I'll bring you a replacement. That one must have had a flaw in it, don't you think, to have broken so easily? I'll have a word with the shop manager. You shan't go without.'

'Goodbye,' she says again, and the moment he is clear of the threshold, presses home the door.

She listens keenly for the sounds of his footsteps and of his car starting up, not moving from the hall.

Put the wind up him, thinks Sonia. That would be the way to do it. Give him a real incentive never to come bothering her again.

She decides on a coffee. Not a cup of instant, but a large cafetière of strong Lavazza. She needs the boost. Sleep won't come easily anyway after that scene tonight. It was a scary experience, it's made her feel starkly exposed; as if, with the explosion of the ornamental plaque over the kitchen floor, the windows and doors of her lovely home blew out, laying her open to all kinds of riff-raff, unreasonable and disrespectful persons. She tells herself to get a grip as she waits for the coffee to brew. Get a grip, Sonia, she repeats as she sips it.

The coffee has a bracing effect, and before she has drained her first cup she has recovered sufficiently to recall certain personal and pertinent characteristics. Namely, that she is resourceful. A woman who has never yet allowed life to get on top of her. To give up in despair just wouldn't be her. It isn't in you, Sonia, she declares to herself. And she recalls a silent remark she made some minutes earlier, perceiving in it the germ of a sound idea. That somehow or other Jason must be warned off.

Further perusal leads her to conclude that she will need assistance. The point being, from whom?

The person of Ronnie Bellamy is permitted to stand in her mind. And following Ronnie some of David's other old friends. Eventually all are dismissed *because* they are David's old friends – she would rather die than hazard a smidgeon of David's respect. She doesn't doubt that Ronnie would promise never to breathe a word afterwards of her difficulty, but she can imagine certain circumstances, boozy back-slapping loose-tongued circumstances, in which the old pals' act might seem more compelling than a promise made to an old pal's ex-spouse. Anyway, instinct warns her never to become even slightly beholden to a member of the opposite. With men you just never know. Once they get the urge, other con-siderations can fly right out of the window – loyalty, decency, even reputation. Look at the way Alistair Rogers tried it on, quite out of the blue, the night of the Rotarian quiz. No, no. Good chum that dear Ronnie is, better not take the chance.

She needs to be certain of absolute discretion. She needs to be certain of sure-fire effectiveness. There-fore, the assistance she requires would probably have an official flavour. How to get it, how to use it, and the many spin-offs from these considerations, now engage her.

She notices at one point that she doesn't feel in the least tired, if anything she feels more wide awake than usual – and somehow extra vigorous, even if she is only sitting down and thinking. She can't have ex-ercized her brain this thoroughly for many a long day – not to mention long night. It's nice to know she can.

*   *   *

'Yes, I remember you very well, Mrs Garrs,' he says, stepping in and going confidently through her hall, looking about him as if to say *So this is what the inside of the house is like; I've always wondered.* 'We last met at a town hall bash. You won first prize in the raffle.' He looks into her sitting room and without waiting for permission goes into it.

'My goodness, you do have a memory for detail.'

'You tend to cultivate one in this job. Very nice, very tasteful,' he comments, looking about the room.

'Thank you.'

'And I remember Mr Garrs, too, though from much further back. He was good enough to support the Riverfields Youth Project, which was partly my baby.'

'Oh yes. David's always had a keen sense of civic duty,' Sonia agrees eagerly.

'So, how can I help? You wanted my advice, an informal chat. A difficulty with a young man, you said; someone you've given a helping hand to, who has since become a pest. Though I did warn you, Mrs Garrs, these are difficult cases to deal with, proof tending to be hard to come by.'

'Ah, well, point taken, Inspector. But as a matter of fact – I didn't want to say this over the phone with it only being a suspicion – but I think it may also be a case of theft.'

'Things gone missing?'

'One thing has. Though I didn't notice till yesterday morning. I was dusting, you see. And the awful thing is, I can't swear to having seen it since the last time I dusted. Mind you, we're only talking about last Thursday morning. I never allow the dust to build, I'm fussy that way. So there it is,' says Sonia, directing a mournful look at the whatnot.

'Um, I'm not with you, Mrs Garrs.'

223

'The gap, Inspector. Where the teapot usually is. A rather valuable teapot. A Clarice Cliff, you know.'

'I can't say the name rings a bell. However, this valuable teapot disappeared—?'

'Between last Thursday morning and yesterday morning. I'd be the last one to cast aspersions, but he did show an interest in that particular teapot. Always picking it up and turning it over. He was quite fixated; even went so far as to consult a book on the teapot's designer. Another thing: no-one else has been in this room, except he and myself. We came in briefly last Friday evening, and I have to say it was not a happy occasion. You see, I'd made up my mind to speak firmly about the way he keeps coming round here, and also about the phone calls. I don't think he took it too well. Perhaps depriving me of the teapot was a form of revenge. Could that be it, do you think, Inspector?'

'Any sign of locks being forced, windows interfered with?'

'None at all.'

'And you're sure no-one else has been in here?'

'No-one else has been in the house. Except my friend Natalie Bellamy, who called on Saturday – that's Mrs Ronald Bellamy, you know, of Bellamy's Motors. But she and I sat in the kitchen. We're very old friends, we don't stand on ceremony.'

'Seems you'd better fill me in on this young man.'

'It's quite a long story. Can I offer you some refreshment?'

'Well, seeing as I'm off duty—'

'It's really sweet of you to spare the time. A lady does occasionally need a little masculine input on a problem I find. Usually David – um, Mr Garrs – would be the one I'd turn to. But he's so far away, a real globe-trotter – business, you know. Though I'd only have to say the word and he'd be on the next plane.'

'Well, let's see if we can solve it without putting Mr Garrs to the inconvenience.'

'Oh, you are kind, Inspector. So what's it to be? Can I interest you at all in a rather special single malt?'

'Let's get this straight,' says Inspector Bascombe while leafing through Jason's copy of *Banking Quarterly*, 'this could've been done another way. Instead of sitting in the car for the past half-hour waiting for you to turn up, I could have walked into the bank this afternoon. I could've asked to speak to your boss, asked for the loan of one of his little side-rooms, told him I needed to interview one of his employees. Jason Caulfield by name, I could've said, been working for you seven or eight months according to my information. Easier for me, doing it like that. Though maybe not too healthy for you.'

Jason is perched on the edge of his bed, his visitor having taken the one and only chair. He listens carefully, catching the policeman's drift, going hot and cold in turns. It seems that one of Sonia's teapots has gone missing. He wanted to phone her at once, hearing this, to express his sympathy and concern. But his informant (surely exceeding his powers) took the phone out of Jason's hand and laid it down on the table, telling him to leave Mrs Garrs alone, that he'd upset her quite enough already by continually phoning her.

He wanted to ask: is that what Sonia said? But somehow couldn't. Instead, 'Was it the Clarice Cliff?' came out.

The inspector lays down the magazine. 'Now, why do you ask that?' he wants to know.

'I'm not sure,' says Jason. 'Except – well, it's the most valuable of her teapots – that's what she said. And I'm sure she's right. People pay good money for a Clarice Cliff.'

'Do they, indeed? Is that what you found? Who'd you sell it to? Local dealer? It'll be easy enough to discover. But it'd be easier for you in the long run if you saved us the trouble.'

'Mm-me?' stutters Jason. 'You think I took it? Sonia doesn't, surely? Look, I have to phone her. This is awful. She must know – I mean, I wouldn't steal from anyone, I've never stolen a thing in my life, but the idea I'd steal from Sonia—'

Jason's voice, having gone hoarse, now gives out. He leaps to his feet, and flings open the door of the wardrobe, turns and pulls out the doors and drawers of the sink unit. 'Help yourself, take a look.' These are the only possible hiding places – other than under the bed, to which Jason now returns to yank up the covers and expose the space between bed and floor. 'Go on, look around.'

But Inspector Bascombe stays put. With scant inter-est, his eyes flicker over the revealed cavities. His expression conveys that he is not a man who would pause for an invitation before examining anything he'd a mind to. 'Word of advice,' he says. 'And I hope you're paying attention?'

Jason swallows and nods. The shock of the occasion is subsiding, leaving him possessed of a clammy fear.

'Leave Mrs Garrs alone. Keep away from her house. Stop phoning her.'

Jason doesn't respond, and the inspector continues, his voice developing an edge. 'What's the matter with you, anyway, hanging about an older woman? Old enough to be your grandmother, I shouldn't wonder. Pestering her, frightening her in her own home. It's not nice being harassed, not nice at all. A very severe view is taken of that sort of thing nowadays. I don't suppose Barclays would be too thrilled, either, if it came to their notice one of their employees is perse-cuting a fifty-year-old woman.'

'I don't! I wouldn't!'

'Listen to me, you nasty little perv. I have it on good authority that that's precisely what you've been doing: phoning her at all hours, pushing letters through her box, turning up on the doorstep with trumped up excuses. What makes you tick, eh? Women your own age not to your taste? Get your kicks bothering nice respectable older ladies like poor Mrs Garrs? It's sick, that, perverted—'

'Stop!' cries Jason. The talk of perversion coupled with mention of the bank has started up in him a new kind of fear, the heart-thumping fear you get in dreams full of wild and unconnected and terrifying happenings. 'I'm not like that. I'm ordinary, normal. I've, I've got a steady girlfriend, same age as me. You go and ask her, yes, ask *her* if I'm perverted. Heather, her name is; works in Wilson's Shoes. She'll soon put you straight. Ask her if I'm a pervert, and she'll laugh her socks off. Yeah, you go and ask Heather—'

He manages to put a break on his tongue which, having run away with him, now seems stuck in a groove. 'You've got it wrong about me and Son— Me and Mrs Garrs,' he says more quietly. 'It was her always ringing *me*. It was her actually gave me the mobile. She'd phone me at work – you can ask them at the bank if you want; several of them took messages. Then quite out of the blue she changed. I admit *then* I started ringing, because it was odd the way she was behaving and I wanted to know why. And all of a sudden she started being nice, her old self again, wanting me to go over and lay carpet in her bathroom. Which I did, naturally, being pleased things were OK. Then the other evening I called round, and damn me if she hadn't gone back to being cold and funny. So you see, it's not me; it's *her*.'

Inspector Bascombe drums his fingers on the table, evidently thinking the matter over. Then he gets to his feet. 'Well, my advice to you, old son, is to keep clear of the lady. Stick with this – Heather, did you say? Wilson's Shoes, eh? Nice shop, Wilson's. Nice class of merchandise. If Mrs Garrs phones again wanting you to lay carpet, tell her you can't. Tell her your girlfriend keeps you fully occupied, thanks. What did she think, anyway, Heather, about you dancing attendance on Mrs Garrs?'

'Well,' says Jason, feeling his face redden. 'Well—'

'Not too keen on the idea, eh?' the inspector interprets. 'Can't say I'm surprised. Right. Keep your nose clean. There'll be eyes on you, lad, know what I mean?' He goes towards the door, telling Jason not to bother coming down.

But at the last moment he looks back. 'A Clarice what was it, the teapot? Clough?'

'Er, Cliff,' Jason says nervously. 'But I didn't take it, you know. Really I didn't.'

The inspector nods – though what is indicated by it Jason can't tell – then softly closes the door behind him.

Jason is lying on his bed. When the kettle comes to the boil he doesn't move. The kettle clicks off. He listens to its dying hum, not wanting a coffee after all. And not fancying the sandwiches either that he brought home with him from the Tasty Bite. Filling the kettle, laying out sandwiches, he was acting out of habit, doing what he normally does when he gets home from work, trying to kid himself that tonight's homecoming wasn't all that unusual. Or maybe acting out of a need to occupy his nervy fingers and focus his reeling mind. Thinking about it now, hunger and thirst seem unimaginable sensations. Only tiredness is compelling. It brought him to the bed and it keeps him here. Keeps him pinned down.

She hasn't had the teapot stolen, of course. Why

should a burglar confine his take to one piece of china? And why that piece of china? Clarice Cliffs may be sought after, but they are not exactly in the commission-a-theft league. No, she decided on the teapot (decided to remove it? hide it?) because of all her possessions it was the only item he had frankly admired and itched to handle. She was aiming straight at him, no messing, by saying she was minus the Clarice Cliff teapot.

He is so damn slow. It's pathetic how slow he can be. First off, when the policeman said the teapot was missing, he was really sorry for her, really upset. Then, when he saw suspicion pointing in his direction, he assumed there'd been a mistake, a misunderstanding that would be cleared up easily if only he were allowed to speak to Sonia. The penny only dropped properly when Inspector What's-it brought up the subject of harassment, implying he'd been pestering Sonia and getting a perverted thrill out of it. He understood then that the teapot was a side issue. Sonia wanted him out of her life and had set about achieving this end ruthlessly. If in the process she had to half-destroy him, it was tough luck.

Prone in the centre of the sagging bed, Jason marvels at Sonia's thoroughness. She really went to town: made out he's a thief and also a pervert. Maybe she'll try to have him done for sexual harassment. If he loses his job it will suit her fine, because then he'd leave town.

What lies behind all this, of course, is the coming visit of her ex-husband – Jason recalls the way she's always gone on about *David*, as if the light shines out of the man's backside. Jason himself was last season's diversion, when there was nothing much doing – no word from the ex-husband, not many from the daughter, social life a bit flat, and jobs round the house so scarce they needed to be invented. Now

something better is coming her way, someone infinitely more interesting. So she wants the decks
cleared. She wants no hide or hair of Jason Caulfield
because he reminds her of a very thin time. She
doesn't want to be reminded. She wants to look
forward, to make her plans, to savour her anticipation.

It is such a thorough-going betrayal – risking
the smashing of his life in order to tidy up her own –
that it's mind-blowing. He recalls how, when he was
flavour of the month, she would express concern for
his health and well-being. Was he eating properly?
Was his bedsit insulated and warm? Did he make sure
that the extra hours he put in at the bank were duly
noticed? Skin-deep concern was all it was. Sonia
playing at Fussy Mummy.

He goes cold saying that to himself, saying Mummy.
The word triggers a leap of his mind, from a dark
swampy sickly sort of area into cold hard light. The
light illuminates an aspect of his mother; an aspect
that has always been there, but from which he has
tended to shield his eyes. He is forced to look at it
now.

His mother didn't just walk out on her husband.
She also walked out on him. Maybe what his father
has always claimed is true: that she went off with a
fancyman, the sort of man who wouldn't want a kid
mucking up his life. But for whatever reason she left,
she could at least have kept in touch with her son.
Why has he been forgotten all these years? Because he
was only a blip in her life. Like he was a blip in
Sonia's.

Oh yes, Sonia and his mother are linked, all right.
But not in the way he's been fooling himself, not in
soft maternal feelings for him and teasing caring
indulgence of him. In wilful betrayal.

Suddenly his mind seems to be slowing down.
Sleep comes sidling, blurring the edges of his

thoughts, soothing and warming and gentling. He lets it wash right over.

Heather. He can't tell whether the name has come to him from a dream or was the first thing his waking mind latched on to. But there it is, the name and Heather herself, all encompassing.

Minutes go by before he realizes he is on the bed, not in it, also that he is fully dressed. A squint at his illuminated alarm tells him the time is half-past four. It's a stale feeling, rising and undressing at this hour. It's a stale feeling, too, when, returned to bed, the events of last evening come flowing back. He experiences each one again: his arrival home to find a plain-clothes police officer waiting, the shock and pain of an alarming interview, and later his sober line of thought, his brutal facing of facts. It is all deeply depressing.

But his feelings on waking were hopeful and re-surgent, he recalls. Not the feelings of someone who is done for, but of someone who is in with a chance. A thumping good chance, in point of fact. Name of Heather. It's a relief to him, remembering this. Hang on to it, he tells himself. Forget the other.

But then it hits him – and he sits up and snatches the alarm clock and resets it to go off a half-hour earlier – that it is absolutely vital, his career could depend on it, to speak to Heather first thing in the morning. He should try to catch her before the shop and the bank open. And arrange to have lunch with her – not in the Tasty Bite but somewhere more private where he can slip an arm round her. Then over lunch he'll say the words she's been desperate to hear for almost as long as he's known her. He'll ask her out. And he'll try to act reasonably cool about it, not give away that now it's his turn to be desperate. That everything depends on her agreeing.

Don't worry about it, he urges himself. Heather will be good as gold. She's a rock, that girl, loyal, dogged. All the knock-backs he's given her, yet she still comes hopefully into the bank most mornings: 'Hi, Jason. Know what you're doing for lunch?' Imagine needing one of the girls at work to see him through a dodgy situation. That sort would run a mile. That sort, in any case, think he's a joke. But then he thinks *they* are a pretty sad joke, only concerned with their appearance, worrying whether their bums look fat, or the new hairstyle suits, or announcing to the world that they wouldn't consider going out with a bloke who didn't own the right type of car. Heather, thank heaven, is not a bit like that. You know where you are with her. Which is why he should feel confident now.

And it's not as if he hasn't wanted to ask her out. They still see each other in the lunch hour two or three times a week. And for some reason – probably it was their exchange of Christmas gifts that did it – they've been better chums lately. He's often thought of asking her out – at least, since Christmas he's thought of it. It was the chance of Sonia phoning that prevented him; he couldn't risk missing her call. Heather asked him to see a film with her the other week, and he really hated having to turn her down. When he said he couldn't, she asked if it was because he was seeing someone else. No, he told her, it wasn't that, and then trotted out the usual excuses: the study he had to do for the banking exams, the overtime he put in. She seemed to accept it, though he wouldn't say she looked specially happy. He couldn't tell her the sad truth: that he waited in every night on the very slender chance of someone relenting sufficiently to give him a call – and not someone who would qualify as a 'someone else', either.

Jason resolves not to mention Sonia to Heather. It shouldn't be necessary. Not if his hunch is correct and any checking up that is done is limited to establishing whether Heather is in truth his girlfriend. All he needs is sufficient time to get that state of affairs established. With luck, the inspector won't be too quick off the mark; there must be more pressing police business. And Heather, he should imagine, will fall in nicely.

Heather. What a godsend! He'd be shitting himself now if it weren't for her. He closes his eyes. And Heather comes down on him, ripe and warm. The relief is wonderful.

14

From the office workers' car-park, Jason walks to the bank. He goes to a discreet door at the side of the main entrance and presses some numbered buttons. As a result the door opens when he pushes on it, and similarly, when he swipes a card through a machine in the wall, an inner door unclicks. In the main banking room he makes for a desk bearing a plastic wedge with the inscription J. CAULFIELD, hailing his colleague Michael on the way, and pausing for a moment at the desk of the new deputy manager Ms Angela Horton who detains him with a professional request. It's business as usual. Jason ensures that in manner and appearance he too is as usual. Inside him, though, he is not as usual. He hasn't been for the past two weeks.

Up until two weeks ago, his main sensation, as he carried out the various arrival-at-work procedures would be eagerness, hunger almost, for whatever the day had in store. The trickier the task, the more complicated and time consuming, the more sharply he relished getting down to it. This keenness could earn him sour looks from Gina and the other young women assistants. But Jason never cared. Management's satisfaction was abundantly clear; it has been officially noted down during his monthly appraisals. He would also be nursing a secret glee at actually belonging to this place, at the yielding of doors to him, at the fact of his name on the desk. With the admittance of the public his sense of pride would receive a further boost. And the bedrock of all these positive feelings was the knowledge that he could cope, that nothing was going to be asked of him that his competence, expertise and intelligence couldn't deal with.

This was how it was every single morning of his employment here. Until two weeks ago, when the bedrock crumbled. Two weeks ago, when Inspector Bascombe waylaid him after work and followed him into his bedsit, and made accusations and threatened to ruin things for Jason at the bank.

The policeman's voice sounds many times in Jason's ears during a working day, hinting that things can be done the hard way, calling him *lad* and *old son*, saying there are eyes on him. Most acutely does Jason sense these eyes. He can be working through a sheet of figures at his desk and feel the back of his neck tingle. He can be dealing with a customer and suddenly lose the thread of the conversation as he imagines an intentness in the way the customer is viewing him. He can be on his way to the manager's office with a printout of figures, and be taken with an absolute necessity to pee – brought on by a conviction that more than one pair of eyes will confront him when he opens the manager's door.

It's not the inspector's wilder imputation that bothers Jason now – the suggestion that Jason's interest in Sonia was somehow perverted – though at the time of their encounter this frightened him more than the accusation of theft. He is sure that by going out with Heather he has put paid to any notion of unhealthy tendencies. In fact, by going out with Heather he seems to have done himself favours all round. During the lunch hour, for instance (always spent in her company) his confidence begins to revive, with the result that afternoons are never as bad as mornings. Returning to work after seeing Heather, he feels less paranoid, more like a normal person.

Even so, he hasn't told Heather about his friendship with Sonia. If he can't altogether account for it himself, how can he expect anyone else to understand? Instead he told her a cock-and-bull story about the likelihood of checks being made on him in the near future, due to the special security requirements of a job he's been asked to do for the bank. It was these requirements, he told her, that had made him hesitate in the first place before committing himself to a steady relationship, knowing any girlfriend of his would come under scrutiny. But Heather, he'd come to realize, was someone who could definitely stand being vetted, and on this basis he'd decided to give in to his inclinations. All she had to do, if anyone approached her with questions concerning himself, was admit honestly and fearlessly to being the girl-friend of Jason Caulfield, employee of Barclays Bank – his steady girlfriend, Jason added; the people doing the vetting would be impressed by steadiness. 'And in any case, that's how I want us to be,' he told her.

Actual tears had sprung in Heather's eyes when he said this. 'Gosh, Jason, oh, Jayce – yeah, I want that, too. Oh, I'm so proud. I mean, you must be brilliant to do a job like that, they must think ever so highly of you. I won't let you down, Jayce; I'd never do that. You can rely on me.'

It seems that so far no approach has been made to Heather. But the more time that elapses, and the more time he puts in with her, the surer he becomes of convincing any snooper on the sexual normality score.

Unfortunately, the elapse of time does nothing to soothe his fears over the other matter. The matter of the teapot. The matter of an accusation of theft hanging over him. Any hint of that and his career would be done for. So it's no wonder he feels edgy at work. Who wouldn't, with their job liable to be snatched from them at any moment?

That sodding teapot. It often rises to his mind's eye. But its decorative motifs in yellow and orange and mauve and green are no longer fresh seeming and spring-like. They are sickly and cloying, like the fruits of rot or disease.

'Dad, can I ask you a favour?'

'You can ask.'

'Run me to the station in the morning – so I don't have to take my car? I'm going out tomorrow night, um, probably till late—' Heather falters. Across the table Janie has her specs trained on her like twin searchlights. She'd have done better to have waited till after supper and caught Dad on his own. But what the hell? 'So I'm, er, stopping over with a girl at work. You know how it is: leave the car at the station overnight, and it's bound to get done over.'

'Well,' says Steve, thinking of the night ahead, most of which he will be spending in the lambing shed.

'I'll run you,' Fran says quickly. And Heather's face turns to her, a face that is changed in some way, though Fran can't quite put her finger on how.

'Thanks, Mum,' Heather smiles. 'That's really terrific.'

A smile is a change in itself, thinks Fran, beaming back.

'You sure, love? I'd do it myself, only it's Ken's night off, my turn with the lambing.'

'Of course I'm sure.'

Forking up fish pie, Fran is dying to ask Heather where she is going, and who she'll be staying with. But she doesn't. She hopes Steve won't either, and to distract him asks how many ewes are expected to

237

lamb over the next twelve or so hours. She doesn't catch his answer though, because it strikes her then how unusual it is for Heather to forget about farm business, to forget her father may well have been up all night and be showered and newly gone to bed by the time she has to leave for work in the morning. Then Janie's voice breaks into her thoughts.

'Oh yeah – staying the night with a girl at work? I'll bet. You know what she's really planning? Planning to shack up with some horrible bloke. Bet you anything.'

'What if I am?' asks Heather.

'See? Told you.'

'I didn't say I am and I didn't say I'm not. Just it's none of your business, little girl.'

'And I can just imagine what sort of bloke. Nerdy. A total anorak. He'd have to be, wouldn't he, to go out with you?'

Fran and Steve have both stopped eating. Both anticipate an almighty cat fight, both feel energy draining from them. To their astonishment, though, a disarming sound comes from Heather, which they only slowly recognize. It's laughter – soft, throaty, secretive.

(Nerdy? Heather is thinking. Just let her wait. Let 'em all wait. She pictures him in the Tasty Bite, wearing the smart suit he wears for work – it's diabolical what that does to her, the fair hair and the dark suit. She pictures him in the pair of chinos she helped him buy, with a T-shirt tucked in and a soft jacket over – the outfit he was wearing a few nights ago in the Pizza Hut. She recalls the straight brows and the blue eyes beneath and the incredibly long lashes; and her fingers recall the feel of his hair – soft with a crisp undertow, like silk. Just wait, she thinks. Wait till they see the quality she's pulled.)

Janie, who was briefly stunned by her failure to get a rise out of her sister, changes tack fast. 'Anyway, men are all a sad waste of time. It's pathetic you'd want to bother. You must be really hard up— What?' she demands, as Heather starts laughing all over again with her eyes on her father.

'Don't take it to heart, Dad. What does she know?'

'Huh,' says Janie, glowering down at her plate. Nothing further occurs to her to say, so she resumes eating.

As also, after an exchange of looks, do Fran and Steve.

It takes Fran a little while to grasp what has happened: Heather has joined the grown-ups. Janie's remarks struck her as those of a kid, unworthy of bother.

Janie is right about one thing, though: Heather does plan to spend the night with a boyfriend. The more she thinks about it, the surer Fran becomes. Heather is planning to sleep – maybe is sleeping already – with some unknown man. Nothing can be done about this, however. Legally, Heather is an adult and at perfect liberty to sleep with whomsoever she pleases. Reminding herself of this, Fran is silently rehearsing for the moment – which will happen as soon as this meal is over – when a worried Steve grabs her and questions her behind some closed door. She can see already that he's eating less rapidly, that his mind's workings have brought a frown to his forehead, that the knowledge is getting there.

No-one wants a second helping. There's cake, Fran reminds them. No-one shows interest in cake either, though only Heather looks genuinely satisfied. 'I'm totally stuffed, Mum, thanks,' she says, stretching luxuriantly. She gets up and starts clearing the table.

Watching her, Fran wonders whether Heather's joining the grown-ups will prove helpful or unhelpful to her hopes for an improved relationship. It's hard to judge. It could mean that the time for mending fences is running out, as Heather becomes more detached from home and more involved with this unknown man – or the man's successors. It could mean, though, if Fran plays this turn of events intelligently, that as two adults they can at last be friends. It could mean a whole new chance.

Heather is so passionate. Sometimes Jason can hardly credit how passionate. Take the other night. They'd seen a film and were walking hand in hand to the multi-storey, when suddenly she just couldn't wait: backed him into a shop recess, jammed him up against the plate glass, cut off his air supply with her mouth, her hands roaming and squeezing.

'Heather,' he protested, soon as he could.

'What?'

'Someone might see.'

'Well? You ought to be glad I love you so much.'

'I am, but—'

'Really glad, honest?'

'Come back to my place and I'll show you how glad.'

'You fancy me, then?'

'You know I do. Come on, let's go.'

But it was Heather who started stripping off the clothes the moment they arrived. Stripping off *his* clothes. 'What about yours?' he said.

'In a minute. Christ, Jason, you're gorgeous—'

She's a big girl, is Heather, her body's like a pneumatic tyre: nice and curvy, big and bouncy, but hard. It must be the farm work she's grown up with, the silage-cutting, bale-hauling, tractor-driving, cattle-herding, sheep-chasing: seems she's had a go at the lot. And what she can do with that body – what she can do with *his* – is out of this world.

There are times, though, when he thinks she'll wear him out. Often she starts on him during the lunch hour. Then after work, if she has her own way, they head straight for the bedsit and it's knickers off almost before the door gets shut. Later they have to dash to the station to catch her train. If it's very late he insists on driving her the seventeen miles to Weston Sowerby Halt where she leaves her car every morning. He doesn't like to think of her exposed, walking through a dark and deserted car-park to collect the single remaining car – even if she is capable of wrestling an average size man to the ground – even if she is capable of freezing the balls off someone she doesn't like the look of. But a drive of thirty-four miles on top of an energetic evening makes one night's sleep seem not enough.

It is worth it though. What an idiot he was to leave it so long, all those months when she was practically begging him. This was Sonia's fault. Sonia giving him ideas. And when he gets those ideas to do with his mother something weird happens, part of him shuts down. Sex, for instance, is something he goes right off, or becomes something he has to get over with quickly in order to continue concentrating on the stuff in his head. The dream in his head. Because that's all it is, a dream. The trouble is, the dream's persistent. If someone new enters his life – not a girlfriend, someone older, someone mature, someone who fires his imagination in a particular way – the dream comes homing back. But maybe he won't be such an easy target in future, now he's with Heather. For just how powerful can a mere dream be? Surely no match for Heather knocking the living daylights out of it.

Which is a very reassuring and hopeful thought.

That's something else about Heather, quite apart from her giving a better time in bed than he ever conjured in his most fevered fantasies: she makes him feel sure-footed, strong. This is due to her thorough-

241

going competence. Everything the girl does, she does well – no fuss, no big production. You have to admire it. And he does admire it, he's grateful for it. It's the most confidence-boosting thing in the world to know all that competence is on your side. To know Heather is.

'Jason,' says Heather. 'You awake, Jayce?'

It's Sunday morning. Sunday morning after a memorable and strenuous Saturday night. Jason murmurs cautiously.

'I forgot to tell you. You know you said someone might come in the shop and maybe ask me some personal questions?'

'Yes?' Jason says, feeling considerably more alert.

'Well, they did. He did. This bloke – tall, oldish, quite handsome with a tache. He came in with his wife. She tried on a pair of shoes – didn't buy 'em, though. Paula was serving her, but I could see it was me he was looking at, clocking the name badge. "Can I help you?" I said. I was serving this woman, but I had a feeling he wanted to speak, so while I was waiting for a Visa check I gave him the opportunity. "I see your name's Heather," he said. "You're not by any chance a friend of Jason Caulfield? Jason mentioned a Heather who works in Wilson's." "You know him, then?" I asked, and he said he had dealings with the bank. "Oh, I see," I said. "Yeah, I'm a friend of his. Matter of fact I'm his girlfriend. Matter of fact—" Oh Christ, you'll never guess what I said next, Jayce. I didn't know I was going to, honest. It just came out, because I really, really wanted to impress him. Impress him for *you*, I mean.'

'What?' cries Jason, clutching a fistful of duvet.

'I said – now promise you won't go mad, Jayce? I said – "Matter of fact we're engaged." And – you know what? – it did seem to impress him. "Congratulations,

Miss—" "Topping," I told him. "Excellent taste on the young man's part, Miss Topping, if I may say so. Good luck to you both." So you see, Jayce, I know I shouldn't have, but it honestly felt like I'd said the right thing.'

'But you did. It was inspired. It was bloody marvellous! Come back here, you tasty trollop—'

Sometime later – though while they are still in bed – Jason thinks over that conversation. This time *engaged* doesn't sound so engaging. It sounds dullish, fusty, behind the times. Surely nowadays people just move in together. 'Of course,' he says, 'all that's in the future.'

'All what, Jayce?'

'What you said. When the man asked you questions in the shop.'

'You mean about being engaged?'

'Mm.'

'But I thought you were pleased, you *sounded* pleased.'

'I am. I'm just saying. Anything official like that would have to be thought out carefully.'

'I know that, silly. We'd have to make plans, job-wise and flat-wise, we'd have to get some money behind us. I'm not daft, I'm not the impractical sort. It's just what we're aiming for, right? Like, between you and me, we know where we're heading. Is that what you meant, Jayce?'

'More or less. 'Course it needn't stop us getting a place together, if one came up.'

''Course not,' Heather says quickly, but with the feeling she missed a piece of the argument somewhere. 'But you're still all right about, you know— What I told the man?'

'Absolutely. Look, don't get me wrong, I'm not objecting *in principle*. I'm just pointing out it's something we don't have to worry about right this minute.'

''Course not,' says Heather. 'Right.'

It isn't going to happen, Fran tells him, as she goes towards the big window in the big bedroom – which is not the bedroom she and Steve use; farmers like a room with a view of the yard, they like to be in a position to keep an eye on their assets. This nevertheless is the best bedroom in the house; it's large and lofty, nicely proportioned, with a principal window overlooking the garden and providing a view of the countryside – fields and copses and horizontal slashes of brown, yellow, purple or blue, depending on the light, the time of day and the season. When Fran comes in here to dust, she often lingers by the large window. The view draws her. She likes to share it with him.

This morning while sharing it, she's telling him about the situation with Heather. It's not going to happen, she says. Heather is not going to let her in. Though amiable and considerate – startlingly amiable and considerate for Heather – she is not of a mind to share her happiness. At any rate, not with her mother.

Do you suppose, she asks, sensing that he has come a little closer, do you suppose we would have ended up like that, you and I, if we'd been able to stay together? Would we have grown distant, just tolerating one another, having no special bond, no notion of what makes the other one tick? Is it possible?

She explores the scenario, tries it out in her head.

It doesn't work. And she knows the reason. It's the way he related to her as a tiny baby, which was quite different to the way Heather related. Or failed to relate.

Heather hardly ever cried. She fed and burped and soiled her nappy regularly and fulsomely without any

244

trouble to herself or anyone else. She didn't smile. She didn't stare. She slept a great deal. Nothing startled or surprised her. A very placid baby, commented Fran's approving mother-in-law.

He, on the other hand, cried often and raucously. 'There goes your one again,' members of staff would grumble to her, as a convulsive row – like an engine that can't quite fire – penetrated the home's corridors. 'I should think you're glad you're not taking him home. Let's hope his new mum and dad don't cop an earful – they might change their minds.' Such comments would follow her as she pelted to the nursery. 'Give him to me,' she'd demand when she got there. (Where did her supreme confidence suddenly come from?) She'd take him in her arms and hold him against her, and immediately he'd be pacified. His dark eyes would stare into hers. 'They can't see much at that age,' a nurse told her. So then, thought his mother, he could smell her, he could hear her heartbeat. And it was the right smell, and the right heartbeat.

Holding him, rocking him, she knew it was out of the question to give him up. Separation would be amputation, severed flesh. It would be unhealable wounds seeping blood and water.

You have to be brave, our Francesca. Think of poor Daddy. Think of his position. It's painful, I know, but these things fade. Be a sensible girl and in a few months' time you'll have forgotten all about it. Thus they promised and pressed her, the mother, the grandmother.

Now, Francesca, you can just stop that. It would be downright wicked of you, thoroughly selfish. Don't you think you've hurt your daddy enough? It's been very stressful for him trying to keep this quiet. Not to mention expensive. It's not twopence-halfpenny, you know, what they charge to look after you in a place like this—

Now then, our Francesca. Daddy's coming to see you this afternoon. So we don't want any nonsense, do we love? Not a word about you-know-what. Wash your hair and put on that pretty new dress I brought you, there's Mummy's sweet girl. Give Daddy a nice bright smile when you see him. Try and remember how good he's been about all this. A little gratitude wouldn't come amiss. It's not every father who's so kind and generous; lots of girls in your position get shown the door—

Just you listen to me, my girl. It's my son we're talking about, and he hasn't worked his fingers to the bone building up a fine business and reputation to see it go up in smoke, ruined by a daughter who's behaved like a slut. Slut's what I said, and slut's what I meant. Your mother's too soft with you, always has been; it's time someone told you straight. I've never seen a man so upset as your father was last night. I thought he was going to have a heart attack. If he hears one more word about you not going through with this adoption, I reckon it'll kill him—

All you do, love, is go in that room and sign some papers. That's all there is to it. It's for the best, believe you me. Matron says they're a lovely couple, comfortably off, a beautiful home, desperate for a baby. It'll have every advantage. I mean, what sort of home could you, a teenager, provide? What sort of life? Go in and sign now, dear, you'll be doing the right thing. Trust Mummy. I can see you to the door but I'm not allowed in. There'll be a lady from the agency waiting, she'll show you where to sign. Chin up now, soon be over. Then you and me and Granny will go home to Daddy. He's ever so anxious, poor lamb. He's full of lovely plans about you helping him in the office. That's what you need, lovey, something to occupy your mind. There you are, in you go, Mummy's good brave girl—

Only one voice ever urged differently. 'They can't

make you give him up,' a nursery nurse – a relief nurse, not a regular – hissed to her one night. 'Not if you don't want to. They can't force you to sign him away.'

But the regular staff, and Matron herself, knew which side their bread was buttered: Mr Spencer was the one contributing to the wage bill, not his daughter. (And possibly the adopting couple, who knows?) Furthermore, the Homes for Unmarried Mothers business was encountering hard times. Half, maybe more, of their potential clientele had been wiped out by the Abortion Act. Soon, there'd only be greenhorns like herself – the sort who'd leave matters too late – and women with scruples, religious and otherwise, available as customers.

The fiercely hissing relief nurse was proved self-evidently wrong. They *could* make her, because they *did*. In the end she was too dazed and incoherent and hurting to resist. Months went by before a riposte occurred to her, the perfect answer to her mother's question about what sort of home she, a teenager, could provide for a baby. *Our sort of home.* If only she'd thought of it in time. If only there'd been someone in her life to prompt her. She has often looked back and regretted this absence – of someone older, experienced, wise, someone from outside the family and therefore detached from the pressures, who might have encouraged her to have faith in her instincts.

Only lately has she understood that the person she has wished for is her middle-aged self. The gaining of wisdom is such a painful waste; by the time you've acquired it, it's too late to be of enormous personal use, and who else around you would want it? Certainly, in Fran's case, her daughters wouldn't (she can imagine how they'd recoil: Oh, Mum, back off!). But waste is endemic, in life, in nature; and you can't live on a farm without being reminded of it. Every May or June Fran is reminded – when the spring lambs go for slaughter, a few of which Fran herself will have bottle-fed. Steve thinks she's a whiz with an orphaned or rejected lamb, or a calf refusing to become weaned. He praises her no end for the loss she saves the farm, not appreciating that her knack comes from caring about the animal in question, that economic considerations wouldn't be enough. The lambs going to market are usually separated from their mothers on the day prior to their journey. Their thin bleats and the baritone plaints of the ewes continue all night long. At daybreak the lorry arrives, and a woolly running stream disappears into its maw. That's fifty or so individual miracles of construction, each going cheaply for chops, shoulder, scrag end. It depends on your point of view, but to Fran it seems blasphemously cheap and wasteful.

No doubt there was plenty of wisdom going to waste when she was sixteen and needing it. But it didn't find her out. No-one with confidence appeared at her elbow. Only the mother and the grandmother pressing their point, which ultimately, for Fran, was the wrong point.

And they were wrong about her forgetting, of course. She's forgotten nothing. It's all amazingly fresh and vivid, even tiny details like the pattern made by hairline scratch marks on the table to the side of the adoption papers. She remembers the sound of her ratchet breath as she took up the pen. And later the sound of his engine-noise crying – getting fainter.

She can hold him against her any time she wants. It's easy. Her arms, breasts, shoulders, neck, cheek, every bit of her knows how he feels. She holds him against her now. Then, with an easy, sliding, emptying sensation, slips him to her side where he looms above her (after all, he'll be several inches taller than she is by now); and for a moment she lets *his* head be the one that leans over.

Definitely our relationship wouldn't have been like mine and Heather's, she says to herself. More like mine and Janie's. But not exactly like, because everyone is unique. We only borrow flesh – the egg, the sperm – in order to slide out into the world as our own never-before, never-again person.

I'm going now, she tells him. Got to see about lunch. Best if I leave you here.

15

Gina is ushering someone towards the manager's office. Jason, happening to glance up at this moment, recognizes who it is. Inspector Bascombe.

No, it isn't. Just someone like him, Jason realizes after longer, calmer observation. His eyes return to the computer screen in front of him. His heart continues to drum in his ears.

But it *could* be the inspector. Later on today, it could. Or tomorrow morning. Or the day after. This idea disrupts his concentration. And suddenly he knows he's been incredibly optimistic imagining the danger is past. Just because Heather exchanged a few words with the man and there was a courteous response to what she told him, it doesn't mean he's in the clear. The exchange may have encouraged a change of heart about him being a weirdo, but could scarcely have had any bearing on whether or not he's a thief. Sonia presumably is still out to get him, still insisting on her teapot's disappearance. For all he knows she has since reported some other of her knick-knacks as stolen and again directed suspicion in his direction. Once that finger has been pointed your way you can never rest entirely easy. Because to some extent you then have 'form'; your name has cropped up during police inquiries.

It's like a blanket dropping over him, having these miserable thoughts. He's been feeling so cheery, too, ever since Heather's report. Serves him right for being a pathetic fool. For believing what he wanted to. For kidding himself.

'Glad to see you took my advice about the chain,' says Inspector Bascombe, speaking through the gap.

'Inspector!' cries Sonia, wishing very heartily that she hadn't taken his advice – or rather, wishing she'd taken the other, more expensive, course he'd suggested and had a spy glass fitted in her stout front door. In which case she wouldn't now be in this horrible position. She wouldn't have opened the door in the first place. What the blazes is he doing here, anyway? It must be more than a fortnight since he spoke to her on the phone saying he didn't anticipate her having any more trouble. She hadn't expected to hear from him further, certainly not to find him on her doorstep. And this time tomorrow, by crikey, David will be here. Somehow she has to make it perfectly clear to Inspector Bascombe that it's not acceptable for him to call on her without invitation.

'If you close the door you'll be able to slip it off,' he suggests helpfully.

'You caught me on the hop,' says Sonia, at last opening the door and reminding herself of the importance of leading him straight through the hall and into the kitchen, thus by-passing the sitting room.

But she soon discovers she has reckoned without his habit of not waiting to be led or directed. He makes his own way down the hall. 'No further bother from our young friend, I take it?'

'Um, Inspector?' calls Sonia.

'I didn't think you would have, not after I had that word with him.'

She hurries after, but short of yelling *not in there* (which would make matters worse) can think of no way of diverting him from his course.

Which takes him right into the sitting room. 'And I'm even more confident now, having met the girl-friend. Mrs Bascombe and I happened to be passing Wilson's Shoes last Saturday morning, and I per-suaded her inside to look around. Thought I'd take the opportunity of satisfying myself on a couple of points. And I must say, I was impressed by the young lady— Hang on a minute. Is that—? That's never the Clarrie What's-its-name teapot?'

'Clarice Cliff. Yes, Inspector. I was about to tell you—'

'Well, well, well. So this is it. An attractive enough piece in its way, I suppose. Well then, Mrs Garrs, I'm all ears.'

Sonia has to sit down; her legs have gone to jelly, she has a nasty suspicion that her cheeks have flamed. And the inspector, having gazed his fill on the Clarice Cliff teapot, sits down also and contemplates Sonia. 'It's quite a turn-up,' he remarks.

'You can say that again,' cries Sonia, making a valiant effort to recover herself. 'It was yesterday morning. I opened the door to fetch in the milk, and there it was on the doorstep. Well, it was a newspaper parcel, but I knew soon as I picked it up the teapot was inside. I suppose what happened was, your little word had its effect. Had him worried. He must have driven over with it during the night. I can't thank you enough, Inspector, because as a matter of fact I'm expecting David, Mr Garrs, tomorrow evening, and I wasn't looking forward to breaking the loss of the teapot to him, I can tell you. He's fond of it, you see. It was a present from his favourite auntie. A wedding present,' she adds, rapidly personalizing the teapot's provenance to add credence to her story, 'our wed-ding, David's and mine—' Her voice trails off, as something the inspector said goes *bong* in her ears, like a clock striking the hour a rather long time after the chimes have sounded. 'Wilson's Shoes, did you say? You mean Jason has a girlfriend in Wilson's Shoes?'

'That's right. Heather. Nice girl.'

'Good gracious me!'

'You know her?'

'I've bought shoes from her. Many times. But I wasn't aware Jason and Heather even knew each other.'

Inspector Bascombe gives a lengthy sigh. 'I have to put it to you, Mrs Garrs, that I'm not at all happy with your hypothesis concerning Jason and this much travelled teapot. I have to put it to you that a false accusation is a serious matter. Very serious indeed.'

'But— Look here, really, Inspector.'

'What I suspect is, you encouraged this young man and when you both ended up at cross purposes—'

'What do you mean *encouraged*? I'm not sure I like the sound of that.'

'You invented this business of the teapot in an attempt to put an end to the difficulty.'

'Are you calling me a liar? How dare you! I'm not used to having my veracity called into question—'

'The story doesn't ring true. I have to say it, Mrs Garrs.'

'*That teapot went missing!*'

Inspector Bascombe sighs again. 'Then take my advice: make it hard for it to go missing again. I should keep it under lock and key if I were you, seeing as it means so much to you and your husband.'

'Ex-husband,' snaps Sonia.

'Oh? I hadn't realized. I'd assumed it was business kept Mr Garrs away so much.'

'That's right. His business keeps him abroad. I can't say more, it's confidential, hush-hush. But business is the reason he and I— I mean, the divorce was merely a practicality. We are still extremely close.'

'I see,' says the inspector, sounding less harsh and rather more kindly. He shakes his head and blows out his cheeks, and at last heaves out of his chair. 'I should get one of those glass-fronted display cabinets, Mrs Garrs. It'd save you all that dusting, too.' He sets off for the front door. Arriving there he pulls it open and is about to step outside when he changes his mind and looks back. 'I'll tell you what's bothering me, shall I? You don't seem to realize the sort of an effect it could have on a young man's career, an accusation like that. Give it some thought.'

Now he does step outside – to Sonia's great relief – though he doesn't say goodbye. His only further utterance comes as he closes the gate behind him: 'A display cabinet with a lock is what you want,' he calls. Then moves away, and is soon blocked from view by next door's tall privet.

Look, says Jason to himself, continuing a never-ending internal argument: would the inspector have been so pleasant, going so far as to send a goodwill message, if he still believed him to be guilty of lifting Sonia's teapot?

Jason is driving home after dropping Heather off at the station. Two days have passed since he almost gave himself a heart attack, imagining it was the inspector he was seeing going towards the manager's office. He's been agitated and depressed ever since. He hasn't even had the heart for sex. Last night he persuaded Heather he needed an early night. And this evening instead of going to the bedsit they went for a Chinese. She was after him of course, as soon as she'd finished her crispy duck. 'I'm really bushed,' he told her. 'Let's talk for a change. Let's just relax. Talk to me, Heather.'

Naturally she chose the farm as a subject, saying she could hardly wait for him to see it, and perhaps it was time he met her parents, and how about tea on Sunday? He said, all right. (Why put it off? He'll have to meet them sometime.) Once the matter was settled he steered her towards the shop as a subject, and eventually got her to describe yet again her meeting with the inspector.

'You're really bothered about that, aren't you?' she said. 'You haven't heard, then, whether they think I'm OK and that?'

Belatedly he remembered what she was referring to – the fictitious vetting procedure. 'Oh, you never get to *hear*, not officially. But I know there's no problem.'

'How?'

'Nods and winks, that sort of thing. So what did he say exactly? Good luck to you both, was it? You sure about that?'

'Yeah. Good luck to you both. I thought at the time it sounded promising – with you starting that special job.'

'You'd just told him we're engaged. He probably meant good luck about that.'

'I expect he meant good luck with the job *and* the engagement. Nice of him, wasn't it?'

Jason arrives in his street and starts looking for a parking space. This is the one snag about seeing Heather of an evening. When he returns from taking her to the station, most of the parking's gone. Tonight, however, he's lucky.

While locking the car and letting himself into the house, he tries to conclude the argument in his head. There's no way a policeman would wish good luck to anyone dodgy, he tells himself firmly. It would go against the grain. ''Course it would,' he says, inadvertently out loud.

'You what, mate?' asks the tenant of one of the first floor rooms who is coming out with a bag of rubbish.

'Er, I said goodnight.'

'Oh,' says the man.

Stop it, Jason silently commands, as he closes the bedsit door behind him. Think about something else for Pete's sake. Think about Heather.

'Jason—'

Oh my God! He might have known this is how it would happen; that after all the false warnings, his skin pricking, his eyes alerted, when the bomb was actually about to drop his sixth sense would be switched off.

Thus run Jason's thoughts, like tumultuous water down a sheer-drop crevice, during the five or six seconds it takes Ms Angela Horton (deputy manager) to deposit next week's work schedule on Jason's desk, notice that Jason looks pale and strained, and arrange in her mind a concerned but not intrusive line of enquiry.

'Feeling all right? You look tired. It's very impressive the amount of work you get through, Jason, but you mustn't push yourself too hard.'

Jason expels his pent-up breath. So this isn't it, the dreaded denouement. He brings up his head, brings out a smile, and listens as she explains at length that everyone has a need for rest and recreation, everyone should take time to prepare healthy and nutritious meals—

Mother! a voice pipes up inside him – or maybe not quite; it's faint, it's weak, it's more a memory of what used to happen when an older woman smiled the way Angela Horton is smiling now, showing her womanly concern, taking an interest in his personal welfare. Older women tend to take this sort of interest, tend to warm to him, and he's such a sucker for it. (Not that Ms Horton is all that much older, ten years at the most. It's her authority – which is greater even than the manager's since she is well up the career ladder at a comparatively young age and obviously heading for heights Mr Whitehouse in his fifties won't reach – that makes the age difference seem greater.) Jason was glad when she was appointed here. She's improved the bank's atmosphere no end. Gina and her colleagues have pulled their socks up, become less bitchy, more serious minded – possibly because they have living proof that women in the bank do get promoted. Straight away Jason recognized Angela Horton as an outstanding person, very efficient, thoroughly competent. Having people like that around him always gives him confidence. She warmed to him (noting his work rate, no doubt), and he warmed to her. But for once in his life he did not go overboard, the odd fluttery feeling and occasional squeak have been ignored and resisted. Perhaps this is due to Heather's influence. Or perhaps due to the stress he is under as a result of going overboard for Sonia. Or perhaps it's simply that he's becoming more mature. Whatever the reason, it's good to know he's got that tendency licked.

No, he smilingly assures Angela Horton, he's not overdoing things, it's nothing like that. It's just he's had a few disturbed nights. There's a bloke in the bedsit next to his who plays CDs late into the night. Soundproofing in the house is non-existent. (This is true, up to a point. The house is seldom without a beat thumping out of one of its rooms. But Jason has only recently noticed this, lying awake with his worries.)

Can't he find a quieter place to live? wonders Ms Horton. And Jason says he's working on it. He doesn't mention the need to have a deposit saved up if you want to secure superior accommodation. He doesn't mention the payments he has to make, servicing the debt he acquired as a student and the hire purchase of his car. But Ms Horton appears to deduce all this anyway. Self-deprecatingly she laughs down her nose. 'It's tough when you're just starting out, as I well remember. Hang on in there, Jason.'

She moves away. 'How about earplugs? You can get them in Boots,' she calls over her shoulder.

It's a shame, thinks Jason, that you can't buy worry plugs.

But back to work.

'This is Jason,' Heather says casually.

Then she moves away from him, leaves him stranded in a room that appears to be full of bodies, full of eyes.

But in fact there are only four people here besides himself and Heather, and one of these comes quickly forward. 'Hello, Jason. I'm Fran, Heather's mother. This is—'

In a dream, Jason shakes hands with Heather's father, Steve, and Heather's grandfather, Hal; he says, 'Hi' to a scowling bespectacled gnome (who is apparently female if the name Janie is an indication), accepts that the cat in the gnome's lap is Mrs Twitten, and finally strokes the head of a tail-thumping retriever who is persuaded to remain prone when addressed as Rosie – all in a dream, because that is the condition he has been plunged into by the overwhelming presence of Heather's mother.

Fran, her name is. She has freckles and dark eyes and masses of dark curly hair and a wide welcoming mouth. But the most arresting thing about her is the way she moves, the way her arms and hands indicate and describe, the way she swoops down beside the dog then rises effortlessly and moves across the room, calling and gesticulating to Heather as she goes: slight and swift and airily poised in long and flowing rust-coloured garments.

And she is Heather's *mother*. It's incredible that

such a creature can be anyone's mother. Does it feel incredible to Heather and Janie? How does it feel? How *would* it feel, if—?

A wave goes through him; a gathering, peaking, swooning wave.

'Come on, lad, sit yourself down. Come and sit by 'ere.'

It's the grandfather speaking to him and clapping the arm of a chair.

Jason goes over. Sits.

There is a problem with Fran. Jason can't work out how to be with her, he can't pick up any clues. So far he's made two attempts. Both failures.

First of all, to keep on the safe side, he accorded Fran the selfsame treatment as Steve and Hal; he was polite, interested, slightly deferential. Then after a bit he allowed a little gallantry to creep into his voice and adopted a look of bashful appreciation. I think you are utterly charming, he aimed to convey.

It was failure number one. All it did was cause Fran to withdraw, to sit further back in her chair and leave the available talking space for others to fill.

Then some while later he got an idea. She's the artistic type, he thought. She'd want something more profound than flattery, however subtle. She'd warm to a sensitive and expressive approach. He munched through a slice of lemon cake and considered his options – various suitable remarks and phrases, and the appropriate manner to adopt while saying them.

His cue seemed to come when she asked if he'd like a second cup of tea. She drained his cup into a china bowl, she poured hot water into the teapot, stirred, waited, then put a dash of milk into his cup and poured a steady stream of tea. The wide-cuffed sleeve of her brown jumper fell back to reveal a slim freckled arm as she returned his cup. Little ceremonies are so important, he commented. They bring grace to everyday life, and a sense of reassurance and continuity.

Failure number two. For Fran simply frowned, a little puzzled frown. This rapidly became a thunderous frown which was directed at Heather's troll-like sister. And troll, by God, was the apposite word, given the face the girl was pulling – eyes rolled up, tongue lolling, upper lip peculiarly distended. 'Ow!' she suddenly squawked. 'That hurt,' she complained.

'Just behave,' Fran hissed – or some such phrase. Obviously he'd missed something.

Now, sipping his tea, he ponders his failure. Maybe ceremonies aren't all that artistic. But he needn't worry about it right now. Something better will come to him eventually.

'Dad, shall we take Jason round the farm while the light's still good?' says Heather.

'Good idea,' says Heather's father.

'I'll come, too,' says Heather's grandfather. 'I can fill the lad in on the history.'

'Oh, all right,' Heather agrees. 'You'll need your boots, then, Jayce. Did you leave them in the car?'

'I'll go and get them,' he says.

From her bedroom window Fran sees them go across the yard. Jason appears to be perfectly normal, acting like any other young man, with Heather's arm linked through his and pulling him into her side. It's hard to be absolutely sure, but she could swear he laughed just now – the half-embarrassed laugh of a young man who has recently become the property of a young woman – probably at something Heather whispered in his ear. She thinks she then saw him straighten suddenly, as if recalling the need to pay respectful attention to the young woman's father and grandfather – certainly Hal is vigorously pointing out a feature of the barn. So there you are, Fran says to herself. An ordinary scene, an ordinary young man. No doubt the reason he behaved oddly at tea was the strain of the occasion.

At the window Fran is physically holding herself in check. An arm is pulled tightly into her waist, a hand is clasping the back of her neck. When she drops her arms and turns to go out of the room, more than her body is released.

I don't like him; there's something about him: the words tumble through her head.

'Muttering again. You want to get a grip, Mum,' observes Janie, who is perched on the blanket chest under the landing window. Mrs Twitten is draped over her shoulder.

'What are you doing here? And don't bring that cat upstairs.'

'I don't bring her, she comes.' Janie springs down, and side by side they go down the wide front-of-house staircase. 'I'm not surprised you're upset,' says Janie, 'Heather bringing home such a terrible plonker.'

Fran comes to a dead stop. 'Now just look here, you were bad enough at tea – after you'd promised me faithfully to behave.'

'I couldn't help it. I mean, I never dreamt he'd be bad as that.'

'Will you stop? Heather is obviously extremely keen, and I won't have her upset. In any case, I don't know what you mean, he seems perfectly all right to me.'

'Fibber! I saw your face, you were thinking same as me. He's not real.'

Fran is silenced. It's uncanny how her younger daughter's callous and jargony language can sometimes put a matter exactly.

*   *   *

Jason, lying in bed, is thinking that he behaved like an idiot. You said you'd got that tendency licked, he reminds himself.

But this is different, another part of him counters. It's not a case of confusing Fran with his mother, or trying to stamp his mother over Fran – a fanciful idea of his mother. He's learned his lesson about that, all right; he's faced the facts and he's not going soft on them. His mother was useless, she was shallow, cruel, not worth losing sleep over. No, it's the fascination of Fran herself that he can't get over. And Fran is, after all, the mother of his girlfriend. So he's entitled to wonder about her just a little, surely? And to hope for some sort of a pleasant relationship.

Unfortunately, Fran doesn't seem to see it that way. She was pretty cool to say the least.

Not to worry, it's early days. And in any case she'd be hard to draw out. She's like one of those retractile creatures that pull into a shell when anything strange approaches. She's— Oh help, she's so—

But the word can't be found.

'I don't think your mother likes me,' worries Jason to Heather.

It's Monday lunchtime. In the churchyard they are sharing sandwiches. Yesterday he paid his second visit to Willow Bank Farm, and found Fran as difficult to read then as on the previous Sunday.

'Oh, *her*,' says Heather. 'Dad likes you, all right. Dad's really great. Don't you think he's great?'

'Oh, I do.'

'I knew you would,' says Heather. 'Grandpa likes you, too. Mind you, Grandpa likes anyone who'll listen to his stories. But it's really terrific that you and Dad hit it off. Come here, gissus a kiss— Jayce? You going off me or something?'

'I'm not going off you or anything, idiot. It's just that

262

it's broad daylight and those women over there are trying to eat their sandwiches.'

'Who's stopping them? Mm, this spicy prawn one's good. Want a bite?'

'N'thanks. Hey though, I wish your mother would like me, too. It really bothers me that she doesn't.'

'Oh I expect she does in her way. She's funny sometimes, really weird. You'll get used to her. Want to give the farm a miss then on Sunday?'

''Course not. I enjoy going. Your mum's a great cook.'

'Oh good. I'm ever so glad you like the farm. I was worried you wouldn't. But I don't want to overdo it, right? If you'd rather go to the flicks or something, just say. Mind you, it does have its attractions. It was great in the Dutch barn.'

'Yes, it was,' grins Jason.

Two days later, Jason, on his way to meet Heather for lunch, sees up ahead a figure that is familiar. It's Sonia. Jason stops. After a second he goes on. He forgets to turn into the lane for the Tasty Bite. He follows Sonia, all the way into Marks & Spencer.

Inside, Sonia is lingering over a rail of women's sweaters. Idly she fingers the articles. It doesn't take a practised salesperson to know the lady's not interested, to know she's filling in time. Or maybe comparing in a pleased sort of way these not-so-hot sweaters with the sort she would buy.

Jason wants to go up to her. He wants to seize her by the arm and pull her round to face him. *What do you mean by it?* he wants to shout, *Telling a policeman I stole your teapot. You must know I wouldn't—*

He doesn't, of course, even though the actions and words are vivid and urgent, even though his limbs and mouth teem with their execution. He doesn't, because the inevitable consequences are also vivid.

MAN ASSAULTS WOMAN IN SHOP the local rag blazes – in capital letters, in leaping flames. An assault charge really would dish him with Barclays. It would with any decent employer.

He turns and goes out into the street.

A few minutes later, with Heather sitting on the opposite side of the table and a plate of pasta under his nose, he breaks into shivering. 'I don't feel so hot,' he says, and puts down his fork. 'I honestly don't think I can eat this, Heather.'

'That's a shame, Jayce, when you've gone and paid for it, and we were going to make do with sarnies this evening.'

'You eat it.'

'After this lot?' She looks at her split jacket potato brimming with grated cheese. 'Oh, all right. I was going to have cherry pie after, but I'll force that down instead. I hope you're not sickening for something. I hope you're not starting a cold.'

'No, I don't think it's that,' says Jason.

Later on in the bank his agitation returns. Prickly heat on the back of his neck causes him to look around, to examine faces. Thoughts of Sonia and the inspector repeatedly break up his concentration. Maybe the inspector was playing with him by sending a message of good luck. Like a cat playing with a mouse. Maybe he hoped to put Jason off guard in the expectation that he'd then commit a further robbery. Maybe that's the way a policeman's mind works.

Bugger the inspector, silently cries Jason. He gets up and heads for the cloakroom. It was such bad luck that Sonia and he were driving that night on the same bit of road at the very same time. And bugger Sonia, he cries, slamming and bolting the lavatory door.

He unzips, then tries to pee. But, God, he can't even manage that. He really has to stop all this worrying. Otherwise he'll make a serious error, like pressing the wrong keys on the computer and wiping out vital customer information. Then he'd get the push, all right, without any help from Inspector Bascombe.

In fits and starts a stream comes out. He zips up, washes and dries his hands, returns to his desk. He has to concentrate, he tells himself. And later on, if his mind insists on taking a wander, he should stick to benign topics. Like visiting the farm with Heather on Sunday – this time for Sunday lunch. Like Heather's provoking mother – now there's a subject that can surely divert him from Sonia and her beastly works.

'I hope Heather doesn't frighten off that young man, dragging him round the farm the way she does.' Steve is saying this to Fran during the afternoon of Jason's third visit.

'So you like him, then?'

'Heather certainly does.'

'But you do, too?'

'I reckon so, don't you? He's personable, speaks up for himself. Speaks very nicely, I must say; he shows Heather up in that respect. And he seems to know what he's talking about – what he was saying about grain prices was interesting. Of course, that was his expertise talking. I should imagine he's got a decent career ahead of him.'

'My goodness, sounds like you've lined him up as a son-in-law.'

'That'll be up to Heather, I should imagine. She's pretty good at giving him orders. She's had him ferrying bales to the cattle – her on the tractor, him on the trailer. He was all right hefting the bales, but he was none too keen on going in with the bullocks – you know what they're like at the moment, pretty frisky, thinking it's time they were let out in the meadow. One of them started kicking up just after he went in.

You should've seen him leap for the door, poor lad. Heather was doubled up, laughing. Still, he takes it in good part, I'll say that for him. Last I saw, they were heading for the Dutch barn. I thought I'd leave 'em to it.'

It must be her, then. Must be. 'I think I'll go and mow the lawn,' she says. 'Talk of the cattle going out reminds me how long the grass is getting.'

Fran shunts the motor-mower round a tricky corner and tells herself that it *isn't* just her, Janie's noticed it too: an embarrassing falseness in Jason's manner to her. But why me? she demands, as she gives the mower its head and goes storming down the lawn's length. What have I done to deserve it?

What she has done, of course, is allowed herself to dislike Jason. Though whether she disliked him instantly from the outset, or later as a result of the odd treatment she was getting, she can't honestly recall – she's been too worried, too bewildered, to think about it coolly. So maybe it is her fault. Maybe, picking up her dislike, he became anxious. Maybe it's anxiety making him obsequious to her one minute, faintly flirtatious the next.

But she can't help wishing Heather had fallen for some other young man. Someone straightforward. Certainly Jason isn't helping her relationship with Heather. Last Monday evening it hit an all-time low.

'Mum, I know nothing I do can ever come up to your high standard,' said Heather, 'but do you think you could do me one small favour? Try not to turn up your nose at Jason? Obviously he has to be a jerk in your eyes, seeing as it's *me* who thinks he's great, seeing as it's *me* he's going out with. But do you have to make it so obvious? For once in your life could you give me a break? Fake it, OK? Make out you think he's all right.'

Fran can't remember what she said at this point, but it was obviously the wrong thing.

'Come off it, Mum. I was no good at school; I mess about on the farm; I work in a shop. All sad disappointments. For some reason you're disappointed with the way *you* turned out, not making it to university, missing out on a posh career. So you think your daughters ought to do it for you. Well sorry, but I'm not up to it. Don't worry, though; I'm sure your precious Janie will see you right.'

It was rubbish, utter rubbish. How Heather performed at school, the work she's chosen to do, was never a disappointment. Nor could Fran have implied that it was.

So how did Heather come to believe otherwise? What did Fran do, what did she say? What careless gesture, silly throwaway remark?

When the lawn is mown, Fran gathers up the corners of the plastic sheet on which she has heaped the grass cuttings. She ties them to form a parcel which she drags up a narrow curving path, out of the garden, onto a patch of rough tree-shrouded ground. Here a low hillock has been formed by the mowings of previous years, previous decades. New young nettles have sprung over it, peppery-smelling. Fran hauls up her parcel, shakes out the sheet, steps down.

It's dim in this place in the late afternoon, dim and dank. Unnoticed, the plastic sheet drops from her fingers.

It's a great relief to her when he joins her at the foot of the mound. A great relief to have him to lean against.

Families! she cries to him. Simply hopeless. People on top of one another, watching and listening and breeding resentments, seeing slights where there aren't any, believing whatever they want to believe, never mind the facts. What did I do, what did I say?

Or was it something Janie said, could that be it? Those girls can be poisonous to one another. Hey— She gives a laugh, but not a happy one: I get the blame for that too I suppose; I am their mother.

Just look at me, she invites. Beating my breast about the child I lost when I can't even handle the kids I've got.

He comes closer, seeming to surround her. Their closeness is velvety, hushed.

But she has to break away, she's virtually drowning. Luckily, there's a tissue in her pocket. She blows her nose and blots her eyes. Then stoops to gather up the plastic sheet.

Maybe it's the result of blood rushing to her head, but while she is bent double groping for the sheet, she suddenly sees how perfectly simple is her problem's solution. Never mind what Heather imagines about this and that, never mind the queasy feeling Jason gives her, never mind whether Jason is or isn't a sound bet for Heather (this is for Heather to decide), never mind any of those murky ifs and buts: all she has to do is *like Jason*. That's it. Everything else then falls into place. Heather will be pleased with her and will forgive the slights Fran has inadvertently given. Jason will be more relaxed and therefore less disconcerting. So darn well like him, she orders herself. Find the good in the lad. There has to be some.

It's simple, it's attainable, it's a godsend. Thank you, thank you, she tells him. It's glaringly obvious, but she would never have got to it without his help. Cutting away the stuff that's hindering you is always the hardest part.

16

It's a stormy night. April going out with a rending of garments and floods of tears, thinks Fran, waking suddenly. She wishes she'd woken sooner, been spared some of her dreams; the howling outside seems a distant continuation of the turmoil her subconscious has been putting her through. She puts out a hand to touch Steve. His side of the bed is empty.

Then she remembers. A cow was threatening to calve tonight, an old stager who has calved twice before. So no need for the vet, Steve said. He could manage alone, though he might be grateful for a bit of help.

'Then wake me if you need me,' Fran told him on her way to bed.

She's out of bed now, and rushing to the window. And yes, the yard lights are on, light is showing at the cowshed windows. She pulls on plenty of warm clothes. Further down the landing she finds Heather's door agape and Heather not in her bed. In the scullery she puts on her boots and waxed jacket, ties the hood under her chin, collects a torch.

The crisis is over: she's deduced this already from the lack of bellowing. The reason she is struggling against wind and rain is to demonstrate that her intentions are good, that it's perfectly possible for her to give up her warm bed on a foul night, and if she didn't do so at the relevant time this is down to Steve for not waking her.

Steve and Heather are sitting in the hay watching a newly born calf learn how to suckle. Fran hesitates in the doorway, just outside the pool of light. She wonders if it is wimpish to show up now when the hard part's over, whether it is fair to intrude into the labourers' reward. It takes her ears quite a while to focus on their voices, and a further while to cotton on that she is the subject of their murmured conversation.

'I just don't want her interfering with me and Jason, that's all. I don't trust her, changing her tune all at once; barely speaking to him one minute, all over him the next. She's being tricky if you ask me. She's up to something.'

'Oh come on, Heather. That's not your mum. What you see is what you get with Fran. I've always said so.'

Well, there's a relief. Steve still thinks well of her, the old love. God, though, she just can't get it right with Heather.

Then another thing strikes her: Steve's idea of her, which shone out when he sprang to her defence. *What you see is what you get*. Good grief, he hasn't a clue. How can he partner a woman for twenty-two years and not pick up her central characteristic: that at least 50 per cent of her life is lived inside her own head?

She decides to slink off.

And that's exactly what it feels like as she treads carefully, with the aid of torchlight along the concrete paths and the stretch of cobbles, keeping close to the shelter of shed and barn walls: slinking, sloping, skulking off.

It's eight o'clock. Sunlight is pressing against the curtains in Sonia's bedroom. She sits blinking on the edge of her bed, fighting an urge to get straight back in. She longs to fall back on the pillow, longs to draw up her legs, longs to pull the duvet up to her chin. Perhaps she should, she had a broken night, there was one heck of a storm; she heard three o'clock strike, she heard four. But no, the light would be a reproof, she'd start feeling guilty, she'd become miserable with herself. Come on, Sonia, you know better than that. Haven't you always said the trouble with half these so-called unemployed people is they can't get up in the morning?

She pushes herself upright, goes to the window on rather groggy legs, and draws back the curtains. What a beautiful May morning, she silently exclaims by way of self-encouragement. Now, how best to use it? Town, the shops, a gossip with a chum? Loads to do in the garden, of course, but the ground will be soggy after the rain in the night. No point dusting, she cleaned the house yesterday from top to bottom. Mind you, the windows could probably do with a shine; there's nothing like strong sunlight for showing you up window-wise.

It's impossible to decide. She'll think it over while she's taking a bath.

But with her body fragrantly submerged, her mind drifts backwards not forwards, it will not be engaged by plans for the day. It wants to indulge in the pastime that it is currently favourite, which is to select from ten wonderful days at the end of March and beginning of April (ten days spent largely with David), a portion of time – an afternoon, say, or an evening – and relive it right now.

And so, while the water cools and her skin puckers, (how she will scold herself when she notices the time that has elapsed!) the essential Sonia is transported to Dublin, to an expensive hotel. Its restaurant, to be precise, where she and David are enjoying lobster and champagne and laughing togetherness.

Though, rather unfortunately, during dessert David gets called away to take a lengthy phone call.

But it doesn't really matter, because he very handsomely makes up for it. While conducting his call he must somehow manage to slip a tip to someone, for the head waiter arrives at Sonia's table with a tall glass of fumy black coffee and proceeds to the delicate operation of floating cream on top. (How typical of David that in the middle of a complicated telephone conversation he should remember her weakness for Irish coffee.) Next a plate of petit fours arrives. The head waiter frequently returns to check on her comfort and to offer discreet snippets of conversation. So by no means does Sonia feel deserted, but treasured and pampered due to the treatment she's getting.

Though, rather unfortunately, on his way back to the restaurant David gets lumbered with a man from Kerry.

But poor David can't help it. The man accosts him, apparently, as he's walking back through the lobby. Naturally he has to bring him to the table, not wanting to leave her alone for another minute, not wanting either to miss out on the chance of a chat with a business contact. Though what the dickens they actually chat about is beyond Sonia; the Kerryman's accent you could cut with a knife, she wonders how David can make head or tail of it. But again, David has a knack of making things lovely. He keeps an arm round her, gives her shoulder little intimate squeezes to convey how much he'd prefer it if he and she were alone. Perhaps the Kerryman also senses this. 'I should let you be with your lovely wife,' he says.

'Ah, Sonia is my ex-wife, I'm very sad to say.'

'You mean you let this lovely lady go? Then you're an eejit, so you are.'

'Life's a bitch,' David sighs. 'If you don't mind I should like to dance with her.'

'Not at all, not at all. I'll be waiting in the bar, so I will.'

And David commandingly steers her from the table.

David is a super dancer, none better. Oh, how the dancing brings it all back, the years when they were young and in love. And the way he holds her, twirls her, leads her, while gazing into her eyes, is just so romantic. They dance for, oh, ten minutes or more. And are still dancing more or less when he leads her out of the room, across the lobby, towards the lift.

'Sorry about boring old business intruding again, my love. Though as usual you're the model of understanding.'

As the lift doors slide together he is blowing her a kiss.

For the first time Jason is staying overnight at Heather's. He has been given a room at the front of the farmhouse which faces the garden. It's the largest bedroom he has ever encountered. Heather's is down the corridor. She says she's going to slip into his once the house is quiet, but the prospect of this is making Jason feel nervous; on the whole he would prefer her not to, he's unsure how her parents would react if they found out – which they might, if one of them went into her room for some reason and saw it was empty. Heather scoffed at his worries. She said they'll probably guess anyway, but won't have the nerve to bring up the subject. This hasn't altogether reassured Jason. It would be a pity to offend Fran, now that her attitude has warmed towards him. More than anything he would hate to do that.

Right now he's in the dining-cum-family room, sitting in front of the television. Heather's father is slumped in a chair and Rosie the retriever is lying full length on the hearth rug. Mr Topping and Rosie are both asleep. Heather herself has gone up for a bath. The hideous Janie is away for the night, thank goodness, staying with a schoolfriend. Where Fran is, Jason doesn't know. But he would dearly like to. Despite her friendliness he has never managed to achieve any time with her alone.

Before supper he caught a glimpse of her going through the paddock with a pail hanging from each arm. Heather said in a bored tone when Jason mentioned the sighting that her mother would be on her way to feed the hens. He wanted so much to leave Heather at that moment and hurry after Fran. He imagined relieving her of the pails, he imagined matching his stride to hers through the grass and sharing the scent of early evening, he imagined how, when the hens had been satisfied, Fran and he would linger and talk. But it was impossible to invent, right on the spot, a plausible reason for doing so.

And now here he is without his minder, perfectly able, thanks to his companions' slumbers, to leave the room unnoticed. But where, if he did so, might Fran be located?

Eventually, deciding the chance is too good to pass up, he slips out of his seat and across the room, quietly opens the door and quietly fastens it behind him.

He steals upstairs. He checks the bathroom, listening at the door to sounds of splashing, then checks the rooms at the back of the house – one that is obviously Janie's and another that is crammed full of boxes and lumber. Then he goes towards the front of the house, passing Heather's room, until he reaches the room that he has been allocated. On the opposite side of the landing is Heather's parents' bedroom. The door to this is not fully closed. He waits outside for a moment, then, detecting no sound, slowly, cautiously, inserts his head. The room is empty, as he'd supposed.

Having drawn a blank on the first floor, he runs softly downstairs to investigate below. The scullery at the back of the house is deserted, and so is the dim bare room they call the dairy. He passes through the kitchen, passes through the hall, then goes along the corridor, passing the door he himself recently closed and also passing the door to the garden. All that remains to be checked is whatever lies behind a closed door near the foot of the front stairs. Reason and instinct persuade him Fran does.

He listens, discounting the faint creaks and thumps of his own internal system. And suddenly is rewarded by a distinct sound: the rustle of paper, unless he is very much mistaken. He grips the door handle. He can't hold back now.

'So this is where you hide yourself!' he cries, gladness at the sight of her pitching his voice at the height of its range.

But people don't burst in on Fran in the parlour. At least, not without some apologetic word – 'Mum, I'm sorry, but,' – to acknowledge their trespass. Not that the parlour is officially Fran's, it's simply understood that this is where she goes to be quiet; 'to read and scribble' is how they put it, no interest being shown in what she reads or scribbles. When Jason bursts in she is disorientated. She can't make sense of his beaming face. The implication of his words strikes her as madness, an impression that is heightened by the shrillness of his voice.

Before the door opened she was miles away, chasing a word that was eluding her: the perfect word, the only word, a word she knows well, a word that had no business to desert her, a word almost on the tip of her tongue—

But then, intrusion. Fran in her chair, notepad on knee and pen in hand, blinks up at him.

'I'm not disturbing you, I hope.' Evidently he assumes he is not, for after closing the door he removes a book from the chair beside her and sits himself down. 'I've been dying for a talk. We never seem to get the opportunity, do we? What're you writing?'

'Poetry,' says Fran.

'Gosh,' says Jason, 'I'm well impressed! I'd no idea. I mean, I guessed you were artistic, but I didn't realize you were a poet.'

Did she really say she was? To this awful youth?

'Er, I'm just, you know, practising. I can't think why I said it.' She can though. Shock made her. 'Look, I'd um be grateful—' She seems to take for ever getting to his name, forcing herself to bring it out in order to be mollifying because to him of all people she has betrayed her secret hope and ambition – 'um Jason, if you'd keep what I said to yourself. I don't normally tell people. I mean, I haven't told anyone, it's a private thing. Your question took me aback.'

'Oh,' says Jason, 'absolutely. It'll be our little secret. I'm touched you confided in me. Rest assured I shan't breathe a word.'

'Right. Thanks.'

She closes up her notepad. She recalls the energy she's expended working herself up to be nice to this young man, and also her reason for doing so. 'You wanted to talk,' she reminds him while summoning up a smile. 'Tell me about life in Aldershot. That's where you're from, isn't it?'

'Yes,' says Jason, regretting that he can't on this occasion rearrange history, having already told Heather the boring truth. Or at least, the version he usually trots out to people his own age or people he's not out to impress. His mother died when he was a

276

little kid, so he hasn't any memories of her, he tells them (because it's easier than saying she cleared off when he was seven years old). His dad brought him up, he continues, and usually leaves it at that – unless it's someone he's totally relaxed with, like Heather, in which case he adds: 'and, boy, did the miserable old git resent it, every last penny he was forced to lay out.' He gives Fran the shorter version. Though he adds as an afterthought that he didn't have a particularly happy childhood since he and his father don't get on.

Fran's heart sinks. He's got problems, she knew it. Heather has helped herself to a load of trouble.

Suddenly she wants him out of the room. There's a cloying falseness to him. She has to ward it off.

'I'm going to make some tea,' she says, cutting into his description of a poem he once wrote at school that earned high marks and a teacher's opinion that it showed promise. 'Fancy a cup? I'll put the kettle on.'

All the way down the hall to the kitchen, holding back only while she looks in on Steve, he continues about this wretched poem. But she mustn't think in these terms, she mustn't be negative. Any minute now Heather will come bouncing downstairs, fresh from her bath, revitalized, sharp as a sniffer dog when it comes to detecting atmosphere or Mum being difficult.

In any case, who hasn't got problems? Who in childhood didn't get at least a spattering of shit as a result of being subject to adult human beings? For Pete's sake, give the lad a chance.

Jason lies in the big iron-framed bed, thinking not so much about Heather (who will be here at any moment; she's always good as her word) so much as Heather plus extensions. Heather and her family, the Toppings. That's Hal, Steve, Fran, Heather and, all right, Janie – plus a cat, a dog, farm animals, many acres and this old house with the two staircases. Families shrink and families grow, they don't stay the same. A large family is a fabulous thing, he's never pictured himself as part of one before. But he does now. His bond with this one is widening. Not only is he Heather's lover; this evening he became Fran's confidant.

If he and Heather ever got married—

His heart misses a beat, as a moving shadow descends on the bed. 'Phew, Heather, you nearly killed me. I didn't hear you come in.'

'So no-one else did, right?' She snuggles into his side. 'Missed me?'

'Lots. Actually, I've been thinking. It's your birthday on Wednesday. What do you say we get engaged?'

'Eh?'

'You want us to be, don't you?'

'Yes, but— I thought we were going to save and that first.'

'We'll save and that after. Go on. Say yes.'

'Gosh, Jayce, you really mean it? With a ring and everything?'

'Of course with a ring.'

'Oh blimey, wow. Yes, *yes*. Hey, I wonder what everyone's going to think?'

Fran thinks Heather is far too young to think of tying herself down. There's a whole world to be explored, people to meet, new things to try.

Heather fixes stony eyes on her. 'So how old were you when you got engaged to Dad?'

Fran, engaged at twenty, married at twenty-one, doesn't reply.

Steve concedes that it's a very good question.

Heather goes over and wraps her arms round him and gives him a kiss. 'Mum did all right,' she says.

Who would blame Steve at that moment for deciding his daughter has excellent judgement? Fran wouldn't. She gives in and smiles, as Heather, still with an arm round her father's neck, moves on to the subject of the farm's future.

Why should Fran be a beggar at the feast?

After tea on the following Sunday, Fran invites Jason to help her feed the hens.

A look of suspicion comes on Heather's face. 'Oh, he doesn't want to do that. Hens are boring. In any case we promised Dad—'

'But I do! I'd love to. Do we collect their eggs as well?'

'Yes, if there are any.'

She knew he'd jump at the chance. She'd banked on it.

'Well, *I'm* not going to let Dad down,' says Heather, tossing her head; and to Fran she hisses, 'I'd like to know what you think you're playing at,' but she doesn't hang around to learn.

They set off in silence. Jason is searching for a way to strike an intimate note. Fran is biding her time.

'Still writing the poems?' he asks at last.

Fran frowns. 'On and off.'

'I'd be ever so flattered if you'd show me one some time.'

By now they are approaching the top of the rise. 'Here we are,' says Fran, as the chicken-run comes into view. She outlines the procedure in front of them, explaining one or two things about the nature and needs of poultry.

When they enter the run, Jason finds the hen presence overwhelming – claws and beaks and feathers and dust, the sweetish thick smell, mad intensity, raucous noise.

Things calm down once the pails are emptied. The hens peck quickly at the grain and softly chunter, some stalk about on the edge of the group, and now and then there's a flurry of feathers as a squabble breaks out. Fran leans back against a post in the wire fence. She fixes her eyes on him.

'Do you love Heather?'

'What? Of course I do.'

'You're sure about that?'

'Don't you believe me? Why do you think I want to marry her, then?'

'I don't know. Tell me.'

Jason stares. 'I can't believe this. I'm hurt. I'm' – (Fran fears he's going to cry, but he doesn't quite) – 'really wounded. Choked. I thought you approved. I thought you liked me.'

'We're not discussing you and me. That's not the issue. I want to know how you feel about Heather. Your true feelings.'

'I love her, of course. I don't know why you ask. I should've thought it was obvious. Christ, Heather's the best thing that's ever happened to me.'

'Then I hope you'll prove a good thing for her. She's my daughter, you see. That's why I need to be clear.'

'I hope I've set your mind at rest?'

'Well I'm glad to have heard you say it.' She pushes off the post. 'OK. Let's see if there are any eggs.'

But Jason can't settle to think about eggs. With Fran faintly hostile to him, how can he think about eggs? How, when it comes to checking the wire fences, can he be bothered to think about foxes? All he wants is to put things right, as right as they were before they set out.

'I do love Heather you know, really and truly,' he insists when they are heading back to the paddock. 'I'd never hurt her. I'm a loyal person.'

'I'm sure you are. Just the natural fears of a mother, that's all. Don't mind me, Jason.'

'But I do. I mind a lot. Hell, you're—'

'Then perhaps you shouldn't. I'd rather you concentrated on Heather, frankly. That's what you're here for, after all. That's why you and I are together now.'

'Yes, but I have to know I have your blessing.'

'If you love Heather and she loves you, then of course you have it. Let's change the subject. Oh look, here comes Janie.'

Along the track on a purple and pink bicycle, Janie comes hurtling. Obediently, Jason marks her progress.

'Hi, Janie,' shrieks Fran.

'Hi, there,' cries Jason.

Without any sort of acknowledgement, Janie goes whooshing past.

Fran turns to him with a grin. 'What a rude little tyke. But she'll grow out of it, I hope.'

The grin is infectious. Jason laughs and feels better. It's like she said, he reassures himself, she just wants to be sure. As any mother would. Any proper mother.

Sonia is heading for Wilson's Shoes. She is wearing a green tweed outfit, rather voluminous, not the sort of thing she usually favours. David bought it for her during their holiday in Dublin, and in Dublin it felt just fine. Here in the shopping centre though, she feels a touch self-conscious. Never mind. At Sunday lunch in a country pub – the sort of occasion her friends the Gillmans often arrange – it will come into its own. Providing, that is, she can lay her hands on the perfect shoes.

Not possessing the appropriate shoes for this outfit is the reason it looks faintly odd on her. This insight came in a flash while she was shining the windows the other morning. She had to dump the Windolene, dump the shammy, fly upstairs. She had to try it on that very moment to judge whether she was right. And by golly she was. Nothing from her vast selection of footwear truly complemented the outfit. Something brogue-ish, with a stacked heel might be the answer. She had a project!

Heather would be the one to consult. But ever since Inspector Bascombe's news about Heather being Jason's girlfriend, Sonia has given a wide berth to Wilson's. This was silly though. Why deprive herself of the services of the one person who understands her problematic arches? Sonia put the outfit in a carrier bag, and got into the car and went into town. Heather said she'd like a few days to think it over. She'd be visiting head office later in the week and would keep Sonia's problem at the back of her mind during the stock presentation. She promised to telephone Sonia as soon as she had something worth trying on and advised that when Sonia next came in, the outfit should be worn. Which is how Sonia comes to be hurrying through the shopping mall in rather conspicuous apparel.

She dodges round a gang of fat mothers, each propelling a pushchair, each with a lighted cigarette. She dodges round weedy whey-faced youths, round slow-moving pensioners and dowdily dressed shoppers and one or two business types. Not a man jack of them is smart-looking, no-one has dash. Except herself, thinks Sonia, darting a sideways look in a window at her reflection.

It's the same sad story outside on the street. The people here are as drab as sparrows; they have no idea, no bezazz. Sonia sighs. Dublin it isn't.

Ah, but here is Wilson's. And there is Heather looking out for her, ready to open the door.

The shoes Heather has found are perfect. The moment Sonia stands up in them she sees they are perfect. The outfit above them is no longer saggy and enveloping, but swingy and stylish. As supporting evidence Heather offers a photograph in a magazine of a woman wearing a very similar two-piece with, it

282

would appear, the selfsame shoes. Sonia's confidence soars. Heather is a marvel. What service!

'Right. You'd better tell me the damage.'

'A hundred and twenty-nine pounds ninety-nine,' says Heather without a blink.

'Crikey,' says Sonia.

'I bet the two-piece was pretty pricey. You wouldn't want to let it down.'

No, she wouldn't. Because to do so would be letting David down. He evidently thinks of her in terms of this sort of price bracket, so why should she quibble? 'Well, dear, you've got me over the proverbial barrel. Only joking. I think you've done wonders. I'm ever so grateful.'

'I'll bring over the doings, then.'

When Heather brings over the Visa machine, she also brings over a pair of shoe trees and a jar of shoe cream. 'Yes, all right,' says Sonia. 'In for a penny—' Then she stops, because at that moment a light from the display shelves seems to ignite one of Heather's fingers. 'My goodness, it's a ring. A dazzler!'

'Oh, yeah,' says Heather, 'we got engaged last week.' She holds out the ring for Sonia's inspection.

'I always say you can't beat a diamond solitaire.' Sonia thinks hard for a moment, then asks, 'Who's the lucky man? Anyone I know?'

'His name's Jason. He works for Barclays in the square.'

'Oh yes, I know the manager. Well, well. I expect he's good-looking, your young man?'

'Mm, he is actually. Tall and slim and fair— Right, Mrs Garrs, if you'd like to sign.'

'Of course.'

Tall and slim and fair, blue eyes, straight brows, nicely spoken – in her head Sonia repeats and enlarges on Heather's description. She's still sitting in her chair, feeling dazed, when Heather returns and hands her a parcel.

'All right, Mrs Garrs?'

'Thank you, yes, I was miles away.'

'If there's anything else you'd like to see—'

'No, no, I've spent quite enough for one morning. Well, Heather, I'm thrilled about the engagement. Did I say congratulations? And thank you for all the trouble you've taken.'

'No trouble at all, Mrs Garrs.' (No trouble at all ringing up a hundred and thirty-odd quid.) 'Any time you're passing I'll be very pleased to help you.'

'I know you will. You're a veritable treasure. See you again soon,' Sonia promises.

Fran walks through the streaming sunlight. A breeze fills her skirt, billows it between her legs and behind them. Undoubtedly the breeze is slanting the willows by the side of the brook; but she takes this on trust, she can't see the willows, the light is too strong for her eyes.

Reaching the yard, she clambers up on the wall to bask for a while. She sits, arms round knees, squinting at cowsheds, fences and troughs. They seem less substantial, as if the light has sucked the solidity from them. She herself feels weightless and airy. Her spirits are high. For the past few days, they haven't been; they've growled in her throat, spat up against her teeth, all because the sun was neglecting this part of the world. But never mind that. Never mind anything. Here for the moment is glorious sunshine.

The light draws her and smooths her out. She imagines herself entirely given up to it, soaring, shimmering, transmuted. The ultimate ecstasy, she thinks. Maybe that's what getting to heaven is.

Soundlessly, yet with a thump, a pair of hands lands on the wall, which Fran can very clearly see in the shadow thrown by her legs. They have knuckles and veins and skin like the joints and ribs and bark of a tree. Old hands formed by earthy labour. They are Hal's hands, of course. Hal has been trailing her almost since she climbed out of bed this morning.

'It's bright out here.'

He wants her to go indoors. He thinks it's time for coffee, coffee drunk with a slice of cake and someone who will listen to a tale or two.

Her legs swing lightly down from the wall. Her feet float her forward. The cat suddenly darts from somewhere and moves across her path, persuading the hairs on the front of her calves that they've been brushed by fur – though the cat was several inches away and travelling fast.

'All right are you, Fran? I'm not in your way?'

'Not at all in my way.'

'Because I don't want to get under your feet.'

She makes the coffee, brings out the cake; they sit at the scrubbed wood table.

'So,' she invites. 'Tell me what you make of Heather's young man.'

He ponders. 'Ah,' he says. 'Urr.' Working up to a considered answer.

'He ent a farm boy,' he comments at last.

'I'm glad you noticed that, Hal.'

His brows shoot up. 'You saying I'm slow?'

'Oh now, as if! Going to stay for lunch?'

'I wouldn't want to put anyone out.'

'You can help me get it then. When you've finished your coffee you can go down the garden and cut me some lettuce.'

'Some ready, is there?'

'The cos wants thinning.'

'That reminds me. Did I ever tell you about the time our Edna fell out with her sister over a lettuce? A

Webb's Wonder it were. Edna had entered it for the village show.'

'You did, Hal, as a matter of fact. But I don't mind hearing it again.'

'It was when we were courting. Terrible hot summer that year. Lettuce were bolting—'

Sonia is guilt stricken. Which is not at all a comfortable feeling. And not one she has often had just cause to suffer, even if she does say so herself.

But oh this business with Jason. She forgot about him for a while. When David was here she never gave him a second's thought. Inspector Bascombe started her on this tack, she supposes. But it was seeing Heather, learning about the engagement, that virtually hooked her mind on the subject.

Now, whenever she works in the garden she's reminded of him – there's the conifer he helped her with, there's the stone he shifted on the rockery. She went into the lumber room the other day and a whole conversation came winging back. *So much rubbishy stuff, Jason.* He was always a good listener. In the kitchen, too, there are reminders, though these are mixed, good and frightful. But it's when she's in the sitting room and her eyes meet the Clarice Cliff teapot that the guilt is worse. Because it's while she's looking at the teapot that a certain scene jumps into her mind. It's herself she sees, her own hands in rubber gloves, wrapping the teapot in newspaper and then in a plastic bag, then carrying it out into the moon-lit garden and digging a hole under the choisya. And then the parting words of Inspector Bascombe sound in her head, about an accusation of theft being detrimental to a young man's career.

But good grief, she never intended to harm his career. She did what she did out of desperation. Because not only was the boy incapable of taking a hint, he was darn well digging his heels in, refusing to allow her the space she needed. And she was expecting *David* for heaven's sake.

All right, he was a sweet little friend to her. But wasn't she a friend to him, paying for his car to be mended, cooking him meals, giving him treats?

At least the inspector is now aware of the teapot's restitution. Though she was rather naughty in that respect too, making out she'd found it on her doorstep, saying Jason must have put it there. But heck, she'd been put on the spot. She was in a very tricky situation. She just hopes no note was made during the inspector's inquiries; after all, she did stipulate it was unofficial advice she was seeking. Unfortunately, one does tend to associate policemen with notebooks. And wouldn't it be just too dreadful for words, if – questions having been asked – a note was made by Jason's boss?

But this is unlikely, most unlikely. Even so, it's quite a jolt to consider that if her accusation *has* affected Jason's career (which she is 99 per cent certain it can't have) this would rub off on Heather.

Now that is just being morbid, Sonia. It's stupid to imagine such far-fetched things.

It's funny those two should have come together. They don't seem an obvious couple – Jason so good-looking and amusing, and Heather so, well, stolid. Mind you, he was never your typical young man of today, he never mentioned football or racing, the club scene wasn't a draw, and when he flicked through a magazine he was more likely to dwell on Delia Smith than Naomi Campbell. So maybe they're suited. She wishes them well with all her heart.

But isn't that a bit hypocritical of her? Isn't it, just a smidgeon?

It would be lovely not to dread them having a certain conversation, the one where Heather mentions a customer called Mrs Garrs, and Jason says, Hang about—

Oh dear, she does hate feeling in the wrong like this. It would be wonderful to put things right in some way – perhaps by suggesting a misunderstanding had occurred, which has since been resolved, and she is sorry indeed for having suspected him. If only some way could be found of conveying this, she would feel so much easier.

Sonia gazes at the Clarice Cliff teapot, and an idea begins to form.

17

It's Saturday evening. Heather and Jason are driving
out of town. Crawling out of town – Jason wanted
them to wait before setting off, and wasn't he right?
But Heather is tired, she's been on her feet since eight
forty-five this morning; she doesn't care how long the
journey takes as long as someone else is changing
the gears and making the decisions: this lane or that?
Ring road or backstreet rat-run? Main road to Weston
Sowerby Halt or winding B road? 'Come on, come *on*,'
growls Jason. Heather, with her eyes shut, puts out a
hand to turn up the volume on the cassette player.
Jason can stand it, she thinks. He's had the day off,
lucky sod.

The weekend trip to Willow Bank Farm is becoming
a habit, Jason muses. There's always someone Heather
wants him to meet. Last Sunday she took him to
church. Afterwards they went for a beer in the village
pub. He's up for inspection. Or is it exhibition? 'I
want to show you off, I want everyone to see what
I've got,' says Heather. Tomorrow some cousins are
coming for lunch. In his heart of hearts, though, he's
enjoying it. He only pulls a face because he senses
this is what the role demands and he wouldn't want
to be thought a wimp.

'Oh yeah, I nearly forgot,' says Heather, sitting up
and turning down the volume. 'We were given an

engagement present today. A customer of mine came in with it specially.'

'That's nice. What is it?'

'Don't know yet. It's all wrapped up in fancy paper, tied with a bow. I thought we'd open it together. Maybe after supper, in front of the others.'

'Good idea.'

Heather puts the volume up again and settles back.

'The present!' cries Heather, suddenly recalling it. She leaves the table and goes out into the hall and retrieves the beribboned parcel from a carrier bag.

'What's this?' asks Steve.

'An engagement present from a grateful customer.' Heather sets it on the table in front of Jason. 'You open it, darling.'

'No, you. It was your customer.'

'Oh, all right.'

'Do your customers normally dish out engagement presents?' Steve asks.

'No, but this is a woman I've put myself out for. She's the type that has to have everything matching, the right shoes and the right bag for each and every outfit. Probably wears matching knickers, too. Just in case.'

'Er, pardon?'

'Sorry, Dad,' says Heather, and Janie sniggers.

'My goodness, she wasn't taking any chances.' When the decorative paper comes off there's a plain cardboard box, and inside the box there is something solid wound lavishly in bubble wrap.

'It's probably breakable,' Fran warns.

'What do you think?' asks Heather, when the gift is finally unwrapped. She sets it in the centre of the table.

'Pooh, a teapot. An old one too, by the look of it,' scoffs Janie.

'Could be a collector's item,' says Fran. 'Pretty.'

'Yeah, I reckon it's sweet. Do you like it, Jayce?'

Jason doesn't answer. In dreams it isn't appropriate to give answers, and Jason knows that he's dreaming. He darts a look behind him, anticipating the next nightmarish instalment – Inspector Bascombe emerging from the television perhaps, to declare he knew the teapot would ultimately be discovered in Jason's possession; Mr Whitehouse, his boss, coming forward, employing the voice of Jason's father to declare the evidence is quite sufficient. *That's it, lad. Sling yer hook.*

'Jayce?' says Heather. Everyone's staring at him.

'What's her name?' he barks.

'Who?'

'The customer. The woman who—' He nods speechlessly at the object that has haunted him for months. With his mind taken up by Heather and Fran he had almost forgotten it. But now it's here, back – not just in his head, before his eyes.

'Mrs Garrs. You don't know her, do you?'

Sonia. It takes his breath away that she can be this ruthless, this determined to get to him. First she invades the bank, now she pursues him amongst the Toppings; dispatches her malevolent token right to the heart of the family table.

'Christ, Jayce, it's only a teapot.'

'Leave him alone. For once he's showing good taste. It's pukey, if you ask me.'

'Nobody did, OK?'

'Girls, girls.'

'It reminds me of something,' he blurts. It's the best he can do.

Then, unexpectedly, blessedly, Fran comes to his rescue.

'Oh, I know what you mean. I've had that sort of experience, too. I bet when you were small there was

291

some Thirties china like this at home. We had a Thirties fruit bowl – diamonds round the rim, triangles down the side. Then years later I saw one just the same in a junk shop, and I suddenly felt utterly miserable. A real *pang*. The way I explained it: when I was little something upsetting must have happened while that fruit bowl was in my line of vision. Perhaps I was getting a good telling off.'

'Poor little Mummy,' says Janie in a mock-baby voice.

'It's all right for you, miss, you don't know you're born.'

'Oh yeah? You nearly shook my brains out once when you were in a mood. We were in the kitchen, remember? I could've been looking at one of the plates on the dresser. Maybe one day I'll see one like it and want to kill myself or something.'

'Dear oh dear,' comments Fran unsympathetically. 'Put the thing away, Heather. Another time you must make some delicious tea in it – Darjeeling or jasmine – and have some happy music playing while Jason's drinking it. Alter the spell.'

'Oh, pass me the sickbag,' cries Janie, jerking away from the table. She clutches her stomach and staggers towards the door making retching noises.

Fran sighs, and Heather tut-tuts, and Steve says, 'That child gets worse.' They rise to their feet. Only Jason remains seated.

Fran reaches across him for used plates. His eyes turning to hers are large and unfocussed.

It must have been something truly awful, she thinks. His mother died, of course. Lord, was that it? And for the first time, exchanging looks, she has fellow-feeling for him.

Jason would prefer to spend the night alone, but a mild disturbance of the air indicates the door opening and closing (he's become alive to these signs now that the room is familiar) and the next moment Heather is bouncing into bed. He tells her he's too tired for it. She doesn't persist, she's tired too. When she falls asleep with the clock under her pillow set to go off at five, he turns onto his side.

What on earth made Sonia send that teapot? What did she mean by it? Has she guessed how the object has preyed on his mind for weeks on end? Maybe she has. And maybe she's sensed that its potency has waned recently; maybe this is her method of gearing up its power. Whatever did he do to incur such fanatical loathing?

It's hard to believe the Sonia he knew is even capable of fanatical loathing. But then it was hard to credit she would accuse him of robbery and sexual harassment, and call in the police. Obviously there's a light and a dark side to Sonia. He didn't invent a light side, did he? Like he invented a light side to his mother. The kindness, generosity, phone calls, the lovely lunches, cosy evenings, fun: he couldn't have invented all that. Unless of course he's mad.

'Wake up, lazybones, it's nearly half-eight. Oo, you look ever so lovely and snugly. I wish I dare hop in. Better not. They saw I was making you a cup of tea. They probably started their stopwatches. Going to sit up? Don't let it get cold. See you later, precious.'

He'll get rid of the damn thing, he decides, as he struggles up into sitting position. He'll smash it and bury the pieces. Or drive round to Sonia's and dump it on her doorstep, very rude note attached. Or take it to the police station and demand to see Inspector Bascombe, taking Heather along as a witness to the fact that it was Sonia who sent it.

But Heather doesn't know about Sonia. And there's

that other matter. What if—? And would—? Oh why—? How the hell—?

One after the other, still without answers, the questions that plagued him half the night return. They swim in his head like fish in a tank. Getting nowhere.

Fran seizes his arm and pulls him along the hall. At the foot of the stairs she turns into the parlour, draws him in, shuts the door. 'Sit down,' she commands.

He's been looking like a ghost all day. Like a shell of a person. Something's happened. Something that's knocked the wind out of his sails. Where was the chattiness that borders on cockiness at lunchtime today? Two new people to impress and he hardly noticed. Far from his usual way of going on, trying out one persona, then another, striving for the one that would most appeal to the current audience, he sat at the table barely speaking, barely eating. Oh, she's had quite enough time to get his number. What he's about is making an impression. Desperate to ingratiate, he'll act just about anything – keen young banker one minute, flippant devil-may-care the next; he'll go from shy but warm to intuitive and deep, then callously streetwise, without batting an eyelid. It's automatic with him. Probably he kids himself as well. All due, no doubt, to the existence of a cold black hole where security and loving approval should've been, back in his childhood.

But today for some reason his player's habit deserted him, left him naked and clueless as a newly hatched bird. So what happened? When he arrived last night he was Jason as usual, full of some mock-horror tale about the journey. He was as usual during supper – until Heather unwrapped that present.

She shifts her chair round till she's facing him. 'The teapot,' she says. 'Tell me about the teapot, Jason.'

He turns a shade whiter. He swallows. She sees him

brace, sees him try on puzzlement, then amusement, then insouciance. 'You can cut out the nonsense,' she warns. 'It doesn't wash with me. I want it straight or not at all. Though I do think it might be a good idea if you told someone. Of course, I could be the wrong person—'

She half rises, meaning to look out of the window and give him time to decide what he wants to do. But he assumes she's going, that following her last remark she's already given up on him.

'No, please! You're probably the only person—'

Surprised, she settles back. 'OK. Let's hear it, then.'

He looks away from her, muttering, 'Don't know if I can.'

'Oh hell, Jason, *try*. Give it a go.'

Once he gets started, it's amazing how the story flows – though in a backwards direction: an explanation of Sonia leads, via Dr Janet Drinkwater, Mrs Pam James and Miss Nyree Purcell, back to his mother (who, he confesses, isn't dead at all, as far as he knows), to his father, to his patchily remembered childhood. For a while the focus is all on a seven-year-old, eight-year-old, ten- twelve- and fifteen-year-old Jason, his mother newly gone, gone for quite a while, then gone altogether, gone for eternity – distance and his particular needs at the time lending her various distortions (he describes the photograph). And his father's voice comes very much to the fore, droning out his pessimistic forecasts, rubbishing everything Jason says and does.

Fran wants to go back to the mother. 'You were seven years old when she left,' she interrupts gently. 'You must have some memories.'

He thinks about it. 'Some,' he agrees. 'There's one where I come home from school—'

'Yes?'

'We had an oval mirror hanging over the sideboard. She was doing her face in it, leaning against the sideboard, jars and tubes heaped all over. I said, "Hello, Mum." She turned round, she was waving this stick of mascara, her face had no expression. "You'll have to get your own tea," she said, "I'm going out." And that's it, really. Except, when I'm going upstairs and when I'm in my bedroom I keep hearing her say it.' He waits, trying to hear it again. 'It's not the words,' he reports slowly. 'I'm not bothered about getting my own tea. It's her voice, how it sounds. There's no love in it.'

This reminds him of another incident: he's much younger now, his mother is pulling him along a street. She's in a really bad mood, she's nearly yanking his arm out of its socket. She's saying, 'Hurry up, you little sod.'

Fran sees her clearly, this discontented young woman. Discontented with her husband who is much older than she is and bitter at the prospect of finding employment outside the army. Discontented with the kid, who is tying her down to a drab life. She craves excitement, she craves pleasure, she's pretty enough to attract men with more life in them than her dour husband. The drawback is the kid, of course, the kid her husband uses to keep her in line. 'Hurry up, you little sod,' she growls, yanking the kid's arm, yanking along her burden.

Jason has gone quiet. While she waits for him to pick up the thread, she reflects on the photograph. She imagines the woman posing for it, tipping her head back and smiling down at the camera, feeling her hair being blown about by the wind. 'Hurry,' she instructs through the teeth of her smile, worried lest hair should blow over her face and cover her features. She's faking happiness for posterity – the way tourists who are stupefied with boredom fake it for a camera, so that people at home, and eventually they themselves, will be reassured that they had a good time. She can guess how the child would see in this photograph everything his needs dictated; not the woman herself with particular characteristics, but human warmth, fun, delight. And motherliness, of course. He'd dwell on these things, they'd become a goal, he'd start looking for them, and every now and then he'd convince himself that he'd caught a glimpse. As in Miss Nyree Purcell and Mrs Pam James and Dr Janet Drinkwater. As in Mrs Sonia Garrs.

'I think what happens is,' says Jason, who has been musing along lines similar to Fran's, 'I can't help looking for my mother in people.'

'Well, don't look at me, I won't be your mother. It's tough enough being Heather's and Janie's,' Fran fires off sharply, unable to restrain herself. She feels bad when she's said it, though. It was a bit unnecessary. But look, isn't the object of this exercise to get him to face reality?

Fortunately, the outburst only serves to jog him towards the point of the story – the teapot business. And so he returns to Sonia, to Sonia and himself, to the beginning of their story, the part where she bumps into his car.

For Fran, listening, there's something about this woman, something in the way he speaks of her and the soft expression that comes on his face, that makes her want to shout and scream. It's lucky that the details come out slowly, because a commentary, almost an alternative version, starts up in her head. She sees this young fellow – bit of a greenhorn, nothing behind him, just started his first job in a strange town, snatched up from the dark and disorientating street to have a warm and wonderful world dangled before him, a world where young people are forgiven their early mistakes, where they

297

are stoked with good food and have the harshness of life softened by tenderness. There is something in all this as Jason elaborates and in the image she's getting of Sonia, that is driving Fran into total frenzy. Because she knows precisely what is going to happen. The woman will tire of Jason. Eventually she'll want a new plaything, some other little diversion. Gritting her teeth, Fran waits for him to get to it.

Sonia, for some reason that clearly bewilders Jason, can't be persuaded to go with him to the pantomime. Put on the spot, she invents some half-baked story about being mauled in a cinema as a teenager. Jason sends Fran an embarrassed look when he's explaining this, as if he knows Sonia's lying. (Well of course she's lying!) Sonia won't answer his telephone calls, won't come to the door. Now she's relenting a little and asking him over, but only to explain that she needs some space. Next there's a painful episode involving a decorative plaque for Sonia's kitchen wall. Jason tries to press it on her: a placatory offering, a form of begging. Fran has to close her eyes.

Then one day after work, Jason finds Inspector Bascombe waiting. 'You mean,' says Fran, trying to control herself, 'she'd been to the *police*?'

His colour rises as he stutters through an account of the subsequent interview. He glosses over the bit where he seeks out Heather, confining himself to the observation that if it weren't for Heather he might have gone out of his mind, what with the fear of losing his job, what with the long drawn-out dread of that.

Poor benighted fellow, thinks Fran: after scrabbling up to the respectable end of the dunghill, by his own efforts entirely and contrary to his father's predictions, he sees his precious job being snatched away.

'Then, last night—'

Fran finishes for him: 'The bloody thing arrives on our supper table.'

He nods. There's a long silence.

Fran thinks that if Sonia Garrs were within reach right now, she'd damn well scrag her. She'd shake her till her teeth rattled.

After a while Jason remembers something important. 'Heather doesn't know about Sonia. I didn't want her to think, you know, there was anything in it.'

'Oh,' says Fran feeling awkward. She thinks it over, and recalls the way Heather will sometimes look at Jason: as if she can't quite credit her luck. Heather would take him whatever he'd been up to, whoever he'd been with: this is Fran's hunch. But probably Jason is right to assume the crucial meaning of the Sonia affair would pass Heather by. Anyway, it's none of Fran's business. Though it's nice to know he cares for Heather's good opinion. 'Sorry, by the way, for biting your head off just now.'

'Did you?' he asks, looking puzzled.

'I sounded off about not being your mother. Mind you, I meant it. Don't ever try it on. If you and Heather ever do get married, I'll still be Fran. Not your mother-in-law, not your mother anything.'

'What do you mean, *ever get married*? Heather and I are engaged, remember? *Fran?*'

She smiles wryly, acknowledging the use of her name, but asking herself: Just who is he staking a claim to here? Heather or herself? Then an inkling comes to her that it doesn't matter: that whether he marries Heather or some other girl, or in the end doesn't get married at all, as far as she is concerned it won't make a difference, she is lumbered anyway. You rub up against someone, sometime in your life, and it just isn't possible to pretend not to notice. Besides (is there such a thing as pure altruism?), she spies a payoff.

'I am trying, you know. I've been struggling like the devil against that, er, tendency,' says Jason, feeling embarrassed. To himself in silent witness, he cites his uncomplicated appreciation of Ms Angela Horton at work and his fearless honesty with Fran tonight.

What did he say? wonders Fran. Ah yes, that he's struggling. Lots of sad old lumber he has to shrug off. Sounds familiar. 'The thing is,' she says slowly, 'we're not, as you suppose, at opposite ends of the pole. It's not *you son, me mother*, even if I am trying to come to your rescue. You mayn't realize it, but we're in similar positions. We both had stuff dumped on us,' (mother*less*ness in his case, mother*hood* in hers – but she's not telling him that) 'and we're both trying to crawl out from under.' (As she speaks, understanding comes to her also on another matter. All the work she's put in, the reading, the thinking, the writing: until this moment she hasn't been totally clear where it was coming from. Now she is. She's been reaching back to whatever was in her before calamity fell, and trying to take that impulse forward.) 'I tell you what, Jason, we'll look out for each other's progress, eh? Give the other one a jolt if we spot any backsliding.'

'Ah,' says Jason, slowly catching her meaning, or at least a portion of it. 'You mean, if you don't keep on writing the poems.'

'And if you start imagining stuff about older women.'

It's a great relief to share a laugh.

Jason, however, soon sobers up. He still has the problem of the teapot.

'Leave it to me,' she says, reading his mind. 'I'll take it back to her. It'll be a pleasure. It was never stolen, of course; she made that up, it was a ruse to get rid of you. To be fair, I expect you made her a bit uneasy. Became a little too intense?'

300

'Maybe,' he shrugs. 'I got really wound up when I sensed her going off me.'

'It mightn't be a great idea for you to return it. Can you give me her address?'

'Sure.'

'Stop worrying, then. I'll make certain it's the end of the matter.'

The end of it, he thinks, and lets out his breath. 'Phew. Thanks.'

Jason says he has a thumping headache. Fran isn't surprised. He says he wouldn't mind going up to bed if it wouldn't be thought rude. Fran guesses he's done all the talking he can bear for one night.

So she makes a big pan of cocoa and sends him off to his room with a brimming mug and two para-cetamol tablets. Then she fills a second mug and takes it up the back stairs to Janie's room.

GCSE exams start in four weeks' time. Twenty-eight days tomorrow to be precise – and Janie is precise, she's been announcing the number of days ever since countdown passed the five-week mark.

'I've brought you some cocoa.'

Janie stares round at her, boggle-eyed, obviously trying to put a name to the intruder.

'Mum,' she says.

'Correct,' Fran says. 'Isn't it about time you packed that in?'

It's a boring question, not worth a reply. Janie blows gently at the surface of her cocoa, and Fran examines her. On one side of her head, the side that's been propped on a hand, her hair appears to be growing upwards; and there's a peak of hair jutting from her forehead at right angles, the bit her fingers twiddle. Her glasses are speckled over, they could do with a clean. She's wearing the same raggy shorts and sour-looking sweatshirt she's had on all weekend.

'Mum,' says Janie, 'how can I be sure all this stuff is actually going in? I mean, it's not like there's a SAVE button on your forehead, wired up to your hands so they can write it all out on exam day, is it? So how do you know? How can you tell when it's safe to stop going over and over?'

'I'll test you tomorrow, if you like,' offers Fran. 'When you come home from school.'

'Yeah, that'd be a help.'

'Why don't you hand me those books to look at so I can think up some questions? Then go and have a soak. You'll sleep better after a bath.'

Janie's lips come together in a high-level pout which she snitches from side to side. Her eyes are calculating. She knows what Fran's up to. But after considering the matter, she decides to be kind, to let her mother win one for a change.

'OK,' she says, folding together text books and notes. She hands them over. 'Everything to do with the Second World War. Have a nice time.'

'Make sure you clean your teeth properly when you've drunk that cocoa.'

'Oh yes, Mummy, I will, and I'll wash behind my ears,' says Janie in a four-year-old's voice.

'Goodnight, then, pet,' says Fran, helping herself to a kiss.

'Goo'night, Mummy, I do love oo.' Her daughter sounds mocking, but hugs her nevertheless.

Later on Fran looks in on Steve and Heather whose television programme has recently ended. Steve is climbing out of his chair. He comes towards her and gives her a kiss, saying he's away to his bed, he's jiggered, and will she put the dog out for him. 'All right,' she agrees, 'but go up quietly. I've just sent Jason up with a couple of tablets. He's not feeling too clever.'

'I was wondering where he'd got to,' says Heather.

Fran waits till Steve has gone, then says, 'I should let the poor fellow get his sleep tonight. If you don't mind my saying.'

Heather doesn't reply. She picks up a magazine.

You went too far, Fran tells herself. She calls the dog over.

'Mum, come and sit down a minute.'

Surprised, Fran sits down. 'Good girl,' she reassures Rosie, who has obediently risen.

'I've been thinking, Mum, about Jason and me. There's something I want to ask. Well, sound you out, really.'

'Yes?'

'It's going to be ages and ages till we can get a place, and I really wish— If there could just be a glimmer of *hope* for the future, it wouldn't seem so bad. And I thought, well, Grandpa, you know, hates living in the bungalow; he's always looking for an excuse to stay in the house.'

'Heather, I'm trying very hard to get some time for myself these days.'

'Oh, I don't blame you. But me and Jayce could help you there. He has every other Saturday off. I can have any day off I like, Monday to Thursday. If we were living in the bungalow, one of us, or both, could easily come and keep Grandpa company, and feed the hens and cook the meals and answer the phone and do some cleaning. So once or even twice a week you could do whatever you wanted.'

'Have you mentioned this to Jason?' Fran asks sharply.

'No.'

'Hal?'

'No.'

'Steve?'

'*No!* I thought you and me could talk it through, that's all. If it upsets you, forget it.'

Fran is impressed. Her daughter actually wants to share something with her. She starts looking at the idea afresh. 'Well, love, it certainly bears thinking about. I can see there could be advantages. But it's very early days, we'd have to see how things go.' She means see how Heather and Jason go, not Hal – which is what Heather assumes.

'Oh, I know he's perfectly OK in the summer. It's come the winter he starts getting miserable.'

'Mm. What do you say we keep this strictly between ourselves and review it in the autumn?'

'Great, Mum. Thanks. That's all I wanted.'

With Heather beaming at her Fran feels invincible all at once. Fit to tackle just about any subject. She strokes the dog, asking it softly if it's ready for bed. Then she remarks casually, as if she's only just thought of it: 'I don't know whether it's because Jason's off-colour, but he's really taken against that teapot. I wonder – Maggie Lake has a stall in the antiques market: should I ask her how much she'd give for it?'

'Terrific idea! Yeah, would you, Mum? You never know, we might get enough to buy a decent stainless steel one.'

'Er, you might,' agrees Fran, burying her nose in Rosie's fur. And there was I, she laughs to herself, all set to forgo a new waxed jacket. At the very least! The housekeeping might just about stand the price of a steel teapot, she reckons, with a bit of jiggery-pokery over the next few weeks.

18

'Mrs Garrs?'

'Can't spare a minute, I'm afraid. I'm on the point of going out.'

Fran wonders what class of person Sonia takes her for. Not a consumer researcher – no clipboard, unsmartly dressed. Is she sufficiently down-at-heel for a Jehovah's Witness? Most likely Sonia assumes she's a raffish door-to-door wanting to sell her something.

'I'm Francesca Topping, mother of Heather; Heather who works in Wilson's Shoes.'

Sonia hesitates.

'Heather who is engaged to Jason Caulfield,' Fran further offers.

'Oh,' says Sonia. 'Oh, yes.'

The door opens wider, revealing Sonia's complete self. It's not an invitation to enter, just a less emphatic barring of the portal.

'I've something for you.'

'Ah,' says Sonia. Some token from Jason, she thinks, some little way of saying: message received, you are forgiven, Sonia. 'Well, I'm relieved about that. You see, there's been a perfectly ridiculous misunder-standing—'

'May I come in?'

'Er, certainly. When I said I was going out, I didn't mean this very minute. Later's what I meant. Would you care for some coffee?'

'Thanks.' She may not get time to drink it, thinks Fran, but the making of it will allow her time to say her piece. She steps inside and Sonia closes the door.

'Come into the kitchen. Please excuse the mess. I had a bridge party last night and it's not very tidy, I'm afraid.'

Fran takes in the gleaming kitchen. How tidy is tidy? she wonders. Apparently, when there are no drinks glasses and small plates on the worktop, judging from Sonia's hasty way with them, sweeping them into the sink.

'Do sit down. So you're Heather's mother. I don't mean to be rude, but I can hardly believe it.'

'She takes after her father's side of the family.'

'Really? Well, as I was saying: there's been the most extraordinary mix-up. I'm so glad Jason cottoned on. I hoped he'd tumble when he saw my little present. And now you'll be able to put him properly in the picture. You see, what happened—' But at this point her visitor suddenly swoops on her shopping bag. As she waits to regain her full attention, Sonia gropes in her head for the handy form of words she has prepared and stowed there.

Fran lifts out a box. 'There it is,' she says, putting it on the table and folding back its flap. 'Right inside. Your teapot.'

Sonia has taken two steps forward – tippy-toe steps, like a child at a party called up to receive a prize. But at the word teapot she holds back, turns rigid. Except for her eyes, which flick and dart as, guesses Fran, a dozen contradictory openings chase through her mind.

Fran uses the silence to take a good look at Sonia. She'd formed a mental picture, but, as usually happens, reality proves different. Sonia is softer and prettier than she'd foreseen, and twinkly – Jason said she enjoyed being teased.

'You've brought it back,' Sonia manages at last.

'I have indeed. So you can put it where it belongs with the rest of your collection.'

'You know about my teapots? I suppose Jason told you.'

Fran nods.

'But he didn't want the Clarice Cliff. Well, I am surprised. He used to be fond of it. I sent it, you see, to show him there were no hard feelings,' – she gives a little embarrassed laugh – 'after our unfortunate misunderstanding, you know. And of course to show Heather how very much I appreciate—'

'Oh, Heather was delighted with it. But Jason was upset, thoroughly shaken in fact, as I should've thought you might have foreseen. Perhaps you intended it.'

'Certainly not. I intended— Well, as a matter of fact, it was a form of apology. You see, as I said just now, there'd been a perfectly stupid—'

'Don't worry, he told me what happened. You accused him of stealing it. You reported him to the police.'

'Oh now, not exactly—'

'Exactly enough to get him quizzed by a police inspector. And to have a threat of dismissal hanging over him for weeks on end. What do you imagine that felt like, eh? Or didn't you think so far ahead? Because, let's not beat about the bush, you did do some pretty fanciful thinking. You dreamed up a plan, a way to be rid of him. That teapot wasn't stolen. I bet it never left this house.'

Just then the kettle comes to the boil – Sonia doesn't move – and eventually switches itself off.

'As far as you were concerned Jason was past his sell-by,' says Fran. 'I suppose you had your eye on some other novelty.'

Sonia takes hold of a chair back, pulls the chair

307

from under the table, gingerly sits down. 'It wasn't like that. Really.' She grips the rim of her sweatshirt – one of the tops she wears to do the housework – and scrumples it tightly. 'I *helped* Jason. I was kind to him. You can ask my friend Mr Bellamy of Bellamy's Motors; he'll bear me out.'

'Oh, I know you behaved handsomely after bumping his car. You didn't let him suffer for it – which I admit most people would, they'd do the minimum they were forced to – I grant you that. But it didn't end there, did it?'

'I liked him. We hit it off. We became firm friends.'

'But not equal friends. You felt perfectly free to dump him when you felt like it, and tell lies about him and put his career at risk. You felt free to give him the fright of his life.'

'Look here,' cries Sonia, firing up. 'He gave me the fright of my life, if you want to know. In this very kitchen.' She looks round, recalling the scene. 'Virtually forced his way in – some silly nonsense about a plaque for the kitchen wall, which I said I didn't want but he insisted I have – like a man possessed, like, well, he could have been *on* something for all I know, he was very hyped up. Then he dropped the blessed thing. It broke in smithereens all over the floor. I was petrified. I thought I was next. I thought *I* was going to end up on the floor in bits.'

In spite of herself Fran can't help a stir of sympathy. 'People under stress can be very off-putting. That was his trouble. He was desperate not to let what was happening actually happen – your dismissing him. You'd made him so welcome, you'd taken to ringing him up, shoving good food into him, showing concern for his welfare. Like a mother, don't you see?'

'No, I do not!' shouts Sonia.

'I suppose he told you his mother died? Well she didn't. She cleared off when he was seven years old. So he's particularly vulnerable to a bit of mother-ing.'

'I can hardly be responsible,' begins Sonia.

'But you have to see it from his angle,' persists Fran. Then, hearing herself, stops. What on earth is she doing? What gives her the right to tell this woman what she has or hasn't to see? She is not so hot her-self in the seeing department – remember Heather's outburst? She is by no means the all-seeing Mrs Wonderful.

'Look, I didn't come here to preach. Sorry. I came to ask you to leave Jason alone. No more presents. And please hang on to that teapot. Heather doesn't know about this, by the way. She reluctantly agreed I could sell the thing, since Jason vehemently disliked it. Fortunately my daughter isn't the curious type. I'm sure when you see her next she'll tell you how much they both love it. I hope you'll be ready for that?'

'Oh, um, yes,' says Sonia, unable to picture herself dropping into Wilson's in the foreseeable future.

'Right.' Fran picks up her empty shopping bag. 'Just to satisfy *my* curiosity,' she says diffidently, 'you couldn't explain why you had to go so far, I suppose? Go for overkill? Risk damaging the lad?'

Sonia might have difficulty seeing Jason's side of things, but she has no trouble at all seeing her visitor's. She is helped to do so by the image that has been troubling her lately: of a woman stealing into the garden at dead of night, burying a piece of china, declaring it to be stolen, denouncing an innocent young man as a thief. Sometimes she can hardly credit that it happened. What made her do such a drastic thing?

'David was coming,' she suddenly blurts. 'I didn't want anything to be in the way. I wanted to clear the decks, I wanted to be totally free. Free to concentrate on David's visit.'

'David?'

'He's my— Well, he was my husband. And he's still – I mean, I know we're divorced, but we're still, we're very, we're extremely *close*.' Her voice goes shrill. She falls silent, bites her lip.

And Fran also is silent, awkwardly clutching her shopping bag.

But the silence for Fran is not complete. Outside is it? Or perhaps in her head? A thin whoop, a distorted echo of Sonia's last words; a hope against hope, pick yourself up and dust yourself down and keep on smiling kind of whoop. A pang strikes her. She knows it's time to go.

At the front door, which she opens for herself, she turns round briefly. 'Goodbye. Good luck,' she offers.

'Oh. Same to you,' says Sonia, catching hold of the door and hanging onto it, watching her visitor walk down her path and out of her life.

Fran drives into town. She has a restless, flat, unfinished feeling. Which serves her right. It's the feeling you get left with after a self-righteous outburst. Nevertheless she'd quite like to be comforted out of it. Of the available candidates for this task, Heather is nearest. Though whether Heather would take it on is another matter.

She parks in the multi-storey and opens her purse. Another reason for wanting to seek out her daughter is guilt; guilt at having deprived her of what was possibly a valuable present. It's a drag being poor, thinks Fran, as she sorts through coins and unravels a single ten-pound note. All right, not *poor*; she can hardly claim that, with acres of land, a hundred head of livestock, valuable machinery, and plenty of living space. Short of the readies, is what she means. It's hard in farming to keep comfortably liquid. She makes for Debenhams to discover what kind of money is at issue here.

A shiny, capacious, heavy-gauge stainless-steel teapot can be had for under twenty quid, she discovers. And twenty quid would be an excellent excuse for dropping in on Heather. She goes out of the shop, heads for the cash-points, hoping that when the moment arrives her pin number will come to her. Also that the machine won't have a seizure when she presents her card.

In the event, the money slides out slickly, two brand new notes. Fran folds them over and buries them deep in her skirt pocket.

Sonia is getting on with the dusting: singing along to Radio One, and bending low and reaching high, darting hither to shake out the cloth and thither to aim the can of spray polish, rubbing and dubbing, and every now and then having a snap thought about her visitor. A strange woman, so intense.

Not someone I could take to, she thinks a little later. Too fierce, too downright.

Untidy as well, the thought comes later still. And the state of her hands! A rather sad person; going downhill fast. Yet she wouldn't mind betting that she could give that woman ten or more years. It pays to look after yourself. Full marks, Sonia, she tells her reflection, as she polishes the glass.

Then the phone rings. She turns off the radio and hurries to answer. 'Oh, Natalie, lovely! How are you, dear?'

Natalie, it seems, is not good at all. Ronnie is cross as two sticks. Maybe she's imagining it, but sometimes she gets the feeling that he doesn't even like her. Their wedding anniversary is coming up soon; they're planning to mark it with a romantic weekend at the Cavendish in Eastbourne. Well, *she's* doing the planning; Ronnie has rather grudgingly agreed to come. The thing is, she'd like something terrific to wear. Sonia has such reliable taste. Has she time to come shopping? That new place they noticed in Leamington Spa might be a good place to start.

'Bless you, darling, I'd love it. As a matter of fact I was having a rather dreary morning. Now stop worrying, Natalie, between us we'll track down the perfect thing. You'll knock Ronnie's eyes out. Shall I drive, or you?'

Natalie says she was so downhearted when she got up this morning she had to take a tablet.

'Then I'd better. What shall we say – about an hour?'

All of that, says Natalie, because to tell the truth she's still in her nightie. Sonia's eyebrows shoot up at this, she thinks of the time, ten past eleven, but she ruthlessly embargoes any hint of criticism in her, 'Very well, dear. Be with you in an hour and a quarter.' She is not one to condemn.

Stepping up her pace, Sonia continues with the dusting. The radio remains switched off: if a slow number came on, or an interesting snippet of news, it might take the edge off her speed. 'There!' she exclaims at last when everywhere is shiny and spotless. She chucks the dusters into the washing machine, puts the spray cans away in their cupboard, then runs upstairs to tackle the next items on her agenda: the selection of suitable clothes, the freshening and tidying of her person.

It's all go, she exclaims to herself. But it's good to keep busy. It's not in her to be idle. Fancy Natalie being still in her nightgown. It's fatal that. Get up and get cracking, that's Sonia's motto. And never mind taking a pill (she's sorry, but that is a practice she cannot condone), if you wake up in the morning with a touch of the miseries (and let's face it, we've all been there sometime in our lives) you do not sit around feeling sorry for yourself. You grit your teeth, you say I – will – be – happy! Then you pick up that duster or gardening fork, and on you jolly well go. Sadly, not everyone possesses the necessary backbone.

Now then, what to wear? Leamington Spa, eh? New shop – so they'll need showing. They'll need to see the moment Sonia walks through the door that clotheswise here comes a lady who knows her onions. She decides on the silk two-piece in pale gold, and removes it from the wardrobe and lays it out on the bed. And the brown shoes with the tortoiseshell buckles; she places these beside the long mirror. Then it's into the bathroom for a bit of a splash (she had the full works when she got up this morning).

That woman, she thinks later when she is seated at her dressing table. That woman who came barging into the house earlier – what was her name? Heather's mother, she said she was, though there was scant sign of a physical resemblance and their attitudes were poles apart; Heather's is unfailingly obliging; the woman's verged on the obnoxious. Where was she? Sonia holds her powder puff still for a moment. Oh yes, the woman who called here earlier this morning. Well, she got it wrong, that woman did, questioning Sonia's motive for befriending Jason, implying there was selfishness in it, using a horrible word. *Novelty.* What a cheek! Good heavens, it's Sonia's nature to take trouble with people, to put herself out. Look at her now. In the middle of a busy morning the telephone rings. It's a friend in distress. What does she do? Drops everything flat to answer a need, that's what. It's the way she's made. It's her caring responsive nature.

She steps into the skirt, zips it up and smooths it down. She steps into the shoes. She puts the day's necessities into the correct handbag. Then puts on the jacket and checks in the mirror the final result. As she is standing there, a sequential observation occurs to her.

In the case of Jason, she thinks, that caring responsive nature of hers led her into a murky area. Perhaps it's been a lesson: look before you leap, be a little more canny in future, Sonia. Because quite frankly – she has to say it – that boy was unworthy. He didn't merit her kindness, her time and her trouble. It's a shame Heather had to get herself mixed up with him. Because it's highly doubtful whether he is worthy of anybody's.

Heather, who is occupied with a customer, looks up when the door opens. Fran, a little nervously, raises her hand in salute. She is encouraged by the sight of her daughter's face brightening.

'Hi, Mum,' Heather says when she is able to come over. 'What are you up to? Doing some shopping?'

'I've sold that teapot. I got twenty pounds. You can get quite a nice one for that in Debenhams. I've been over to check.'

'Hey, great, twenty quid! Tell you what – forget the teapot – let's blow it on lunch, you and me. We've never done that.'

'Aren't you meeting Jason?'

'I'll send over a message. I can see him tonight. Go on.'

'I'm game if you are,' says Fran.

'Great. Call for me at one?'

'Right-oh. See you later.'

'See you, Mum.'

Fran walks on air to the end of the street. She walks to the square and climbs the steps to the church.

Under the portico a young woman is resting in the right-hand niche. She sits cross-legged on the stone slab, smoking a cigarette and lolling an arm over the handle of an empty pushchair while her toddler chases up and down. As Fran turns the handle on the west door and the heavy wood swings inwards, the toddler runs up eagerly, wanting a glimpse inside.

'Oi,' shouts his mother. 'You can't go in there.'

Fran wouldn't be surprised if an internal voice said much the same to John Clare: *you can't go in there*. For the interior is grand, the pews – there is a second elevated tier of them – are high and forbidding; memorials to the worthy line the walls; the richly ornamented chancel and sanctuary form an awe-inspiring pinnacle. Perhaps these trepidations were also imagined by whoever placed a bust of John Clare not within the main body of the church but in the gloomy passageway just inside the west door.

It is to the bust that Fran goes first, to look again at the face she knows by heart. At the wide down-turned lips, at the overhanging brows drawing together in an upwards slant and seeming to convey bewilderment; at the flower in the button hole, plucked, Fran imagines, in the asylum gardens as he walked out that morning or from an overgrown verge along the route.

Now is past since last we met, she says to him under her breath, using his own phrase, remembering the last time she was here and other times before, contrasting her feelings then with the way she is today.

In a while she opens the door into the nave. Steps inside and goes to sit in one of the pews.

There was a time in her life when she went right off John Clare. Took against him. It was when she was still raw after the birth, but before she started compensating by partying and sleeping with as many young men as she could get her hands on. During that time she read a great deal, for escape mostly; but for nostalgia's sake she also read John Clare and far more widely than she'd been able to as a schoolgirl. And she learned that there were many more Marys than the special Mary; and an Ann Foot and an Eliza Phillips, an Isabella, a Susan, a Bessey, and scores of unnamed ones: *a crowd of blooming girls*, he gloated. *I loved and wooed them in the field* – just as she'd been loved and wooed – fucked in the field. Then off he went, she imagined, on to the next, and soon to a further rapturous outpouring. It was alienating. She felt all of a sudden on the other side of the fence. (How many by-blows did John Clare father?) Objectified as she felt she was, it seemed not her place to identify with the writer. So she didn't any more. She cast him out.

Until a few years later when she went to live at Willow Bank Farm, and the verses she'd committed to memory as a child sprang to her mind with new vitality. Every time she put her nose out of the door it seemed John Clare spoke to her. Her heart softened towards him. We can all become victims, she excused him, and herself.

Fran still remembers how it felt to become a victim. Particularly she remembers the surprise. It usually happens by accident: there you are minding your own business when some*thing* or some*one*, not necessarily with intent or malice or forethought, acts like an airborne tip-up lorry, discharging exactly over the point you are passing. There's a good chance, of course, that if it weren't for stupidity, gullibility or ignorance, you mightn't be passing that point in the first place – and if it weren't for the habit you'd developed of living life to a large and clamorous extent inside your own head.

It's years, though, since she thought of herself *as* a victim. She thinks of herself nowadays as the opposite, someone who is stronger than most by virtue of having survived the condition – taken some damage but survived. Which is why she knows she can be

316

good for Jason. She can keep an eye on him from the background; she can encourage, she can scold; she can apply affection when needed, with a light hand. Crucially, she can give the unspoken undertaking that she won't go away and she won't shut him out. Someone has to give it. Otherwise he'll never rest, part of him will be always on the lookout, and the pattern will again proceed: Jason making a nuisance of himself, Jason getting hurt when the focus of his inappropriate attention understandably withdraws. Not that it's a job she would necessarily have applied for. But underneath her resignation there's a kind of relish. And of course there's the pay-off: it allows her to make another of her pacts with fate. *I'll do a good job on this one; you do a good job on mine*, she is able to call to the unknown woman who has reared her son. It doesn't make sense from a logical view of time, but it feels like sense. And it's no more eccentric than the pact she made many years ago, that has been her mainstay ever since. Which can be explained, more or less, as follows:

If she, Fran, will accept the pain of *not knowing* (not knowing whether he is thriving, whether he is treated with love and intelligence, whether he is glad to be alive), fate will ensure that he *is* all these things.

So every time she hurts it's a reminder that he's fine.

When she senses his arrival, senses he is drawing close, she doesn't speak.

Don't speak it, *write* it, she thinks.

A prickly sensation twitches the fingers of her right hand – her writing hand – and a mixture of hunger and satisfaction stirs pleasantly inside her. Yesterday's effort wasn't bad. Tonight's will be better.

At least she never formed any mental picture of him. She is glad about that. Because if one day he does apply to the Adoption Contact Register and is given her letter and decides to seek her out, she will have no adjustments to make. The sight of him will be pure pleasure.

Time must be getting on. She squints at her watch. Yes, it's time to go and meet Heather.

On the way out she chucks John Clare under his chin.

MR BRIGHTLY S EVENING OFF
Kathleen Rowntree

'A WRITER WITH AN UNUSUALLY SHARP EYE, AND
A PARTICULAR EAR FOR THE UNDERTONES
AND DISHARMONIES THAT DISTURB LIFE
IN A SMALL COMMUNITY'
The Times

To Mrs Parminter, elderly and living alone, Mr Brightly is a
handsome man of taste and sensibility who finds time in his
busy life to visit her on his evening off. To his wife, Ginny,
Dick is a good provider whose clever business deals promise
her the lifestyle she aspires to. For Cressida, struggling to
look after her disabled son, Richard is a knight in shining
armour. And Nanette, whose personal services he once
bought, now pays Ricki for his financial wizardry. Only the
new-broom vicar, finding discrepancies in the church funds,
begins to suspect that the respected treasurer may be a
rogue.

Which is the true Mr Brightly? Events and revelations lead
Mrs Parminter, Ginny, Cressida and Nanette – and the vicar
– each to their own conclusion.

'KATHLEEN ROWNTREE IS AN UNDERRATED
NOVELIST AND SHE IS AT HER BEST IN THIS
ELEGANT VILLAGE COMEDY'
Max Davidson, *Daily Telegraph*

'EXCELLENT'
Jane Hardy, *Sunday Times*

0552 99733 1

BLACK SWAN

A SELECTED LIST OF FINE WRITING
AVAILABLE FROM BLACK SWAN

99313	1	OF LOVE AND SHADOWS	Isabel Allende	£6.99
99766	8	EVERY GOOD GIRL	Judy Astley	£6.99
99619	X	HUMAN CROQUET	Kate Atkinson	£6.99
99755	2	WINGS OF THE MORNING	Elizabeth Falconer	£6.99
99760	9	THE DRESS CIRCLE	Laurie Graham	£6.99
99774	9	THE CUCKOO'S PARTING CRY	Anthea Halliwell	£5.99
99681	5	A MAP OF THE WORLD	Jane Hamilton	£6.99
99736	6	KISS AND KIN	Angela Lambert	£6.99
99771	4	MALLINGFORD	Alison Love	£6.99
99689	0	WATERWINGS	Joan Marysmith	£6.99
99709	9	THEORY OF MIND	Sanjida O'Connell	£6.99
99506	1	BETWEEN FRIENDS	Kathleen Rowntree	£6.99
99325	5	THE QUIET WAR OF REBECCA SHELDON		
			Kathleen Rowntree	£6.99
99584	3	BRIEF SHINING	Kathleen Rowntree	£6.99
99561	4	TELL MRS POOLE I'M SORRY	Kathleen Rowntree	£6.99
99606	8	OUTSIDE, LOOKING IN	Kathleen Rowntree	£6.99
99608	4	LAURIE AND CLAIRE	Kathleen Rowntree	£6.99
99732	3	A PRIZE FOR SISTER CATHERINE	Kathleen Rowntree	£6.99
99733	1	MR BRIGHTLY'S EVENING OFF	Kathleen Rowntree	£6.99
99763	3	GARGOYLES AND PORT	Mary Selby	£6.99
99781	1	WRITING ON THE WATER	Jane Slavin	£6.99
99753	6	AN ACCIDENTAL LIFE	Titia Sutherland	£6.99
99700	5	NEXT OF KIN	Joanna Trollope	£6.99
99780	3	KNOWLEDGE OF ANGELS	Jill Paton Walsh	£6.99
99673	4	DINA'S BOOK	Herbjørg Wassmo	£6.99
99723	4	PART OF THE FURNITURE	Mary Wesley	£6.99
99761	7	THE GATECRASHER	Madeleine Wickham	£6.99
99797	8	ARRIVING IN SNOWY WEATHER	Joyce Windsor	£6.99